DEEP DOWN
A Tale of the Cornish Mines

R.M. BALLANTYNE

Frontispiece by John Betancourt. Based on a painting.

DEEP DOWN

A Tale of the Cornish Mines

R.M. Ballantyne

WILDSIDE PRESS

INTRODUCTION

Robert Michael Ballantyne (1825–1894) was a Scottish author who published more than 100 books. He was also an accomplished artist and exhibited some of his water-colours at the Royal Scottish Academy.

Ballantyne was born in Edinburgh, the ninth of ten children (and the youngest son), to Alexander and Anne Ballantyne. His father was a newspaper editor and printer in the family firm of "Ballantyne & Co" based at Paul's Works on the Canongate. His uncle, James Ballantyne, was the printer for Scottish author Sir Walter Scott. A banking crisis in 1825 resulted in the collapse of the Ballantyne printing business the following year with debts of £130,000,which led to a decline in the family's fortunes.

Robert Ballantyne went to Canada at the age of 16 and spent five years working for the Hudson's Bay Company. He traded with the local Native Americans for furs, which required him to travel by canoe and sleigh to the areas occupied by the modern-day provinces of Manitoba, Ontario, and Quebec—experiences that formed the basis of his novel *Snowflakes and Sunbeams* (1856). His longing for family and home during that period impressed him to start writing letters to his mother. Ballantyne recalled in his autobiographical *Personal Reminiscences in Book Making* (1893) that "To this long-letter writing I attribute whatever small amount of facility in composition I may have acquired."

In 1847 Ballantyne returned to Scotland to discover that his father had died. He published his first book the following year, *Hudson's Bay: or, Life in the Wilds of North America*, and for some time was employed by the publishers Messrs Constable. In 1856 he gave up business to focus on his literary career and began the series of adventure stories for the young with which his name is popularly associated.

The Young Fur-Traders (1856), *The Coral Island* (1857), *The World of Ice* (1859), *Ungava: a Tale of Eskimo Land* (1857), *The Dog*

Crusoe (1860), *The Lighthouse* (1865), *Fighting the Whales* (1866), *Deep Down* (1868), *The Pirate City* (1874), *Erling the Bold* (1869), *The Settler and the Savage* (1877), and more than 100 other books followed in regular succession, his rule being to write as far as possible from personal knowledge of the scenes he described. *The Gorilla Hunters: A tale of the wilds of Africa* (1861) shares three characters with The Coral Island: Jack Martin, Ralph Rover and Peterkin Gay. Here Ballantyne relied factually on Paul du Chaillu's Exploration in Equatorial Guinea, which had appeared early in the same year.

The Coral Island remains the most popular of the Ballantyne novels still read and remembered today, but because of a mistake he made in that book—he gave an incorrect thickness of coconut shells—he prioritized research on his subjects for later books. For instance, he spent time living with the lighthouse keepers at the Bell Rock before writing *The Lighthouse*, and he spent time with the tin miners of Cornwall while researching *Deep Down*.

In 1866 he married Jane Grant, with whom he had three sons and three daughters. He spent his later years in Harrow, London, before moving to Italy for the sake of his health, possibly suffering from undiagnosed Ménière's disease. He died in Rome in 1894 and was buried in the Protestant Cemetery there.

One of the young men influenced by Ballantyne's novels was Robert Louis Stevenson (1850–94). Stevenson was so impressed with the story of *The Coral Island* (1857) that he based portions of his most famous book, *Treasure Island* (1881), on themes found in Ballantyne's classic novel.

—Karl Wurf
Rockville, Maryland

DEEP DOWN

A Tale of the Cornish Mines

CHAPTER I.

Begins the Story with a Peculiar Meeting.

Necessity is the mother of invention. This is undoubtedly true, but it is equally true that invention is not the only member of necessity's large family. Change of scene and circumstance are also among her children. It was necessity that gave birth to the resolve to travel to the end of the earth — of English earth at all events — in search of fortune, which swelled the bosom of yonder tall, well-favoured youth, who, seated uncomfortably on the top of that clumsy public conveyance, drives up Market-Jew Street in the ancient town of Penzance. Yes, necessity — stern necessity, as she is sometimes called — drove that youth into Cornwall, and thus was the originating cause of that wonderful series of events which ultimately led to his attaining — but hold! Let us begin at the beginning.

It was a beautiful morning in June, in that period of the world's history which is ambiguously styled "Once-upon-a-time," when the "Kittereen" — the clumsy vehicle above referred to — rumbled up to the Star Inn and stopped there. The tall, well-favoured youth leapt at once to the ground, and entered the inn with the air of a man who owned at least the half of the county, although his much-worn grey shooting costume and single unpretentious portmanteau did not indicate either unusual wealth or exalted station.

In an off-hand hearty way, he announced to landlord, waiters, chamber-maids, and hangers-on, to all, indeed, who might choose to listen, that the weather was glorious, that coaches of all kinds, especially Kittereens, were detest-able machines of torture, and that he meant to perform the remainder of his journey on foot.

He inquired the way to the town of St. Just, ordered his luggage to be for-warded by coach or cart, and, with nothing but a stout oaken cudgel to encumber him, set out on his walk of about seven miles, with the determination of compensating himself for previous hours of forced inaction and constraint by ignoring roads and crossing the country like an Irish fox-hunter.

Acting on the presumptuous belief that he could find his way to any part of the world with the smallest amount of direction, he naturally missed the right road at the outset, and instead of taking the road to St. Just, pursued that which leads to the Land's End.

The youth, as we have observed, was well-favoured. Tall, broad-shouldered, deep-chested, and athletic, with an active step, erect gait, and clear laughing eye, he was one whom a recruiting-sergeant in the Guards would have looked upon with a covetous sigh. Smooth fair cheeks and chin told that boyhood was scarce out of sight behind, and an undeniable *some thing* on the upper lip declared that manhood was not far in advance.

Like most people in what may be termed an uncertain stage of existence, our hero exhibited a variety of apparent contradictions. His great size and mus-cular strength and deep bass voice were those of a man, while the smooth skin, the soft curling hair, and the rollicking gladsome look were all indicative of the boy. His countenance, too, might have perplexed a fortune-teller. Sometimes it was grave almost to sternness, at other times it sparkled with delight, exhibiting now an expression that would have befitted a sage on whose decisions hung the fate of kingdoms, and anon displaying a dash of mischief worthy of the wildest boy in a village school.

Some of the youth's varied, not to say extravagant, actions and expressions, were perhaps due to the exhilarating brilliancy of the morning, or to the appearance of those splendid castles which his mind was actively engaged in building in the air.

The country through which he travelled was at first varied with trees and bushes clothed in rich foliage; but soon its aspect changed, and ere long he pursued a path which led over a wide extent of wild moorland covered with purple heath and gorse in golden-yellow bloom. The ground, too, became so rough that the youth was fain to confine himself to the highroad; but being of an explorative disposition, he quickly diverged into the lanes, which in that part of Cornwall were, and still are, sufficiently serpentine and intricate to mislead a more experienced traveller. It soon began to dawn upon the youth's mind that he was wandering in a wrong direction, and when he suddenly discovered a solitary cottage on the right hand, which he had previously observed on the left, he made up his mind to sacrifice his independence and condescend to ask for guidance.

Lightly leaping a wall with this intent, he crossed two fields, and stooped as he looked in at the low doorway of the cottage, from the interior of which there issued the loud cries of a child either in great pain or passion.

A sturdy little boy seated on a stool, and roaring like a young bull, while an elderly woman tried to comfort him, was the sight which met his gaze.

"Can you show me the road to St. Just?" inquired our adventurer.

"St. Just, sur?" said the woman, stepping out in front of the door, "why, you're on the way to St. Buryan, sure. Ef you do keep on the right of the hill over theere, you'll see the St. Just road."

A yell of unparalleled ferocity issued at this moment from the cottage, and it was found that the noisy urchin within, overcome by curiosity, had risen to ascertain who the stranger outside could be, and had been arrested by a pang of agony.

"Aw dear, aw dear, my poor booy," exclaimed the woman, endeavouring gently to press the boy down again on the stool, amid furious roaring.

"What's wrong with him?" asked our traveller, entering the apartment.

"He's tumbled off the wall, dear booy, an' semen to me he's scat un shoulder very bad."

"Let me have a look at him," said the youth, sitting down on the edge of a bed which stood at one end of the room, and drawing the child between his knees. "Come, little man, don't shout so loud; I'll put it all right for you. Let me feel your shoulder."

To judge from the immediate result, the young man seemed to put it all wrong instead of "all right," for his somewhat rough manipulation of the boy's shoulder produced such a torrent of screams that the pitying woman had much ado to restrain herself from rushing to the rescue.

"Ah!" exclaimed the youth in grey, releasing his victim; "I thought so; he has broken his collarbone, my good woman; not a serious matter, by any means, but it will worry him for some time to come. Have you got anything to make a bandage of?"

"Sur?" said the woman.

"Have you a bit of rag — an old shirt or apron? — anything will do."

The woman promptly produced a cotton shirt, which the youth tore up into long strips. Making a pad of one of these, he placed it under the boy's arm-pit despite of sobs and resistance. This pad acted as a fulcrum on which the arm rested as a lever. Pressing the elbow close to the boy's side he thus forced the shoulder outwards, and, with his left hand, set the bone with its two broken ends together. To secure it in this position he bound the arm pretty firmly to the boy's body, so that he could not move a muscle of the left arm or shoulder.

"There," said the youth, assisting his patient to put on his shirt, "that will keep all straight. You must not on any account remove the bandage for some weeks."

"How long, sur?" exclaimed the woman in surprise.

"For some weeks; but that will depend on how the little fellow gets on. He may go about and use his right arm as he pleases, but no more climbing on walls for some time to come. Do you hear, little man?"

The urchin, whose pain was somewhat relieved, and who had moderated down to an occasional deep sob, said "Iss."

"You're a doctor, sur, I think?" said the woman.

"Yes, I am; and I'll come to see you again, so be careful to attend to my directions. Good-morning."

"Good mornin', sur, an' thank 'ee!" exclaimed the grateful dame as the youth left the house, and, leaping the low enclosure in front of it, sped over the moor in the direction which had been pointed out to him.

His resolution to ignore roads cost our traveller more trouble than he had anticipated, for the moor was very rugged, the brambles vexatious, and the spines of the gorse uncommonly sharp. Impediments of every kind were more numerous than he had been accustomed to meet with even on the heath-clad hills of Scotland, with which — although "the land of the mountain and the flood" was not that of his birth — he had from childhood been familiar.

After a good deal of vigorous leaping and resolute scrambling, he reached one of those peculiar Cornish lanes which are so deeply sunk in the ground, and edged with such high solid walls, that the wayfarer cannot in many places see the nature of the country through which he is passing. The point at which he reached the lane was so overgrown with gorse and brambles that it was necessary to search for a passage through them. This not being readily found, he gave way to the impetuosity of his disposition, stepped back a few paces, cleared the obsta-cles with a light bound, and alighted on the edge of the bank, which gave way under his weight, and he descended into the lane in a shower of stones and dust, landing on his feet more by chance than by dexterity.

A shout of indignation greeted the traveller, and, turning abruptly round, he beheld a stout old gentleman stamping with rage, covered from head to foot with dust, and sputtering out epithets of opprobrium on the hapless wight who had thus unintentionally bespattered him.

"Ugh! hah! you young jackanapes — you blind dumbledory — ugh! What mean you by galloping over the country thus like a wild ass — eh?"

A fit of coughing here interrupted the choleric old gentleman, in the midst of which our hero, with much humility of demeanour, many apologies, and pro-testations of innocence of intention to injure, picked up the old gentleman's hat, assisted him to brush his clothes with a bunch of ferns, and in various other ways sought to pacify him.

The old man grumbled a good deal at first, but was finally so far mollified as to say less testily, while he put on his hat, "I warrant me, young man, you are come on some wild-goose chase to this out-o'-the-way region of the land in search of the picturesque — eh? — a dauber on canvas?"

"No, sir," replied the youth, "I profess not to wield the pencil or brush, although I admit to having made feeble efforts as an amateur. The scalpel is more to my taste, and my object in coming here is to visit a relative. I am on my way to St. Just; but, having wandered somewhat out of my road, have been obliged to strike into bypaths, as you see."

"As I *see*, young man! — yes, and as I *feel*," replied the old gentleman, with some remains of asperity.

"I have already expressed regret for the mischance that has befallen you," said the youth in grey somewhat sternly, for his impulsive spirit fired a little at the continued ill-humour of the old gentleman. "Perhaps you will return good for evil by pointing out the way to St. Just. May I venture to ask this favour of you?"

"You may venture, and you *have* ventured; and it is my belief, young man, that you'll venture many a thing before this world has done with you; however, as you are a stranger in these parts, and have expressed due penitence for your misdeed, though I more than half doubt your sincerity, I can do no less than point out the road to St. Just, whither I will accompany you at least part of the way; and, young sir, as you have taken pretty free liberty with *me* this morning, may I take the liberty of asking *you* the name of your relative in St. Just? I am well acquainted with most of the inhabitants of that town."

"Certainly," replied the youth. "The gentleman whom I am going to visit is my uncle. His name is Donnithorne."

"What! Tom Donnithorne?" exclaimed the old gentleman, in a tone of sur-prise, as he darted a keen glance from under his bushy eyebrows at his com-panion. "Hah! then from that fact I gather that you are Oliver Trembath, the young doctor whom he has been expecting the last day or two. H'm — so old Tom Donnithorne is your uncle, is he?"

The youth in grey did not relish the free and easy, not to say patronising, tone of his companion, and felt inclined to give a sharp answer, but he restrained his feelings and replied, – "He is, and you are correct in your supposition regarding myself. Do you happen to know my uncle personally?"

"Know him personally!" cried the old gentleman with a sardonic laugh; "Oh yes, I know him intimately – intimately; some people say he's a very good fellow."

"I am glad to hear that, for to say truth –"

He paused abruptly.

"Ha! I suppose you were going to say that you have heard a different account of him – eh?"

"Well, I *was* going to observe," replied Oliver, with a laugh, "that my uncle is rather a wild man for his years – addicted to smuggling, I am told, and somewhat given to the bottle; but it is well known that tattlers give false reports, and I am delighted to hear that the old boy is not such a bad fellow after all."

"Humph!" ejaculated the other. "Then you have never seen him, I suppose?"

"No, never; although I am a Cornishman I have seen little of my native county, having left it when a little boy – before my uncle came to live in this part of the country."

"H'm – well, young man, I would advise you to beware of that same uncle of yours."

"How!" exclaimed the youth in surprise; "did you not tell me just now that he is a very good fellow?"

"No, sir, I did not. I told you that *some* people say he is a very good fellow, but for myself I think him an uncommonly bad man, a man who has done me great injury in his day –"

"It grieves me to hear you say so," interrupted Oliver, whose ire was again roused by the tone and manner of his companion.

"A decidedly bad man," continued the old gentleman, not noticing the interruption, "a thorough rascal, a smuggler, and a drunkard, and –"

"Hold, sir!" cried the youth sternly, as he stopped and faced the old gentleman, "remember that you speak of my relative. Had you been a younger man, sir –"

Again the youth paused abruptly.

"Go on, sir," said the old gentleman ironically, "you would have pommelled me to a jelly with your cudgel, I suppose; is that it? – acting somewhat in the spirit of your kinsman, that same smuggling and tippling old scoundrel, who –"

"Enough, sir," interrupted the young man angrily; "we part company here."

So saying, he vaulted over the wall that separated the road from the moor, and hurried away.

"Take the first turn to the left, and keep straight on, else you'll lose yourself aga-a-a-in," roared the old gentleman, "and my compliments to the rascally old smugg-le-e-r-r!"

"The old scoundrel!" muttered the youth as he hurried away.

"The young puppy!" growled the old gentleman as he jogged along. "Given to smuggling and the bottle indeed — humph! the excitable jackanapes! But I've given him a turn in the wrong direction that will cool his blood somewhat, and give me leisure to cool mine too, before we meet again."

Here the old gentleman's red countenance relaxed into a broad grin, and he chuckled a good deal, in the midst of a running commentary on the conduct and appearance of his late companion, from the disjointed sentences of which it might have been gathered that although his introduction to the young doctor had been unfortunate, and the succeeding intercourse stormy, his opinion of him was not altogether unfavourable.

CHAPTER II.

Shows what Astonishing Results may follow from taking the Wrong Road.

Before Oliver Trembath had advanced half a mile on his path, he had cooled sufficiently to experience some regret at having been so quick to take offence at one who, being evidently an eccentric character, should not, he thought, have been broken with so summarily. Regrets, however, had come too late, so he endeavoured to shake off the disagreeable feelings that depressed him, and, the more effectually to accomplish this, burst forth into a bravura song with so much emphasis as utterly to drown, and no doubt to confound, two larks, which, up to that time, had been pouring their melodious souls out of their little bodies in the bright blue sky above.

Presently he came to a part of the moor where two roads diverged – one to the right and the other to the left. Recalling the shout of advice which the old gentleman had given him in parting, he took that which led to the left, and was gratified, on gaining an eminence a short distance in advance, to see in the far distance a square turret, which he concluded was that of the church of St. Just.

Keeping this turret in view, the youth stepped out so vigorously that he soon reached the small town that clustered round the church, and going up to the first man he met, said, "This is the town of St. Just, I suppose, is it not?"

"No, et is'n; thee's come the wrang road, sur," replied the rustic. "This es Sennen church-town. St. Just es up over th' hill theere."

Oliver Trembath's first feeling was one of surprise; this was followed by annoyance, which quickly degenerated into anger as it flashed into his mind that the old gentleman might possibly have led him wrong on purpose.

"How far is it to St. Just?" he inquired.

"'Bout six miles, sur."

"Then I suppose I am not far from the Land's End?" said Oliver after a pause.

"No, not fur," replied the man. "Et do lie straight before 'ee."

Thanking the man, Oliver started off at a smart pace, resolving, before proceeding to St. Just, to visit this extreme western point of England – a visit to which he had often looked forward with pleasant anticipation.

During the last hour of his walk the sun had been obscured by clouds, but, just as he approached the cliffs, the clouds separated, and a golden flood rushed over the broad Atlantic, which now lay spread out before him in all its wide majesty as far as the eye could see.

"A good omen!" cried the youth with a shout, as he hurried towards the shore, intending to fling off his garments and bathe in the mighty ocean, which, from the place where he first beheld it, appeared to be smooth and still as a mill-pond. But Oliver was compelled to restrain his ardour, for on nearing the sea he found that he stood on the summit of high cliffs, beyond which the Land's End stretched in a succession of broken masses of granite, so chafed and shattered by the action of the sea, and so curiously split, as to resemble basaltic columns. To reach the outermost of those weatherworn sentinels of Old England, required some caution on the part of our traveller, even although well used to scaling the rocky heights of Scottish mountains, and when he did at last plant his foot on the veritable Land's End, he found that it was a precipice apparently sixty feet high, which descended perpendicularly into deep water. His meditated bathe was therefore an impossibility, for those glassy undulations, which appeared so harmless at a distance, gathered slow and gradual height as they approached the land, and at last, assuming the form of majestic waves, flung themselves with a grand roar on the stern cliffs which they have battered so long in vain, and round which — always repulsed but never conquered — they seethed in milky foam.

With glistening eye, and heaving breast, and mantling colour, the young doctor stood long and motionless on this extreme point of land — absorbed in admiration of the glorious scene before him. Often had he beheld the sea in the firths and estuaries of the North, but never till now had he conceived the grandeur of the great Atlantic. It seemed to him as if the waves of those inland seas, when tossed by wild storms, were but rough miniature copies of the huge billows which arose before him, without apparent cause, and, advancing without rush or agitation, fell successively with solemn roar at his feet, awakening irresistibly within him deep and new thoughts of the Almighty Creator of earth and sea.

For many minutes he stood entranced, his mind wandering in a species of calm delight over the grand scene, but incapable of fixing itself definitely on any special feature — now sweeping out to where the Scilly Isles could be seen resting on the liquid horizon, anon following the flight of circling seagulls, or busy counting the innumerable ships and boats that rested on the sea, but ever and anon recurring, as if under the influence of fascination, to that rich turmoil of foam which boiled, leaped, and churned, around, beneath, and above the mighty breakers.

Awaking at last from his trance, Oliver tore himself from the spot, and hastened away to seek the nearest strip of sand where he might throw off his clothes and plunge into the boiling surf.

He proceeded in a southerly direction, impatiently expecting at every step to discover some spot suitable for his purpose, but he had taken a long and rapid walk before he found a break in those wild cliffs which afforded him the opportunity of descending to the water's edge. Here, on a narrow strip of sand, he undressed and leaped into the waves.

Well was it for Oliver that day that he had been trained in all manly exercises, that his "wind" was good, that his muscles were hard, his nerves well strung, and, above all, that in earliest youth he had learned to swim.

Misjudging, in his ignorance, the tremendous power of the surf into which he sprang, and daring to recklessness in the conscious possession of unusual strength and courage, he did not pause to look or consider, but at once struck out to sea. He was soon beyond the influence of the breaking waves, and for some time sported in the full enjoyment of the briny Atlantic waters. Then turning towards the shore he swam in and was speedily tossing among the breakers. As he neared the sandy beach and felt the full power of the water on his partially exhausted frame, he experienced a slight feeling of anxiety, for the thunder of each wave as it fell and rushed up before him in seething foam, seemed to indicate a degree of force which he had not realised in his first vigorous plunge into the sea. A moment more and a wave caught him in its curling crest, and swept him onwards. For the first time in his life, Oliver Trembath's massive strength was of no avail to him. He felt like a helpless infant. In another instant the breaker fell and swept him with irresistible violence up the beach amid a turmoil of hissing foam. No sooner did he touch the ground than he sprang to his feet, and staggered forward a few paces but the returning rush of water swept sand and stones from beneath his feet, carried his legs from under him, and hurled him back into the hollow of the succeeding wave, which again rolled him on the sand.

Although somewhat stunned, Oliver did not lose consciousness or self-possession. He now fully realised the extreme danger of his position, and the thought flashed through his brain that, at the farthest, his fate must be decided in two or three minutes. Acting on a brave spirit, this thought nerved him to desperate effort. The instant he could plant his feet firmly he bounded forwards, and then, before the backward rush of water had gathered strength, fell on his knees, and dug his fingers and toes deep into the sand. Had the grasp been on something firm he could easily have held on, but the treacherous sand crumbled out of his grasp, and a second time he was carried back into the sea.

The next time he was cast on the beach he felt that his strength was failing; he staggered forward as soon as he touched bottom, with all the energy of one who avails himself of his last chance, but the angry water was too strong for him. Feeling that he was being overpowered, he cast his arms up in the air, and gave utterance to a loud cry. It was not like a cry of despair, but sounded more like what one might suppose would be the shout of a brave soldier when compelled to give way — fighting — before the might of overwhelming force. At that moment a hand caught the young man's wrist, and held it for a few seconds in a powerful grasp. The wave retreated, a staggering effort followed, and the next moment Oliver stood panting on the beach grasping the rough hand of his deliverer.

"Semen to me you was pretty nigh gone, sur," said the man, who had come thus opportunely to the rescue, as he wrung the sea-water from his garments.

He was a man of middle height, but of extremely powerful frame, and was habited in the garb of a fisherman.

"Truly I had been gone altogether but for your timely assistance; may God reward you for it!" said Oliver earnestly.

"Well, I don't think you would be so ready to thank me if you did knaw I had half made up my mind to lev 'ee go."

Oliver looked at the man in some surprise, for he spoke gruffly, almost angrily, and was evidently in earnest.

"You are jesting," said he incredulously.

"Jestin'; no I ain't, maister. Do 'ee see the boat out over?" he said, pointing to a small craft full of men which was being rowed swiftly round a point not more than half a mile distant; "the villains are after me. They might as well have tried to kitch a cunger by the tail as nab Jim Cuttance in one of his dens, if he hadn't bin forced by the softness of his 'art to pull a young fool out o' the say. You'll have to help me to fight, lad, as I've saved your life. Come, follow me to the cave."

"But — my clothes —" said Oliver, glancing round him in search of his garments.

"They're all safe up here; come along, sur, an' look sharp."

At any other time, and in other circumstances, Oliver Trembath's fiery spirit would have resented the tone and manner of this man's address, but the feeling that he owed his life to him, and that in some way he appeared to be the innocent cause of bringing misfortune on him, induced him to restrain his feelings and obey without question the mandate of his rescuer. Jim Cuttance led the way to a cave in the rugged cliffs, the low entrance to which was concealed by a huge mass of granite. The moment they entered several voices burst forth in abuse of the fisherman for his folly in exposing himself; but the latter only replied with a sarcastic laugh, and advised his comrades to get ready for action, for he had been seen by the enemy, who would be down on them directly. At the same time he pointed to Oliver's clothes, which lay in a recess in the side of the cavern.

The youth dressed himself rapidly, and, while thus engaged, observed that there were five men in the cavern, besides his guide, with whom they retired into the farthest recess of the place, and entered into animated and apparently angry, though low-toned, conversation. At length their leader, for such he evidently was, swung away from them, exclaiming, with a laugh, "Well, well, he's a good recruit, and if he should peach on we — us can —"

He concluded the sentence with a significant grunt.

"Now, sur," he said, advancing with his comrade towards Oliver, who was completing his toilet, "they'll be here in ten minutes, an' it is expected that you will lend we a hand. Here's a weapon for you."

So saying, he handed a large pistol to Oliver, who received it with some hesitation.

"I trust that your cause is a good one," he said. "You cannot expect me to fight for you, even though I am indebted to you for my life, without knowing against whom I fight, and why."

At this a tall thick-set man suddenly cocked his pistol, and uttering a fierce oath swore that if the stranger would not fight, he'd shoot him through the head.

"Silence, Joe Tonkin!" cried Jim Cuttance, in a tone that at once subdued the man.

Oliver, whose eyes had flashed like those of a tiger, drew himself up, and said — "Look at me, lads; I have no desire to boast of what I can or will do, but I assure you it would be as easy to turn back the rising tide as to force me to fight against my will — except, indeed, with yourselves. As I have said, I owe my life to your leader, and apparently have been the innocent means of drawing his enemies upon him. Gratitude tells me to help him if I can, and help him will if the cause be not a bad one."

"Well spoken, sur," said the leader, with an approving nod; "see to the weapons, Maggot, and I'll explain it all to the gentleman."

So saying, he too Oliver aside, told him hurriedly that the men who ere expected to attack them were fishermen belonging to a neighbouring cove, whose mackerel nets had been accidentally cut by his boat some weeks ago, and who were bent on revenge, not believing that the thing had been done by accident.

"But surely you don't mean to use firearms against them in such a quarrel?" said Oliver.

A sort of humorous smile crossed the swarthy countenance of the man as he replied —

"They will use pistols against we."

"Be that as it may," said Oliver; "I will never consent to risk taking the life of a countryman in such a cause."

"But you can't fight without a weapon," said the man; "and sure, if 'ee don't shut them they'll shut you."

"No matter, I'll take my chance," said Oliver; "my good cudgel would have served me well enough, but it seems to have been swept away by the sea. Here, however, is a weapon that will suit me admirably," he added, picking up a heavy piece of driftwood that lay at his feet.

"Well, if you scat their heads with that, they won't want powder and lead," observed the other with a grin, as he rose and returned to the entrance of the cave, where he warned his comrades to keep as quiet as mice.

The boat which had caused so much angry discussion among the men of the cave had by this time neared the beach, and one of the crew stood up in the bow to guide her into the narrow cove, which formed but a slight protection, even in calm weather, against the violence of that surf which never ceases to grind at the hard rocks of West Cornwall. At length they effected a landing, and the crew, consisting of nine men armed with pistols and cutlasses, hurried up to the cliffs and searched for the entrance to the cavern.

While the events which have been related were taking place, the shades of evening had been gradually creeping over land and sea, and the light was at that time scarcely sufficient to permit of things being distinguished clearly beyond a few yards. The men in the cavern hid themselves in the dark recesses on each side of the entrance, ready for the approaching struggle.

Oliver crouched beside his rescuer with the piece of driftwood by his side. Turning suddenly to his companion, he said, in an almost inaudible whisper —

"Friend, it did not occur to me before, but the men we are about to fight with will recognise me again if we should ever chance to meet; could I not manage to disguise myself in some way?"

"If you get shut," replied his companion in the same low tone, "it won't matter much; but see here — shut your eyes."

Without further remark the man took a handful of wet earth and smeared it over Oliver's face, then, clapping his own "sou'-wester" on his head, he said, with a soft chuckle, "There, your own mother wouldn't knaw 'ee!"

Just then footsteps were heard approaching, and the shadow of a man was seen to rest for a moment on the gravel without. The mouth of the cave was so well hidden, however, that he failed to observe it, and passed on, followed by several of his comrades. Suddenly one of them stopped and said —

"Hold on, lads, it can't be far off, I'm sartin' sure; I seed 'em disappear hereabouts."

"You're right," cried Jim Cuttance, with a fierce roar, as he rushed from the cavern and fired full at the man who had spoken. The others followed, and a volley of shots succeeded, while shouts of defiance and anger burst forth on all sides. Oliver sprang out at the same moment with the leader, and rushed on one of the boat's crew with such violence that his foot slipped on a piece of seaweed and precipitated him to the ground at the man's feet; the other, having sprung forward to meet him was unable to check himself, tripped over his shoulders, and fell on the top of him. The man named Maggot, having been in full career close behind Oliver, tumbled over both, followed by another man named John Cock. The others, observing them down, rushed with a shout to the rescue, just as Oliver, making a superhuman effort, flung the two men off his back and leaped to his feet. Maggot and the boatman also sprang up, and the latter turned and made for the boat at full speed, seeing that his comrades, overcome by the suddenness of the onset, were in retreat, fighting as they went.

All of them succeeded in getting into the boat unharmed, and were in the act of pushing off, when Jim Cuttance, burning with indignation, leaped into the water, grasped the bow of the boat, and was about to plunge his cutlass into the back of the man nearest him, when he was seized by a strong hand from behind and held back. Next moment the boat was beyond his reach.

Turning round fiercely, the man saw that it was Oliver Trembath who had interfered. He uttered a terrible oath, and sprang on him like a tiger; Oliver stood firm, parried with the piece of driftwood the savage cut which was made at his head, and with his clenched left hand hit his opponent such a blow on the chest as laid him flat on the sand. The man sprang up in an instant, but instead of renewing the attack, to Oliver's surprise he came forward and held out his hand, which the youth was not unwilling to grasp.

"Thank 'ee, sur," he said, somewhat sternly, "you've done me a sarvice; you've prevented me committin' two murders, an' taught me a lesson I never knaw'd afore — that Jim Cuttance an't invulnerable. I don't mind the blow, sur — not I. It wor gov'n in feer fight, an' I was wrang."

"I'm glad to find that you view the matter in that light," said Oliver with a smile, "and, truly, the blow was given in self-defence by one who will never forget that he owes you his life."

A groan here turned the attention of the party to one of their number who had seated himself on a rock during the foregoing dialogue.

"What! not hurt, are 'ee, Dan?" said his leader, going towards him.

To this Dan replied with another groan, and placed his hand on his hip.

His comrades crowded round him, and, finding that he was wounded and suffering great pain, raised him in their arms and bore him into the cavern, where they laid him on the ground, and, lighting a candle, proceeded to examine him.

"You had better let me look at him, lads," said Oliver, pushing the men gently aside, "I am a surgeon."

They gave place at once, and Oliver soon found that the man had received a pistol-ball in his thigh. Fortunately it had been turned aside in its course, and lay only a little way beneath the skin, so that it was easily extracted by means of a penknife.

"Now, friends," said Oliver, after completing the dressing of the wound, "before I met with you I had missed my way while travelling to St. Just. Will one of you direct me to the right road, and I shall bid you good-night, as I think you have no further need of my services."

The men looked at their leader, whom they evidently expected to be their spokesman.

"Well, sur, you have rendered we some help this hevenin', both in the way o' pickin' out the ball an' helpin' to break skulls as well as preventin' worse, so we can do no less than show 'ee the road; but hark 'ee, sur," here the man became very impressive, "ef you do chance to come across any of us in your travels, you had better not knaw us, 'xcept in an or'nary way, d'ye understand? an' us will do the same by thee."

"Of course I will act as you wish," said Oliver with a smile, "although I do not see why we should be ashamed of this affair, seeing that we were the party attacked. There is only one person to whom I would wish to explain the reason of my not appearing sooner, because he will probably know of the arrival in Penzance this morning of the conveyance that brought me to Cornwall."

"And who may that be?" demanded Jim Cuttance.

"My uncle, Thomas Donnithorne of St. Just," said Oliver.

"Whew!" whistled the fisherman in surprise, while all the others burst into a hearty fit of laughter.

"Why do you laugh?" asked Oliver.

"Oh, never mind, sur, it's all right," said the man with a chuckle. "Iss, you may tell Thomas Donnithorne; there won't be no harm in tellin' he — oh, dear no!"

Again the men laughed loud and long, and Oliver felt his powers of forbearance giving way, when Cuttance said to him: "An' you may tell all his friends too, for they're the right sort. Come now, Maggot here will show 'ee the way up to St. Just."

So saying, the stout fisherman conducted the young surgeon to the mouth of the cavern, and shaking hands with him left him to the guidance of the man named Maggot, who led him through several lanes, until he reached the highroad between Sennen church-town and St. Just. Here he paused; told his companion to proceed straight on for about four miles or so, when he would reach the town, and bade him good-night.

"And mind 'ee, don't go off the road, sur," shouted Maggot, a few seconds after the young man had left him, "if 'ee don't want to fall down a shaft and scat your skull."

Oliver, not having any desire to scat his skull, whatever that might be, assured the man that he would keep to the road carefully.

The moon shone clear in a cloudless sky, covering the wide moor and the broad Atlantic with a flood of silver light, and rendering the road quite distinct, so that our traveller experienced no further difficulty in pursuing his way. He hurried forward at a rapid pace, yet could not resist the temptation to pause frequently and gaze in admiration on the scene of desolate grandeur around him. On such occasions he found it difficult to believe that the stirring events of the last few hours were real. Indeed, if it had not been that there were certain uneasy portions of his frame — the result of his recent encounter on the beach — which afforded constant and convincing evidence that he was awake, he would have been tempted to believe that the adventures of that day were nothing more than a vivid dream.

CHAPTER III.

Introduces a few more Characters and Homely Incidents.

It was late when our hero entered the little town of St. Just, and inquired for the residence of his uncle, Thomas Donnithorne. He was directed to one of the most respectable of the group of old houses that stood close to the venerable parish church from which St. Just derives its title of "Church-town."

He tapped at the door, which was opened by an elderly female.

"Does Mr. Thomas Donnithorne live here?" asked Oliver.

"Iss, sur, he do," answered the woman; "walk in, sur."

She ushered him into a small parlour, in which was seated a pretty, little, dark-eyed, rosy-cheeked girl, still in, or only just out of, her teens. Oliver was so taken aback by the unexpected sight that he stood gazing for a moment or two in rather stupid silence.

"Your name is Oliver Trembath, I presume," said the girl, rising and laying down the piece of needlework with which she was occupied.

"It is," replied Oliver, in some surprise, as he blundered out an apology for his rudeness.

"Pray sit down, sir," said the girl; "we have been expecting you for some time, and my uncle told me to act the part of hostess till his return."

"Your uncle!" exclaimed Oliver, whose self-possession, not to say impudence, returned immediately; "if Thomas Donnithorne be indeed your uncle, then, fair maid, you and I must needs be cousins, the which, I confess, fills me with satisfaction and also with somewhat of surprise, for up to this hour I have been ignorant of my good fortune in being related to so — so —"

"I made a mistake, sir," said the girl, interrupting a speech which was evidently verging towards impropriety, "in calling Mr. Donnithorne uncle to you, who are not aware, it seems, that I am only an adopted niece."

"Not aware of it! Of course not," said Oliver, throwing himself into a large armchair, while his fair companion busied herself in spreading the board for a substantial meal. "I could not be aware of much that has occurred in this distant part of the kingdom, seeing that my worthy uncle has vouchsafed to write me only two letters in the course of my life; once, many years ago, to condole with me — in about ten lines, address and signature included — on the death of my dear mother; and once again to tell me he had procured an appointment for me as assistant-surgeon in the mining district of St. Just. He must have been equally uncommunicative to my mother, for she never mentioned your existence. However, since I have now made the agreeable discovery, I trust that you will dispense with ceremony, and allow me at once to call you cousin. By the way, you have not yet told me your name."

The maiden, who was charmingly unsophisticated, replied that her name was Rose Ellis, and that she had no objection whatever to being called cousin without delay.

"Well, cousin Rose," said Oliver, "if it be not prying into secrets, I should like to know how long it is since my uncle adopted you."

"About nineteen years ago," replied Rose.

"Oh!" said Oliver remonstratively, "before you were born? impossible!"

Rose laughed — a short, clear, little laugh which she nipped in the bud abruptly, and replied —

"Well, it was only a short time after I was born. I was wrecked on this coast" — the expressive face here became very grave — "and all on board our ship perished except myself."

Oliver saw at once that he had touched on a tender subject, and hastened to change it by asking a number of questions about his uncle, from which he gradually diverged to the recent events in his own history, which he began to relate with much animation. His companion was greatly interested and amused. She laughed often and heartily in a melodious undertone, and Oliver liked her laugh, for it was peculiar, and had the effect of displaying a double row of pretty little teeth, and of almost entirely shutting up her eyes. She seemed to enjoy a laugh so much that he exerted all his powers to tickle her risible faculties, and dwelt long and graphically on his meeting with the irascible old gentleman in the lane. He was still busy with this part of the discourse when a heavy step was heard outside.

"There's my uncle," exclaimed Rose, springing up.

A moment after the door opened, and in walked the identical irascible old gentleman himself!

If a petrified impersonation of astonishment had been a possibility, Oliver Trembath would, on that occasion, have presented the phenomenon. He sat, or rather lay, extended for at least half a minute with his eyes wide and his mouth partly open, bereft alike of the powers of speech and motion.

"Heyday, young man!" exclaimed the old gentleman, planting his sturdy frame in the middle of the floor as if he meant then and there to demand and exact an ample apology, or to inflict condign and terrible chastisement, for past misdeeds; "you appear to be making yourself quite at home — eh?"

"My *dear* sir!" exclaimed Oliver, leaping up with a look of dismay; "how can I express my — my — but is it, *can* it be possible that you are Mr. Donnithorne — m — my — uncle?"

Oliver's expression, and the look of amazement on the countenance of Rose Ellis, who could not account for such a strange reception of her newly-found cousin, proved almost too much for the old gentleman, whose eyes had already begun to twinkle.

"Ay, young man, I am Tom Donnithorne, your uncle, the vile, old, smug-gling, brandy-loving rascal, who met his respectful nephew on the road to St. Just" — at this point Rose suddenly pressed her hand over her mouth, darted to her own apartment in a distant corner of the house, and there, seated on her little bed, went into what is not inaptly styled fits of laughter — "and who now," continued the old gentleman, relaxing into a genial smile, and grasping his nephew's hand, "welcomes Oliver Trembath to his house, with all his heart and soul; there, who will say after that, that old Donnithorne does not know how to return good for evil?"

"But, my dear uncle," began Oliver, "allow me to explain —"

"Now, now, look at that — kept me hours too late for supper already, and he's going to take up more time with explanations," cried the old gentleman, flinging himself on the chair from which Oliver had risen, and wiping his bald pate with a red silk handkerchief. "What can you explain, boy, except that you met an angry old fellow in a lane who called your uncle such hard names that you couldn't help giving him a bit of your mind — there, there, sit down, sit down. — Hallo!" he shouted, starting up impulsively and thrusting his head into the passage, "Rose, Rose, I say, where are you? — hallo!"

"Coming, uncle — I'm here."

The words came back like an echo, and in another minute Rose appeared with a much-flushed countenance.

"Come along, lass, let's have supper without delay. Where is aunty? Rout her out, and tell that jade of a cook that if she don't dish up in five minutes I'll — I'll — . Well, Oliver, talking of explanations, how comes it that you are so late?"

"Because I took the wrong road after leaving you in the lane," replied the youth, with a significant glance at his uncle, whose eyes were at the moment fixed gravely on the ground.

"The wrong road — eh?" said Mr. Donnithorne, looking up with a sly glance, and then laughing. "Well, well, it was only *quid pro quo*, boy; you put a good deal of unnecessary earth and stones over my head, so I thought it was but fair that I should put a good deal more of the same under your feet, besides giving you the advantage of seeing the Land's End, which, of course, every youth of intelligence must take a deep interest in beholding. But, sure, a walk thither, and thence to St. Just, could not have detained you so long?"

"Truly no," replied Oliver; "I had a rencontre — a sort of adventure with fishermen, which —"

"Fishermen!" exclaimed Mr. Donnithorne in surprise; "are ye sure they were not smugglers — eh?"

"They said they were fishermen, and they looked like such," replied Oliver; "but my adventure with them, whatever they were, was the cause of my detention, and I can only express my grief that the circumstance has incommoded your household, but, you see, it took some time to beat off the boat's crew, and then I had to examine a wound and extract —"

"What say you, boy!" exclaimed Mr. Donnithorne, frowning, "beat off a boat's crew — examine a wound! Why, Rose, Molly, come hither. Here we have a young gallant who hath begun life in the far west in good style; but hold, here comes my excellent friend Captain Dan, who is no friend to the smugglers; he is to sup with us tonight; so we will repress our curiosity till after supper. Let me introduce you, Oliver to my wife, your Aunt Molly, or, if you choose to be respectful, Aunt Mary."

As he spoke, a fat, fair, motherly-looking lady of about five-and-forty entered the room, greeting her husband with a rebuke, and her nephew with a smile.

"Never mind him, Oliver," said the good lady; "he is a vile old creature. I have heard all about your meeting with him this forenoon, and only wish I had been there to see it."

"Listen to that now, Captain Dan," cried Mr. Donnithorne, as the individual addressed entered the room; "my wife calls me — me, a staid, sober man of fifty-five — calls me a vile old creature. Is it not too bad? really one gets no credit nowadays for devoting oneself entirely to one's better half; but I forget: allow me to introduce you to my nephew, Oliver Trembath, just come from one of the Northern Universities to fight the smugglers of St. Just — of which more anon. Oliver, Captain Hoskin of Botallack, better known as Captain Dan. Now, sit down and let's have a bit of supper."

With hospitable urgency Mr. Donnithorne and his good dame pressed their guests to do justice to the fare set before them, and, during the course of the meal, the former kept up a running fire of question, comment, and reply on every conceivable subject, so that his auditors required to do little more than eat and listen. After supper, however, and when tumblers and glasses were being put down, he gave the others an opportunity of leading the conversation.

"Now, Oliver," he said, "fill your glass and let us hear your adventures. What will you have — brandy, gin, or rum? My friend, Captain Dan here, is one of those remarkable men who don't drink anything stronger than ginger-beer. Of course you won't join *him*."

"Thank you," said Oliver. "If you will allow me, I will join your good lady in a glass of wine. Permit me, Aunt Mary, to fill —"

"No, I thank you, Oliver," said Mrs. Donnithorne good-humouredly but firmly, "I side with Captain Dan; but I'll be glad to see you fill your own."

"Ha!" exclaimed Mr. Donnithorne, "Molly's sure to side with the opponent of her lawful lord, no matter who or what he be. Fill your own glass, boy, with what you like — cold water, an it please you — and let us drink the good old Cornish toast, 'Fish, tin, and copper,' our three staples, Oliver — the bone, muscle, and fat of the county."

"Fish, tin, and copper," echoed Captain Dan.

"In good sooth," continued Mr. Donnithorne, "I have often thought of turning teetotaller myself, but feared to do so lest my wife should take to drinking, just out of opposition. However, let that pass — and now, Oliver, open thy mouth, lad, and relate those surprising adventures of which you have given me a hint."

"Indeed, uncle, I do not say they are very surprising, although, doubtless, somewhat new to one who has been bred, if not born, in comparatively quiet regions of the earth."

Here Oliver related circumstantially to his wondering auditors the events which befell him after the time when he left his uncle in the lane — being interrupted only with an occasional exclamation — until he reached the part when he knocked down the man who had rescued him from the waves, when Mr. Donnithorne interrupted him with an uncontrollable burst.

"Ha!" shouted the old gentleman; "what! knocked down the man who saved your life, nephew? Fie, fie! But you have not told us his name yet. What was it?"

"His comrades called him Jim, as I have said; and I think that he once referred to himself as Jim Cuttance, or something like that."

"What say you, boy?" exclaimed Mr. Donnithorne, pushing back his chair and gazing at his nephew in amazement. "Hast fought side by side with Jim Cuttance, and then knocked him down?"

"Indeed I have," said Oliver, not quite sure whether his uncle regarded him as a hero or a fool.

The roar of laughter which his answer drew from Captain Dan and his uncle did not tend to enlighten him much.

"Oh! Oliver, Oliver," said the old gentleman, on recovering some degree of composure, "you should have lived in the days of good King Arthur, and been one of the Knights of the Round Table. Knocked down Jim Cuttance! What think'ee, Captain Dan?"

"I think," said the captain, still chuckling quietly, "that the less our friend says about the matter the better for himself."

"Why so?" inquired Oliver quickly.

"Because," replied his uncle, with some return of gravity, "you have assisted one of the most notorious smugglers that ever lived, to fight his Majesty's coastguard — that's all. What say you, Molly — shall we convict Oliver on his own confession?"

The good lady thus appealed to admitted that it was a serious matter, but urged that as Oliver did the thing in ignorance and out of gratitude, he ought to be forgiven.

"*I* think he ought to be forgiven for having knocked down Jim Cuttance," said Captain Dan.

"Is he then so notorious?" asked Oliver.

"Why, he is the most daring smuggler on the coast," replied Captain Dan, "and has given the preventive men more trouble than all the others put together. In fact, he is a man who deserves to be hanged, and will probably come to his proper end ere long, if not shot in a brawl beforehand."

"I fear he stands some chance of it now," said Mr. Donnithorne, with a sigh, "for he has been talking of erecting a battery near his den at Prussia Cove, and openly defying the Government men."

"You seem to differ from Captain Dan, uncle, in reference to this man," said Oliver, with a smile.

"Truly, I do, for although I condemn smuggling — ahem!" (the old gentleman cast a peculiar glance at the captain), "I don't like to see a sturdy man hanged or shot — and Jim Cuttance is a stout fellow. I question much whether you could find his match, Captain Dan, amongst all your men?"

"That I could, easily," said the captain with a quiet smile.

"Pardon me, captain," said Oliver, "my uncle has not yet informed me on the point. May I ask what corps you belong to?"

"To a sturdy corps of tough lads," answered the captain, with another of his quiet smiles — "men who have smelt powder, most of 'em, since they were little boys — live on the battlefield, I may say, almost night and day — spring more mines in a year than all the soldiers in the world put together — and shorten their lives by the stern labour they undergo; but they burn powder to raise, not to waste, metal. Their uniform is red, too, though not quite so red, nor yet so elegant, as that of the men in his Majesty's service. I am one of the underground captains, sir, of Botallack mine."

Captain Dan's colour heightened a very little, and the tones of his voice became a little more powerful as he concluded this reply; but there was no other indication that the enthusiastic soul of one of the "captains" of the most celebrated mine in Cornwall was moved. Oliver felt, however, the contact with a kindred spirit, and, expressing much interest in the mines, proceeded to ask many questions of the captain, who, nothing loath, answered all his queries, and explained to him that he was one of the "captains," or "agents," whose duty it was to superintend the men and the works below the surface — hence the title of "underground;" while those who super-intended the works above ground were styled "grass, or surface captains." He also made an appointment to conduct the young doctor underground, and go over the mine with him at an early date.

While the party in old Mr. Donnithorne's dwelling were thus enjoying themselves, a great storm was gathering, and two events, very different from each other in character, were taking place — the one quiet, and apparently unimportant, the other tremendous and fatal — both bearing on and seriously influencing the subjects of our tale.

CHAPTER IV.

At Work under the Sea.

Chip, chip, chip — down in the dusky mine! Oh, but the rock at which the miner chipped was hard, and the bit of rock on which he sat was hard, and the muscles with which he toiled were hard from prolonged labour; and the lot of the man seemed hard, as he sat there in the hot, heavy atmosphere, hour after hour, from morn till eve, with the sweat pouring down his brow and over his naked shoulders, toiling and moiling with hammer and chisel.

But stout David Trevarrow did not think his lot peculiarly hard. His workshop was a low narrow tunnel deep down under the surface of the earth — ay, and deep under the bottom of the sea! His daily sun was a tallow candle, which rose regularly at seven in the morning and set at three in the afternoon. His atmosphere was sadly deficient in life-giving oxygen, and much vitiated by gunpowder smoke. His working costume consisted only of a pair of linen trousers; his colour from top to toe was red as brick-dust, owing to the iron ore around him; his food was a slice of bread, with, perchance, when he was unusually luxurious, the addition of a Cornish pasty; and his drink was water. To an inexperienced eye the man's work would have appeared not only hard but hopeless, for although his hammer was heavy, his arm strong, and his chisel sharp and tempered well, each blow produced an apparently insignificant effect on the flinty rock. Frequently a spark of fire was all that resulted from a blow, and seldom did more than a series of little chips fly off, although the man was of herculean mould, and worked "with a will," as was evident from the kind of gasp or stern expulsion of the breath with which each blow was accompanied. Unaided human strength he knew could not achieve much in such a process, so he directed his energies chiefly to the boring of blast-holes, and left it to the mighty power of gunpowder to do the hard work of rending the rich ore from the bowels of the unwilling earth. Yes, the work was very hard, probably the hardest that human muscles are ever called on to perform in this toiling world; but again we say that David Trevarrow did not think so, for he had been born to the work and bred to it, and was blissfully ignorant of work of a lighter kind, so that, although his brows frowned at the obstinate rock, his compressed lips smiled, for his thoughts were pleasant and far away. The unfettered mind was above ground roaming in fields of light, basking in sunshine, and holding converse with the birds, as he sat there chip, chip, chipping, down in the dusky mine.

Stopping at last, the miner wiped his brow, and, rising, stood for a few moments silently regarding the result of his day's work.

"Now, David," said he to himself, "the question is, what shall us do — shall us keep on, or shall us knack?"

He paused, as if unable to answer the question. After a time he muttered, "Keep on; it don't look promisin', sure 'nuff, an' it's poor pay; but it won't do to give in yet."

Poor pay it was indeed, for the man's earnings during the past month had been barely ten shillings. But David Trevarrow had neither wife, child, nor mother to support, so he could afford to toil for poor pay, and, being of a remarkably hopeful and cheery disposition, he returned home that afternoon resolved to persevere in his unproductive toil, in the hope that at last he should discover a good "bunch of copper," or a "keenly lode of tin."

David was what his friends and the world styled unfortunate. In early man-hood he had been a somewhat wild and reckless fellow — a noted wrestler, and an adept in all manly sports and games. But a disappointment in love had taught him very bitterly that life is not all sunshine; and this, coupled with a physical injury which was the result of his own folly, crushed his spirit so much that his comrades believed him to be a "lost man."

The injury referred to was the bursting of a blood-vessel in the lungs. It was, and still is, the custom of the youthful miners of Cornwall to test their strength by racing up the almost interminable ladders by which the mines are reached. This tremendous exertion after a day of severe toil affected them of course very severely, and in some cases seriously. Many an able-bodied man has by this means brought himself to a premature end. Among others, David Trevarrow excelled and suffered. No one could beat him in running up the ladders; but one day, on reaching the surface, blood issued from his mouth, and thenceforth his racing and wrestling days were ended, and his spirit was broken. A long illness succeeded. Then he began to mend. Slowly and by degrees his strength returned, but not his joyous spirit. Still it was some comfort to feel able for work again, and he "went underground" with some degree of his old vigour, though not with the light heart or light step of former days; but bad fortune seemed to follow him everywhere. When others among his comrades were fortunate in finding copper or tin, David was most unaccountably unsuccessful. Accidents, too, from falls and explosions, laid him up more than once, and he not only acquired the character of an unlucky man from his friends, but despite a natu-rally sanguine temperament, he began himself to believe that he was one of the unluckiest fellows in the world.

About this time the followers of that noble Christian, John Wesley, began to make an impression on Cornwall, and to exert an influence which created a mighty change in the hearts and manners of the people, and the blessed effects of which are abundantly evident at the present day — to the rejoicing of every Christian soul. One of those ministers of our Lord happened to meet with David Trevarrow, and was the means of opening his eyes to many great and pre-viously unknown truths. Among others, he convinced him that "God's ways are not as man's ways;" that He often, though not always, leads His people by thorny paths that they know not of, but does it in love and with His own glory in their happiness as the end in view; that the Lord Jesus Christ must be to a man "the chiefest among ten thousand, and altogether lovely," else He is to him nothing at all, and that he could be convinced of all these truths only by the Holy Spirit.

It were vain to attempt to tell all that this good man said to the unhappy miner, but certain it is that from that time forth David became himself again – and yet not himself. The desire to wrestle and fight and race returned in a new form. He began to wrestle with principalities and powers, to fight the good fight of faith, and to run the race set before him in the gospel. The old hearty smile and laugh and cheery disposition also returned, and the hopeful spirit, and so much of the old robust health and strength, that it seemed as if none of the evil effects of the ruptured blood-vessel remained. So David Trevarrow went, as of old, daily to the mine. It is true that riches did not flow in upon him any faster than before, but he did not mind that much, for he had discovered another mine, in which he toiled at nights after the day's toil was over, and whence he extracted treasure of greater value than copper or tin, or even gold – treasure which he scattered in a Sabbath school with liberal hand, and found himself all the richer for his prodigality.

Occasionally, after prolonged labour in confined and bad air, a faint trace of the old complaint showed itself when he reached the top of the ladders, but he was not now depressed by that circumstance as he used to be. He was past his prime at the period of which we write, and a confirmed bachelor.

To return from this digression: David Trevarrow made up his mind, as we have said, to "go on," and, being a man of resolute purpose, he went on; seized his hammer and chisel, and continued perseveringly to smite the flinty rock, surrounded by thick darkness, which was not dispelled but only rendered visible by the feeble light of the tallow candle that flared at his side.

Over his head rolled the billows of the Atlantic; the whistling wind howled among the wild cliffs of the Cornish coast, but they did not break the deep silence of the miner's place of midnight toil. Heaven's artillery was rending the sky, and causing the hearts of men to beat slow with awe. The great boulders ground the pebbles into sand as they crashed to and fro above him, but he heard them not – or if he did, the sound reached him as a deep-toned mysterious murmur, for, being in one of the low levels, with many fathoms of solid rock between him and the bottom of the superincumbent sea, he was beyond the reach of such disturbing influences, tremendous though they were.

The miner was making a final effort at his unproductive piece of rock, and had prolonged his toil far into the night.

Hour after hour he wrought almost without a moment's respite, save for the purpose, now and then, of trimming his candle. When his right arm grew tired, he passed the hammer swiftly to his left hand, and, turning the borer with his right, continued to work with renewed vigour.

At last he paused, and looking over his shoulder called out – "Zackey, booy."

The sound died away in a hollow echo through the retiring galleries of the mine, but there was no reply.

"Zackey, booy, are 'ee slaipin'?" he repeated.

A small reddish-coloured bundle, which lay in a recess close at hand, uncoiled itself like a hedgehog, and, yawning vociferously, sat up, revealing the fact that the bundle was a boy.

"Ded 'ee call, uncle?" asked the boy in a sleepy tone.

"Iss did I," said the man; "fetch me the powder an' fuse, my son."

The lad rose, and, fetching out of a dark corner the articles required, assisted in charging the hole which his uncle had just finished boring. This was the last hole which the man intended to blast that night. For weeks past he had laboured day after day — sometimes, as on the present occasion, at night — and had removed many tons of rock, without procuring either tin or copper sufficient to repay him for his toil, so that he resolved to give it up and remove to a more hopeful part of the mine, or betake himself to another mine altogether. He had now bored his last hole, and was about to blast it. Applying his candle to the end of the fuse, he hastened along the level to a sufficient distance to afford security, warning his nephew as he passed.

Zackey leaped up, and, scrambling over the debris with which the bottom of the level was covered, made good his retreat. About a minute they waited in expectancy. Suddenly there was a bright blinding flash, which lit up the rugged sides of the mine, and revealed its cavernous ramifications and black depths. This was accompanied by a dull smothered report and a crash of falling rock, together with a shower of debris. Instantly the whole place was in profound darkness.

"Aw, booy," exclaimed the miner; "we was too near. It have knacked us in the dark."

"So't have, uncle; I'll go an' search for the box."

"Do, my son," said David.

In those days lucifer matches had not been invented, and light had to be struck by means of flint, steel, and tinder. The process was tedious compared with the rapid action of congreves and vestas in the present day. The man chipped away for full three minutes before he succeeded in relighting his candle. This done, the rock was examined.

"Bad still, Uncle David?" inquired the boy.

"Iss, Zackey Maggot, so we'll knack'n, and try the higher mine tomorrow." Having come to this conclusion Uncle David threw down the mass of rock which he held in his brawny hands, and, picking up his implements, said, "Get the tools, booy, and lev us go to grass."

Zackey, who had been in the mine all day, and was tired, tied his tools at each end of a rope, so that they might be slung over his shoulder and leave his hands free. Trevarrow treated his in the same way, and, removing his candle from the wall, fixed it on the front of his hat by the simple process of sticking thereto the lump of clay to which it was attached. Zackey having fixed his candle in the same manner, both of them put on their red-stained flannel shirts and linen coats, and traversed the level until they reached the bottom of the ladder-shaft. Here they paused for a few moments before commencing the long wearisome ascent of almost perpendicular ladders by which the miners descended to their work or returned "to grass," as they termed the act of returning to the surface.

It cost them more than half an hour of steady climbing before they reached the upper part of the shaft and became aware that a storm was raging in the regions above. On emerging from the mouth of the shaft or "ladder road," man and boy were in a profuse perspiration, and the sharp gale warned them to hasten to the moor-house at full speed.

Moor-houses were little buildings in which miners were wont to change their wet underground garments for dry clothes. Some of these used to be at a considerable distance from the shafts, and the men were often injured while going to them from the mine, by being exposed in an overheated state to cutting winds. Many a stout able-bodied miner has had a chill given him in this way which has resulted in premature death. Moor-houses have now been replaced by large drying-houses, near the mouths of shafts, where every convenience is provided for the men drying their wet garments and washing their persons on coming to the surface.

Having changed their clothes, uncle and nephew hastened to St. Just, where they dwelt in the cottage of Maggot, the blacksmith. This man, who has already been introduced to the reader, was brother-in-law to David, and father to Zackey.

When David Trevarrow entered his brother-in-law's cottage, and told him of his bad fortune, and of his resolution to try his luck next day in the higher mine, little did he imagine that his change of purpose was to be the first step in a succession of causes which were destined to result, at no very distant period, in great changes of fortune to some of his friends in St. Just, as well as to many others in the county.

CHAPTER V.

Describes a Wreck and some of its Consequences.

While the miner had been pursuing his toilsome work in the solitude and silence of the level under the sea, as already described, a noble ship was leaping over the Atlantic waves — homeward bound — to Old England.

She was an East-Indiaman, under close-reefed sails, and although she bent low before the gale so that the waves almost curled over her lee bulwarks, she rose buoyantly like a seagull, for she was a good ship, stout of plank and sound of timber, with sails and cordage to match.

Naturally, in such a storm, those on board were anxious, for they knew that they were drawing near to land, and that "dear Old England" had an ugly sea-board in these parts — a coast not to be too closely hugged in what the captain styled "dirty weather, with a whole gale from the west'ard," so a good lookout was kept. Sharp eyes were in the foretop looking out for the guiding rays of the Long-ships lighthouse, which illumine that part of our rocky shores to warn the mariner of danger and direct him to a safe harbour. The captain stood on the "foge's'l" with stern gaze and compressed lip. The chart had been consulted, the bearings correctly noted, calculations made, and leeway allowed for. Everything in fact that could be done by a commander who knew his duty had been done for the safety of the ship — so would the captain have said probably, had he lived to be questioned as to the management of his vessel. But everything had *not* been done. The lead, strange to say, had not been hove. It was ready to heave, but the order was delayed. Unaccountable fatality! The only safe guide that remained to the good ship on that wild night was held in abeyance. It was deemed unnecessary to heave it yet, or it was troublesome, and they would wait till nearer the land. No one now can tell the reasons that influenced the captain, but *the lead was not used*. Owing to similar delay or neglect, hundreds upon hundreds of ships have been lost, and thousands of human lives have been sacrificed!

The ship passed like a dark phantom over the very head of the miner who was at work many fathoms below the bottom of the sea.

"Land, ho!" came suddenly in a fierce, quick shout from the mast-head.

"Starboard! starboard — hard!" cried the captain, as the roar of breakers ahead rose above the yelling of the storm.

Before the order was obeyed or another word spoken the ship struck, and a shriek of human terror followed, as the foremast went by the board with a fearful crash. The waves burst over the stern, sweeping the decks fore and aft. Wave after wave lifted the great ship as though it had been a child's toy, and dashed her down upon the rocks. Her bottom was stove in, her planks and timbers were riven like matchwood. Far down below man was destroying the flinty rock, while overhead the rock was destroying the handiwork of man! But the destruction in the one case was slow, in the other swift. A desperate but futile effort was made by the crew to get out the boats, and the passengers, many of whom were women and children, rushed frantically from the cabin to the deck, and clung to anything they could lay hold of, until strength failed, and the waves tore them away.

One man there was in the midst of all the terror-stricken crew who retained his self-possession in that dread hour. He was a tall, stern old man with silver locks — an Indian merchant, one who had spent his youth and manhood in the wealthy land collecting gold — "making a fortune," he was wont to say — and who was returning to his fatherland to spend it. He was a thinking and calculating man, and in the anticipation of some such catastrophe as had actually overtaken him, he had secured some of his most costly jewels in a linen belt. This belt, while others were rushing to the boats, the old man secured round his waist, and then sprang on deck, to be swept, with a dozen of his fellow-passengers, into the sea by the next wave that struck the doomed vessel. There was no one on that rugged coast to lend a helping hand. Lifeboats did not then, as now, nestle in little nooks on every part of our dangerous coasts. No eye was there to see nor ear to hear, when, twenty minutes after she struck, the East-Indiaman went to pieces, and those of her crew and passengers who had retained their hold of her uttered their last despairing cry, and their souls returned to God who gave them.

It is a solemn thought that man may with such awful suddenness, and so unexpectedly, be summoned into the presence of his Maker. Thrice happy they who, when their hearts grow chill and their grasps relax as the last plank is rending, can say, "Neither death, nor life, nor any other creature, is able to separate us from the love of God, which is in Christ Jesus our Lord."

The scene we have described was soon over, and the rich cargo of the East-Indiaman was cast upon the sea and strewn upon the shore, affording much work for many days to the coastguard, and greatly exciting the people of the district — most of whom appeared to entertain an earnest belief in the doctrine that everything cast by storms upon their coast ought to be considered public property. Portions of the wreck had the name "Trident" painted on them, and letters found in several chests which were washed ashore proved that the ship had sailed from Calcutta, and was bound for the port of London. One little boy alone escaped the waves. He was found in a crevice of the cliffs the following day, with just enough vitality left to give a few details of the wreck. Although all possible care was bestowed on him, he died before night.

Thus sudden and complete was the end of as fine a ship as ever spread her canvas to the breeze. At night she had been full of life — full of wealth; in the morning she was gone — only a few bales and casks and broken spars to represent the wealth, and stiffened corpses to tell of the life departed. So she came and went, and in a short time all remnants of her were carried away.

One morning, a few weeks after the night of the storm, Maggot the smith turned himself in his bed at an early hour, and, feeling disinclined to slumber, got up to look at the state of the weather. The sun was just rising, and there was an inviting look about the morning which induced the man to dress hastily and go out.

Maggot was a powerfully-built man, rough in his outer aspect as well as in his inner man, but by no means what is usually termed a bad man, although, morally speaking, he could not claim to be considered a good one. In fact, he was a hearty, jolly, reckless fisherman, with warm feelings, enthusiastic temperament, and no principle; a man who, though very ready to do a kind act, had no particular objection to do one that was decidedly objectionable when it suited his purpose or served his present interest. He was regarded by his comrades as one of the greatest madcaps in the district. Old Maggot was, as we have said, a blacksmith to trade, but he had also been bred a miner, and was something of a fisherman as well, besides being (like most of his companions) an inveterate smuggler. He could turn his hand to almost anything, and was "everything by turns, but nothing long."

Sauntering down to Priests Cove, on the south of Cape Cornwall, with his hands in his pockets and his sou'-wester stuck carelessly on his shaggy head, he fell in with a comrade, whom he hailed by the name of John Cock. This man was also a fisherman, *et cetera*, and the bosom friend and admirer of Maggot.

"Where bound to this mornin', Jack?" inquired Maggot.

"To fish," replied John.

"I go with 'ee, booy," said Maggot.

This was the extent of the conversation at that time. They were not communicative, but walked side by side in silence to the beach, where they launched their little boat and rowed out to sea.

Presently John Cock looked over his shoulder and exclaimed — "Maggot, I see summat."

"Do 'ee?"

"Iss do I."

"What do un look like?"

"Like a dead corp."

"Aw, my dear," said Maggot, "lev us keep away. It can do no good to we."

Acting on this opinion the men rowed past the object that was floating on the sea, and soon after began to fish; but they had not fished long when the dead body, drifted probably by some cross-current, appeared close to them again. Seeing this they changed their position, but ere long the body again appeared.

"P'raps," observed Maggot, "there's somethin' in its pockets."

As the same idea had occurred to John Cock, the men resolved to examine the body, so they rowed up to it and found it to be that of an elderly man, much decomposed, and nearly naked. A very short examination sufficed to show that the pockets of such garments as were still upon it were empty, and the men were about to let it go again, when Maggot exclaimed —

"Hold fast, Jack, I see somethin' tied round the waist of he; a sort o' belt it do seem."

The belt was quickly removed and the body released, when it sank with a heavy plunge, but ere long reappeared on the surface. The fishermen rowed a considerable distance away from it, and then shipped their oars and examined the belt, which was made of linen. Maggot sliced it up as he would have ripped up a fish, and laid bare, to the astonished gaze of himself and his friend, a number of glittering gems of various colours, neatly and firmly embedded in cotton, besides a variety of rings and small brooches set with precious stones.

"Now, I tell 'ee," said Maggot, "'tis like as this here will make our fortin', or else git we into trouble."

"Why, whatever shud we git into trouble 'bout it for?" said John Cock. "'Tis like as not they ain't real — only painted glass, scarce wuth the trouble o' car'in' ashore."

"Hould thy tongue, thee g'eat chucklehead," replied Maggot; "a man wouldn't go for to tie such stuff round his waist to drown hisself with, I do know, if they worn't real. Lev us car' 'em to Maister Donnithorne."

John Cock replied with a nod, and the two men, packing up the jewels, pulled in-shore as fast as possible. Hauling their boat beyond the reach of the surf, they hastened to St. Just, and requested a private audience of Mr. Donnithorne.[1]

That excellent gentleman was not unaccustomed to give private audiences to fishermen, and, as has been already hinted at the beginning of this tale, was reported to have private dealings with them also — of a very questionable nature. He received the two men, however, with the hearty air of a man who knows that the suspicions entertained of him by the calumnious world are false.

"Well, Maggot," said Mr. Donnithorne, "what is your business with me? You are not wont to be astir so early, if all be true that is reported of 'ee."

"Plaise, sur," said Maggot, with a glance at Rose Ellis, who sat sewing near the window, "I'm come to talk 'bout private matters — if —"

"Leave us, Rose dear, for a little," said the old gentleman.

As soon as she was out of the room Maggot locked the door, a proceeding which surprised Mr. Donnithorne not a little, but his surprise was much greater when the man drew a small parcel from the breast of his rough coat, and, unrolling it, displayed the glittering jewels of which he had so unexpectedly become possessed.

"Where got you these?" inquired Mr. Donnithorne, turning them over carefully.

"Got 'em in the say — catched 'em, sure 'nough," said Maggot.

"Not with a baited hook, I warrant," said the old gentleman. "Come, my son, let's hear all about it."

Maggot explained how he had obtained the jewels, and then asked what they were worth.

"I can't tell that," said Mr. Donnithorne, shaking his head gravely. "Some of them are undoubtedly of value; the others, for all I know, may not be worth

---

1 It may be well here to inform the reader that the finding of the jewels as here described, and the consequences which followed, are founded on fact.

much."

"Come now, sur," said Maggot, with a confidential leer, "it's not the fust time we have done a bit o' business. I 'spose I cud claim salvage on 'em?"

"I don't know that," said the old gentleman; "you cannot tell whom they belonged to, and I suspect Government would claim them, if — But, by the way, I suppose you found no letters — nothing in the shape of writing on the body?"

"Nothin' whatsomever."

"Well, then, I fear that —"

"Come now, sur," said Maggot boldly; "'spose you gives John and me ten pounds apaice an' kape 'em to yourself to make what 'ee can of 'em?"

Mr. Donnithorne shook his head and hesitated. Often before had he defrauded the revenue by knowingly purchasing smuggled brandy and tobacco, and by providing the funds to enable others to smuggle them; but then the morality of that day in regard to smuggling was very lax, and there were men who, although in all other matters truly honest and upright, could not be convinced of the sinfulness of smuggling, and smiled when they were charged with the practice, but who, nevertheless, would have scorned to steal or tell a downright lie. This, however, was a very different matter from smuggling. The old gentleman shrank from it at first, and could not meet the gaze of the smuggler with his usual bold frank look. But the temptation was great. The jewels he suspected were of immense value, and his heart readily replied to the objections raised by his conscience, that after all there was no one left to claim them, and he had a much better right to them, in equity if not in law, than Government; and as to the fellows who found them — why, the sum they asked would be a great and rich windfall to them, besides freeing them from all further trouble, as well as transferring any risk that might accrue from their shoulders to his own.

While the old gentleman was reasoning thus with himself, Maggot stood anxiously watching his countenance and twisting the cloth that had enclosed the jewellery into a tight rope, as he shifted his position uneasily. At length old Mr. Donnithorne said —

"Leave the jewels with me, and call again in an hour from this time. You shall then have my answer."

Maggot and his friend consented to this delay, and left the room.

No sooner were they gone than the old gentleman called his wife, who naturally exclaimed in great surprise on beholding the table covered with such costly trinkets —

"Where *ever* did you get these, Tom?"

Mr. Donnithorne explained, and then asked what she thought of Maggot's proposal.

"Refuse it," said she firmly.

"But, my dear —"

"Don't 'but' about it, Tom. Whenever a man begins to 'but' with sin, it is sure to butt him over on his back. Have nothing to do with it, *I* say."

"But, my dear, it is not dishonest —"

"I don't know that," interrupted Mrs. Donnithorne vigorously; "you think that smuggling is not dishonest, but I do, and so does the minister."

"What care *I* for the minister?" cried the old gentleman, losing his temper; "who made *him a* judge of my doings?"

"He is an expounder of God's Word," said Mrs. Donnithorne firmly, "and holds that 'Thou shalt not steal' is one of the Ten Commandments."

"Well, well, he and I don't agree, that's all; besides, has he never expounded to you that obedience to your husband is a virtue? a commandment, I may say, which you are —"

"Mr. Donnithorne," said the lady with dignity, "I am here at your request, and am now complying with your wishes in giving my opinion."

"There, there, Molly," said the subdued husband, giving his better half a kiss, "don't be so sharp. You ought to have been a lawyer with your powerful reasoning capacity. However, let me tell you that you don't understand these matters —"

"Then why ask my advice, Tom?"

"Why, woman, because an inexplicable fatality leads me to consult you, although I know well enough what the upshot will be. But I'm resolved to close with Maggot."

"I knew you would," said Mrs. Donnithorne quietly.

The last remark was the turning-point. Had the good lady condescended to be *earnest* in her entreaties that the bargain should not be concluded, it is highly probable her husband would have given in; but her last observation nettled him so much that he immediately hoisted a flag of defiance, nailed it to the mast, and went out in great indignation to search for Maggot. That individual was not far off. The bargain was completed, the jewels were locked up in one of the old gentleman's secret repositories, and the fishermen, with ten pounds apiece in their pockets, returned home.

CHAPTER VI.

Treats of the Miner's Cottage, Work, and Costume.

Maggot's home was a disordered one when he reached it, for his youngest baby, a fat little boy, had been seized with convulsions, and his wife and little daughter Grace, and son Zackey, and brother-in-law David Trevarrow, besides his next neighbour Mrs. Penrose, with her sixteen children, were all in the room, doing their best by means of useless or hurtful applications, equally useless advice, and intolerable noise and confusion, to cure, if not to kill, the baby.

Maggot's cottage was a poor one, his furniture was mean, and there was not much of it; nevertheless its inmates were proud of it, for they lived in comparative comfort there. Mrs. Maggot was a kind-hearted, active woman, and her husband — despite his smuggling propensities — was an affectionate father. Usually the cottage was kept in a most orderly condition; but on the present occasion it was, as we have said, in a state of great confusion.

"Fetch me a bit of rag, Grace," cried Mrs. Maggot, as her husband entered.

"Here's a bit, old 'ooman," said Maggot, handing her the linen cloth in which the jewels had been wrapped up, and which he had unconsciously retained in his hands on quitting Mr. Donnithorne — "Run, my dear man," he added, turning to John Cock, "an' fetch the noo doctor."

John darted away, and in a quarter of an hour returned with Oliver Trembath, who found that the baby had weathered the storm by the force of its own constitution, despite the adverse influences that were around it. He therefore contented himself with clearing the place of intruders, and prescribing some simple medicine.

"Are you going to work?" inquired Oliver of David Trevarrow, observing that the man was about to quit the cottage.

"Iss, sur — to Botallack."

"Then I will accompany you. Captain Dan is going to show me over part of the mine today. Good-morning, Mrs. Maggot, and remember my directions if this should happen to the little fellow again."

Leaving the cottage the two proceeded through the town to the north end of it, accompanied by Maggot, who said he was going to the forge to do a bit of work, and who parted from them at the outskirts of the town.

"Times are bad with you at the mines just now," said Oliver as they walked .

"Iss sur, they are," replied Trevarrow, in the quiet tone that was peculiar to him; "but, thank God, we do manage to live, though there are some of us with a lot o' child'n as finds it hard work. The Bal^2 ain't so good as she once was."

"I suppose that you have frequent changes of fortune?" said Oliver.

2   The mine.

The miner admitted that this was the case, for that sometimes a man worked underground for several weeks without getting enough to keep his family, while at other times he might come on a bunch of copper or tin which would enable him to clear £50 or more in a month.

"If report says truly," observed Oliver, "you have hit upon a 'keenly lode,' as you call it, not many days ago."

"A do look very well now, sur," replied the miner, "but wan can never tell. I did work for weeks in the level under the say without success, so I guv it up an went to Wheal Hazard, and on the back o' the fifty-fethom level I did strike 'pon a small lode of tin 'bout so thick as my finger. It may get better, or it may take the bit in its teeth and disappear; we cannot tell."

"Well, I wish you good luck," said Oliver; "and here comes Captain Dan, so I'll bid you good-morning."

"Good-morning, sur," said the stout-limbed and stout-hearted man, with a smile and a nod, as he turned off towards the moor-house to put on his mining garments.

Towards this house a number of men had been converging while Oliver and his companion approached it, and the former observed, that whatever colour the men might be on entering it, they invariably came out light red, like lobsters emerging from a boiling pot.

In Botallack mine a large quantity of iron is mingled with the tin ore. This colours everything in and around the mine, including men's clothes, hands, and faces, with a light rusty-red. The streams, of course, are also coloured with it, and the various pits and ponds for collecting the fluid mud of tin ore seem as if filled with that nauseous compound known by the name of "Gregory's Mixture."

In the moor-house there were rows of pegs with red garments hung thereon to dry, and there were numerous broad-shouldered men dressing and undressing — in every stage of the process; while in a corner two or three were washing their bodies in a tank of water. These last were men who had been at work all night, and were cleansing themselves before putting on what we may term their home-going clothes.

The mining dress is a very simple, and often a very ragged affair. It consists of a flannel shirt, a pair of linen trousers, a short coat of the same, and a hat in the form of a stiff wide-awake, but made so thick as to serve the purpose of a helmet to guard the head from the rocks, etc. Clumsy ankle-boots complete the costume. As each man issued from the house, he went to a group of wooden chests which lay scattered about outside, and, opening his own, took from it a bag of powder, some blasting fuse, several iron tools, which he tied to a rope so as to be slung over his shoulder, a small wooden canteen of water, and a bunch of tallow candles. These last he fastened to a button on his breast, having previously affixed one of them to the front of his hat.

Thus accoutred, they proceeded to a small platform close at hand, with a square hole in it, out of which protruded the head of a ladder. This was the "ladder road." Through the hole these red men descended one by one, chatting and laughing as they went, and disappeared, leaving the moor-house and all around it a place of solitude.

Captain Dan now prepared to descend this ladder road with Oliver Trembath.

CHAPTER VII.

Tells of the Great Mine and of a Royal Dive under the Sea.

Botallack, to the dark depths of which we are now about to descend, is the most celebrated mine in the great mining county of Cornwall. It stands on the sea coast, a little more than a mile to the north of St. Just. The region around it is somewhat bleak and almost destitute of trees. In approaching it, the eyes of the traveller are presented with a view of engine-houses, and piles of stones and rubbish, in the midst of which stand a number of uncouth yet picturesque objects, composed of boards and timber, wheels, ropes, pulleys, chains, and suchlike gear. These last are the winding erections of the shafts which lead to the various mines, for the whole region is undermined, and Botallack is only one of several in St. Just parish. Wherever the eye turns, there, in the midst of green fields, where rocks and rocky fences abound, may be seen, rising prominently, the labouring arms, or "bobs," of the pump and skip engines, and the other machinery required in mining operations; while the ear is assailed by the perpetual clatter of the "stamps," or ore-crushing machines, which never cease their din, day or night, except on Sundays.

Botallack, like all the other mines, has several "shafts" or entrances to the works below, such as Boscawen Shaft, Wheal Button, Wheal Hazard, Chicornish Shaft, Davis Shaft, Wheal Cock, etc., the most interesting of which are situated among the steep rugged cliffs that front and bid defiance to the utmost fury of the Atlantic Ocean.

From whatever point viewed, the aspect of Botallack mine is grand in the extreme. On the rocky point that stretches out into the sea, engines with all their fantastic machinery and buildings have been erected. On the very summit of the cliff is seen a complication of timbers, wheels, and chains sharply defined against the sky, with apparently scarce any hold of the cliff, while down below, on rocky ledges and in black chasms, are other engines and beams and rods and wheels and chains, fastened and perched in fantastic forms in dangerous-looking places.

Here, amid the most savage gorges of the sea and riven rocks – half clinging to the land, half suspended over the water – is perched the machinery of, and entrance to, the most singular shaft of the mine, named the "Boscawen Diagonal Shaft." This shaft descends under the sea at a steep incline. It is traversed, on rails, by an iron carriage called the "gig," which is lowered and drawn up by steam power. Starting as it does from an elevated position in the rocks that are close to the edge of the sea, and slanting down through the cape, *outward* or seaward, this vehicle descends only a few fathoms when it is *under the ocean's bed*, and then its further course is far out and deep down – about two-thirds of a mile out, and full 245 fathoms down! The gig conveys the men to and from their work – the ore being drawn up by another iron carriage. There is (or rather there was, before the self-acting brake was added) danger attending the descent of this shaft, for the rope, although good and strong, is not immaculate, as was proved terribly in the year 1864 — when it broke, and the gig flew down to the bottom like lightning, dashing itself to pieces, and instantly killing the nine unfortunate men who were descending at the time.

Nevertheless, the Prince and Princess of Wales did not shrink from descending this deep burrow under the sea in the year 1865.

It was a great day for St. Just and Botallack that 24th of July on which the royal visit was paid. Great were the expectation and preparation on all hands to give a hearty welcome to the royal pair. The ladies arrayed themselves in their best to do fitting honour to the Princess; the balmaidens donned their holiday-attire, and Johnny Fortnight[3] took care, by supplying the poor mine-girls with the latest fashions, that their appearance should be, if we may be allowed the word, *splendiferous*! The volunteers, too, turned out in force, and no one, looking at their trim, soldierly aspect, could have believed them to be the same miners who were wont to emerge each evening through a hole in the earth, red as lobsters, wet, ragged, and befouled — in a word, surrounded by a halo of dishevelment, indicative of their rugged toils in the regions below.

Everywhere the people turned out to line the roads, and worthily receive the expected visitors, and great was the cheering when they arrived, accompanied by the Duke and Duchess of Sutherland, the Earl of Mount Edgecumbe, Lady de Grey, Lord and Lady Vivian, General Knollys, and others, but louder still was the cheer when the Princess rode down the steep descent to the cliffs in a donkey-carriage.

The Botallack cliffs themselves, however, were the central point, not only of the interest, but of the grandeur of the scene, for here were presented such a view and combination as are not often witnessed — nature in one of her wildest aspects, combined with innumerable multitudes of human beings swayed by one feeling of enthusiastic loyalty. Above, on every attainable point, projection, and eminence, men and women clustered like gay flies on the giant cliffs, leaving immense gaps here and there, where no foot might venture save that of a bird. Midway, on the face of the precipice, clung the great beams and supports of the Boscawen Diagonal Shaft, with the little gig perched on them and the royal party seated therein, facing the entrance to the black abyss — the Princess arrayed in a white flannel cloak trimmed with blue, and a straw hat with a blue ribbon round it, and the Prince clad in miner's costume. Underneath, a dizzy depth to gaze down, lay the rugged boulders of the shore, with the spray of the Atlantic springing over them.

Deafening was the cheer when the gig at last entered the shaft and disappeared, and intense the anxiety of the vast multitude as they watched the descent — in imagination, of course, for nothing could be seen but the tight

---

3   The packmen are so styled because of their visits being paid fortnightly.

wire-rope uncoiling its endless length, and disappearing like a thin snake down the jaws of some awful sea-monster that had climbed so far up the cliffs to meet and devour it! Now they are at the shore; now passing under the sea; fairly under it by this time; a few minutes more and they have reached the spot where yonder seagull is now wheeling above the waves, wondering what new species of bird has taken possession of its native cliffs. Five minutes are passed — yet still descending rapidly! They must be half a mile out from the land now — half of a mile out on the first part of a submarine tunnel to America! "Old England is on the lee," but they are very much the reverse of afloat; solid rock is above, on either side and below — so close to them that the elbows must not be allowed to protrude over the edge of their car, nor the head be held too high. Here even royalty must stoop — not that we would be understood to imply that royalty cannot stoop elsewhere. Those who dwell in Highland cottages could contradict us if we did! Presently the rope "slows" — the lower depths are reached, and now for some time there is patient waiting, for it is understood that they are examining the "levels," where the stout men of Cornwall tear out the solid rock in quest of copper and tin.

After a time the thin snake begins to ascend; they are coming up now, but not so fast as they went down. It is about ten minutes before the gig emerges from that black hole and bears the Prince and Princess once more into the light of day.

Yes, it was a great day for Botallack, and it will dwell long in the memories of those who witnessed it — especially of that fortunate captain of the mine who had the honour of conducting the Princess on the occasion, and of whose enthusiasm in recalling the event, and in commenting on her intelligence and condescension, we can speak from personal observation.

But, reader, you will say, What has all this to do with our story?

Nothing — we admit it frankly — nothing whatever in a direct way; nevertheless, indirectly, the narrative may possibly arouse in you greater interest in the mine down which we are about to conduct you — not by the same route as that taken by the Prince and Princess (for the Boscawen Shaft did not exist at the period of our tale), but by one much more difficult and dangerous, as you shall see.

Before we go, however, permit us to add to the offence of digression, by wandering still further out of our direct road. There are a few facts regarding Botallack and mining operations, without a knowledge of which you will be apt at times to misunderstand your position.

Let us suppose that a mine has been already opened; that a "lode" — that is, a vein of quartz with metal in it — has been discovered cropping out of the earth, and that it has been dug down upon from above, and dug in upon from the sea-cliffs. A shaft has been sunk — in other words, a hole excavated — let us say, two or three hundred yards inland, to a depth of some forty or fifty fathoms — near the sea-level. This shaft is perhaps nine feet by six wide. The lode, being a layer of quartz, sometimes slopes one way, sometimes another, and is occasionally perpendicular. It also varies in its run or direction a little here and there, like a wildish horse, being sometimes met by other lodes, which, like bad companions, divert it from the straight course. Unlike bad companions, however, they increase its value at the point of meeting by thickening it. Whatever course the lode takes, the miner conscientiously follows suit. His shaft slopes much, little, or not at all, according to the "lie of the lode."

It is an ancient truism that water must find its level. Owing to this law, much water accumulates in the shaft, obliging the miner to erect an engine-house and provide a powerful pumping-engine with all its gear, at immense cost, to keep the works dry as he proceeds. He then goes to the shore, and there, in the face of the perpendicular cliff, a little above the sea-level, he cuts a horizontal tunnel about six feet high by three broad, and continues to chisel and blast away the solid rock until he "drives" his tunnel a quarter of a mile inland, which he will do at a rate varying from two to six feet per week, according to the hardness of the rock, until he reaches the shaft and thus provides an easy and inexpensive passage for the water without pumping. This tunnel or level he calls the "Adit level." But his pumping-engine is by no means rendered useless, for it has much to do in hauling ore to the surface, etc. In process of time, the miner works away all the lode down to the sea-level, and must sink the shaft deeper — perhaps ten or twenty fathoms — where new levels are driven horizontally "on the lode," and water accumulates which must be pumped up to the Adit level, whence it escapes to the sea.

Thus down, down, he goes, sinking his shaft and driving his levels on — that is, always following the lode *ad infinitum*. Of course he must stop before reaching the other side of the world! At the present time Botallack has progressed in that direction to a depth of 245 fathoms. To those who find a difficulty in realising what depth that really is, we would observe that it is equal to more than three and a half times the height of St. Paul's Cathedral in London, nearly four times the height of St. Rollox chimney in Glasgow, and considerably more than twice the height, from the plain, of Arthur's Seat, near Edinburgh.

When the levels have been driven a considerable distance from the shaft, the air naturally becomes bad from want of circulation. To remedy this evil, holes, or short shafts, called "winzes," are sunk at intervals from the upper to the lower levels. These winzes are dangerous traps for the unwary or careless, extending frequently to a depth of ten or fifteen fathoms, and being bridged across by one or two loose planks. Ladders are fixed in many of them to facilitate progress through the mine. When a miner drives the end of his level so far that the air will not circulate, a new winze is usually sunk down to him from the level above. The circulation is thus extended, and the levels progress further and further right and left until they occupy miles of ground. The levels and shafts of Botallack, if put together, would extend to not less than forty miles, and the superficial space of ground, on and beneath which the mine lies, is above 260 acres.

When the lode is rich, and extends upwards or downwards, it is cut away from between levels, in a regular systematic manner, strong beams being placed to support temporary platforms, on which the miners may stand and work as they ascend. When they have cut all the lode away up to the level above them, a false timber bottom is made to replace the rocky bottom of the level which is being removed. Thus, in traversing the old workings of a mine one suddenly comes to great caverns, very narrow, but of such immense height above and depth below that the rays of your candle cannot penetrate the darkness. In such places the thick short beams that were used by the old miners are seen extending from side to side of the empty space, disappearing in dim perspective. Woe betide the man who stumbles off his narrow plank, or sets his foot on an insecure beam in such places! Where such workings are in progress, the positions of the miners appear singularly wild and insecure. The men stand in the narrow chasm between the granite walls above each others' heads, slight temporary platforms alone preserving them from certain death, and the candles of those highest above you twinkling like stars in a black sky.

In these underground regions of Botallack, above three hundred men and boys are employed, some of whom work occasionally by night as well as by day. On the surface about two hundred men, women, and boys are employed "dressing" the ore, etc.

Other mines there are in the great mining centres of Cornwall – Redruth, St Just, St. Austell, and Helston, which are well worthy of note – some of them a little deeper, and some richer than Botallack. But we profess not to treat of all the Cornish mines; our object is to describe one as a type of many, if not all, and as this one runs farthest out beneath the sea, is deeper than most of the others, and richer than many, besides having interesting associations, and being of venerable antiquity, we hold it to be the one most worthy of selection.

With a few briefly stated facts we shall take final leave of statistics.

As we have said, the Boscawen shaft measures 245 fathoms. The ladder-way by which the men ascend and descend daily extends to 205 fathoms. It takes a man half an hour to reach the bottom, and fully an hour to climb to the surface. There are three pumping and seven winding engines at work – the largest being of 70 horse-power. The tin raised is from 33 to 35 tons a month. The price of tin has varied from £55 to £90 per ton. In time past, when Botallack was more of a copper than a tin-mine, a fathom has been known to yield £100 worth of ore, and a miner has sometimes broken out as much as £300 worth in one month.

The mine has been worked from time immemorial. It is known to have been wrought a hundred years before it was taken by the present company, who have had it between thirty and forty years, and, under the able direction of the present manager and purser, Mr. Stephen Harvey James, it has paid the shareholders more than £100,000. The profit in the year 1844 was £24,000. At the termination of one period of working it left a profit of £300,000. It has experienced many vicissitudes of fortune. Formerly it was worked for tin, and at one period (1841) was doing so badly that it was about to be abandoned, when an unlooked for discovery of copper was made, and a period of great prosperity again set in, during which many shareholders and miners made their fortunes out of Botallack.

Thus much, with a humble apology, we present to the reader, and now resume the thread of our narrative.

CHAPTER VIII.

Down, Down, Down.

Before descending the mine Captain Dan led Oliver to the counting-house, where he bade him undress and put on miner's clothing.

"I'll need a biggish suit," observed Oliver.

"True," said Captain Dan; "we are obliged usually to give visitors our smallest suits. You are an exception to the rule. Indeed, I'm not sure that I have a pair of trousers big enough for — ah yes, by the way, here is a pair belonging to one of our captains who is unusually stout and tall; I dare say you'll be able to squeeze into 'em."

"All right," said Oliver, laughing, as he pulled on the red garments; "they are wide enough round the waist, at all events. Now for a hat."

"There," said the captain, handing him a white cotton skull-cap, "put that on."

"Why, what's this for?" said Oliver.

"To keep *that* from dirtying your head," replied the other, as he handed his companion a thick felt hat, which was extremely dirty, on the front especially, where the candle was wont to be fixed with wet clay. "Now, then, attach these two candles to that button in your breast, and you are complete. — Not a bad miner to look at," said Captain Dan with a smile of approval.

The captain was already equipped in underground costume, and the dirty disreputable appearance he presented was, thought Oliver, a wonderful contrast to his sober and gentlemanly aspect on the evening of their first meeting at his uncle's table.

"I'll strike a light after we get down a bit — so come along," said Captain Dan, leaving the office and leading the way.

On reaching the entrance to the shaft, Oliver Trembath looked down and observed a small speck of bright light in the black depths.

"A man coming up — wait a bit," said the captain in explanation.

Presently a faint sound of slow footsteps was heard; they grew gradually more distinct, and ere long the head and shoulders of a man emerged from the hole. Perspiration was trickling down his face, and painting him, streakily, with iron rust and mud. All his garments were soaking. He sighed heavily on reaching the surface, and appeared to inhale the fresh air with great satisfaction.

"Any more coming?"

"No, Captain Dan," replied the man, glancing with some curiosity at the tall stranger.

"Now, sir, we shall descend," said the captain, entering the shaft.

Oliver followed, and at once plunged out of bright sunshine into subdued light. A descent of a few fathoms brought them to the bottom of the first ladder. It was a short one; most of the others, the captain told him, were long ones. The width of the shaft was about six feet by nine. It was nearly perpendicular, and the slope of the ladders corresponded with its width — the head of each resting against one side of it, and the foot against the other, thus forming a zigzag of ladders all the way down.

At the foot of the first ladder the light was that of deep twilight. Here was a wooden platform, and a hole cut through it, out of which protruded the head of the second ladder. The Captain struck a light, and, applying it to one of the candles, affixed the same to the front of Oliver's hat. Arranging his own hat in a similar way, he continued the descent, and, in a few minutes, both were beyond the region of daylight. When they had got a short way down, probably the distance of an ordinary church-steeple's height below the surface, Oliver looked up and saw the little opening far above him, shining brightly like a star. A few steps more and it vanished from view; he felt that he had for the first time in his life reached the regions of eternal night.

The shaft varied in width here and there; in most places it was very narrow — about six feet wide — but, what with cross-beams to support the sides, and prevent soft parts from falling in, and other obstructions, the space available for descent was often not more than enough to permit of a man squeezing past.

A damp smell pervaded the air, and there was a strange sense of contraction and confinement, so to speak, which had at first an unpleasant effect on Oliver. The silence, when both men paused at a ladder-foot to trim candles or to rest a minute, was most profound, and there came over the young doctor a sensation of being buried alive, and of having bid a final farewell to the upper earth, the free air, and the sunshine, as they went down, down, down to the depths below.

At last they reached a "level" or gallery, by which the ladder-shaft communicated with the pump-shaft.

Here Captain Dan paused and trimmed Oliver's candle, which he had thrust inadvertently against a beam, and broken in two.

"You have to mind your head here, sir," said the captain, with a quiet smile; "'tis a good place to learn humility."

Oliver could scarce help laughing aloud as he gazed at his guide, for, standing as he did with the candle close to his face, his cheeks, nose, chin, forehead, and part of the brim of his hat and shoulders were brought into brilliant light, while the rest of him was lost in the profound darkness of the level behind, and the flame of his candle rested above his head like the diadem of some aristocratic gnome.

"How far down have we come?" inquired Oliver.

"About eighty fathoms," said the captain; "we shall now go along this level and get into the pump-shaft, by which we can descend to the bottom. Take care of your feet and head as you go, for you'll be apt to run against the rocks that hang down, and the winzes are dangerous."

"And pray what are winzes?" asked Oliver as he stumbled along in the footsteps of his guide, over uneven ground covered with débris. — "Ah! hallo! stop!"

"What's wrong?" said the captain, looking back, and holding up his candle to Oliver's face.

"Candle gone again, captain; I've run my head on that rock. Lucky for me that your mining hats are so thick and hard, for I gave it a butt that might have done credit to an ox."

"I told you to mind your head," said Captain Dan, relighting the candle; "you had better carry it in your hand in the levels, it will light your path better. Look out now — here is a winze."

The captain pointed to a black yawning hole, about six or seven feet in diameter, which was bridged across by a single plank.

"How deep does it go?" asked the youth, holding up his candle and peering in; "I can't see the bottom."

"I dare say not," said the captain, "for the bottom is ten fathoms down, at the next level."

"And are all the winzes bridged with a single plank in this way?"

"Why, no, some of 'em have two or three planks, but they're quite safe if you go steady."

"And, pray, how many such winzes are there in the mine?" asked Oliver.

"Couldn't say exactly, without thinkin' a bit," replied the captain; "but there are a great number of 'em — little short of a hundred, I should say — for we have a good many miles of levels in Botallack, which possesses an underground geography as carefully measured and mapped out as that of the surface."

"And what would happen," asked Oliver, with an expression of half-simulated anxiety, "if you were to fall down a winze and break your neck, and my candle were to get knocked or blown out, leaving me to find my way out of a labyrinth of levels pierced with holes sixty feet deep?"

"Well, it's hard to say," replied Captain Dan with much simplicity.

"Go on," said Oliver, pursing his lips with a grim smile, as he followed his leader across the narrow bridge.

Captain Dan continued his progress until he reached the pump-shaft, the proximity of which was audibly announced by the slow ascent and descent of a great wooden beam, which was styled the "pump-rod." Alongside, and almost touching it, for space was valuable there, and had to be economised, was the iron pipe — nearly a foot in diameter — which conveyed the water from the mine to the "Adit level."

The slow-heaving plunge, of about ten feet in extent, and the sough or sigh of the great beam, with the accompanying gurgle of water in the huge pipe, were sounds that seemed horribly appropriate to the subterranean scene. One could have imagined the mine to be a living giant in the last throes of death by drowning. But these were only one half of the peculiarities of the place. On the other side of the shaft an arrangement of beams and partially broken boards formed the traversing "ways" or tube, up which were drawn the kibbles — these last being large iron buckets used for lifting ore to the surface.

In the present day, machinery being more perfect, the ancient kibble has been to some extent supplanted by skips, or small trucks with wheels (in some cases iron boxes with guiding-rods), which are drawn up smoothly, and without much tear and wear; but in the rough times of which we write, the sturdy kibble used to go rattling up the shaft with deafening noise, dinting its thick sides, and travelling with a jovial free-and-easy swing that must have added considerably to the debit side of the account of working expenses. Between the pump-rod and the kibble-way there was just room for the ladders upon which Captain Dan, followed by Oliver, now stepped. This shaft was very wet, water dropped and spirted about in fine spray everywhere, and the rounds of the ladders were wet and greasy with much-squeezed slime.

It would seem as though the kibbles had known that a stranger was about to descend and had waited for him, for no sooner did Oliver get on the ladder than they began to move — the one to ascend full, and the other to descend empty.

"What's that?" exclaimed Oliver.

"It's only the kibbles," replied Captain Dan.

Before the captain could explain what kibbles were, these reckless buckets met, with a bang, close to Oliver's cheek, and rebounded on the beams that protected him from their fury. Naturally the young man shrank a little from a noise so loud and so near. He was at once scraped down on the other side by the pump-rod! Drawing himself together as much as possible, and feeling for once the disadvantage of being a large man, he followed his leader down, down, ever down, into the profounder depths below.

All this time they had not met with a miner, or with any sign of human life — unless the pump and kibbles could be regarded as such — for they had been hitherto traversing the old levels and workings of the mine, but at last, during one of their pauses, they heard the faint sound of chip, chip, chip, in the far distance.

"Miners?" inquired Oliver.

Captain Dan nodded, and said they would now leave the shaft and go to where the men were at work. He cautioned his companion again to have regard to his head, and to mind his feet. As they proceeded, he stopped ever and anon to point out some object of peculiar interest.

"There's a considerable space above and below you here, sir," said the captain, stopping suddenly in a level which was not more than three feet wide.

Oliver had been so intent on his feet, and mindful of the winzes, that he had failed to observe the immense black opening overhead. It extended so high above him, and so far forward and backward in the direction of the level, that its boundaries were lost in an immensity of profoundly dark space. The rocky path was also lost to view, both before and behind them, so that the glare of their lights on the metallic walls rendered the spot on which they stood a point of brilliancy in the midst of darkness. Only part of a great beam was visible here and there above them, as if suspended in the gloom to render its profundity more apparent.

This, Captain Dan explained, was the space that had once been occupied by a rich lode of ore, all of which had been removed years ago, to the great commercial advantage of a past generation.

Soon after passing this the captain paused at a deep cutting in the rock, and, looking sadly at it for a few minutes, said — "It was here that poor Trevool lost his life. He was a good lad, but careless, and used to go rattling along the levels with his light in his hat and his thoughts among the stars, instead of carrying the light in his hand and looking to his feet. He fell down that winze and broke his back. When we got him up to grass he was alive, but he never spoke another word, and died the same night."

"Poor fellow!" said Oliver; "I suppose your men have narrow escapes sometimes."

"They have, sir, but it's most always owin' to carelessness. There was a cousin of that very lad Trevool who was buried with a comrade by the falling in of a shaft and came out alive. I was there at the time and helped to dig him out."

Captain Dan here stopped, and, sticking his candle against the wet wall of the mine, sat down on a piece of rock, while our hero stood beside him. "You see," said he, "we were sinking a shaft, or rather reopening an old one, at the time, and Harvey, that was the man's name, was down working with a comrade. They came to a soft bit o' ground, an' as they cut through it they boarded it up with timbers across to prevent it slipping, but they did the work hastily. After they had cut down some fathoms below it, the boarding gave way, and down the whole thing went, boards, timbers, stones, and rubbish, on their heads. We made sure they were dead, but set to, nevertheless, to dig them out as fast as possible — turning as many hands to the work as could get at it. At last we came on them, and both were alive, and not very much hurt! The timbers and planks had fallen over them in such a way as to keep the stones and rubbish off. I had a talk with old Harvey the other day on this very subject. He told me that he was squeezed flat against the side of the shaft by the rubbish which buried him, and that he did not lose consciousness for a moment. A large stone had stuck right above his head, and this probably saved him. He heard us digging down to him, he said, and when we got close he sang out to hold on, as the shovel was touching him. Sure enough this was the case, for the next shovelful of rubbish that was lifted revealed the top of his head! We cleared the way to his mouth as carefully as we could, and then gave him a drop of brandy before going on with the work of excavation. His comrade was found in a stooping position, and was more severely bruised than old Harvey, but both of them lived to tell the tale of their burial, and to thank God for their deliverance. Yes," continued the captain, detaching his candle from the wall and resuming his walk, "we have narrow escapes sometimes. — Look here, doctor, did you ever see a rock like that?"

Captain Dan pointed to a place in the side of the rocky wall which was grooved and cut as if with a huge gouge or chisel, and highly polished. "It was never cut by man in that fashion; we found it as you see it, and there's many of 'em in the mine. We call 'em slinking slides."

"The marks must have been caused when the rocks were in a state of partial fusion," observed Oliver, examining the place with much curiosity.

"I don't know as to that, sir," said the captain, moving on, "but there they are, and some of 'em polished to that extent you could almost see your face in 'em."

On turning the corner of a jutting rock a light suddenly appeared, revealing a pair of large eyes and a double row of teeth, as it were gleaming out of the darkness. On drawing nearer, this was discovered to be a miner, whose candle was at some little distance, and only shone on him partially.

"Well, Jack, what's doing?" asked the captain.

The man cast a disconsolate look on a large mass of rock which lay in the middle of the path at his feet. He had been only too successful in his last blasting, and had detached a mass so large that he could not move it.

"It's too hard for to break, Captain Dan."

"Better get it into the truck," said the captain.

"Can't lift it, sur," said the man, who grudged to go through the tedious process of boring it for a second blast.

"You must get it out o' that, Jack, at all events. It won't do to let it lie there," said the captain, passing on, and leaving the miner to get out of his difficulty as best he might.

A few minutes more and they came on a "pare" of men (in other words, a band of two or more men working together) who were "stopeing-in the back of the level," as they termed the process of cutting upwards into the roof.

"There's a fellow in a curious place!" said Oliver, peering up through an irregular hole, in which a man was seen at work standing on a plank supported by a ladder. He was chiselling with great vigour at the rock over his head, and immediately beyond him another man stood on a plank supported by a beam of timber, and busily engaged in a similar occupation. Both men were stripped to the waist, and panted at their toil. The little chamber or cavern in which they worked was brilliantly illuminated by their two candles, and their athletic figures stood out, dark and picturesque, against the light glistering walls.

"A curious place, and a singular man!" observed the captain; "that fellow's family is not a small one. — Hallo! James Martin."

"Hallo! Captain Dan," replied the miner, looking down.

"How many children have you had?"

"How many child'n say 'ee?"

"Ay, how many?"

"I've had nineteen, sur, an' there's eight of 'em alive. Seven of 'em came in three year an six months, sur — three doubles an' a single, but them uns are all gone dead, sur."

"How old are you, Jim?"

"Forty-seven, sur."

"Your brother Tom is at work here, isn't he?"

"Iss, in the south level, drivin' the end."

"How many children has Tom had, Jim?"

"Seventeen, sur, an' seven of 'em's alive; but Tom's only thirty-eight years old, sur."[4]

"Good-morning, Jim."

"Good-morning, Captain Dan," replied the sturdy miner, resuming his work.

"Good specimens of men these," said the captain, with a quiet smile, to Oliver. "Of course I don't mean to say that all the miners hereabouts are possessed of such large families — nevertheless there are, as I dare say you have observed, a good many children in and about St. Just!"

Proceeding onward they diverged into a branch level, where a number of men were working overhead; boring holes into the roof and burrowing upwards. They all drove onwards through flinty rock by the same slow and toilsome process that has already been described — namely, by chipping with the pick, driving holes with the borer, and blasting with gunpowder.

As the Captain and Oliver traversed this part of the mine they had occasionally to squeeze past small iron trucks which stood below holes in the sides of the level, down which ever and anon masses of ore and débris came from the workings above with a hard crashing noise. The ore was rich with tin, but the metal was invisible to any but trained eyes. To Oliver Trembath the whole stuff appeared like wet rubbish.

Suddenly a low muffled report echoed through the cavernous place. It was followed by five or six similar reports in succession.

"They are blasting," said Captain Dan.

As he spoke, the thick muddy shoes and brick-dust legs of a man appeared coming down the hole that had previously discharged ore. The man himself followed his legs, and, alighting thereon, saluted Captain Dan with a free-and-easy "Good-morning." Another man followed him; from a different part of the surrounding darkness a third made his appearance, and others came trooping in, until upwards of a dozen of them were collected in the narrow tunnel, each with his tallow candle in his hand or hat, so that the place was lighted brilliantly. They were all clad in loose, patched, and ragged clothes. All were of a uniform rusty-red colour, each with his broad bosom bared, and perspiration trickling down his besmeared countenance.

Here, however, the uniformity of their appearance ended, for they were of all sizes and characters. Some were robust and muscular; some were lean and wiry; some were just entering on manhood, with the ruddy hue of health shining through the slime on their smooth faces; some were in the prime of life, pale from long working underground, but strong, and almost as hard as the iron with which they chiselled the rocks. Others were growing old, and an occasional

---

4   Reader, allow us to remark that this is a fact. Indeed, we may say here, once for all, that all the *important* statements and incidents in this tale are facts, or founded on facts, with considerable modification, but without intentional exaggeration.

cough told that the "miners' complaint" had begun its fatal undermining of the long-enduring, too-long-tried human body. There were one or two whose iron constitutions had resisted the evil influences of wet garments, bad air, and chills, and who, with much of the strength of manhood, and some of the colour of youth, were still plying their hammers in old age. But these were rare specimens of vigour and longevity; not many such are to be found in Botallack mine. The miner's working life is a short one, and comparatively few of those who begin it live to a healthy old age. Little boys were there, too, diminutive but sturdy urchins, miniature copies of their seniors, though somewhat dirtier; proud as peacocks because of being permitted at so early an age to accompany their fathers or brothers underground, and their bosoms swelling with that stern Cornish spirit of determination to face and overcome great difficulties, which has doubtless much to do with the excessive development of chest and shoulder for which Cornish miners, especially those of St. Just, are celebrated.[5]

It turned out that the men had all arranged to fire their holes at the same hour, and assemble in a lower level to take lunch, or, as they term it, "kroust," while the smoke should clear away. This rendered it impossible for the captain to take his young companion further into the workings at that part of the mine, so they contented themselves with a chat with the men. These sat down in a row, and, each man unrolling a parcel containing a pasty or a thick lump of cake with currants in it, commenced the demolition thereof with as much zeal as had previously been displayed in the demolition of the rock. This frugal fare was washed down with water drawn from little flat barrels or canteens, while they commented lightly, grumblingly, or laughingly, according to temperament, on the poor condition of the lode at which they wrought. We have already said that in mining, as in other things, fortune fluctuates, and it was "hard times" with the men of Botallack at that period.

Before they had proceeded far with their meal, one of the pale-faced men began to cough.

"Smoke's a coming down," he said.

"We shall 'ave to move, then," observed another.

The pouring in of gunpowder smoke here set two or three more a-coughing, and obliged them all to rise and seek for purer — perhaps it were better to say less impure — air in another part of the level, where the draught kept the smoke away. Here, squatting down on heaps of wet rubbish, and sticking their candles against the damp walls, they continued their meal, and here the captain and Oliver left them, retraced their steps to the foot of the shaft, and began the ascent to the surface, or, in mining parlance, began to "return to grass."

5   It has been stated to us recently by a volunteer officer, that at battalion parade, when companies were equalised in numbers, the companies formed by the men of St. Just required about four paces more space to stand upon than the other volunteers. No one who visits a St. Just miner at his underground toil will require to ask the reason why.

Up, up, up — the process now was reversed, and the labour increased tenfold. Up they went on these nearly perpendicular and interminable ladders, slowly, for they had a long journey before them; cautiously, for Oliver had a tendency to butt his head against beams, and knock his candle out of shape; carefully, for the rounds of the ladders were wet and slimy and a slip of foot or hand might in a moment have precipitated them into the black gulf below; and pantingly, for strength of limb and lung could not altogether defy the influence of such a prolonged and upright climb.

If Oliver Trembath felt, while descending, as though he should *never* reach the bottom, he felt far more powerfully as if reaching the top were an event of the distant future — all the more that the muscles of his arms and legs, unused to the peculiar process, were beginning to feel rather stiff. This feeling, however, soon passed away, and when he began to grow warm to the work, his strength seemed to return and to increase with each step — a species of revival of vigour in the midst of hard toil with which probably all strong men are acquainted.

Up they went, ladder after ladder, squeezing through narrow places, rubbing against wet rocks and beams, scraping against the boarding of the kibble-shaft, and being scraped by the pump-rods until both of them were as wet and red and dirty as any miner below.

As he advanced, Oliver began to take note of the places he had passed on the way down, and so much had he seen and thought during his sojourn underground, that, when he reached the level where he first came upon the noisy kibbles, and made acquaintance with the labouring pump-rod, he almost hailed the spot as an old familiar landmark of other days!

A circumstance occurred just then which surprised him not a little, and tended to fix this locality still more deeply on his memory. While he was standing in the level, waiting until the captain should relight and trim his much and oft bruised candle, the kibbles began their noisy motion. This was nothing new now, but at the same time the shout of distant voices was heard, as if the gnomes held revelry in their dreary vaults. They drew gradually nearer, and Oliver could distinguish laughter mingled with the sound of rapidly approaching footsteps.

"Foolish lads!" ejaculated Captain Dan with a smile, and an expression that proved he took some interest in the folly, whatever it might be.

"What is it?" inquired Oliver.

"They are racing to the kibble. Look and you shall see," replied the other.

Just then a man who had outrun his comrades appeared at the place where the level joined the shaft, just opposite. Almost at the same moment the kibble appeared flying upwards. The miner leaped upon it, caught and clung to the chain as it passed, and shouted a defiant adieu to his less fortunate comrades, who arrived just in time to witness him disappear upwards in this rapid manner "to grass."

"That's the way the young ones risk their lives," said the captain, shaking his head remonstratively; "if that young fellow had missed the kibble he would have been dashed to pieces at the bottom of the shaft."

Again Captain Dan said "Foolish lads," and shook his head so gravely that Oliver could not help regarding him with the respect due to a sedate, fatherly sort of man; but Oliver was young and unsophisticated, and did not know at the time that the captain had himself been noted in his youth as an extremely reckless and daring fellow, and that a considerable spice of the daring remained in him still!

Diverging to the right at this point Captain Dan led Oliver to an old part of the mine, where there were a couple of men opening up and extending one of the old levels. Their progress here was very different from what it had been. Evidently the former miners had not thought it worth their while to open up a wide passage for themselves, and Oliver found it necessary to twist his broad shoulders into all sorts of positions to get them through.

The first level they came to in this part was not more than three feet high at the entrance.

"A man can't hold his head very high here, sir," said his guide.

"Truly no, it is scarce high enough for my legs to walk in without any body above them," said Oliver. "However, lead the way, and I will follow."

The captain stooped and made his way through a winding passage where the roof was so low in many places that they were obliged to bend quite double, and the back and neck of the young doctor began to feel the strain very severely. There were, however, a few spots where the roof rose a little, affording temporary relief. Presently they came to the place where the men were at work. The ground was very soft here; the men were cutting through *soft* granite! — a condition of the stone which Oliver confessed he had never expected to see. Here the lights burned very badly.

"What can be the matter with it?" said Oliver, stopping for the third time to trim the wick of his candle.

Captain Dan smiled as he said, "You asked me, last night, to take you into one of the levels where the air was bad — now here you are, with the air so bad that the candle will hardly burn. It will be worse before night."

"But I feel no disagreeable sensation," said Oliver. "Possibly not, because you are not quite so sensitive as the flame of a candle, but if you remain here a few hours it will tell upon you. Here are the men — you can ask them."

The two men were resting when they approached. One was old, the other middle-aged. Both were hearty fellows, and communicative. The old one, especially, was ruddy in complexion and pretty strong.

"You look well for an old miner," said Oliver; "what may be your age?"

"About sixty, sur."

"Indeed! you are a notable exception to the rule. How comes it that you look so fresh?"

"Can't say, sur," replied the old man with a peculiar smile; "few miners live to my time of life, much less do they go underground. P'raps it's because I neither drink nor smoke. Tom there, now," he added, pointing to his comrade with his thumb, "he ain't forty yit, but he's so pale as a ghost; though he is strong 'nuff."

"And do you neither drink nor smoke, Tom?" inquired Oliver.

"Well, sur, I both smokes and drinks, but I do take 'em in moderation," said Tom.

"Are you married?" asked Oliver, turning again to the old man.

"Iss, got a wife at hum, an' had six child'n."

"Don't you find this bad air tell on your health?" he continued.

"Iss, sur. After six or seven hours I do feel my head like to split, an' my stummik as if it wor on fire; but what can us do? we must live, you knaw."

Bidding these men goodbye, the captain and Oliver went down to another level, and then along a series of low galleries, in some of which they had to advance on their hands and knees, and in one of them, particularly, the accumulation of rubbish was so great, and the roof so low, that they could only force a passage through by wriggling along at full length like snakes. Beyond this they found a miner and a little boy at work; and here Captain Dan pointed out to his companion that the lodes of copper and tin were rich. Glittering particles on the walls and drops of water hanging from points and crevices, with the green, purple, and yellow colours around, combined to give the place a brilliant metallic aspect.

"You'd better break off a piece of ore here," said Captain Dan.

Oliver took a chisel and hammer from the miner, and applying them to the rock, spent five minutes in belabouring it with scarcely any result.

"If it were not that I fear to miss the chisel and hit my knuckles," he said, "I think I could work more effectively."

As he spoke he struck with all his force, and brought down a large piece, a chip of which he carried away as a memorial of his underground ramble.

"The man is going to fire the hole," said Captain Dan; "you'd better wait and see it."

The hole was sunk nearly two feet deep diagonally behind a large mass of rock that projected from the side of the level. It was charged with gunpowder, and filled up with "tamping" or pounded granite, Then the miner lighted the fuse and hastened away, giving the usual signal, "Fire!" The others followed him to a safe distance, and awaited the result. In a few minutes there was a loud report, a bright blinding flash, and a concussion of the air which extinguished two of the candles. Immediately a crash followed, as the heavy mass of rock was torn from its bed and hurled to the ground.

"That's the way we raise tin and copper," said Captain Dan; "now, doctor, we had better return, if you would not be left in darkness, for our candles are getting low."

"Did you ever travel underground in the dark?" inquired Oliver.

"Not often, but I have done it occasionally. Once, in particular, I went down the main shaft in the dark, and gave a miner an awful fright. I had to go down in haste at the time, and, not having a candle at hand, besides being well acquainted with the way, I hurried down in the dark. It so chanced that a man named Sampy had got his light put out when about to ascend the shaft, and, as he also was well acquainted with the way, he did not take the trouble to relight.

There was a good deal of noise in consequence of the pump being at work. When I had got about half-way down I put my foot on something that felt soft. Instantly there was uttered a tremendous yell, and my legs at the same moment were seized by something from below. My heart almost jumped out of my mouth at this, but as the yell was repeated it flashed across me I must have trod on some one's fingers, so I lifted my foot at once, and then a voice, which I knew to be that of Sampy, began to wail and lament miserably.

"'Hope I haven't hurt 'ee, Sampy?' said I.

"'Aw dear! aw dear! aw, my dear!' was all that poor Sampy could reply.

"'Let us go up, my son,' said I, 'and we'll strike a light.'

"So up we went to the next level, where I got hold of the poor lad's candle and lighted it.

"'Aw, my dear!' said Sampy, looking at his fingers with a rueful countenance; 'thee have scat 'em all in jowds.'"

"Pray," interrupted Oliver, "what may be the meaning of 'scat 'em all in jowds'?

"Broke 'em all in pieces," replied Captain Dan; "but he was wrong, for no bones were broken, and the fingers were all right again in the course of a few days. Sampy got a tremendous fright, however, and he was never known to travel underground without a light after that."

Continuing to retrace their steps, Captain Dan and Oliver made for the main shaft. On the way they came to another of those immense empty spaces where a large lode had been worked away, and nothing left in the dark narrow void but the short beams which had supported the working stages of the men. Here Oliver, looking down through a hole at his feet, saw several men far below him. They were at work on the "end" in three successive tiers — above each other's heads.

"You've seen two of these men before," said Captain Dan.

"Have I?"

"Yes, they are local preachers. The last time you saw the upper one," said Captain Dan with a smile, "you were seated in the Wesleyan chapel, and he was in the pulpit dressed like a gentleman, and preaching as eloquently as if he had been educated at college and trained for the ministry."

"I should like very much to go down and visit them," said Oliver.

"'Tis a difficult descent. There are no ladders. Will your head stand stepping from beam to beam, and can you lower yourself by a chain?"

"I'll try," said Oliver.

Without more words Captain Dan left the platform on which they had been walking, and, descending through a hole, led his companion by the most rugged way he had yet attempted. Sometimes they slid on their heels down places that Oliver would not have dreamed of attempting without a guide; at other times they stepped from beam to beam, with unknown depths below them.

"Have a care here, sir," said the captain, pausing before a very steep place. "I will go first and wait for you."

So saying, he seized a piece of old rusty chain that was fastened into the rock, and swung himself down. Then, looking up, he called to Oliver to follow.

The young doctor did so, and, having cautiously lowered himself a few yards, he reached a beam, where he found the captain holding up his candle, and regarding him with some anxiety. Captain Dan appeared as if suspended in mid-air. Opposite to him, in the distance, the two "local preachers" were hard at work with hammer and chisel, while far below, a miner could be seen coming along the next level, and pushing an iron truck full of ore before him.

A few more steps and slides, and then a short ascent, and Oliver stood beside the man who had preached the previous Sunday. He worked with another miner, and was red, ragged, and half-clad, like all the rest, and the perspiration was pouring over his face, which was streaked with slime. Very unlike was he at that time to the gentlemanly youth who had held forth from the pulpit. Oliver had a long chat with him, and found that he aspired to enter the ministry, and had already passed some severe examinations. He was self-taught, having procured the loan of books from his minister and some friends who were interested in him. His language and manners were those of a gentleman, yet he had had no advantages beyond his fellows.

"My friend there, sir, also hopes to enter the ministry," said the miner, pointing, as he spoke, to a gap between the boards on which he stood.

Oliver looked down, and there beheld a stalwart young man, about a couple of yards under his feet, wielding a hammer with tremendous vigour. His light linen coat was open, displaying his bared and muscular bosom.

"What! is *he* a local preacher also?"

"He is, sir," said the miner, with a smile.

Oliver immediately descended to the stage below, and had a chat with this man also, after which he left them at their work, wondering very much at the intelligence and learning displayed by them; for he remembered that in their sermons they had, without notes, without hesitation, and without a grammatical error, entered into the most subtle metaphysical reasoning (rather too much of it indeed!), and had preached with impassioned (perhaps too impassioned) eloquence, quoting poets and prose writers, ancient and modern, with the facility of good scholars — while they urged men and women to repent and flee to Christ, with all the fervour of men thoroughly in earnest. On the other hand, he knew that their opportunities for self-education were not great, and that they had to toil in the meantime for daily bread, at the rate of about £3 a month!

Following Captain Dan, Oliver soon reached the ladder-way.

While slowly and in silence ascending the ladders; they heard a sound of music above them.

"Men coming down to work, singing," said the captain, as they stood on a cross-beam to listen.

The sounds at first were very faint and inexpressibly sweet. By degrees they became more distinct, and Oliver could distinguish several voices singing in harmony, keeping time to the slow measured tread of their descending steps. There seemed a novelty, and yet a strange familiarity, in the strains as they were wafted softly down upon his ear, until they drew near, and the starlike candles of the miners became visible. Their manly voices then poured forth in full strength the glorious psalm-tune called "French," which is usually sung in Scotland to the beautiful psalm beginning, "I to the hills will lift mine eyes."

The men stopped abruptly on encountering their captain and the stranger. Exchanging a few words with the former, they stood aside on the beams to let them pass. A little boy came last. His small limbs were as active as those of his more stalwart comrades, and he exhibited no signs of fatigue. His treble voice, too, was heard high and tuneful among the others as they continued their descent and resumed the psalm. The sweet strains retired gradually, and faded in the depths below as they had first stolen on the senses from above; and the pleasant memory of them still remained with the young doctor when he emerged from the mine through the hole at the head of the shaft, and stood once more in the blessed sunshine!

CHAPTER IX.

Treats of Difficulties to be Overcome.

One afternoon a council — we may appropriately say of war — was held in St. Just. The scene of the council was the shop of Maggot, the blacksmith, and the members of it were a number of miners, the president being the worthy smith himself, who, with a sledge-hammer under his arm in the position of a short crutch, occupied the chair, if we may be allowed so to designate the raised hearth of the forge.

The war with poverty had not been very successfully waged of late, and, at the time of which we write, the enemy had apparently given the miners a severe check, in the way of putting what appeared to be an insuperable obstacle in their path.

"Now, lads," said Maggot, with a slap on the leathern apron that covered his knees, "this is the way on it, an' do 'ee be quiet and hould yer tongues while I do spaik."

The other men, of whom there were nearly a dozen, nodded and said, "Go on, booy; thee's knaw tin, sure;" by which expression they affirmed their belief that the blacksmith was a very knowing fellow.

"You do tell me that you've come so close to water that you're 'fraid to go on? Is that so?"

"Iss, iss," responded the others.

"Well, I'll hole into the house, ef you do agree to give un a good pitch," said Maggot.

"Agreed, one and all," cried the miners.

In order that the reader may understand the drift of this conversation, it is necessary to explain that the indefatigable miner, David Trevarrow, whom we have already introduced in his submarine workshop, had, according to his plan, changed his ground, and transferred his labour to a more hopeful part of the mine.

For some time previous the men had been at work on a lode which was very promising, but they were compelled to cease following it, because it approached the workings of an old part of the mine which was known to be full of water. To tap this old part, or as the miners expressed it, to "hole into this house of water," was, they were well aware, an exceedingly dangerous operation. The part of the mine to which we allude was not under the sea, but back a little from the shore, and was not very deep at that time. The "adit" — or water-conducting — level by which the spot was reached commenced at the cliffs, on a level with the seashore, and ran into the interior until it reached the old mine, about a quarter of a mile inland. Here was situated the "house," which was neither more nor less than a number of old shafts and levels filled with water. As they had approached the old mine its near proximity was made disagreeably evident by the quantity of moisture that oozed through the crevices in the rocks — moisture which ere long took the form of a number of tiny rills — and at last began to spirt out from roof and sides in such a way that the miners became alarmed, and hesitated to continue to work in a place where they ran the most imminent risk of being suddenly drowned and swept into the sea, by the bursting of the rocks that still withstood the immense pressure of the confined water.

It was at this point in the undertaking that David Trevarrow went to examine the place, and made the discovery of a seam — a "keenly lode" — which had such a promising appearance that the anxiety of the miners to get rid of this obstructive "house" was redoubled.

It was at this point, too, that the council of which we write was held, in order to settle who should have the undesirable privilege of constituting the "forlorn hope" in their subterranean assault.

Maggot, who was known to be one of the boldest, and, at the same time, one of the most utterly reckless, men in St. Just, was appealed to in the emergency, and, as we have seen, offered to attack the enemy single-handed, on condition that the miners should give him a "pitch" of the good lode they had found — that is, give him the right to work out a certain number of fathoms of ore for himself.

They agreed to this, but one of them expressed some doubt as to Maggot's courage being equal to the occasion.

To this remark Maggot vouchsafed no other reply than a frown, but his friend and admirer John Cock exclaimed in supreme contempt — "What! Maggot afear'd to do it! aw, my dear, hould tha tongue."

"But he haven't bin to see the place," urged the previous speaker.

"No, my son," said Maggot, turning on the man with a look of pity, "but he can go an' see it. Come, lads, lev us go an' see this place of danger."

The miners rose at once as Maggot threw his forehammer on a heap of coals, put on his hat, and strode out of the forge with a reckless fling. A few minutes sufficed to bring them to the beach at the mouth of the adit.

It was a singularly wild spot, close under those precipitous cliffs on which some of the picturesque buildings of Botallack mine are perched — a sort of narrow inlet or gorge which from its form is named the Narrow Zawn. There was nothing worthy of the name of a beach at the place, save a little piece of rugged ground near the adit mouth, which could be reached only by a zigzag path on the face of the almost perpendicular precipice.

Arrived here, each man lighted a candle, wrapped the customary piece of wet clay round the middle of it, and entered the narrow tunnel. They advanced in single file, James Penrose leading. The height of the adit permitted of their walking almost upright, but the irregularity of the cuttings rendered it necessary that they should advance carefully, with special regard to their heads. In about a quarter of an hour they reached a comparatively open space — that is to say, there were several extensions of the cutting in various directions, which gave the place the appearance of being a small cavern, instead of a narrow tunnel. Here the water, which in other parts of the adit flowed along the bottom, ran down the walls and spirted in fine streams from the almost invisible crevices of the rock, thus betraying at once the proximity and the power of the pent-up water.

"What think'ee now, my son?" asked an elderly man who stood at Maggot's elbow.

After a short pause, during which he sternly regarded the rocks before him, the smith replied, "*I'll do it,*" in the tone and with the air of a man who knows that what he has made up his mind to do is not child's play.

The question being thus settled, the miners retraced their steps and went to their several homes.

Entering his cottage, the smith found his little girl Grace busily engaged in the interesting process of nursing the baby. He seated himself in a chair by the fireside, smoked his pipe, and watched the process, while his wife busied herself in preparing the evening meal.

Oh! but the little Maggot was a big baby — a worthy representative of his father — a true chip of the old block, for he was not only fat, riotous, and muscular, but very reckless, and extremely positive. His little nurse, on the contrary, was gentle and delicate; not much bigger than the baby, although a good deal older, and she had a dreadful business of it to keep him in order. All her efforts at lifting and restraining him were somewhat akin to the exertion made by wrestlers to throw each other by main force, and her intense desire to make baby Maggot "be good" was repaid by severe kicks on the shins, and sundry dabs in the face with, luckily, a soft, fat pair of fists.

"Sit 'ee quiet, now, or I'll scat oo nose," said the little nurse suddenly, with a terrible frown.

It need scarcely be said that she had not the remotest; intention of carrying out this dreadful threat to smash the little Maggot's nose. She accompanied it, however, with a twist that suddenly placed the urchin in a sitting posture, much to his own surprise, for he opened his eyes very wide, drew his breath sharply, and appeared to meditate a roar. He thought better of it, however, and relapsed into goodness just as the door opened, and David Trevarrow entered.

"Oh, uncle David," cried little Grace, jumping up and running towards him, "do help me nuss baby."

"What's the matter with the cheeld — bad, eh? Fetch un to me and I'll cure him."

There was no necessity to fetch baby, for that obstreperous individual entertained an immense regard for "Unkil Day," and was already on his fat legs staggering across the floor to him with outstretched arms. Thereafter he only required a pair of wings to make him a complete cherub.

Little Grace, relieved of her charge, at once set to work to assist her mother in household matters. She was one of those dear little earnest creatures who of their own accord act in a motherly and wifely way from their early years. To look at little Grace's serious thoroughgoing face, when she chanced to pause in the midst of work, and meditate what was to be done next, one might imagine that the entire care of the household had suddenly devolved upon her shoulders. In the matter of housewifery little Grace was almost equal to big Grace, her respected mother; in downright honesty and truthfulness she greatly excelled her.

The description of Maggot's household, on that evening, would be very incomplete were we to omit mention of Zackey Maggot. That young man — for man he deemed himself, and man he was, in all respects, except the trifling matters of years, size, and whiskers — that young man entered the room with his uncle, and, without deigning to change his wet red garments, sat him down at his father's feet and caught hold of a small black kitten, which, at the time, lay sound asleep on the hearth, and began to play with it in a grave patronising way, as though his taking notice of it at all were a condescension.

That black kitten, or Chet, as it was usually styled, was accustomed to be strangled the greater part of the morning by the baby. Most of the afternoon it was worried by Zackey, and, during the intervals of torment, it experienced an unusually large measure of the vicissitudes incident to kitten life — such as being kicked out of the way by Maggot senior, or thrown or terrified out of the way by Mrs. Maggot, or dashed at by stray dogs, or yelled at by passing boys. The only sunshine of its life (which was at all times liable to be suddenly clouded) was when it slept, or when little Grace put it on her soft neck, tickled its chin, and otherwise soothed its ruffled spirit, as only a loving heart knows how. A bad memory seemed to be that kitten's chief blessing. A horror of any kind was no sooner past than it was straightway forgotten, and the facetious animal would advance with arched back and glaring eyes in defiance of an incursive hen, or twirl in mad hopeless career after its own miserable tail!

"'Tis a keenly lode," said Maggot, puffing his pipe thoughtfully.

"Iss," assented David Trevarrow, also puffing his pipe, at the clouds issuing from which baby gazed with endless amazement and admiration; "it's worth much, but it isn't worth your life."

"Sure, I ain't goin' to give my life for't," replied Maggot.

"But you're goin' to risk it," said David, "an' you shouldn't, for you've a wife an' child'n to provide for. Now, I tell 'ee what it is: you lev it to me. *I'll* hole to the house. It don't matter much what happens to me."

"No, 'ee won't," said Maggot stoutly; "what I do promise to do I *will* do."

"But if you die?" said David.

"Well, what if I do? we have all to come to that some day, sooner or later."

"Are you prepared to die?" asked Trevarrow earnestly.

"Now, David, don't 'ee trouble me with that. 'Tis all very well for the women an' child'n, but it don't suit me, it don't, so lev us have no more of it, booy. I'll do it tomorrow, that's fixed, so now we'll have a bit supper."

The tone in which Maggot said this assured David that further conversation would be useless, so he dropped the subject and sat down with the rest of the family to their evening meal.

CHAPTER X.

Shows how Maggot made a Desperate Venture, and what Flowed from it.

"A wilful man must have his way" is a proverb the truth of which was illustrated by the blacksmith on the following day.

David Trevarrow again attempted to dissuade him from his purpose, and reiterated his offer to go in his stead, but he failed to move him. Mrs. Maggot essayed, and added tears to her suasion, as also did little Grace; but they failed too — the obdurate man would not give way. The only one of his household who did not attempt to dissuade him (excepting, of course, the baby, who cared nothing whatever about the matter) was Zackey. That urchin not only rejoiced in the failure of the others to turn his father from his purpose, but pleaded hard to be allowed to go with him, and share his danger as well as glory. This, however, was peremptorily denied to the young aspirant to fame and a premature death by drowning in a dark hole.

Early in the forenoon Maggot and his friends proceeded to the shore, where they found a number of miners and others assembled near the adit mouth — among them our hero Oliver Trembath, Mr. Donnithorne, and Mr. Cornish, at that time the purser and manager of Botallack mine.

The latter gentleman accosted Maggot as he came forward, and advised him to be cautious. Of course the smith gave every assurance that was required of him, and immediately prepared himself to make the dangerous experiment.

Supplying himself with a number of tallow candles, a mining hammer, and other tools, Maggot stripped to the waist, and jestingly bidding his friends farewell, entered the mouth of the tunnel, and disappeared. The adit level, or tunnel, through which he had to pass to the scene of his operations, was, as we have said, about a quarter of a mile in length, about six feet high, and two and a half feet wide. It varied in dimensions here and there, however, and was rough and irregular throughout.

For the first hundred yards or so Maggot could see well enough to grope his way by the daylight which streamed in at the entrance of the adit, but beyond this point all was intense darkness; so here he stopped, and, striking a light by means of flint, steel, and tinder, lit one of his candles. This he attached to a piece of wet clay in the usual fashion, except that he placed the clay at the lower end of the candle instead of round the middle of it. He then stuck it against the rock a little above the level of his head. Lighting another candle he advanced with it in his hand. Walking, or rather wading onward (for the stream was ankle-deep) far enough to be almost beyond the influence of the first candle, he stopped again and stuck up another. Thus, at intervals, he placed candles along the entire length of the adit, so that he might have light to guide him in his race from the water which he hoped to set free. This precaution was necessary, because, although he meant to carry a candle in his hat all the time, there was a possibility — nay, a strong probability — that it would be blown or drowned out.

Little more than a quarter of an hour brought him to the scene of his intended adventure. Here he found the water spirting out all round, much more violently than it had been the day before. He did not waste much time in consideration, having made up his mind on the previous visit as to which part of the rock he would drive the hole through. Sticking his last candle, therefore, against the driest part of the wall that could be found, he seized his tools and commenced work.

We have already said that Maggot was a strong man. As he stood there, naked to the waist, holding the borer with his left hand, and plying the hammer with all his might with the other, his great breadth of shoulder and development of muscle were finely displayed by the candlelight, which fell in brilliant gleams on parts of his frame, while the rest of him was thrown into shadow, so deep that it would have appeared black, but for the deeper shade by which it was surrounded — the whole scene presenting a grand Rembrandt effect.

It is unnecessary to say that Maggot wrought with might and main. Excited somewhat by the novelty and danger of his undertaking, he felt relieved by the violence of his exertion. He knew, besides, that the candles which were to light him on his return were slowly but surely burning down. Blow after blow resounded through the place incessantly. When the smith's right arm felt a very little wearied — it was too powerful to be soon or greatly exhausted — he shifted the hammer to his left hand, and so the work went on. Suddenly and unexpectedly the borer was driven to its head into the hole by a tremendous blow. The rock behind it had given way. Almost at the same instant a large mass of rock burst outwards, followed by a stream of water so thick and violent that it went straight at the opposite side of the cavern, against which it burst in white foam. This, rebounding back and around, rushed against roof and sides with such force that the whole place was at once deluged.

Maggot was knocked down at the first gush, but leaped up and turned to fly. Of course both candles — that in his hat as well as that which he had affixed to the wall — were extinguished, and he was at once plunged in total darkness, for the rays of the next light, although visible, were too feeble to penetrate with any effect to the extremity of the adit. Blinded by rushing water and confused by his fall, the smith mistook his direction, and ran against the side of the level with such violence that he fell again, but his sturdy frame withstood the shock, and once more he sprang to his feet and leaped along the narrow tunnel with all the energy of desperation.

Well was it for Maggot at that hour that his heart was bold and his faculties cool and collected, else then and there his career had ended. Bending forward and stooping low, he bounded away like a hunted deer, but the rush of water was so great that it rapidly gained on him, and, by concealing the uneven places in the path, caused him to stumble. His relay of candles served him in good stead; nevertheless, despite their light and his own caution, he more than once narrowly missed dashing out his brains on the low roof. On came the water after the fugitive, a mighty, hissing, vaulting torrent, filling the level behind, and leaping up on the man higher and higher as he struggled and floundered on for life. Quickly, and before quarter of the distance to the adit mouth was traversed, it gurgled up to his waist, swept him off his legs, and hurled him against projecting rocks. Once and again did he succeed in regaining his foothold, but in a moment or two the rising flood swept him down and hurled him violently onward, sporting with him on its foaming crest until it disgorged him at last, and cast him, stunned, bruised, and bleeding, on the seashore.

Of course the unfortunate man's friends had waited for him with some impatience, and great was their anxiety when the first of the flood made its appearance. When, immediately after, the battered form of their comrade was flung on the beach, they ran forward and bore him out of the stream.

Oliver Trembath being on the spot, Maggot wae at once attended to, and his wounds bound up.

"He'll do; he's all right," said Oliver, on completing the work — "only got a few cuts and bruises, and lost a little blood, but that won't harm him."

The expression of anxiety that had appeared on the faces of those who stood around at once vanished on hearing these reassuring words.

"I knaw'd it," said John Cock energetically. "I knaw'd he couldn't be killed — not he."

"I trust that you may be right, Oliver," said old Mr. Donnithorne, looking with much concern on the pale countenance of the poor smith, who still lay stretched out, with only a slight motion of the chest to prove that the vital spark had not been altogether extinguished.

"No fear of him, he's sure to come round," replied Oliver; "come, lads, up with him on your backs."

He raised the smith's shoulder as he spoke. Three tall and powerful miners promptly lent their aid, and Maggot was raised shoulder-high, and conveyed up the steep, winding path that led to the top of the cliff.

"It would never do to lose Maggot," murmured Mr. Donnithorne, as if speaking to himself while he followed the procession beside Mr. Cornish; "he's far too good a —"

"A smuggler — eh?" interrupted the purser, with a laugh.

"Eh, ah! did I say smuggler?" cried Mr. Donnithorne; "surely not, for of all vices that of smuggling is one of the worst, unless it be an overfondness for the bottle. I meant to have said that he is too valuable a man for St. Just to lose — in many ways; and you know, Mr. Cornish, that he is a famous wrestler — a man of whom St. Just may be justly proud."

Mr. Donnithorne cast a sly glance at his companion, whom he knew to be partial to the ancient Cornish pastime of wrestling. Indeed, if report said truly, the worthy purser had himself in his youthful days been a celebrated amateur wrestler, one who had never been thrown, even although he had on more than one occasion been induced in a frolic to enter the public ring and measure his strength with the best men that could be brought against him. He was long past the time of life when men indulge in such rough play, but his tall commanding figure and huge chest and shoulders were quite sufficient to warrant the belief that what was said of him was possible, while the expression of his fine massive countenance, and the humorous glance of his clear, black eye, bore evidence that it was highly probable.

"'Twould be foul injustice," said the purser with a quiet laugh, "if I were to deny that Maggot is a good man and true, in the matter of wrestling; nevertheless he is an arrant rogue, and defrauds the revenue woefully. But, after all he is only the cat's-paw; those who employ him are the real sinners — eh, Mr. Donnithorne?"

"Surely, surely," replied the old gentleman with much gravity; "and it is to be hoped that this accident will have the effect of turning Maggot from his evil ways."

The purser could not refrain from a laugh at the hypocritical solemnity of the old gentleman, who was, he well knew, one of the very sinners whom he condemned with such righteous indignation, but their arrival at Maggot's cottage prevented further conversation on the subject at that time.

Mrs. Maggot, although a good deal agitated when her husband's almost inanimate and bloody form was carried in and laid on the bed, was by no means overcome with alarm. She, like the wives of St. Just miners generally, was too well accustomed to hear of accidents and to see their results, to give way to wild fears before she had learned the extent of her calamity; so, when she found that it was not serious, she dried her eyes, and busied herself in attending to all the little duties which the occasion required. Little Grace, too, although terribly frightened, and very pale, was quite self-possessed, and went about the house assisting her mother ably, despite the tendency to sob, which she found it very difficult to overcome. But the baby behaved in the most shameful and outrageous manner. His naughtiness is almost indescribable. The instant the door opened, and his father's bloody face was presented to view, baby set up a roar so tremendous that a number of dogs in the neighbourhood struck in with a loud chorus, and the black kitten, startled out of an innocent slumber, rushed incontinently under the bed, faced about, and fuffed in impotent dismay!

But not only did baby roar — he also fell on the floor and kicked, thereby rendering his noise exasperating, besides exposing his fat person to the risk of being trod upon. Zackey was therefore told off as a detachment to keep this enemy in check, a duty which he performed nobly, until his worthy father was comfortably put to bed, after which the friends retired, and left the smith to the tender care of his own family.

"He has done good service anyhow," observed Mr. Donnithorne to his nephew, as he parted from him that evening; "for he has cleared the mine of water that it would have cost hundreds of pounds and many months to pump out."

CHAPTER XI.

Shows that Music hath Charms, and also that
it sometimes has Disadvantages.

One morning, not long after his arrival at St. Just, the young doctor went out to make a round of professional visits. He had on his way to pass the cottage of his uncle, which stood a little apart from the chief square or triangle of the town, and had a small piece of ground in front. Here Rose was wont to cultivate her namesakes, and other flowers, with her own fair hands, and here Mr. Thomas Donnithorne refreshed himself each evening with a pipe of tobacco, the flavour of which was inexpressibly enhanced to him by the knowledge that it had been smuggled.

He was in the habit of washing the taste of the same away each night, before retiring to rest, with a glass of brandy and water, hot, which was likewise improved in flavour by the same interesting association.

The windows of the cottage were wide open, for no Atlantic fog dimmed the glory of the summer sun that morning, and the light air that came up from the mighty sea was fresh and agreeably cool.

As Oliver approached the end of the cottage he observed that Rose was not at her accustomed work in the garden, and he was about to pass the door when the tones of a guitar struck his ear and arrested his step. He was surprised, for at that period the instrument was not much used, and the out-of-the-way town of St. Just was naturally the last place in the land where he would have expected to meet with one. No air was played — only a few chords were lightly touched by fingers which were evidently expert. Presently a female voice was heard to sing in rich contralto tones. The air was extremely simple, and very beautiful — at least, so thought Oliver, as he leaned against a wall and listened to the words. These, also, were simple enough, but sounded both sweet and sensible to the listener, coming as they did from a woman's lips so tunefully, and sounding the praises of the sea, of which he was passionately fond:

> "I love the land where acres broad
> Are clothed in yellow grain;
> Where cot of thrall and lordly hall
> Lie scattered o'er the plain.
> Oh! I have trod the velvet sod
> Beneath the beechwood tree;
> And roamed the brake by stream and lake
> Where peace and plenty be.
> But more than plain,
> Or rich domain,
> I love the bright blue sea!
>
> "I love the land where bracken grows

And heath-clad mountains rise;
Where peaks still fringed with winter snows
Tower in the summer skies.
Oh! I have seen the red and green
Of fir and rowan tree,
And heard the din of flooded linn,
With bleating on the lea.
But better still
Than heath-clad hill
I love the stormy sea!"

The air ceased, and Oliver, stepping in at the open door, found Rose Ellis with a Spanish guitar resting on her knee. She neither blushed nor started up nor looked confused — which was, of course, very strange of her in the circumstances, seeing that she is the heroine of this tale — but, rising with a smile on her pretty mouth, shook hands with the youth.

"Why, cousin," said Oliver, "I had no idea you could sing so charmingly."

"I am fond of singing," said Rose.

"So am I, especially when I hear such singing as yours; and the song, too — I like it much, for it praises the sea. Where did you pick it up?"

"I got it from the composer, a young midshipman," said Rose sadly; at the same time a slight blush tinged her brow.

Oliver felt a peculiar sensation which he could not account for, and was about to make further inquiries into the authorship of the song, when it occurred to him that this would be impolite, and might be awkward, so he asked instead how she had become possessed of so fine a guitar. Before she could reply Mr. Donnithorne entered.

"How d'ee do, Oliver lad; going your rounds — eh? — Come, Rose, let's have breakfast, lass, you were not wont to be behind with it. I'll be bound this gay gallant — this hedge-jumper with his eyes shut — has been praising your voice and puffing up your heart, but don't believe him, Rose; it's the fashion of these fellows to tell lies on such matters."

"You do me injustice, uncle," said Oliver with a laugh; "but even if it were true that I am addicted to falsehood in praising women, it were impossible, in the present instance, to give way to my propensity, for Truth herself would find it difficult to select an expression sufficiently appropriate to apply to the beautiful voice of Rose Ellis!"

"Hey-day, young man," exclaimed Mr. Donnithorne, as he carefully filled his pipe with precious weed, "your oratorical powers are uncommon! Surely thy talents had been better bestowed in the Church or at the Bar than in the sick-room or the hospital. Demosthenes himself would have paled before thee, lad — though, if truth must be told, there is a dash more sound than sense in thine eloquence."

"Sense, uncle! Surely your own good sense must compel you to admit that Rose sings splendidly?"

"Well, I won't gainsay it," replied Mr. Donnithorne, "now that Rose has left the room, for I don't much care to bespatter folk with too much praise to their faces. The child has indeed a sweet pipe of her own. By the way, you were asking about her guitar when I came in; I'll tell you about that.

"Its history is somewhat curious," said Mr. Donnithorne, passing his fingers through the bunch of gay ribbons that hung from the head of the instrument. "You have heard, I dare say, of the burning of Penzance by the Spaniards more than two hundred years ago; in the year 1595, I think it was?"

"I have," answered Oliver, "but I know nothing beyond the fact that such an event took place. I should like to hear the details of it exceedingly."

"Well," continued the old gentleman, "our country was, as you know, at war with Spain at the time; but it no more entered into the heads of Cornishmen that the Spaniards would dare to land on our shores than that the giants would rise from their graves. There was, indeed, an old prediction that such an event would happen, but the prediction was either forgotten or not believed, so that when several Spanish galleys suddenly made their appearance in Mounts Bay, and landed about two hundred men near Mousehole, the inhabitants were taken by surprise. Before they could arm and defend themselves, the Spaniards effected a landing, began to devastate the country, and set fire to the adjacent houses.

"It is false," continued the old man sternly, "to say, as has been said by some, that the men of Mousehole were seized with panic, and that those of Newlyn and Penzance deserted their houses terror-stricken. The truth is, that the suddenness of the attack, and their unprepared condition to repel it, threw the people into temporary confusion, and forced them to retreat, as, all history shows us, the best and bravest will do at times. In Mousehole, the principal inhabitant was killed by a cannon-ball, so that, deprived of their leading spirit at the critical moment when a leader was necessary, it is no wonder that at *first* the fishermen were driven back by well-armed men trained to act in concert. To fire the houses was the work of a few minutes. The Spaniards then rushed on to Newlyn and Penzance, and fired these places also, after which they returned to their ships, intending to land the next day and renew their work of destruction.

"But that night was well spent by the enraged townsmen. They organised themselves as well as they could in the circumstances, and, when day came, attacked the Spaniards with guns and bows, and that so effectively, that the Dons were glad to hoist their sails and run out of the bay.

"Well, you must know there was one of the Spaniards, who, it has been said, either from bravado, or vanity, or a desire to insult the English, or from all three motives together, brought a guitar on shore with him at Mousehole, and sang and played to his comrades while they were burning the houses. This man left his guitar with those who were left to guard the boats, and accompanied the others to Penzance. On his return he again took his guitar, and, going up to a high point of the cliff, so that he might be seen by his companions and heard by any of the English who chanced to be in hiding near the place, sang several songs of defiance at the top of his voice, and even went the length of performing a Spanish dance, to the great amusement of his comrades below, who were embarking in their boats.

"While the half-crazed Spaniard was going on thus he little knew that, not three yards distant from him, a gigantic Mousehole fisherman, who went by the name of Gurnet, lay concealed among some low bushes, watching his proceedings with an expression of anger on his big stern countenance. When the boats were nearly ready to start the Spaniard descended from the rocky ledge on which he had been performing, intending to rejoin his comrades. He had to pass round the bush where Gurnet lay concealed, and in doing so was for a few seconds hid from his comrades, who immediately forgot him in the bustle of departure, or, if they thought of him at all, each boat's crew imagined, no doubt, that he was with one of the others.

"But he never reached the boats. As he passed the bush Gurnet sprang on him like a tiger and seized him round the throat with both hands, choking a shout that was coming up, and causing his eyes to start almost out of his head. Without uttering a word, and only giving now and then a terrible hiss through his clenched teeth, Gurnet pushed the Spaniard before him, keeping carefully out of sight of the beach, and holding him fast by the nape of the neck, so that when he perceived the slightest symptom of a tendency to cry out he had only to press his strong fingers and effectually nip it in the bud.

"He led him to a secluded place among the rocks, far beyond earshot of the shore, and there, setting him free, pointed to a flat rock and to his guitar, and hissed, rather than said, in tones that could neither be misunderstood nor gainsaid —

"'There, dance and sing, will 'ee, till 'ee bu'st!'

"Gurnet clenched his huge fist as he spoke, and, as the Spaniard grew pale, and hesitated, he shook it close to his face — so close that he tapped the prominent bridge of the man's nose, and hissed again, more fiercely than before —

"'Ye haaf saved bucca, ye mazed totle, that can only frighten women an' child'n, an burn housen; thee'rt fond o' singin' an' dancin' — dance now, will 'ee, ye gurt bufflehead, or ef ye waant I'll scat thee head in jowds, an' send 'ee scrougin' over cliffs, I will.'[6]

"The fisherman's look and action were so terrible whilst he poured forth his wrath, which was kept alive by the thought of the smouldering embers of his own cottage, that the Spaniard could not but obey. With a ludicrous compound of fun and terror he began to dance and sing, or rather to leap and wail, while Gurnet stood before him with a look of grim ferocity that never for a moment relaxed.

"Whenever the Spaniard stopped from exhaustion Gurnet shouted 'Go on,' in a voice of thunder, and the poor man, being thoroughly terrified, went on until he fell to the ground incapable of further exertion.

"Up to this point Gurnet had kept saying to himself, 'He is fond o' dancin'

---

6   In justice to the narrator it is right to say that these words are not so
     bad as they sound.

an' singin', let un have it, then,' but when the poor man fell his heart relented. He picked him up, threw him across his shoulder as if he had been a bolster, and bore him away. At first the men of the place wanted to hang him on the spot, but Gurnet claimed him as his prisoner, and would not allow this. He gave him his liberty, and the poor wretch maintained himself for many a day as a wandering minstrel. At last he managed to get on board of a Spanish vessel, and was never more heard of, but he left his guitar behind him. It was picked up on the shore, where he left it, probably, in his haste to get away.

"The truth of this story, of course, I cannot vouch for," concluded Mr. Donnithorne, with a smile, "but I have told it to you as nearly as possible in the words in which I have often heard my grandfather give it — and as for the guitar, why, here it is, having been sold to me by a descendant of the man who found it on the seashore."

"A wonderful story indeed," said Oliver — "*if true.*"

"The guitar you must admit is at least a fact," said the old gentleman.

Oliver not only admitted this, but said it was a sweet-sounding fact, and was proceeding to comment further on the subject when Mr. Donnithorne interrupted him —

"By the way, talking of sweet sounds, have you heard what that gruff-voiced scoundrel Maggot — that roaring bull of Bashan — has been about lately?"

"No, I have not," said Oliver, who saw that the old gentleman's ire was rising.

"Ha! lad, that man ought to be hanged. He is an arrant knave, a smuggler — a — an ungrateful rascal. Why, sir, you'll scarcely believe it: he has come to me and demanded more money for the jewels which he and his comrade sold me in fair and open bargain, and because I refused, and called him a few well-merited names, he has actually gone and given information against me as possessor of treasure, which of right, so they say, belongs to Government, and last night I had a letter which tells me that the treasure, as they call it, must be delivered up without delay, on pain of I don't know what penalties. Penalties, forsooth! as if I hadn't been punished enough already by the harassing curtain-lectures of my over-scrupulous wife, ever since the unlucky day when the baubles were found, not to mention the uneasy probings of my own conscience, which, to say truth, I had feared was dead altogether owing to the villainous moral atmosphere of this smuggling place, but which I find quite lively and strong yet — a matter of some consolation too, for although I do have a weakness for cheap 'baccy and brandy, being of an economical turn of mind, I don't like the notion of getting rid of my conscience altogether. But, man, 'tis hard to bear!"

Poor Mr. Donnithorne stopped here, partly owing to shortness of breath, and partly because he had excited himself to a pitch that rendered coherent speech difficult.

"Would it not be well at once to relieve your conscience, sir," suggested Oliver respectfully, "by giving up the things that cause it pain? In my profession we always try to get at the root of a disease, and apply our remedies there."

"Ha!" exclaimed the old gentleman, wiping his heated brow, "and lose twenty pounds as a sort of fee to Doctor Maggot, who, like other doctors I wot of, created the disease himself, and who will certainly never attempt to alleviate it by returning the fee."

"Still, the disease may be cured by the remedy I recommend," said Oliver.

"No, man, it can't," cried the old gentleman with a perplexed expression, "because the dirty things are already sold and the money is invested in Botallack shares, to sell which and pay back the cash in the present depressed state of things would be utter madness. But hush! here comes my better half, and although she *is* a dear good soul, with an unusual amount of wisdom for her size, it would be injudicious to prolong the lectures of the night into the early hours of morning."

As he spoke little Mrs. Donnithorne's round good-looking face appeared like the rising sun in the doorway, and her cheery voice welcomed Oliver to breakfast.

"Thank you, aunt," said Oliver, "but I have already breakfasted more than an hour ago, and am on my way to visit my patients. Indeed, I have to blame myself for calling at so early an hour, and would not have done so but for the irresistible attraction of a newly discovered voice, which —"

"Come, come, youngster," interrupted Mr. Donnithorne, "be pleased to bear in remembrance that the voice is connected with a pair of capital ears, remarkable for their sharpness, if not their length, and at no great distance off, I warrant."

"You do Rose injustice," observed Mrs. Donnithorne, as the voice at that moment broke out into a lively carol in the region of the kitchen, whither its owner had gone to superintend culinary matters. "But tell me, Oliver, have you heard of the accident to poor Batten?"

"Yes, I saw him yesterday," replied the doctor, "just after the accident happened, and I am anxious about him. I fear, though I am not quite certain, that his eyesight is destroyed."

"Dear! dear! — oh, poor man," said Mrs. Donnithorne, whose sympathetic heart swelled, while her blue eyes instantly filled with tears. "It is so very sad, Oliver, for his delicate wife and four young children are entirely dependent upon him and his two sons — and they found it difficult enough to make the two ends meet, even when they were all in health; for it is hard times among the miners at present, as you know, Oliver; and now — dear, dear, it is very, *very* sad."

Little Mrs. Donnithorne said nothing more at that time, but her mind instantly reverted to a portly basket which she was much in the habit of carrying with her on her frequent visits to the poor and the sick — for the good lady was one of those whose inclinations as well as principles lead them to "consider the poor."

It must not be imagined, however, that the poor formed a large class of the community in St. Just. The miners of that district, and indeed all over Cornwall, were, and still are, a self-reliant, independent, hard-working race, and as long as tough thews and sinews, and stout and willing hearts, could accomplish anything, they never failed to wrench a subsistence out of the stubborn rocks which contain the wealth of the land. Begging goes very much against the grain of a Cornishman, and the lowest depth to which he can sink socially, in his own esteem, is that of being dependent on charity.

In some cases this sentiment is carried too far, and has degenerated into pride; for, when God in His wisdom sees fit, by means of disabling accident or declining health, to incapacitate a man from labour, it is as honourable in him to receive charity as it is (although not always sufficiently esteemed so) a high privilege and luxury of the more fortunate to give.

Worthy Mrs. Donnithorne's charities were always bestowed with such delicacy that she managed, in some mysterious way, to make the recipients feel as though they had done her a favour in accepting them. And yet she was not a soft piece of indiscriminating amiability, whose chief delight in giving lay in the sensations which the act created within her own breast. By no means. None knew better than she when and where to give money, and when to give blankets, bread, or tea. She was equally sharp to perceive the spirit that rendered it advisable for her to say, "I want you to do me a favour — there's a good woman now, you won't refuse me, etc.," and to detect the spirit that called forth the sharp remark, accompanied with a dubious smile and a shake of her fat forefinger, "There now, see that you make better use of it *this* time, else I shall have to scold you."

Having received a message for poor Mrs. Batten, the miner's wife, the doctor left the cottage, and proceeded to pay his visits. Let us accompany him.

CHAPTER XII.

In which Oliver gets "a Fall," and sees some of the Shadows of the Miner's Life.

In crossing a hayfield, Oliver Trembath encountered the tall, bluff figure, and the grave, sedate smile of Mr. Cornish, the manager.

"Good-morning, doctor," said the old gentleman, extending his hand and giving the youth a grasp worthy of one of the old Cornish giants; "do you know I was thinking, as I saw you leap over the stile, that you would make a pretty fair miner?"

"Thanks, sir, for your good opinion of me," said Oliver, with a smile, "but I would rather work above than below ground. Living the half of one's life beyond the reach of sunlight is not conducive to health."

"Nevertheless, the miners keep their health pretty well, considering the nature of their work," replied Mr. Cornish; "and you must admit that many of them are stout fellows. You would find them so if you got one of their Cornish hugs."

"Perhaps," said Oliver, with a modest look, for he had been a noted wrestler at school, "I might give them a pretty fair hug in return, for Cornish blood flows in my veins."

"A fig for blood, doctor; it is of no avail without knowledge and practice, as well as muscle. *With* these, however, I do acknowledge that it makes weight — if by 'blood' you mean high spirit."

"By the way, how comes it, sir," said Oliver, "that Cornishmen are so much more addicted to wrestling than other Englishmen?"

"It were hard to tell, doctor, unless it be that they feel themselves stronger than other Englishmen, and being accustomed to violent exertion more than others, they take greater pleasure in it. Undoubtedly the Greeks introduced it among us, but whether they practised it as we now do cannot be certainly ascertained."

Here Mr. Cornish entered into an enthusiastic account of the art of wrestling; related many anecdotes of his own prowess in days gone by, and explained the peculiar method of performing the throw by the heel, the toe, and the hip; the heave forward, the back-heave, and the Cornish hug, to all of which the youth listened with deep interest.

"I should like much to witness one of your wrestling-matches," he said, when the old gentleman concluded; "for I cannot imagine that any of your peculiar Cornish hugs or twists can be so potent as to overturn a stout fellow who is accustomed to wrestle in another fashion. Can you show me one of the particular grips or twists that are said to be so effective?"

"I think I can," replied the old gentleman, with a smile, and a twinkle in his eye; "of course the style of grip and throw will vary according to the size of the man one has to deal with. Give me hold of your wrist, and plant yourself firmly on your legs. Now, you see, you must turn the arm – so, and use your toe – thus, so as to lift your man, and with a sudden twist – there! That's the way to do it!" said the old gentleman, with a chuckle, as he threw Oliver head foremost into the middle of a haycock that lay opportunely near.

It is hard to say whether Mr. Cornish or Oliver was most surprised at the result of the effort – the one, that so much of his ancient prowess should remain, and the other, that he should have been so easily overthrown by one who, although fully as large a man as himself, had his joints and muscles somewhat stiffened by age.

Oliver burst into a fit of laughter on rising, and exclaimed, "Well done, sir! You have effectually convinced me that there is something worth knowing in the Cornish mode of wrestling; although, had I known what you were about to do, it might not perhaps have been done so easily."

"I doubt it not," said Mr. Cornish with a laugh; "but that shows the value of 'science' in such matters. Good-morning, doctor. Hope you'll find your patients getting on well."

He waved his hand as he turned off, while Oliver pursued his way to the miners' cottages.

The first he entered belonged to a man whose chest was slightly affected for the first time. He was a stout man, about thirty-five years of age, and of temperate habits – took a little beer occasionally, but never exceeded; had a good appetite, but had caught cold frequently in consequence of having to go a considerable distance from the shaft's mouth to the changing-house while exhausted with hard work underground and covered with profuse perspiration. Often he had to do this in wet weather and when bitterly cold winds were blowing – of late he had begun to spit blood.

It is necessary here to remind the reader that matters in this respect – and in reference to the condition of the miner generally – are now much improved. The changing-houses, besides being placed as near to the several shafts as is convenient, are now warmed with fires, and supplied with water-troughs, so that the men have a comfortable place in which to wash themselves on coming "to grass," and find their clothes thoroughly dried when they return in the morning to put them on before going underground. This renders them less liable to catch cold, but of course does not protect them from the evil influences of climbing the ladders, and of bad air. Few men have to undergo such severe toil as the Cornish miner, because of the extreme hardness of the rock with which he has to deal. To be bathed in perspiration, and engaged in almost unremitting and violent muscular exertion during at least eight hours of each day, may be said to be his normal condition.

Oliver advised this man to give up underground work for some time, and, having prescribed for him and spoken encouragingly to his wife, left the cottage to continue his rounds.

Several cases, more or less similar to the above, followed each other in succession; also one or two cases of slight illness among the children, which caused more alarm to the anxious mothers than there was any occasion for. These latter were quickly but good-naturedly disposed of, and the young doctor generally left a good impression behind him, for he had a hearty, though prompt, manner and a sympathetic spirit.

At one cottage he found a young man in the last stage of consumption. He lay on his lowly bed pale and restless – almost wishing for death to relieve him of his pains. His young wife sat by his bedside wiping the perspiration from his brow, while a ruddy-cheeked little boy romped about the room unnoticed – ignorant that the hour was drawing near which would render him fatherless, and his young mother a widow.

This young man had been a daring, high-spirited fellow, whose animal spirits led him into many a reckless deed. His complaint had been brought on by racing up the ladders – a blood-vessel had given way, and he had never rallied after. Just as Oliver was leaving him a Wesleyan minister entered the dwelling.

"He won't be long with us, doctor, I fear," he said in passing.

"Not long, sir," replied Oliver.

"His release will be a happy one," said the minister, "for his soul rests on Jesus; but, alas! for his young wife and child."

He passed into the sickroom, and the doctor went on.

The next case was also a bad one, though different from the preceding. The patient was between forty and fifty years of age, and had been unable to go underground for several years. He was a staid, sober man, and an abstemious liver, but it was evident that his life on earth was drawing to a close. He had been employed chiefly in driving levels, and had worked a great deal in very bad air, where the candles could not be made to burn unless placed nine or ten feet behind the spot where he was at work. Indeed, he often got no fresh air except what was blown to him, and only a puff now and then. When he first went to work in the morning the candle would not keep alight, so that he had to take his coat and beat the air about before going into the level, and, after a time, went in when the candles could be got to burn by holding them on one side, and teasing out the wick very much. This used to create a great deal of smoke, which tended still further to vitiate the air. When he returned "to grass" his saliva used to be as black as ink. About five years before giving up underground work he had had inflammation of the lungs, followed by blood-spitting, which used to come on when he was at work in what he called "poor air," or in "cold-damp," and he had never been well since.

Oliver's last visit that day was to the man John Batten; who had exploded a blast-hole in his face the day before. This man dwelt in a cottage in the small hamlet of Botallack, close to the mine of the same name. The room in which the miner lay was very small, and its furniture scanty; nevertheless it was clean and neatly arranged. Everything in and about the place bore evidence of the presence of a thrifty hand. The cotton curtain on the window was thin and worn, but it was well darned, and pure as the driven snow. The two chairs were old, as was also the table, but they were not rickety; it was obvious that they owed their stability to a hand skilled in mending and in patching pieces of things together. Even the squat little stool in the side of the chimney corner displayed a leg, the whiteness of which, compared with the other two, told of attention to small things. There was a peg for everything, and everything seemed to be on its peg. Nothing littered the well-scrubbed floor or defiled the well-brushed hearthstone, and it did not require a second thought on the part of the beholder to ascribe all this to the tidy little middle-aged woman, who, with an expression of deep anxiety on her good-looking countenance, attended to the wants of her injured husband.

As Oliver approached the door of this cottage two stout youths, of about sixteen and seventeen respectively, opened it and issued forth.

"Good-morning, lads! Going to work, I suppose?" said Oliver.

"Iss, sur," replied the elder, a fair-haired ruddy youth, who, like his brother, had not yet sacrificed his colour to the evil influence of the mines; "we do work in the night corps, brother and me. Father is worse today, sur."

"Sorry to hear that," said the doctor, as he passed them and entered the cottage, while the lads shouldered their tools and walked smartly down the lane that led to Botallack mine.

"Your husband is not quite so well today, I hear," said the doctor, going to the side of the bed on which the stalwart form of the miner lay.

"No, sur," replied the poor woman; "he has much pain in his eyes today, but his heart is braave, sur; I never do hear a complaint from he."

This was true. The man lay perfectly still, the compressed lip and the perspiration that moistened his face alone giving evidence of the agony he endured.

"Do you suffer much?" inquired the doctor, as he undid the bandages which covered the upper part of the man's face.

"Iss, sur, I do," was the reply.

No more was said, but a low groan escaped the miner when the bandage was removed, and the frightful effects of the accident were exposed to view. With intense anxiety Mrs. Batten watched the doctor's countenance, but found no comfort there. A very brief examination was sufficient to convince Oliver that the eyes were utterly destroyed, for the miner had been so close to the hole when it exploded that the orbs were singed by the flame, and portions of unburnt powder had been blown right into them.

"Will he see — a *little*, sur?" whispered Mrs. Batten.

Oliver shook his head. "I fear not," he said in a low tone.

"Speak out, doctor," said the miner in firm tones, "I ain't afeard to knaw it."

"It would be unkind to deceive you," replied Oliver sadly; "your eyes are destroyed."

No word was spoken for a few minutes, but the poor woman knelt by her husband's side, and nestled close to him. Batten raised his large brown hand, which bore the marks and scars of many a year of manly toil, and laid it gently on his wife's head.

"I'll never see thee again, Annie," he murmured in a low deep tone; "but I see thee face now, lass, as I *last* saw it, wi' the smile of an angel on't — an' I'll see it so till the day I die; bless the Lord for that."

Mrs. Batten rose and went softly but quickly out of the room that she might relieve her bursting heart without distressing her husband, but he knew her too well to doubt the reason of her sudden movement, and a faint smile was on his lips for a moment as he said to Oliver — "She's gone to weep a bit, sur, and pray. It will do her good, dear lass."

"Your loss is a heavy one — very heavy," said Oliver, with hesitation in his tone, for he felt some difficulty in attempting to comfort one in so hopeless a condition.

"True, sur, true," replied the man in a tone of cheerful resignation that surprised the doctor, "but it might have been worse; 'the Lord gave, and the Lord hath taken away, blessed be the name of the Lord!'"

Mrs. Batten returned in a few minutes, and Oliver left them, after administering as much comfort as he could in the circumstances, but to say truth, although well skilled in alleviating bodily pains, he was incapable of doing much in the way of ministering to the mind diseased. Oliver Trembath was not a medical missionary. His mother, though a good, amiable woman, had been a weak, easy-going creature — one of those good-tempered, listless ladies who may be regarded as human vegetables, who float through life as comfortably as they can, giving as little trouble as possible, and doing as little good as is compatible with the presence of even nominal Christianity. She performed the duties of life in the smallest possible circle, the centre of which was herself, and the extremity of the radii extending to the walls of her garden. She went to church at the regulation hours; "said her prayers" in the regulation tone of voice; gave her charities in the stated way, at stated periods, with a hazy perception as to the objects for which they were given, and an easy indifference as to the success of these objects — the whole end and aim of her wishes being attained in, and her conscience satisfied by, the act of giving. Hence her son Oliver was not much impressed in youth with the power or value of religion, and hence he found himself rather put out when his common sense told him, as it not unfrequently did, that it was his duty sometimes to administer a dose to the mind as well as to the body.

But Oliver was not like his mother in any respect. His fire, his energy, his intellectual activity, and his impulsive generosity he inherited from his father. Amiability alone descended to him from his mother — an inheritance, by the way, not to be lightly esteemed, for by it all his other qualities were immeasurably enhanced in value. His heart had beat in sympathy with the mourners he had just left, and his manly disposition made him feel ashamed that the lips which could give advice glibly enough in regard to bandages and physic, and which could speak in cheery, comforting tones when there was hope for his patient, were sealed and absolutely incapable of utterance when death approached or hopeless despair took possession of the sufferer.

Oliver had felt something of this even in his student life, when the solemnities of sickness and death were new to him; but it was pressed home upon him with peculiar power, and his manhood was often put to the blush when he was brought into contact with the Wesleyan Methodism of West Cornwall, where multitudes of men and women of all grades drew comfort from the Scriptures as readily and as earnestly as they drew water from their wells — where religion was mingled with everyday and household duties — and where many of the miners and fishermen preached and prayed, and comforted ne another with God's Word, as vigorously, as simply, and as naturally as they hewed a livelihood from the rocks or drew sustenance from the sea.

CHAPTER XIII.

Treats of Spirits and of Sundry Spirited Matters and Incidents.

One sunny afternoon Mrs. Maggot found herself in the happy position of having so thoroughly completed her round of household work that she felt at leisure to sit down and sew, while little Grace sat beside her, near the open door, rocking the cradle.

Baby, in blissful unconsciousness of its own existence, lay sound asleep with a thumb in its mouth; the resolute sucking of that thumb having been its most recent act of disobedience.

Little Grace was flushed, and rather dishevelled, for it had cost her half an hour's hard wrestling to get baby placed in recumbent somnolence. She now sought to soothe her feelings by tickling the chin of the black kitten — a process to which that active creature submitted with purring satisfaction.

"Faither's long of coming hum, mother," said little Grace, looking up.

"Iss," replied Mrs. Maggot.

"D'ee knaw where he is?" inquired Grace.

"No, I doan't," replied her mother.

It was evident that Mrs. Maggot was not in the humour for conversation, so Grace relapsed into silence, and devoted herself to the kitten.

"Is that faither?" said Grace, after a few minutes, pointing to the figure of a man who was seen coming over the distant moor or waste land which at that period surrounded the town of St. Just, though the greater part of it is now cultivated fields.

"It isn' like un," said Mrs. Maggot, shading her eyes with her hand; "sure, it do look like a boatsman.[7]"

The men of the coastguard were called "boatsmen" at that time.

"Iss, I do see his cutlash," said little Grace; "and there's another man comin' down road to meet un."

"Haste 'ee, Grace," cried Mrs. Maggot, leaping up and plucking her last-born out of the cradle, "take the cheeld in to Mrs. Penrose, an' bide theer till I send for 'ee — dost a hear?"

Plucked thus unceremoniously from gentle slumber to be plunged head-long and without preparation into fierce infantine war, was too much for baby Maggot; he uttered one yell of rage and defiance, which was succeeded by a lull — a sort of pause for the recovery of breath — so prolonged that the obedient Grace had time to fling down the horror-struck Chet, catch baby in her arms, and bear him into the neighbouring cottage before the next roar came forth. The youthful Maggot was at once received into the bosom of the Penrose family, and

---

7   The men of the coastguard were called "boatsmen" at that time.

succeeding yells were smothered by eight out of the sixteen Penroses who chanced to be at home at the time.

That Mrs. Maggot had a guilty conscience might have been inferred from her future proceedings, which, to one unacquainted with the habits of her husband, would have appeared strange, if not quite unaccountable. When baby was borne off, as related, she seized a small keg, which stood in a corner near the door and smelt strongly of brandy, and, placing it with great care in the vacant cradle, covered it over with blankets. She next rolled a pair of stockings into a ball and tied on it a little frilled night-cap, which she disposed on the pillow, with the face pretty well down, and the back of the head pretty well up, and so judiciously and cleverly covered it with bedclothes that even Maggot himself might have failed to miss his son, or to recognise the outlines of a keg. A bottle half full of brandy, with the cork out, was next placed on the table to account for the odour in the room, and then Mrs. Maggot sat down to her sewing, and rocked the cradle gently with her foot, singing a sweet lullaby the while. Ten minutes later, two stout men of the coastguard, armed with cutlasses and pistols, entered the cottage. Mrs. Maggot observed that they were also armed with a pick and shovel.

"Good-hevenin', missus; how dost do?" said the man who walked foremost, in a hearty voice.

"Good-hevenin', Eben Trezise; how are *you*?" said Mrs. Maggot.

"Braave, thank 'ee," said Trezise; "we've come for a drop o' brandy, missus, havin' heard that you've got some here, an' sure us can smell it — eh?"

"Why, iss, we've got wan small drop," said Mrs. Maggot, gently arranging the clothes on the cradle, "that the doctor have order for the cheeld. You're welcome to a taste of it, but plaise don't make so much noise, for the poor cheeld's slaipin'."

"He'll be smothered, I do think, if you don't turn his head up a bit, missus," said the man; "hows'ever you've no objection to let Jim and me have a look round the place, I dessay?"

Mrs. Maggot said they were welcome to do as they pleased, if they would only do it quietly for the sake of the "cheeld;" so without more ado they commenced a thorough investigation of the premises, outside and in. Then they went to the smithy, where Mrs. Maggot knew her husband had concealed two large kegs of smuggled liquor on the hearth under a heap of ashes and iron debris, but these had been so cleverly, yet carelessly, hidden that the men sat down on the heap under which they lay, to rest and wipe their heated brows after their fruitless search.

"Hast 'ee found the brandy?" inquired Mrs. Maggot, with a look of innocence, when the two men returned.

"Not yet," replied Eben Trezise; "but we've not done. There's a certain shaft near by that has got a bad name for drinkin', missus; p'raps you may have heard on it? Its breath do smell dreadful bad sometimes."

Both men laughed at this, and winked to each other, while Mrs. Maggot smiled, and, with a look of surprise, vowed that she had not heard of the disreputable shaft referred to.

Despite her unconcerned look, however, Mrs. Maggot felt anxious, for she was aware that her husband had recently obtained an unusually large quantity of French brandy and tobacco from the Scilly Islands, between which and the coasts of Cornwall smuggling was carried on in a most daring and extensive manner at the time of our story, and she knew that the whole of the smuggled goods lay concealed in one of those numerous disused shafts of old mines which lie scattered thickly over that part of the country. Maggot's absence rendered her position still more perplexing, but she was a woman of ready wit and self-reliance, and she comforted herself with the knowledge that the brandy lay buried far down in the shaft, and that it would take the boatsmen some time to dig to it — that possibly they might give up in despair before reaching it.

While the men went off to search for the shaft, and while Mrs. Maggot was calmly nursing her spirited little baby, Maggot himself, in company with his bosom friend John Cock, was sauntering slowly homeward along the cliffs near Kenidjack Castle, the ruins of which occupy a bold promontory a little to the north of Cape Cornwall. They had just come in sight of the tin-mine and works which cover Nancharrow valley from the shore to a considerable distance inland, where stand the tall chimneys and engine-houses, the whims and varied machinery of the extensive and prolific old tin-mine named Wheal Owles.

The cliffs on which the two men stood are very precipitous and rugged — rising in some places to a height of about 300 feet above the rocks where the waters of the Atlantic roll dark and deep, fringing the coast with a milky foam that is carried away by the tide in long streaks, to be defiled by the red waters which flow from Nancharrow valley into Porth Ledden Cove.

This cove is a small one, with a narrow strip of sand on its shore. At its northern extremity is a deep narrow gorge, into which the waves rush, even in calm weather, with a peculiar sound. In reference to this it is said that the waves "buzz-and-go-in," hence the place has been named Zawn Buzzangein. The sides of the Zawn are about sixty feet high, and quite precipitous. In one part, especially, they overhang their base. It was here that Maggot and his friend stopped on their way home, and turned to look out upon the sea.

"No sign o' pilchers yet," observed Maggot, referring to the immense shoals of pilchards which visit the Cornish coasts in the autumn of each year, and form a large portion of the wealth of the county.

"Too soon," replied John Cock.

"By the way, Jack," said Maggot, "wasn't it hereabouts that the schooner went ashore last winter?"

"Iss, 'twor down theer, close by Pullandeese," replied the other, pointing to a deep pool in the rocks round which the swell of the Atlantic broke in white foam. "I was theere myself. I had come down 'bout daylight — before others were stirring, an' sure 'nuff there she lay, on the rocks, bottom up, an' all the crew lost. We seed wan o' them knackin' on the rocks to the north, so we got ropes an' let a man down to fetch un up, but of coorse it was gone dead."

"That minds me, Jack," said Maggot, "that I seed a daw's nest here the last time I come along, so lev us go an' stroob that daw's nest."

"Thee cusn't do it," said John Cock.

Maggot laughed, and said he not only could but would, so he ran down to the neighbouring works and returned with a stout rope, which he fixed firmly to a rock at the edge of the overhanging cliff.

We have already said that Maggot was a noted madcap, who stuck at nothing, and appeared to derive positive pleasure from the mere act of putting his life in danger. No human foot could, by climbing, have reached the spot where the nest of the daw, or Cornish chough, was fixed — for the precipice, besides being perpendicular and nearly flat, projected a little near the top, where the nest lay in a crevice overhanging the surf that boiled and raged in Zawn Buzzangein. Indeed, the nest was not visible from the spot where the two men stood, and it could only be seen by going round to the cliffs on the opposite side of the gorge.

Without a moment's hesitation Maggot swung himself over the edge of the precipice, merely cautioning his comrade, as he did so, to hold on to the rope and prevent it from slipping.

He slid down about two yards, and then found that the rock overhung so much that he was at least six feet off from the crevice in which the young daws nestled comfortably together, and no stretch that he could make with his legs, long though they were, was sufficient to enable him to get on the narrow ledge just below the nest. Several times he tried to gain a footing, and at each effort the juvenile daws — as yet ignorant of the desperate nature of man — opened their little eyes to the utmost in undisguised amazement. For full five minutes Maggot wriggled and the daws gazed, and the anxious comrade above watched the vibrations and jerks of the part of the rope that was visible to him while he listened intently. The bubbles on Zawn Buzzangein, like millions of watery eyes, danced and twinkled sixty feet below, as if in wonder at the object which swung wildly to and fro in mid-air.

At last Maggot managed to touch the rock with the extreme point of his toe. A slight push gave him swing sufficient to enable him to give one or two vigorous shoves, by which means he swung close to the side of the cliff. Watching his opportunity, he planted both feet on the narrow ledge before referred to, stretched out his hands, pressed himself flat against the rock, let go the rope, and remained fast, like a fly sticking to a wall.

This state of comparative safety he announced to his anxious friend above by exclaiming — "All right, *John* – *I've* got the daws."

This statement was, however, not literally true, for it cost him several minutes of slow and careful struggling to enable him so to fix his person as to admit of his hands being used for "stroobing" purposes. At length he gained the object of his ambition, and transferred the horrified daws from their native home to his own warm but unnatural bosom, in which he buttoned them up tight. A qualm now shot through Maggot's heart, for he discovered that in his anxiety to secure the daws he had let go the rope, which hung at a distance of full six feet from him, and, of course, far beyond his reach.

"Hullo! John," he cried.

"Hullo!" shouted John in reply.

"I've got the *daws*," said Maggot, "but I've lost the *rope!*"

"Aw! my dear," gasped John; "have 'ee lost th' rope?"

It need scarcely be said that poor John Cock was dreadfully alarmed at this, and that he eagerly tendered much useless advice — stretching his neck the while as far as was safe over the cliff.

"I say, John," shouted Maggot again.

"Hullo!" answered John.

"I tell 'ee what: I'm goin' to jump for th' rope. If I do miss th' rope, run thee round to Porth Ledden Cove, an' tak' my shoes weth 'ee; I'll be theere before 'ee."

Having made this somewhat bold prediction, Maggot collected all his energies, and sprang from his narrow perch into the air, with arms and hands wildly extended. His effort was well and bravely made, but his position had been too constrained, and his foothold too insecure, to admit of a good jump. He missed the rope, and, with a loud cry, shot like an arrow into the boiling flood below.

John Cock heard the cry and the plunge, and stood for nearly a minute gazing in horror into Zawn Buzzangein. Presently he drew a deep sigh of relief, for Maggot made his appearance, manfully buffeting the waves. John watched him with anxiety while he swam out towards the sea, escaped the perpendicular sides of the Zawn, towards which the breakers more than once swept him, doubled the point, and turned in towards the cove. The opposite cliffs of the gorge now shut the swimmer out from John's view, so he drew another deep sigh, and picking up his comrade's shoes, ran round with all his might to Porth Ledden Cove, where, true to his word, having been helped both by wind and tide, Maggot had arrived before him.

"Are 'ee safe, my dear man?" was John's first question.

"Iss," replied Maggot, shaking himself, "safe enough, an' the daws too, but semmen to me they've gone dead."

This was too true. The poor birds had perished in their captor's bosom.

CHAPTER XIV.

Continues to treat of Spirits, and shows the Value of Hospitality.

Having accomplished the feat narrated in the last chapter Maggot proceeded with his friend towards the town. On their way they had to pass the mouth of an old shaft in which both of them chanced to be much interested at that time, inasmuch as it contained the produce of a recent smuggling expedition on a large scale, consisting of nearly a hundred tubs of brandy. The liquor had been successfully brought ashore and concealed in the mine, and that night had been fixed on for its removal. Mules had been provided, and about fifty men were appointed to meet at a certain spot, at a fixed hour, to carry the whole away into the neighbouring towns.

Maggot and his comrade began to converse about the subject that was uppermost in their minds, and the former increased his pace, when John Cock drew his attention to the fact that the sun was getting low.

"The boys will be mustering now," said John, "an' them theere daws have kep' us late enough already."

"They do say that the boatsmen are informed about the toobs," observed Maggot.

"More need to look alive," said John.

"Hallo!" exclaimed Maggot suddenly; "there's some wan in the shaft!"

He pointed to a neighbouring mound of rubbish, on which, just as he spoke, a man made his appearance.

Without uttering a word the smugglers sauntered towards the mound, assuming a careless air, as though they were passing that way by chance. On drawing near they recognised Ebenezer Trezise, the coastguard-man.

"Good-hevening, sur," said Maggot; "semmen as if you'd found a keenly lode."

"Why, iss, we've diskivered a noo vein," said Trezise with a sly smile, "and we're sinkin' a shaft here in the hope o' raisin' tin, or *somethin'*."

"Ha! hope you'll let John an' me have a pitch in the noo bal, won't 'ee?" said Maggot with a laugh.

"Oh, cer'nly, cer'nly," replied the boatsman; "if you'll lend us a hand to sink the shaft. You appear to have been in the water, and 'twill warm 'ee."

"No, thank 'ee," replied Maggot; "I've bin stroobin' a daw's nest under cliff, an' I fell into the say, so I'm goin' hum to dry myself, as I'm afeared o' kitchin' cold, being of a delikit constitootion. But I'll p'raps lend thee a hand afterwards."

Maggot nodded as he spoke, and left the place at a slow saunter with his comrade, followed by the thanks and good-wishes of the boatsman, who immediately returned to the laborious task of clearing out the old shaft.

"They've got the scent," said Maggot when out of earshot; "but we'll do 'em yet. Whenever thee gets on the leeside o' that hedge, John, do 'ee clap on all sail for Balaswidden, where the boys are waitin', an' tell 'em to be ready for a call. I'll send Zackey, or wan o' the child'n to 'ee."

John went off on his errand the moment he was out of sight of the boatsmen, and Maggot walked smartly to his cottage.

"Owld ooman," he said, commencing to unbutton his wet garments, "do 'ee git ready a cup o' tay, as fast as you can, lass; we shall have company tonight."

"Company!" exclaimed Mrs. Maggot in surprise; "what sort o' company?"

"Oh! the best, the best," said Maggot with a laugh; "boatsmen no less — so look sharp. Zackey booy, come here."

Zackey put down the unfortunate black kitten (which immediately sought comfort in repose) and obeyed his father's summons, while his mother, knowing that her husband had some plot in his wise head, set about preparing a sumptuous meal, which consisted of bread and butter, tea and fried mackerel, and Cornish pasty.

"Zackey, my son," said Maggot while he continued his toilet.

"Iss, father."

"I want 'ee to come down to the owld shaft with me, an' when I give 'ee the ward cut away as hard as thee legs can spank to Balaswidden, an' fetch the lads that are theere to the owld shaft. They knaw what to do, but tell 'em to make so little noise as they can. Dost a hear, my son?"

"Iss, faither," replied Zackey, with a wink of such profound meaning that his sire felt quite satisfied he was equal to the duty assigned him.

"Now, doan't 'ee wag tongue more than enough," continued Maggot; "and go play with the chet till I'm ready."

The urchin at once descended like a thunderbolt on the black kitten, but that marvellous animal had succeeded in snatching five minutes' repose, which seemed to be amply sufficient to recruit its energies, for it began instantly to play — in other words to worry and scratch the boy's hand — with the utmost glee and good humour.

In a few minutes Maggot and his son went out and hastened to the old shaft, where they found the boatsmen still hard at work with pick and shovel clearing away the rubbish.

"You haven't found a bunch o' copper yet, I dessay?" said Maggot with a grin.

"No, not yet, but we shan't be long," replied Eben Trezise with a knowing smile.

"It's warm work," observed Maggot, as he looked down the hole, and saw that what the boatsman said was true, and that they would not be long of reaching the spot where the liquor had been concealed.

Trezise admitted that it *was* warm work, and paused to wipe his heated brow.

"I wish we had a drop o' water here," he said, looking up.

"Ha!" exclaimed Maggot; "not much chance o' findin' water in *that* hole, I do think — no, nor brandy nuther."

"Not so sure o' that," said Trezise, resuming his work.

"Now, et *is* a shame to let 'ee die here for want of a drop o' water," said Maggot in a compassionate tone; "I'll send my booy hum for some."

The boatsmen thanked him, and Zackey was ordered off to fetch a jug of water; but his father's voice arrested him before he had gone a hundred yards.

"Hold on a bit, my son. — P'raps," he said, turning to Trezise, "you'd come up hum with me and have a dish o' tay? Missus have got it all ready."

The invitation appeared to gratify the boatsmen, who smiled and winked at each other, as though they thought themselves very clever fellows to have discovered the whereabouts of a hidden treasure, and to be refreshed in the midst of their toil by one whom they knew to be a noted smuggler, and whom they strongly suspected of being concerned in the job they were at that time endeavouring to frustrate. Throwing down their tools they laughingly accepted the invitation, and clambered out of the shaft.

"Now's your time," whispered Maggot with a nod to his hopeful son, and then added aloud —

"Cut away, Zackey booy, an' tell mother to get the tay ready. Run, my son, let us knaw what thee legs are made of."

"He's a smart lad," observed Trezise, as Zackey gave his father an intelligent look, and dashed away at the top of his speed.

"Iss, a clever cheeld," assented Maggot.

"Bin down in the mines, I dessay?" said Trezise.

"Iss, oh iss; he do knaw tin," replied Maggot with much gravity.

In a few minutes the two coastguard-men were seated at Mrs. Maggot's well-supplied board, enjoying the most comfortable meal they had eaten for many a day. It was seasoned, too, with such racy talk, abounding in anecdote, from Maggot, and such importunate hospitality on the part of his better half, that the men felt no disposition to cut it short. Little Grace, too, was charmingly attentive, for she, poor child, being utterly ignorant of the double parts which her parents were playing, rejoiced, in the native kindliness of her heart, to see them all so happy. Even the "chet" seemed to enter into the spirit of what was going on, for, regardless of the splendid opportunity that now presented itself of obtaining repose to its heart's content, that black ball of concentrated essence of mischief dashed wildly about the floor and up the bed-curtains, with its back up and its tail thickened, and its green eyes glaring defiance at everything animate, inanimate, or otherwise, insomuch that Maggot made sundry efforts to quell it with the three-legged stool — and Mrs. Maggot followed suit with a dish-clout — but in vain!

Meanwhile, men and mules and horses were converging by many paths and lanes towards the old shaft, and the shaft itself was apparently endued with the properties of a volcano, for out of its mouth issued a continuous shower of dust and stones, while many stalwart arms laid bare the mine beneath, and tossed up the precious "tubs" of brandy.

Before the pleasant little tea-party in Maggot's cottage broke up the whole were scattered abroad, and men and mules and horses sped with their ill-gotten gains across the furze-clad moors.

"Sure it's early to break up," said Maggot, when the boatsmen at last rose to take their leave; "there's no fear o' the bunches o' copper melting down there, or flyin' away."

"There's no saying," replied Eben Trezise; "you've heerd as well as we of lodes takin' the bit in their teeth an' disappearing — eh?"

"Well, iss, so they do sometimes; I'll not keep 'ee longer; good-hevenin' to 'ee," said Maggot, going outside the door and wishing them all manner of success as they returned to the old shaft.

Reader, shall we follow the two knowing fellows to that shaft? Shall we mark the bewildered expression of amazement with which they gazed into it, and listen to the wild fiendish laugh of mingled amusement and wrath that bursts from them in fitful explosions as the truth flashes into their unwilling minds? No; vice had triumphed over virtue, and we deem it a kindness to your sensitive nature to draw a veil over the scene of her discomfiture.

CHAPTER XV.

Introduces a Stranger, describes a Picnic, and reveals some
Secrets of Mining.

Somewhere in the vicinity of that magnificent piece of coast scenery in West Cornwall, known by the name of Gurnard's Head, there sauntered, one fine afternoon, a gentleman of tall, commanding aspect. All the parts of this gentleman were, if we may so speak, *prononcé*. Everything about him savoured of the superlative degree. His head and face were handsome and large, but their size was not apparent because of the capacity of his broad shoulders and wide chest. His waist was slender, hair curly and very black, only to be excelled by the intense blackness of his eyes. His nose was prominent; mouth large and well shaped; forehead high and broad; whiskers enormous; and nostrils so large as to appear dilated. He was a bony man, a powerful man — also tall and straight, and a little beyond forty. He was to all appearance a hero of romance, and his mind seemed to be filled with romantic thoughts, for he smiled frequently as he gazed around him from the top of the cliffs on the beautiful landscape which lay spread out at his feet.

Above him there were wild undulating slopes covered with rich green gorse; below were the cliffs of Gurnard's Cove, with rocky projections that resemble the castellated work of man's hand, and intermingled therewith much of the *matériel* connected with the pilchard fishery, with masses of masonry so heavy and picturesque as to resemble Nature's handiwork. Beyond lay the blue waters of the Atlantic, which at that time were calm almost as a mill-pond, studded with a hundred sails, and glittering in sunshine.

The spot appeared a beautiful solitude, for no living thing was visible save the romantic gentleman and a few seagulls and sheep. The pilchard fishery had not yet commenced, and the three or four fishermen who pitched and repaired their boats on the one little spot of sand that could be seen far below on that rugged coast appeared like mice, and were too far distant to break the feeling of solitude — a feeling which was not a little enhanced by the appearance, on a spot not far distant, of the ruined engine-house of a deserted mine.

It was indeed a lovely afternoon, and a beautiful scene — a very misanthrope would have gazed on it with an approach at least to benignity. No wonder that George Augustus Clearemout smiled on it so joyously, and whisked his walking-cane vigorously in the exuberance of his delight.

But, strange to say, his smile was always brightest, and the cane flourished most energetically, when he turned his eyes on the ruined mine! He even laughed once or twice, and muttered to himself as he looked at the picturesque object; yet there seemed nothing in its appearance calculated to produce laughter. On the contrary, there were those alive whom the sight of it might have reduced to tears, for, in its brief existence, it had raised uncommonly little tin or copper, although it had succeeded in sinking an immense amount of gold! Nevertheless Mr. Clearemout chuckled every time he looked at the ruin, and appeared very much tickled with the thoughts to which it gave rise.

"Yes! the very thing! capital!" he muttered to himself, turning again and again to the object of his admiration, "couldn't be better – ha! ha! most suitable; yes, it will do for 'em, probably it will *do* 'em - do 'em," (he repeated the phrase two or three times with a greater display of white teeth at each utterance of it), "a most superb name – Wheal Do-em – ha! ha! Spell it with two o's to make it look more natural, and ensure correct pronunciation – Wheal Dooem – nothing could be finer, quite candid and above-board – no one can call it a swindle."

This last idea caused Mr. Clearemout to break into the loudest laugh in which he had hitherto indulged, and he was about to repeat it, when the appearance of a phaeton at a turn of the carriage road reduced him to gravity.

The vehicle contained a party of ladies and gentlemen from St. Just, among whom were Rose Ellis, Mrs. Donnithorne and her husband, Oliver Trembath, and Mr. William Grenfell, a gentleman of property in the neighbourhood.

As it approached the spot where Mr. Clearemout stood, the horse swerved at a sheep which started out from behind a furze bush, and then backed so rapidly that the hind-wheels were on the point of passing over the edge of the road, when the tall stranger sprang to its head, and led it gently forward.

The danger was not great, for the road at the place was elevated little above the sward, but it was sufficiently so to warrant a profusion of thanks from the occupants of the vehicle, and a pressing invitation to Mr. Clearemout to join the picnic party then and there assembling.

"You see, we're not all here," said Mr. Donnithorne, bustling about energetically, as he pulled baskets and bottles from the body of the vehicle, while Oliver assisted the ladies to alight; "there's another machineful coming, but we have lots of grub for all, and will only be too glad of your company, Mr. – Mr. – what did you say?"

"Clearemout," interposed that gentleman, with a bow and a bland smile that quite took Mr. Donnithorne by storm.

"Ah, yes, glad to have you, Mr. Clearemout; why, our necks might all have been broken but for you. Rose, my dear, do look after this basket. There – thanks – how hot it is, to be sure! Mr. Clearemout – Mr. Grenfell; no introduction – only to let you know his name – my wife – niece, Rose – Oliver Trembath, and all the rest; there, dispense with ceremony on a picnic always. That's the chief fun of it."

While the lively old gentleman ran on thus, and collected the baskets together, Mr. Grenfell, who was a tall, gentlemanly man of about sixty, with a grave, aristocratic countenance and polite manner, assured Mr. Clearemout that he was happy to make the acquaintance of a man who had rendered them such opportune service, whereupon Mr. Clearemout declared himself to be fortunate in being present at such a juncture, and protested that his service was a trifle in itself, although it had led to an introduction which was most gratifying. Then, turning with much urbanity of manner to the ladies, he entered into conversation with them.

"Here they come!" shouted old Mr. Donnithorne, as another carriage drove up.

"The rest of our party," said Mr. Grenfell, turning to Mr. Clearemout; "friends from St. Just."

The carriage stopped as he spoke, and a number of ladies and gentlemen descended therefrom, and mingled their congratulations at the narrow escape which had just been made, with thanks to the dark stranger, and with orders, questions, counter-orders, and explanations innumerable, about baskets to be carried and places to be selected.

The picnic, we need scarcely say, very much resembled picnics in general. All were in good spirits — elated with the splendour of the day, the beauty of the views, and the freshness of the sea-breeze that sprang up soon after their arrival. The only one whose feelings were not absolutely unruffled was Oliver Trembath. That youth was afflicted with an unaccountable dislike to the dark stranger which rendered him somewhat uncomfortable. As for the stranger, he made himself extremely agreeable — told anecdotes, sang songs, and became an immaculate waiter on the whole company, handing about plates, glasses, knives, etc., etc., as deftly as if he were dealing a pack of cards. Above all, he was a good listener, and not only heard other people's stories out to the end, but commented on them as one who had been interested. With all this, he was particularly attentive to Rose Ellis, but so guarded was he that no one noticed the attentions as being peculiar except Rose herself, and Oliver Trembath, who, for the first time in his life, to his great surprise and displeasure, felt the demon of jealousy tormenting his breast.

But in the midst of all this, Mr. George Augustus Clearemout displayed an insatiable curiosity in regard to mines and miners. Whatever might be the subject of conversation for the time, he invariably took the first opportunity of returning to his favourite theme with one or another of the party, as occasion served.

Ashamed of the feelings which troubled him, Oliver Trembath resolved to take the bold and manly step of stifling them, by making himself agreeable to the object of his dislike. Accordingly, he availed himself of an opportunity when the party broke up into groups to saunter about the cliffs, and entered into converse with the stranger on the subject of mines.

"You appear to take much interest in mining, I think," said he, as they walked out on the promontory together.

"I do indeed," replied Clearemout; "the mines of Cornwall have ever been a subject of deep interest to me, and the miners I regard as a race of men singularly endowed with courage and perseverance."

"Your opinion of them is correct," said Oliver. "Have you ever seen them at work?"

"No, I have only just arrived in the county, but I hope to visit the mines ere long."

"When you do," said Oliver with enthusiasm, "your opinion of them will be strengthened, for their endurance underground, and their perseverance in a species of labour which taxes their muscular power as well as their patience to the uttermost, surpasses anything I have either seen or heard of. England does not fully appreciate, because she is not minutely acquainted with, the endurance and courage of her Cornish miners. The rocks through which they have to cut are so hard and unyielding that men who had not been trained from childhood to subdue them would lose heart altogether at the weight of toil and the small return for it. Sometimes, indeed, miners are fortunate, and here, as elsewhere, lucky hits are made, but for the most part their gains are barely sufficient for their wants; and whether they are lucky or unlucky in that respect, the toil is always hard — so hard that few of them retain health or strength sufficient to go underground beyond the age of forty-five, while hundreds of them find an early grave, owing to disease resulting from their peculiar work, or to accidents. These last are usually occasioned by the bursting out of collections of water which flood the mines, or the fall of masses of timber, or the premature explosion of blast-holes. At other times the men lose hold of the ladders — 'fall away' from them, as they express it — or stumble into a winze, which is a small shaft connecting level with level, in which latter case death is almost certain to ensue, many of the winzes being sixty feet deep. In St. Just you will see many poor fellows who have been blinded or maimed in the mines. Nevertheless Cornish miners are a contented, uncomplaining race of men, and Cornwall is justly proud of them."

"I am much interested in what you tell me," said Clearemout; "in fact I have come here for the purpose of making inquiry into mines and mining concerns."

"Then you will find this to be the very place for you," said Oliver. "My uncle, Mr. Donnithorne, and Mr. Grenfell, and Mr. Cornish are intimately acquainted with mining in all its phases, and will, I am certain, be happy to give you all the information in their power. As to the people of St. Just and its neighbourhood, you will find them most agreeable and hospitable. I can speak from personal experience, although I have only been a short time among them."

"I doubt it not," replied Mr. Clearemout with a bland smile; "my own limited experience goes far to corroborate what you say, and I hope to have the pleasure of still further testing the truth of your observations."

And Mr. George Augustus Clearemout did test their truth for several weeks after the picnic. He was received with kindness and hospitality everywhere; he was taken down into the mines by obliging agents, and was invited to several of the periodical business dinners, called "account-dinners," at which he met shareholders in the mines, and had an opportunity of conversing with men of note and wealth from various parts of the county. He dwelt, during his stay, with old Mr. Donnithorne, and, much to the surprise if not pleasure of Rose, proved himself to be a proficient on the guitar and a good musician.

At length the dark gentleman took his departure for London, whither we shall follow him, and watch his proceedings for a very short time, before returning to the principal scene of our tale.

Almost immediately on his arrival in the great city, he betook himself to the West End, and there, in a fashionable square, solicited an interview with an old lady, whose principal noteworthy points were that she had much gold and not much brains. She was a confiding old lady, and had, on a previous occasion, been quite won by the insinuating address of the "charming Mr. Clearemout," who had been introduced to her by a noble lord.

To this confiding old lady George Augustus painted Cornish mines and mining in the most glowing colours, and recommended her to invest in a mine a portion of her surplus funds. The confiding old lady had no taste for speculation, and was rather partial to the three per cent. consols, but George Augustus was so charmingly persuasive that she could not help giving in — so George proposed little plans, and opened up little prospects, and the confiding old lady agreed to all the little plans without paying much regard to the little prospects.

After this Mr. Clearemout paid another visit in another West End square — this time to a gentleman. The gentleman was young and noble, for Clearemout styled him "My lord." Strange to say he also was of a confiding nature — very much so indeed — and appeared to be even more completely under the influence of George Augustus than the confiding old lady herself.

For the benefit of this young gentleman Mr. Clearemout painted the same picture in the same glowing colours, which colours seemed to grow warmer as the sun of success rose upon it. He added something about the value of a name, and referred to money as being a matter of small consequence in comparison. The young lord, like the old lady, agreed to everything that was proposed to him, except the proposal to advance money. On that point he was resolute, but Clearemout did not care much about obtaining money from the confiding young gentleman. His name was as good as gold, and would enable him to screw money out of others.

After this the dark man paid a visit to several other friends at the West End, all of whom were more or less confiding — some with selfish, others with unselfish, dispositions — but all, without exception, a little weak intellectually. These had the same glowing pictures of a Cornish mine laid before them, and most of them swallowed the bait whole, only one or two being content to nibble.

When afternoon began to merge into evening Mr. Clearemout paid a last visit for the day — but not in the West End, rather nearer to the City — to a gentleman somewhat like himself, though less prepossessing, for whose benefit he painted no glowing picture of a mine, but to whom he said, "Come, Jack, I've made a pretty good job of it; let's go and have a chop. If your luck has equalled mine the thing is done, and Wheal Dooem, as I have named the sweet little thing, will be going full swing in a couple of weeks — costing, perhaps, a few hundreds to put it in working order, with a trifle thereafter in the shape of wages to a man and a boy to coal the fire, and keep the thing moving with as much noise as possible to make a show, and leaving a pretty little balance of some twenty or thirty thousand at the credit of the Company, for you and me to enjoy in the meantime — *minus* a small sum for rent of office, clerk's salary, gas and coal, etc., as long as the bubble lasts."

Thus did this polite scoundrel go about from house to house getting up a

Cornish Mining Company on false pretences (as other polite scoundrels have done before, and doubtless as others will do again), bringing into unmerited disrepute those genuine and grand old mines of Cornwall which have yielded stores of tin and copper, to the enriching of the English nation, ever since those old-world days when the Phoenicians sailed their adventurous barks to the "Cassiterides" in quest of tin.

While these things were being done in London, a terrible catastrophe happened in Botallack mine, which threw a dark cloud for some time over more than one lowly cottage in St. Just.

CHAPTER XVI.

Describes "Holing to a House of Water" and its Terrible Consequences.

One morning, about seven o'clock, George and James, the two fair-haired sons of poor John Batten of Botallack, started for their work as usual. They were in high spirits, having obtained a good "pitch" on last setting-day, and things were looking well.

They put on their underground clothing at the changing-house, and with several spare candles attached to buttons on the breasts of their coats, and their tools slung over their shoulders, walked towards the head of the ladder-shaft. At the mouth of the shaft they paused for a moment and glanced round. The sky was bright, the landscape green, and the sun lit up many a distant sail on the Atlantic.

"I do wish," said the younger with a slight sigh, "that our work was more in the sunshine?"

"You'll never be a true miner, Jimmy, if 'ee go hankerin' after the sun like that," said his brother with a laugh, as he stepped on the ladder and began to descend.

Jimmy took a last look at the rising sun, and followed him close without replying. The lads were soon beyond the reach of daylight.

This was the last they ever saw of earthly sunshine. In a few minutes there came a low soft sound up the shaft; it was the lads singing one of Wesley's beautiful hymns. They had been taught to sing these by their mother from their infancy, and usually beguiled the tedium of the long descent of the ladders by singing one or two of them.

Arrived at their place of work the brothers threw down their tools, fixed their candles against the walls of the level, and began the labour of the day.

Other men were in that part of the mine at the time, and the brothers found that a message had been sent to one of the captains requesting him to come and examine the place, as the men were becoming uneasy at the increasing flow of water from the walls. One miner, named John Nicols, was "driving an end," that is, extending the level lengthwise, and two others were "stopeing," or cutting up into the roof in pursuit of a promising little lode. They were using hammer and pick in soft ground when the water trickled through to them.

It was well known that they were approaching an old part of the mine which had not been worked for thirty years. The drainage of the ground was not, however, accurately known, therefore questions had been put to experienced miners as to the probable condition of this "untapped land." The answer was that, as far as was known, the old mine was full of "deads," that is, of rubbish, and that there was therefore, in all probability, no gathering of water in it.

Just at that moment one of the captains entered the level, accompanied by Oliver Trembath. The latter had been called to see a patient near the mine, and chanced to be with the captain when he was summoned. Being anxious to see the place, and the nature of the danger that threatened, he had descended along with him.

Before the captain had time to put a question, and while the men were still picking cautiously at the soft ground, the flow of water suddenly increased. Recognising probable danger, a lad named Oats called to his father, who was at the "end" of the level with Nicols. At the same moment the water forced a gap in the wall three feet long by about half a foot wide, and burst in upon them with terrific violence. All turned and fled. Oats and his son, with the captain and Nicols, made for the nearest shaft – which was about eighty yards distant – and escaped, but the brothers Batten and Oliver were thrown down and swept away. One desperate effort was made by Oliver to outstrip the rushing stream; but the candles had been blown out, and, not stooping sufficiently low, he dashed his head against an overhanging rock, and fell. He retained sufficient consciousness, however, to be aware that a desperate struggle for life must be made, and, without knowing what he did, or at what he aimed, he fought with the strength of a giant in thick darkness against the chaotic flood; but his strength soon gave way, and in a few seconds he became insensible.

That a terrible catastrophe had occurred was at once known to all the men in the mine by the roar of the rushing water. In order that the reader may clearly understand the situation, it is necessary to explain that the accident occurred in one of the *upper* levels, at or near its extremity. At the same depth there were many of these underground passages, running in various directions, and several miles in extent, some of them being worked, but most of them old and used up – all the ore having been extracted from them. At various depths below this level other levels had been cut – also running in various directions, and of several miles' extent. These successive levels were not only connected and communicated with by the main shafts of the mine, but by "winzes" or smaller shafts which connected level with level in many places. Some of these were used as ladder-ways, but others had been cut merely for the purpose of securing ventilation. In many parts of these lower levels miners were at work – some, in following the course of promising lodes, "stopeing," or cutting overhead, some cutting downwards, some "driving ends" or extending the levels, and others sinking winzes to keep up the ventilation as they pushed further and further from the shafts or throats, down which flowed the life-giving air.

By all of these men the dreaded sounds above – which reached the profounder depths with the muffled but deep-toned roar of a distant storm – were well understood and well heard, for the pent-up waters, in their irresistible fury, carried before them the pent-up atmosphere, and sent it through the low and narrow levels as if through the circling tubes of a monster trumpet, which, mingled with the crash of hurling timbers, rocks, and débris, created a mighty roar that excelled in hideous grandeur the prolonged peals of loud thunder.

Every man dropped his tools, and ran to the nearest shaft for his life. It was not, indeed, probable that the flood would fill all the wide-extended ramifications of the vast mine, but no one knew for certain where the catastrophe had occurred, or how near the danger might be to the spot where he laboured. Enough for each that death was dealing terrible destruction somewhere *overhead*, and that, unless every muscle were strained to the uttermost, the pathway might be filled up, and his retreat cut off. The rush was swiftly but not easily made. Those who have never traversed the levels of a Cornish mine may perhaps fancy, on hearing of levels six feet high, and about two and a half feet broad, on the average, that the flight might resemble the rush of men through the windings and turnings of the intricate passages in a stupendous old castle. But it was far otherwise. The roofs, walls, and floors of these levels were irregular, not only in direction, but in height and form. There was no levelling or polishing-off anywhere. It was tunnelling of the roughest kind. Angles and projections remained as the chisel, the pick, and the blasting-powder had left them. Here, the foot tripped over a lump, or plunged into a hollow; there, the head narrowly missed a depending mass of rock, or the shoulder grazed a projecting one. Elsewhere, pools of water lay in the path, and at intervals the yawning chasm of a winze appeared, with one or two broken planks to bridge the gulf, of twenty, forty, or sixty feet, that descended to the levels below. Sometimes it was possible to run with the head stooped a little; generally the back had to be bent low – often double; and occasionally progress could only be made on hands and knees – this, too, with a candle to be guarded from blasts of air or dripping water, and trimmed, lest it should go out and leave the place in total darkness.

But long-continued habit and practice had made the men so familiar with the place, and so nimble in their movements, that they traversed the levels with wonderful rapidity, and most of them ascended the shaft of the mine in safety.

Some, however, escaped with the utmost difficulty, and a few there were – chiefly among those who had been near to or immediately below the scene of the outbreak – who perished miserably.

At the first rush the water had almost filled the level where it occurred, and, sweeping onward about eight fathoms to a winze, plunged down and partly over it. The greater part, however, went down to the eighty-five fathom level. East of this a man named Anguin, with his two sons, William and James – youths of about twenty years of age – were at work. They heard the roar of the approaching torrent, and the father and younger son James rushed towards the winze, intending to ascend the ladder. Before they reached it the flood was pouring down with deafening noise. The least harmful part of the cataract was the water, for the current now carried along with it stones, pieces of timber, and rubbish. To encounter all this might have caused the stoutest hearts to quail, but miners can never calculate the probable extent of an inundation. They might, indeed, by remaining in the roof of the level, escape; but, on the other hand, if the flood should be great enough to fill the place, they would certainly be drowned. Father and son, therefore, preferred to make a desperate effort to save their lives. They dashed into the flood and made a grasp at the ladder, but before their hands touched the first round they were beaten down and swept away dead corpses. William, on the other hand, climbed to a cross-piece of timber, where he remained until the water abated, which it did in a very short time, for events of this kind are for the most part awfully sudden and brief as well as fatal. Then, descending, he groped his way in the dark over the very spot where his father and brother lay dead — fearfully mutilated and covered with rubbish — and escaped up the shaft.

In a still lower level two brothers were at work. Miners usually work in couples — sometimes in larger numbers — and brothers frequently go together. They were in a winze about thirty fathoms from the engine-shaft. Being overtaken by the flood they were washed *down*, to the next level, and along it nearly to the shaft. As the torrent tore past this place, bearing splintered timber, stones, and rubbish along with it, an iron wagon was caught up and flung across the level. This formed a barricade, against which the brothers were dashed. The elder of these brothers was afterwards found alive here, and carried to the surface; but he was speechless, and died twenty minutes after being brought up. When the dead body of the younger and weaker brother was recovered, it was found to be dreadfully shattered, nearly every bone being crushed.

In the same level, two men — John Paul and Andrew Teague — hearing the rush of the advancing torrent above their head, made for a shaft, went up it against a heavy fall of water, and escaped.

A man named Richard — a powerful man and a cool experienced miner, who had faced death in almost every form — was at work in one of the lowest levels with his son William, a youth of twenty-one, and his nephew, a lad of seventeen, who was the sole support of a widowed mother with six children. They were thirty fathoms from one of the winzes down which the water streamed. On hearing the roar Richard cautioned the younger men to be prompt, but collected. No time was to be lost, but rash haste might prove as fatal as delay. He sent them on in front of him, and they rushed under and past the winze, where they were nearly crushed by the falling water, and where, of course, their candles were extinguished, leaving them in midnight darkness. This last was not so serious a matter to the elder Richard as, at first sight, it might appear. He knew every foot of the ground they had to traverse, with all its turnings, yawning chasms, and plank bridges, and could have led the way blindfold almost as easily as with a light. As they neared the shaft he passed the younger men, and led the way to prevent them falling into it. At this time the water raged round them as high as their waists. The nephew, who was weak, in consequence of a fever from which he had not quite recovered, fell, and, passing the others unobserved, went down the shaft and was lost. The escape of Richard and his son was most wonderful. William was a stout fellow, but the father much more so. They were driven at first into the shaft, but there the fall of water was so great that they could do nothing more than cling to the ladder. By this cataract they were beaten back into the level, but here the water rose around them so quickly and with such force as to oblige them to make another effort to ascend.

There was a crevice in the roof of the level here, in which the father had left part of his supply of candles and a tinder-box. He succeeded in reaching these, and in striking a light, which revealed to them the full horrors of their situation. It was with difficulty that the candle could be kept burning by holding it close to the roof under a projecting piece of rock which sheltered it partially from the dashing spray.

"Let us try again!" shouted the father.

The noise was so great that it was with difficulty they could make each other hear.

"It's all over with we," cried the son; "let us pray, faither."

The father urged his son, however, to make another effort, as the water had risen nearly to their waists, and prevailed on him to do so, getting on the ladder himself first, in order to bear the brunt of the falling water and thus break its force to his son. As the water below was now rising swiftly William only held the light long enough to enable his father to obtain a secure footing on the ladder, when he dropped it and followed him. So anxious was the youth to escape from the danger that menaced him from below, that he pressed eagerly up against his father. In doing so, he over-reached the rounds of the ladder on which his father trod, and, almost at every step, the latter unwittingly planted his heavy-nailed boots on the son's hands, lacerating them terribly. To avoid this was impossible. So heavy was the descending flood, that it was only his unusually great strength which enabled the father to advance slowly up against it. The son, being partially sheltered by his father's body, knew not the power against which he had to contend, and, being anxious to go up faster, pressed too closely on him, regardless, in his alarm, of the painful consequences. Masses of stone, wood, and rubbish, dashed down the shaft and grazed their shoulders, but providentially none struck them severely. Thus, slowly and painfully, did they ascend to a height of eighty-four feet, and were saved.

In another part of the mine, below the level where the accident occurred, James Penrose, whom we have already introduced to the reader, was at work with John Cock. The latter having taken a fancy to try mining for a time instead of smuggling — just by way of a change — had joined the former in working a "pitch" in Botallack mine. These men were peculiarly situated. They were in a level which the water entered, not by flowing along or descending, but, by rising up through a winze. On hearing the noise they ran to this winze, and, looking down, saw the water boiling and roaring far below. They were about to pass on to the shaft when Penrose observed a dark object moving on the ladder. It came slowly up.

"Hallo! John," cried Penrose, "stay a bit; here's some one on the ladder."

John Cock returned, and they both stooped to afford help. In another moment Oliver Trembath, drenched and bleeding, and covered with mud, stood, or rather reeled, before them. It was evident that he was only half conscious, and scarcely able to stand. But they had no time to speak — scarcely to think — for the water was already boiling up through the winze like a huge fountain, and filling the level. They seized Oliver by the arms and dragged him hastily towards the nearest winze that led upward. Here they found water pouring down like rain, and heard its thunders above them, but the stream was not sufficient to retard their progress up the winze, which they ascended with comparative ease. Penrose and Cock were surprised at this, but the small quantity of water was soon accounted for by the fact that the hatch or trap-door of the winze had been closed; and thus, while it prevented the great body of water above from descending, also effectually shut off the only way of escape. They were therefore compelled to descend again to the level, in which the water was now rising rapidly.

Oliver leaned against the rock, and stood in apathetic silence. Penrose tried to rouse him, but failed. His injuries had rendered him almost in capable of coherent speech, and his replies showed that his mind was rambling on the necessity of making haste and struggling hard.

James Penrose, who was a "class-leader" and a local preacher among the Wesleyans, and mentally much superior to his comrades, now proved beyond a doubt that his God was to him "a very present help in trouble." Both he and Cock knew, or at least believed, that death was certain to overtake them in a few minutes, for both before and behind retreat was cut off, and the water was increasing with frightful rapidity. Observing that Cock looked anxious, Penrose turned and said earnestly — "John, you and I shall be dead in a few minutes.

"For myself I have no fear, for my peace is already made with God, through Jesus Christ — blessed be His name — but, oh! John, you do know that it is not so with you. Turn, John, turn, even now, to the Lord, who tells you that 'though thy sins be as scarlet they shall be as white as snow,' and that '*now* is the day of salvation,' if you will only repent, and believe on Him!"

"Pray for un, James," said Cock, whose face betrayed his fears.

Penrose at once clasped his hands, and, closing his eyes, prayed for his comrade with such fervour that his voice rose loud and strong above the turmoil of the flood. He was still engaged in prayer when the water drove them from the level, and compelled them to re-ascend the winze. Here John Cock began to pray for himself in agonising tones. By this time Oliver had partially recovered, and suggested that they should ascend the winze to the top. Penrose assured him that it was useless to do so; but, while he was still speaking, he observed that the water ceased to rise, and began quickly to abate. In fact, all that we have taken so long to describe — from the outburst to the termination of the great rush — took place within half an hour.

The noise overhead now grew less and less, until it almost ceased. They then ascended to the trap-door and tried to force it open, but failed. They shouted, however, and were heard, ere long, by those who had escaped and had returned to the mine to search for their less fortunate companions. The trap-door was opened, strong and willing hands were thrust down the dark winze to the rescue, and in a few seconds the three men were saved.

The danger was past — but several lives had been lost in the terrible catastrophe.

CHAPTER XVII.

Touches on the Causes of Accidents: Oliver in a New Light and his Uncle in a sad one.

That was a sad day in St. Just which followed the event related in the last chapter. Many a heart-broken wail was heard round the mouths of the shafts, as the remains of those who perished were brought to the surface, and conveyed to their former homes.

Saddest of all perhaps was the procession that marched slowly to the cottage of blind John Batten, and laid the two fair-haired lads before their stricken parents. Tears were wrung from the strongest men there when they beheld the agonised but tearless mother guide her husband's hand to their faces that he might for the last time feel the loved ones whom, she said in the bitterness of her grief, "he should never see more."

"Never see more, dear lass!" he replied with a sad smile, "how can thee say so? Shall we not behold their dear faces again when we see our blessed Lord face to face?"

Thus the Christian miner comforted himself and his sorrowing family.

It is right to add that such catastrophes are not of frequent occurrence in the mines. The danger of "holing to a house of water," is so great and so well known that the operation is usually conducted with great care, and accident is well guarded against.

Nevertheless, an occasional act of carelessness will now and then result in a terrible disaster. A catastrophe, similar in all its chief features to that which has been related in the last chapter, happened in North Levant mine many years ago, and in the burying-ground of the Wesleyan Chapel of St. Just may be seen a tombstone, which bears record of the sad event as follows:

Sacred to the memory of **James**, *aged* 20, *and* **John**, *aged* 15 *years, sons of James and Nanny Thomas of Bollowall, in this Parish, who were drowned (with three others) by the holing to a house of water in North Levant Mine on the* 1st *of April* 1867.

A "house" of much larger dimensions, and containing a much greater body of water than that which caused the latest destruction of life in North Levant mine, was cleared of water not long ago in Botallack. The agents knew of its existence, for, the whole region both above and below ground being measured off and planned, they could lay their finger on the exact spot where they knew that an old mine existed. They kept a large borer, six feet long, going constantly before them as they cut their way towards the point of danger. The result was that when the borer at last pierced through to the old mine, there were six feet of solid rock between them and the water. Through the small hole the water flowed, and thus the mine was slowly but safely drained. In the other case, the ground happened to be soft, and had been somewhat recklessly cut away.

Of course, there are occasions – proving the truth of the proverb that "accidents will happen in the best regulated families" – in which neither foresight nor precaution can prevent evil; but these are comparatively few. Sometimes the cupidity of a miner will lead him, for the sake of following a rich lode, to approach too near and too recklessly to danger, despite the vigilance of captains, and cause considerable risk to the mine as well as to themselves. Such was the case once long ago at Botallack, when the miners below the sea cut away the rock to within three or four feet of the water, and actually made a small hole through so that they had to plug it up with a piece of wood.

This is a fact which we can vouch for, having seen the plug, and heard the boulders rattling loudly over our head with each successive wave; but there is no danger here, because the cutting under the sea is narrow, and the rock solid and intensely hard.

Such also was the case, not many years since, at Levant mine, where the men working in the levels under the sea drove upwards until the salt water began to trickle through to them in alarming quantities – insomuch that the other miners struck work, and refused to go again into the mine, unless the workings in that part were stopped, and the place made secure. This was accordingly done, and the men returned to the mine. The danger here was really great, because the cutting that had been made was wide, and the ground overhead comparatively soft.

But, to return to our tale.

For many days after the catastrophe Oliver Trembath lay in his bed suffering from severe cuts and bruises, as well as from what must have been, as nearly as possible, concussion of the brain, for he had certainly been washed down one of the winzes, although he himself retained only a confused recollection of the events of that terrible day, and could not tell what had befallen him. At length, however, he became convalescent, and a good deal of his old vigour returned.

During this period of illness and convalescence Oliver had been constrained by old Mr. Donnithorne to take up his abode in his house, and the young doctor could not have experienced more attention and kindness from the old couple if he had been their son. Rose Ellis, too, did her best to cheer him, and, as we need scarcely add, was wonderfully successful in her efforts!

It was during this period that Oliver made the acquaintance of a young man of St. Just, named Charles Tregarthen – a congenial spirit – and one who was, besides, a thorough gentleman and an earnest Christian. With this youth he formed a sincere friendship, and although the subject of religion was never obtrusively thrust upon him by young Tregarthen, it entered so obviously into all his thoughts, and shone so clearly in his words and conduct, that Oliver's heart was touched, and he received impressions at that time which never left him.

Oliver and his friend were sitting one forenoon in Mr. Donnithorne's dining-room, which commanded an extensive view of green fields and grass-covered stone walls, with the beams and machinery of mines on the horizon, and the blue sea beyond. They were planning a short walking tour, which it was thought would be of great benefit to Oliver in that stage of his recovery, when old Mr. Donnithorne entered the room with a somewhat perturbed expression of countenance.

"How are you, Charlie my boy?" he said. "Oliver, I want to have a few minutes' talk with you in my room on business; I know Charlie will excuse you."

"I was on the point of taking leave at any rate," said Tregarthen with a smile, as he grasped Oliver's hand; "think over our plan, like a good fellow; I am sure Mr. Donnithorne will approve of it, and I'll look in tomorrow forenoon to hear what decision you come to."

"Oliver," said Mr. Donnithorne, sitting down opposite the invalid when his friend had left, and frowning portentously, "d'you know I'm a ruined man?"

"I trust not, uncle," replied Oliver with an incredulous smile, supposing that the old gentleman was jesting.

"Yes, but I am," he repeated with tremendous gravity. "At all events, I shall be ere long. These – these – vile jewels will be the death of me."

Having thus broken the ice Mr. Donnithorne went on with much volubility of utterance and exasperation of tone to explain that legal proceedings had been instituted for the recovery of the jewels which he had purchased from the fishermen; that things seemed almost certain to go against him; and that in all probability he should be compelled to sell his estate in order to refund the money.

"But can you not sell your shares in Botallack and refund with the proceeds?" said Oliver.

"No, I cannot," replied the old gentleman. "You know that at present these shares are scarcely saleable except at a ruinous discount, and it would be a pity to part with them just now, seeing that there is some hope of improvement at this time. There is nothing for it but to sell my estate, and I don't think there will be enough left to buy butter to my bread after this unhappy affair is settled, for it amounts to some thousands of pounds."

"Indeed, uncle! how comes it that they found out the value of them?"

"Oh, simply enough, Oliver, but strangely too. You must know that Maggot, the scoundrel (and yet not such a scoundrel either, for the fellow informed on me in a passion, without having any idea of the severity of the consequences that would follow) – Maggot, it seems, kept the cloth belt in which the jewels were found tied round the owner's waist, and there happened to be a piece of parchment sewed up in the folds of it, in which the number and value of the jewels were enumerated. This belt was ferreted out by the lawyers, and the result is that, as I said before, I shall be a ruined man. Verily," added Mr. Donnithorne, with a look of vexation, as he stumped up and down the room with his hands thrust deep into his breeches pockets, "verily, my wife was a true prophetess when she told me that my sin would be sure to find me out, and that honesty was the best policy. 'Pon my conscience, I'm half inclined to haul down my colours and let her manage me after all!"

"I am much concerned at what you tell me," said Oliver, "and I regret now very deeply that the few hundreds which I possessed when I came here — and which you know are all my fortune — have also been invested in Botallack shares, for they should have been heartily at your service, uncle."

"Don't trouble yourself about your hundreds, lad," said the old gentleman testily; "I didn't come here to ask assistance from you in that way, but to tell you the facts of the case, and ask you to do me the favour to carry a letter to my lawyer in Penzance, and inquire into the condition of a mine I have something to do with there — a somewhat singular mine, which I think will surprise as well as interest you; will you do this, for me, lad?"

"Most willingly," replied Oliver. "You heard my friend Charlie Tregarthen speak of our intention to go on a walking tour for a couple of days; now, if you have no objection, he and I will set off together without delay, and make Penzance our goal, going round by the Land's End and the coast."

"So be it, Oliver, and don't hurry yourselves, for the business will wait well enough for a day or two. But take care of yourself, lad; don't go swimming off the Land's End again, and above all things avoid smugglers. The scoundrels! they have been the ruin of me, Oliver. Not bad fellows in their way either, but unprincipled characters — desperately regardless of the national laws; and — and — keep clear of 'em, I advise you strongly — have nothing to do with 'em, Oliver, my son."

So saying the old gentleman left the room, shaking his head with profound gravity.

CHAPTER XVIII.

Tells of King Arthur and other more or less Fabulous Matters.

Next day Oliver Trembath and his friend Charles Tregarthen, before the sun had mounted his own height above the horizon, were on their way to the Land's End.

The young men were admirably suited to each other. Both were well educated, and possessed similar tastes, though their temperaments were dissimilar, and both were strong athletic youths — Oliver's superiority in this latter respect being at that time counterbalanced by his recent illness, which reduced him nearly to a level with his less robust companion.

Their converse was general and desultory until they reached the Land's End, on the point of which they had resolved to breakfast.

"Now, Oliver, we have purchased an appetite," said Tregarthen, throwing down a wallet in which he carried some provisions; "let us to work."

"Stay, Charlie, not here," said Oliver; "let us get out on the point, where we shall have a better view of the cliffs on either side of the Land's End. I love a wide, unobstructed view."

"As you will, Oliver; I leave you to select our table, but I pray you to remember that however steady your head may have been in days of yore when you scaled the Scottish mountains, the rough reception it has met with in our Cornish mines has given it a shake that renders caution necessary."

"Pshaw! Charlie, don't talk to me of caution, as if I were a timid old woman."

"Nay, then, I talk of it because you are *not* a timid old woman, but a reckless young man who seems bent on committing suicide. Yonder is a grassy spot which I think will suit you well."

He pointed to a level patch of sward on the neck of land that connects the outlying and rugged promontory which forms the extreme Land's End with the cliffs of the mainland. Here they spread their meal, and from this point they could see the cliffs and bays of the iron-bound shore extending on the one hand towards Cape Cornwall, and on the other towards that most romantic part of the coast known by the somewhat curious name of Tolpedenpenwith, where rocks and caverns are found in such fantastic fashion that the spot has become justly celebrated for picturesque grandeur. At their feet, far below, the great waves (caused by the swell, for there was no wind) boomed in solemn majesty, encircling the cliffs with a lace-work of foam, while on the horizon the Scilly Islands could be seen shimmering faintly. A bright sun shone on the unruffled sea, and hundreds of ships and boats lay becalmed on its breast.

"'Tis a splendid scene!" said Oliver, sitting down beside his friend.

"It is indeed, and reminds me of the sea of glass before the great white throne that we read of in Revelation. It is difficult to imagine or to believe that the peaceful water before us, lying between this spot and the Scilly Islands yonder, was once a land full of verdure and life — yet such tradition tells us was the case."

"You mean, I suppose, the fabled land of Lionesse?" said Oliver.

"Yes; you have heard the story of its destruction, I suppose?"

"Not I," said Oliver, "so if you have a mind to tell it me while I satisfy the cravings of an unusually sharp appetite I'll consider you a most obliging fellow. Pass me the knuckle of ham — thanks — and the bread; now go ahead."

"'Tis a romantic story," said Tregarthen.

"All the better," replied Oliver.

"And terrible," added Tregarthen.

"It won't spoil my appetite," said his friend.

"Well, then, I'll tell it — to the best of my ability." The youth then began the following legend, pausing ever and anon during the narration to swallow a piece of bread or a mouthful of cold tea, which constituted the principal elements of their frugal meal.

"You must know that, once upon a time, long, long ago, in those ancient days before Norman or Dane had invaded this land, while Britain still belonged to the British, and King Arthur held his court in Tintagel's halls, there was a goodly land, named Lethowsow or the Lionesse, extending a distance of thirty miles between this cape and yonder shadowy islets which seem to float like cirrus clouds on the horizon. It is said that this land of Lionesse was rich and fertile, supporting many hundreds of families, with large flocks and herds. There were no fewer than forty churches upon it, from which it follows that there must have been a considerable population of well-doing people there.

"About the time of the events which I am going to narrate, King Arthur's reign was drawing to a close. Treason had thinned the ranks of the once united and famous knights of the Round Table. It is true that Sir Kaye, the seneschal, remained true, and Sir Ector de Mans, and Sir Caradoc, and Sir Tristram, and Sir Lancelot of the Lake, of whom it was said that 'he was the kindest man that ever struck with sword; and he was the goodliest person that ever rode among the throng of knights; and he was the meekest man, and the gentlest, that did ever eat in hall among ladies; and he was the sternest knight to his mortal foe that ever laid lance in rest.' But many seats at the Round Table that once were filled by brave warriors had become empty, and among these, that of Prince Mordred, who, it was rumoured, meant to declare open war against his royal cousin and benefactor.

"One night King Arthur sat at the Round Table in Tintagel Castle with his knights gathered round him, and Queen Guenever with her maidens by his side. At the beginning of the feast the king's brow was clouded, for, although there was no lack of merriment or song, there was a want of the free-hearted courtesy and confidence of former days. Still the semblance of unabated good-fellowship was kept up, and the evening passed in gaiety until its close, when the king rose to retire. Taking in his hand a golden cup to pledge his guests, he was about to drink, when a shudder passed through his frame, and he cast the goblet away, exclaiming, 'It is not wine, but blood! My father Merlin is among us, and there is evil in the coming days. Break we up our court, my peers! It is no time for feasting, but rather for fasting and for prayer.'

"The king glanced with a dark frown at the chair of his kinsman Mordred, but it was not empty! A strange, indistinct, shadowy form rested on it. It had no human shape, but a dreadful outline of something unearthly. Awe-struck and silent, the company at once broke up.

"On the following day, news of Mordred's revolt arrived at Tintagel Castle, and day after day fresh rumours reached it of foes flocking in numbers to the rebel standard. The army increased as it advanced, but, strange to say, King Arthur showed no disposition to sally forth and meet the traitor. It seemed as if his brave heart had quailed at last, and his good sword Excalibur had lost its magic virtue. Some thought that he doubted the fidelity of those who still remained around him. But, whatever the cause might have been, King Arthur made no preparation, and indicated no feeling or intention. He lay still in his castle until the rebels had approached to the very gates. There was something terrible in this mysterious silence of the king, which had a tendency to overawe the rebels as they drew near, and remembered that they were about to match themselves against warriors who had grown old in fellowship with victory.

"When the main body of the invaders appeared, the great bell of the fortress at last rang out a stirring peal, and before the barbican the trumpets sounded to horse. King Arthur then with his knights and men-at-arms, the best warriors of Britain, arose and sallied forth to fight in their last battle.

"Next evening a broken band of horsemen alone remained to tell of the death of their king and the destruction of all their hopes. They numbered several hundreds, but their hacked armour, jaded steeds, and gaping wounds told that they were unfit to offer battle to any foe. They were in full flight, bearing a torn banner, still wet with the blood of King Arthur; yet they fled unwillingly, as men who were unused to retreat, and scarce knew how to comport them in the novel circumstances. Their course was in the direction of the Lionesse, the tract of country called in the Cornish tongue Lethowsow. On they dashed, without uttering a word, over the bleak moors before them. Sometimes they halted to drink at a spring or tighten their girths, and occasionally a man fell behind from sheer exhaustion. At night they encamped, after a hard ride of thirty miles. Next morning the flight was resumed, but the vindictive Mordred still thundered on in pursuit. Ere long they heard a trumpet sounding in their rear, and King Arthur's men halted for a few minutes, with the half-formed design of facing the foe and selling their lives dearly. While they paused in gloomy irresolution, gazing sternly on the advancing host, whose arms flashed back the rays of the morning sun, a mist rose up between them and their foes. It was a strange shadowy mist, without distinct form, yet not without resemblance to something ghostly. The knights at once recognised it as the shade of Merlin, the Great Wizard! Slowly the cloud uprose between the pursuers and pursued, effectually protecting the latter; nevertheless, although baffled, the former did not give up the chase.

"At last Mordred reached a lofty slope, from the top of which he descried his enemies retreating across the land of Lionesse. Mad with rage, he descended to the plain, where soft sunlight shone through luxuriant glades and across the green pastures, gladdening the hearts of man and beast. Nature was all peaceful, and gloriously beautiful, but Mordred's eyes saw it not, his heart felt not the sweet influences. The bitterness induced by hatred and an evil conscience reigned within, as he urged his steed furiously onward.

"Suddenly a terrible change occurred in the atmosphere, which became oppressively sultry and horrible, while low muttering thunders were heard, and heavings of the earth felt. At the same time the cloud gradually condensed in front of Mordred, and, assuming a distinct form, stood before him in the person of Merlin the Wizard. For a few seconds they stood face to face, frowning on each other in awful silence. Then Merlin raised his arm, and immediately the thunders and confused mutterings increased, until the earth began to undulate and rend as if the foundations of the world were destroyed. Great fissures appeared, and the rocks welled up like the waves of the sea. With a cry of agony the pursuers turned to fly. But it was too late. Already the earth was rent into fragments; it upheaved convulsively for a few seconds; then sank beneath the level of the deep, and the ocean rushed wildly over the land, leaving nothing behind to mark the spot where land had been, save the peaked and barren rocks you see before you, with the surge beating continually around them."

"A most extraordinary tale, truly," said Oliver. "Do you believe it has any foundation?"

"I believe not the supernatural parts of it, of course," replied Tregarthen; "but there is *something* in the fact that the land of Cornwall has unquestionably given up part of its soil to the sea. You are aware, I suppose, that St. Michael's Mount, the most beautiful and prominent object in Mounts Bay, has been described as 'a hoare rock in a wood,' about six miles from the sea, although it now stands in the bay; and this idea of a sunken land is borne out by the unquestionable fact that if we dig down a few feet into the sand of the shore near Penzance, we shall come on a black vegetable mould, full of woodland *detritus*, such as branches, leaves of coppice wood, and nuts, together with carbonised roots and trunks of forest trees of larger growth; and these have been found as far out as the lowest tide would permit men to dig! In addition to this, portions of land have been overwhelmed by the sea near Penzance, in the memory of men now alive."

"Hum!" said Oliver, stretching out his huge limbs like a giant basking in the sunshine, "I dare say you are correct in your suppositions, but I do not profess to be an antiquary, so that I won't dispute the subject with you. At the same time, I may observe that it does seem to me as if there were a screw loose somewhere in the historical part of your narrative, for methinks I have read, heard, or dreamt, that King Arthur was Mordred's uncle, not his cousin, and that Mordred was slain, and that the king was the victor, at the fatal field of Camelford, although the victory was purchased dearly — Arthur having been mortally wounded and carried back to Tintagel to die there. But, of course, I won't pretend to doubt the truth of your narrative because of such trifling discrepancies. As to the encroachment of the sea on the Cornish coast, and the evidences thereof in Mounts Bay, I raise no objection thereto, but I cannot help thinking that we want stronger proof of the existence of the land of Lionesse."

"Why, Oliver," said Tregarthen, laughing, "you began by saying that you would not dispute the subject with me, and in two minutes you have said enough to have justified a regular attack on my part, had I been so disposed. However, we have a long road before us, so I must protest against a passage of arms just now."

Having finished breakfast, the two friends proceeded along the coast a few miles to Tolpedenpenwith. Here, in the midst of the finest scenery on the coast, they spent the greater part of the day, and then proceeded to Penberth Cove, intending to secure a lodging for the night, order supper, and, while that was in preparation, pay a visit to the famous Logan Rock.

Penberth Cove is one of the prettiest little vales in the west of Cornwall. It is enriched with groups of trees and picturesque cottages, and possesses a luxuriant growth of shrubs and underwood, that almost conceals from view the streamlet, which is the chief cause of its fertility.

There were also, at the time we write of, one or two houses which, although not public inns, were open for the entertainment of travellers in a semi-private fashion. Here, therefore, our excursionists determined to put up for the night, with the widow of a fisherman who had perished in a storm while engaged in the herring fishery off the Irish coast. This good woman's chief physical characteristic was rotundity, and her prominent mental attribute good-humour. She at once received the gentlemen hospitably, and promised to prepare supper for them while they went to visit the far-famed Logan or Logging Rock, which lay in the vicinity.

This rock is one of those freaks of nature which furnish food for antiquaries, points of interest to strangers, and occupation to guides. Every one who goes to the Land's End must needs visit the Logan Rock, if he would "do" the country properly; and if our book were a "Guide to Cornwall," we should feel bound to describe it with much particularity, referring to its size, form, weight, and rocking quality, besides enlarging on the memorable incident in its career, when a wild officer of the navy displaced it from its pivot by means of seamen and crowbars, and was thereafter ordered to replace it (a herculean task, which he accomplished at great cost) on pain of we know not what penalties. But, as we make no pretensions to the important office of a guide, we pass this lion by, with the remark that Oliver and his friend visited it and rocked it, and then went back to Penberth Cove to sup on pilchards, after which followed a chat, then bed, sound sleep, daybreak and breakfast, and, finally, the road to Penzance, with bright sunshine, light hearts, and the music of a hundred larks ringing in the sky.

CHAPTER XIX.

Small Talk and some Account of Cornish Fairies.

"What a splendid country for a painter of cliffs!" observed Oliver, as the friends walked briskly along; "I wonder much that our artists do not visit it more frequently."

"Perhaps they find metal more attractive nearer home," replied Tregarthen; "all the world has not fallen so violently in love with furze-clad moorland and rugged sea-cliffs as you seem to have done. Besides, the country is somewhat remote. Mayhap when a railway runs into it, which will doubtless be the case before many years pass by, we shall see knights of the brush pitching their white tents on the Land's End; meanwhile we have a few promising young men of our own who bid fair to rival the great Opie himself. You have heard of him, of course?"

"I have heard of him indeed, and seen some of his works, but I'm ashamed to confess that, having left Cornwall when very young, and been a dweller in the far north of the kingdom ever since, I have only known the facts that he was a celebrated Cornish artist, and became the President of the Royal Academy. Can you tell me anything of his personal history?"

"Not much, but I can give you a brief outline of his career. John Opie was the son of a carpenter of St. Agnes, near Truro, and was discovered and extracted, like a 'bunch' of rich ore, from the midst of the tin-mines, by Dr. Wolcot — who was celebrated under the name of Peter Pindar. The doctor first observed and appreciated Opie's talent, and, resolving to bring him into notice, wrote about him until he became celebrated as the 'Cornish Wonder.' He also introduced people of note to the artist's studio in London, many of whom sat for their portraits. These gave so much satisfaction that the reputation of the 'Cornish Wonder' spread far and wide, and orders came pouring in upon him, insomuch that he became a rich man and a Royal Academician, and ultimately President of the Academy. He married an authoress, and his remains were deposited in St. Paul's Cathedral, near to those of Sir Joshua Reynolds. I have heard my grandfather say that he met him once in the town of Helston, and he described him as somewhat rough and unpolished, but a sterling, kind-hearted man."

"Did he paint landscape at all?" inquired Oliver.

"Not much, I believe. He devoted himself chiefly to portraits."

"Well, now," said Oliver, looking round him; "it strikes me that this is just the country for a landscape painter. There is nowhere else such fine cliff scenery, and the wild moors, which remind me much of Scotland, are worthy of being sketched by an able brush."

"People have curiously different opinions in reference to the moors which you admire so much," said Tregarthen. "A clergyman who lived and wrote not very long ago, came to Cornwall in search of the picturesque, and he was so disappointed with what he termed a barren, desolate region, that he stopped suddenly on the road between Launceston and Bodmin, and turned his back on Cornwall for ever. As might be expected, such a man gave a very false idea of the country. On the other hand, a more recent writer, commenting on the first, speaks of his delight — after having grown somewhat tired of the almost too rich and over-cultivated scenery of Kent — on coming to what he styled 'a sombre apparition of the desert in a corner of green England,' and dwells with enthusiasm on 'these solitudes, and hills crowned with rugged rocks, classical heaths and savage ravines, possessing a character of desolate grandeur.' But this writer did more. He travelled through the country, and discovered that it possessed other and not less beautiful features; that there were richly clothed vales and beautiful rivulets, cultivated fields and prolific gardens, in close proximity to our grand cliffs and moors."

"He might have added," said Oliver, "that plants and flowers flourish in the open air here, and attain to a size, and luxuriance which are rare in other parts of England. Why, I have seen myrtles, laurels, fuchsias, pomegranates, and hortensias forming hedges and growing on the windows and walls of many houses. To my mind Cornwall is one of the finest counties in England — of which Flora herself has reason to be proud, and in which fairies as well as giants might dwell with much delight."

"Spoken like a true Cornishman!" said Tregarthen, laughing; "and in regard to the fairies I may tell you that we are not without a few of them, although giants confessedly preponderate."

"Indeed!" said Oliver; "pray whereabouts do they dwell?"

"You have heard of the Gump, I suppose?"

"What! the barren plain near Carn Kenidjack, to the north of St. Just?"

"The same. Well, this is said to be a celebrated haunt of the pixies, who have often led benighted travellers astray, and shown them wonderful sights. Of course one never meets with any individual who has actually seen them, but I have frequently met with those who have assured me they had known others who had conversed with persons who had seen fairies. One old man, in particular, I have heard of, who was quite convinced of the reality of a fairy scene which he once witnessed.

"This old fellow was crossing the Gump one evening, by one of the numerous paths which intersect it. It was summer-time. The sun had gone down beyond the sea-line, and the golden mists of evening were merging into the quiet grey that hung over the Atlantic. Not a breath of wind passed over land or sea. To the northward Chun Castle stood darkly on the summit of the neighbouring hill, and the cromlech loomed huge and mysterious; southward were traces of mystic circles and upright stones, and other of those inexplicable pieces of antiquity which are usually saddled on the overladen shoulders of the Druids. Everything, in fact — in the scene, the season, and the weather — contributed to fill the mind of the old man with romantic musings as he wended his way over the barren moor. Suddenly there arose on the air a sound of sweet, soft music, like the gentle breathings of an Aeolian harp. He stopped and gazed around with looks of mingled curiosity and surprise, but could see nothing unusual. The mysterious sounds continued, and a feeling of alarm stole over him, for twilight was deepening, and home was still far distant. He attempted to advance, but the music had such a charm for him that he could not quit the spot, so he turned aside to discover, if possible, whence it came. Presently he came to a spot where the turf was smoother and greener than elsewhere, and here the most wonderful and enchanting scene met his gaze. Fairies innumerable were before him; real live fairies, and no mistake. Lying down on the grass, the old man crept cautiously towards them, and watched their proceedings with deep interest. They were evidently engaged in the pleasant occupation of holding a fair. There were stalls, tastefully laid out and decorated with garlands of flowers. On these were spread most temptingly all the little articles of fairy costume. To be sure the said costume was very scanty, and to all appearance more picturesque than useful; nevertheless there was great variety. Some wore heath-bells jauntily stuck on their heads; some were helmeted with golden blossoms of the furze, and looked warlike; others had nothing but their own luxuriant hair to cover them. A few of the lady fairies struck the old man as being remarkably beautiful, and one of these, who wore an inverted tulip for a skirt, with a small forget-me-not in her golden hair, seemed to him the very picture of what his old Molly had been fifty years before. It was particularly noticeable that the stalls were chiefly patronised by the fairy fair sex, with the exception of one or two which were much frequented by the men. At these latter, articles were sold which marvellously resembled cigars and brandy, and the old man declared that he saw them smoke the former, and that he smelt the latter; but as he had himself been indulging a little that evening in smuggled spirits and tobacco, we must regard this as a somewhat ungenerous statement on his part, for it is ridiculous to suppose that fairies could be such senseless creatures as to smoke or drink! They danced and sang, however, and it was observed that one young man, with a yellow night-cap and a bad cold, was particularly conspicuous for his anxiety to be permitted to sing.

"The music was naturally the great attraction of the evening. It consisted of a large band, and although some of the performers used instruments made of reeds, and straws, and other hollow substances, cut into various forms and lengths, most of them had noses which served the purpose of musical instruments admirably. Indeed, the leader of the band had a prolongation of the nose so like to a flesh-coloured clarionet, that it might easily have been mistaken for the real thing, and on this he discoursed the most seraphic music. Another fairy beside him had a much longer nose, which he used as a trombone with great effect. This fellow was quite a character, and played with such tremendous energy that, on more than one occasion, he brought on a fit of sneezing, which of course interrupted the music, and put the clarionet in a passion. A stout old misshapen gnome, or some such creature, with an enormous head, served for the big drum. Four fairies held him down, and a fifth belaboured his head with a drumstick. It sounded wonderfully hollow, and convinced the old man that it was destitute of brains, and not subject to headache.

"All the time that the old man gazed at them, troops of fairies continued to arrive, some on the backs of bats, from which they slipped as they whirred past;

others descending, apparently, on moonbeams. The old man even fancied that he saw one attempting to descend by a starbeam, which, being apparently too weak to support his weight, broke, and let him down with a crash into the midst of a party who were very busy round a refreshment stall, where a liberal supply of mountain dew was being served out; but the old man never felt quite sure upon this point, for, at sight of the mountain dew, he felt so thirsty that he determined to taste it. Fixing his eyes on the stall, he suddenly threw his hat into the midst of the party, and made a dash at it; but, to his intense disappointment, the vision was instantly dispelled, and nothing was to be seen on the spot but a few snails creeping over the wet grass, and gossamer threads bespangled with dewdrops."

"A very pretty little vision," exclaimed Oliver, "and not the first that has been prematurely dispelled by too ardent a pursuit of strong drink! And now, Charlie, as you appear to be in the vein, and we have still some distance to go, will you tell me something about the giants, and how it came to pass that they were so fond of roaming about Cornwall?"

"Their fondness for it, Oliver, must be ascribed to the same cause as your own — just because it is a lovable place," said Tregarthen; "moreover, being a thinly-peopled county, they were probably not much disturbed in their enjoyment of it. To recount their surprising deeds would require a longer space of time than is just now at our disposal, but you have only to look round, in passing through the country, to understand what a mighty race of men they were. There are 'giants' quoits,' as you know, without end, some of which have the marks of the fingers and thumbs with which they grasped them. Their strength may be estimated by the fact that one of these quoits is no less than forty feet long and twenty wide, and weighs some hundreds of tons. It would puzzle even your strong arm to toss such a quoit! One of these giants was a very notable fellow. He was named 'Wrath,' and is said to have been in the habit of quenching his thirst at the Holy Well under St. Agnes's Beacon, where the marks of his hands, made in the solid granite while he stooped to drink, may still be seen. This rascal, who was well named, is said to have compelled poor St. Agnes, in revenge for her refusing to listen to his addresses, to carry in her apron to the top of Beacon Hill the pile of stones which lies there. But here we are at Penzance, so we shall have done with fiction for the present, and revert to matters of fact. You have business with a lawyer, I believe, and I have business for a short time with a friend. Let us appoint a time and place of meeting."

"What say you to the Wherry Mine at two o'clock?" said Oliver. "It is probable that my business will be concluded by that time, when we can go and see this mine together. My uncle seems to set great store by it, because of an old prophecy to the effect that some day or other it will enrich somebody!"

"Why, that prophecy has been fulfilled long ago," said Tregarthen, with a laugh. "The mine was a bold undertaking, and at one time paid well, but I fear it won't do so again. However, let us meet there; so farewell, old boy, till two."

CHAPTER XX.

The Mine in the Sea.

True to their appointment, young Tregarthen and Oliver Trembath met at the western end of the town of Penzance, close to the sea-beach, where a mass of buildings and a chimney indicated the position of the Wherry Mine.

Oliver's countenance betrayed anxiety as he came forward.

"Nothing wrong, I hope?" said Tregarthen.

"Well, I can't say exactly that things are wrong; but, at the same time, I don't know that they are altogether right."

"Much the same thing," said Tregarthen, smiling; "come, Oliver, unbosom yourself, as novelists say. It will do you good, and two heads, you know, are better than one."

"It's not easy to unbosom myself, old fellow," returned Oliver, with a troubled look; "for my poor uncle's affairs are in a perplexed condition, and I hate explanations, especially when I don't understand the nature of what I attempt to explain, so we'll not talk about it, please, till after our visit to the mine. Let it suffice to say that that notorious smuggler Jim Cuttance is concerned in it, and that we must go to Newlyn this afternoon on a piece of business which I shall afterwards disclose. Meanwhile, where is this mine?"

"Lift up your eyes and behold," said Tregarthen, pointing to an object which was surrounded by the sea, and stood above two hundred yards from the beach.

"What! that martello-towerlike object?" exclaimed Oliver in much surprise.

"Even so," replied Tregarthen, who thereupon proceeded to give his friend a history and description of the mine — of which the following is the substance:

At the western extremity of the sea beach at Penzance there is a reef of sunken rocks which shows its black crest above water at low tide. It was discovered that this reef contained tin, and the people of the town attacked it with hammers and chisels, when each receding tide left it exposed, as long as the seasons would permit, until the depth became unmanageable. After having been excavated a few fathoms the work was abandoned.

Fortunately for the progress of this world there exist a few enterprising men whom nothing can discourage, who seem to be spurred on by opposition, and to gather additional vigour and resolution from increasing difficulties. These men are not numerous, but the world is seldom without a few of them; and one made his appearance in Penzance about the end of last century, in the person of a poor miner named Thomas Curtis. This man conceived the bold design of sinking a shaft through this water-covered rock, and thus creating a mine not only *under*, but *in* the sea.

With the energy peculiar to his class he set to work. The distance of the rock from the beach was about two hundred and forty yards; the depth of water above it at spring tides about nineteen feet. Being exposed to the open sea, a considerable surf is raised on it at times by the prevailing winds, even in summer; while in winter the sea bursts over with such force as to render all operations on it impossible.

That Curtis was a man of no common force of character is obvious from the fact that, apart from the difficulties of the undertaking, he could not expect to derive any profit whatever from his labour for several years. As the work could only be carried on during the short period of time in which the rock was above water, and part of this brief period must necessarily be consumed each tide in pumping out the water in the excavation, it of course progressed slowly. Three summers were consumed in sinking the pump-shaft. After this a framework, or caisson, of stout timber and boards, was built round the mouth of the shaft, and rendered watertight with pitch and oakum. It rose to a height of about twelve feet above the surface of the sea, and was strengthened and supported by stout bars, or buttresses of timber. A platform was placed on the top, and a windlass, at which four men could work, was fixed thereon. This erection was connected with the shore by a stage or "wherry" erected on piles. The water was cleared out; the men went "underground," and, with the sea rolling over their heads, and lashing wildly round the turret which was their only safeguard from terrible and instant destruction, they hewed daily from the submarine rock a considerable portion of tin.

These first workers, however, had committed an error in carrying on their operations too near the surface, so that water permeated freely through the rock, and the risk of the pressure above being too great, for it rendered the introduction of immense supporting timbers necessary. The water, too, forced its way through the shaft during the winter months, so that the regular working of the mine could not be carried on except in summer; nevertheless, this short interval was sufficient to enable the projector to raise so much ore that his mine got the reputation of being a profitable adventure, and it was wrought successfully for many years.

About the end of the century the depth of the pump-shaft was about four fathoms, and the roof had been cut away to the thinness of three feet in some places. Twelve men were employed for two hours at the windlass in hauling the water, while six others were "teaming" from the bottom into the pump. When sufficient water had been cleared away the men laboured at the rock for six hours – in all, eight hours at a time. The prolific nature of the mine may be gathered from the fact that in the space of six months ten men, working about one tenth of that time – less than three weeks – broke about £600 worth of ore. During one summer £3,000 worth of tin was raised!

A steam-engine was ultimately attached to the works, and the mine was sunk to a depth of sixteen fathoms, but the expense of working it at length became so great that it was abandoned – not, however, before ore to the amount of £70,000 had been raised from under the sea!

At the time of our tale another effort had been made to work the Wherry Mine, and great expectations had been raised, but these expectations were being disappointed. Our unfortunate friend Mr. Donnithorne was among the number of those who had cause to regret having ventured to invest in the undertaking, and it was to make inquiries in regard to certain unfavourable rumours touching the mine that Oliver Trembath had been sent to Penzance.

After inspecting Wherry Mine the two friends walked along the shore together, and Oliver explained the nature of the difficulties in which his uncle was involved.

"The fact is, Charlie," he said, "an old fish-purchaser of Newlyn named Hitchin is one of the principal shareholders in this concern. He is as rich, they say, as Croesus, and if we could only prevail on him to be amiable the thing might be carried on for some time longer with every hope of a favourable result, for there can be no doubt whatever that there is plenty of tin in the mine yet, and the getting of it out is only a question of time and capital."

"A pretty serious question — as most speculators find," said Tregarthen, laughing; "you appear to think lightly of it."

"Well, I don't pretend to know much about such matters," replied Oliver, "but whatever may be the truth of the case, old Hitchin refuses to come forward. He says that he is low in funds just now, which nobody seems to believe, and that he owes an immense sum of money to Jim Cuttance, the smuggler, for what, of course, he will not tell, but we can have no difficulty in guessing. He says that Cuttance is pressing him just now, and that, therefore, he cannot afford to advance anything on the mine. This being the case it must go down, and, if it does, one of the last few gleams of prosperity that remain to my poor uncle will have fluttered away. This must be prevented, if possible, and it is with that end in view that I purpose going to Newlyn this afternoon to see Hitchin and bring my persuasive powers to bear on him."

"H'm, not of much use, I fear," said Tregarthen. "Hitchin is a tough old rascal, with a hard heart and a miserly disposition. However, it may be worth while to make the attempt, for you have a very oily tongue, Oliver."

"And you have an extremely impudent one, Charlie. But can you tell me at what time the mackerel boats may be expected this evening, for it seems the old fellow is not often to be found at home during the day, and we shall be pretty sure to find him on the beach when the boats arrive?"

Thus appealed to, Tregarthen cast a long look at the sea and sky.

"Well, I should say, considering the state of the tide and the threatening appearance of the sky, we may expect to see them at six o'clock, or thereabouts."

"That leaves us nearly a couple of hours to spare; how shall we spend it?" said Oliver.

"Go and have a look at this fine old town," suggested Tregarthen. "It is worth going over, I assure you. Besides the town hall, market, museum, etc., there are, from many points of the surrounding eminences, most superb views of the town and bay with our noble St. Michael's Mount. The view from some of the heights has been said by some visitors to equal that of the far-famed Bay of Naples itself."

"Part of this I have already seen," said Oliver, "the rest I hope to live to see, but in the meantime tin is uppermost in my mind; so if you have no objection I should like to have a look at the tin-smelting works. What say you?"

"Agreed, by all means," cried Tregarthen; "poor indeed would be the spirit of the Cornishman who did not feel an interest in tin!"

CHAPTER XXI.

Treats of Tin-Smelting and other Matters.

There is something grand in the progress of a mechanical process, from its commencement to its termination. Especially is this the case in the production of metals, nearly every step in the course of which is marked by the hard, unyielding spirit of *vis inertiae* on the one hand, and the tremendous power of intelligence, machinery, and manual dexterity on the other.

Take, for example, the progress of a mass of tin from Botallack.

Watch yonder stalwart miner at work, deep in the bowels of the mine. Slowly, with powerful blows, he bores a hole in the hard rock. After one, two, or three hours of incessant toil, it is ready for the powder. It is charged; the match is applied; the man takes shelter behind a projection; the mass is rent from its ancient bed, and the miner goes off to lunch while the smoke is clearing away. He returns to his work at length, coughing, and rubbing his eyes, for smoke still lingers there, unable, it would seem, to find its way out; and no wonder, lost as it is in intricate ramifications at the depth of about one thousand five hundred feet below the green grass! He finds but a small piece of ore – perhaps it is twice the size of his head, it may be much larger, but, in any case, it is an apparently poor return for the labour expended. He adds it, however, to the pile at his side, and when that is sufficiently large fills a little iron wagon, and sends it up "to grass" through the shaft, by means of the iron "kibble." Here the large pieces of ore are broken into smaller ones by a man with a hammer; as far as the inexperienced eye can distinguish he might be breaking ordinary stones to repair the road! These are then taken to the "stamps."

Those who have delicate nerves would do well to keep as far as possible from the stamps of a tin-mine! Enormous hammers or pounders they are, with shanks as well as heads of malleable-iron, each weighing, shank and head together, seven hundredweight. They are fearful things, these stamps; iron in spirit as well as in body, for they go on for ever – night and day – wrought by a steam-engine of one hundred horse-power, as enduring as themselves. The stamps are so arranged as to be self-feeders, by means of huge wooden troughs with sloping bottoms, into which the ore is thrown in quantities sufficient to keep them constantly at work without requiring much or constant attendance. Small streams of water trickle over the ore to keep it slowly sliding down towards the jaws, where the stamps thunder up and down alternately. A dread power of pounding have they, truly; and woe be to the toe that should chance to get beneath them!

The rock they have to deal with is, as we have said, uncommonly hard, and it enters the insatiable mouth of the stamps about the size of a man's fist, on the average, but it comes out from these iron jaws so exceeding fine as to be incapable of thickening the stream of reddish-yellow water that carries it away. The colour of the stream is the result of iron, with which the tin is mingled.

The particles of tin are indeed set free by the stamps from solid bondage, but they are so fine as to be scarcely visible, and so commingled with other substances, such as iron, copper, sulphur, etc., that a tedious process of separation has yet to be undergone before the bright metal can be seen or handled.

At the present time the stream containing it is poured continuously on several huge wooden tables. These tables are each slightly raised in the centre where the stream falls, so that all the water runs off, leaving the various substances it contains deposited on the table, and these substances are spread over it regularly, while being deposited, by revolving washers or brushes.

Tin, being the heaviest of all the ingredients contained in the stream, falls at once to the bottom, and is therefore, deposited on the head or centre of the table; iron, being a shade lighter, is found to lodge in a circle beyond; while all other substances are either spread over the outer rim or washed entirely away. When the tables are full — that is, coated with what appears to be an earthy substance up wards of a foot in depth — the rich tin in the centre is carefully cut out with shovels and placed in tubs, while the rest is rewashed in order that the tin still mingled with it may be captured — a process involving much difficulty, for tin is so very little heavier than iron that the lighter particles can scarcely be separated even after repeated and careful washings.

In old times the tin was collected in large pits, whence it was transferred to the hands of balmaidens (or mine-girls) to be washed by them in wooden troughs called "frames," which somewhat resembled a billiard table in form. Indeed, the frames are still largely employed in the mines, but these and the modern table perform exactly the same office — they wash the refuse from the tin.

Being finally cleansed from all its impurities, our mass of tin bears more resemblance to brown snuff than to metal. An ignorant man would suppose it to be an ordinary earthy substance, until he took some of it in his hand and felt its weight. It contains, however, comparatively little foreign substance. About seventy per cent. of it is pure tin, but this seventy per cent. is still locked up in the tight embrace of thirty per cent, of refuse, from which nothing but intense fire can set it free.

At this point in the process, our mass of tin leaves the rough hand of the miner. In former days it was divided among the shareholders in this form — each receiving, instead of cash, so many sacks of tin ore, according to the number of his shares or "doles," and carrying it off on mule or horse back from the mine, to be smelted where or by whom he pleased. But whether treated in this way, or, as in the present day, sold by the manager at the market value, it all comes at last to the tin-smelter, whose further proceedings we shall now follow, in company with Oliver and his friend.

The agent of the smelting company — a stout, intelligent man, who evidently did "knaw tin" — conducted them first to the furnaces, in the neighbourhood of which were ranged a number of large wooden troughs or bins, all more or less filled with tin ore. The ore got from different mines, he said, differed in quality, as well as in the percentage of tin which it contained. Some had much iron mixed with it, in spite of all the washings it had undergone; some had a little copper and other substances; while some was very pure. By mixing the tin of different mines, better metal could be procured than by simply smelting the produce of each mine separately. Pointing to one of the bins, about three yards square, he told them it contained tin worth £1,000. There was a large quantity of black sand in one of the bins, which, the agent said, was got by the process of "streaming." It is the richest and best kind of tin ore, and used to be procured in large quantities in Cornwall — especially in ancient times — being found near the surface, but, as a matter of course, not much of that is to be found now, the land having been turned over three times in search of it. This black sand is now imported in large quantities from Singapore.

The agent then conducted his visitors to the testing-house, where he showed them the process of testing the various qualities of tin ore offered, to the House for sale. First he weighed out twenty parts of the ore, which, as we have said, resembled snuff. This, he remarked, contained about five-sixths of pure tin, the remaining one-sixth being dross. He mixed it with four parts of fine coal dust, or culm, and added a little borax — these last ingredients being intended to expedite the smelting process. This compound was put into a crucible, and subjected to the intense heat of a small furnace for about twenty minutes. At the end of that time, the agent seized the crucible with a pair of tongs, poured the metal into an iron mould, and threw away the dross. The little mass of tin thus produced was about four inches long, by half an inch broad, and of a dull bluish-grey colour. It was then put into an iron ladle and melted, as one would melt lead when about to cast bullets, but it was particularly noteworthy here, that a very slight heat was required. To extract the metal from the tin ore, a fierce heat, long applied, was necessary, but a slight heat, continued for a few minutes, sufficed to melt the metal. This remelted metal was poured into a stone mould, where it lay like a bright little pool of liquid silver. In a few seconds it solidified, retaining its clear purity in all its parts.

"That," said the agent, "is tin of the very best quality. We sell it chiefly to dyers, who use it for colouring purposes, and for whom no tin but the best is of any use. I will now show you two other qualities — namely, second and inferior."

He went to a small cupboard as he spoke, and took therefrom a small piece of tin which had already gone through the smelting process in the crucible above described. Melting this in the ladle, he poured it into the mould, where it lay for a few moments, quite bright and pure, but the instant it solidified, a slight dimness clouded its centre.

"That," explained the agent, "is caused by a little copper which they have failed to extract from the tin. Such tin would not do for the dyers, but it is good for the tin-plate makers, who, by dipping thin sheets of iron into molten tin, produce the well-known tin-plates of which our pot-lids and pans, etc., are manufactured. This last bit, gentlemen," he added, taking a third piece of tin from the cupboard, "is our worst quality."

Having melted it, he poured it into the mould, where it assumed a dull, half-solid appearance, as if it were a liquid only half frozen — or, if you prefer it, a solid in a half molten state.

"This is only fit to mix with copper and make brass," said the agent, throwing down the mould. "We test the tin ore twice — once to find out the quantity of metal it contains, and again to ascertain its quality. The latter process you have seen — the former is just the same, with this difference, that I am much more careful in weighing, measuring, etc. Every particle of dross I would have collected and carefully separated from any metal it might contain; the whole should then have been reweighed, and its reduction in the smelting process ascertained. Thus, if twenty parts had been the weight of tin ore, the result might perhaps have been fourteen parts of metal and six parts of dross. And now, gentlemen, having explained to you the testing process, if you will follow me, I will show you the opening of one of our furnaces. The smelting-furnace just shows the testing process on a large scale. Into this furnace, six hours ago," he said, pointing to a brick erection in the building to which he led them, "we threw a large quantity of tin ore, mingled with a certain proportion of culm. It is smelted and ready to be run off now."

Here he gave an order to a sturdy man, who, with brawny arms bared to the shoulders, stood close at hand. He was begrimed and hairy — like a very Vulcan.

Seizing an iron poker, Vulcan probed the orifice of the furnace, and forthwith there ran out a stream of liquid fire, which was caught in an iron bowl nearly four feet in diameter. The intense heat of this pool caused the visitors to step back a few paces, and the ruddy glow shone with a fierce glare on the swart, frowning countenance of Vulcan, who appeared to take a stern delight in braving it.

Oliver's attention was at once attracted to this man, for he felt convinced that he had seen his face before, but it was not until he had taxed his memory for several minutes that the scene of his adventure with the smugglers near the Land's End flashed upon him, when he at once recognised him as the man named Joe Tonkin, who had threatened his life in the cavern. From a peculiar look that the man gave him, he saw that he also was recognised.

Oliver took no further notice of him at the time, however, but turned to watch the flow of the molten tin.

When the iron cauldron was almost full, "slag," or molten refuse began to flow and cover the top of the metal. The hole was immediately plugged up by Vulcan, and the furnace cleared out for the reception of another supply of ore. The surface of the tin was now cleared of slag, after which it was ladled into moulds and allowed to cool. This was the first process completed; but the tin was still full of impurities, and had to undergo another melting and stirring in a huge cauldron. This latter was a severe and protracted operation, which Vulcan performed with tremendous power and energy.

In reference to this, it may interest the reader to mention a valuable discovery which was the result of laziness! A man who was employed in a tin-smelting establishment at this laborious work of stirring the molten metal in order to purify it, accidentally discovered that a piece of green wood dropped into it had the effect of causing it to bubble as if it were boiling. To ease himself of some of his toil, he availed himself of the discovery, and, by stirring the metal with a piece of green wood, caused such a commotion that the end in view was accomplished much more effectually and speedily than by the old process. The lazy man's plan, we need scarcely add, is now universally adopted.

The last operation was to run the metal into moulds with the smelter's name on them, and these ingots, being of portable size, were ready for sale.

While the agent was busily engaged in explaining to Charles Tregarthen some portions of the work, Oliver stepped aside and accosted Joe Tonkin.

"So, friend," he said, with a smile, "it seems that smuggling is not your only business?"

"No, sur, it ain't," replied Joe, with a grin. "I'm a jack-of-all-trades — a smelter, as you do see, an' a miner *also*, when it suits me."

"I'm glad to hear it, my man, for it gives you a chance of coming in contact with better men than smugglers — although I'm free to confess that there *is* some good among them too. I don't forget that your comrade Jim Cuttance hauled me out of the sea. Where is he?"

"Don't knaw, sur," replied Tonkin, with an angry frown; "he and I don't pull well together. We've parted now."

Oliver glanced at the man, and as he observed his stern, proud expression of face, and his huge, powerful frame, he came to the conclusion that Cuttance had met a man of equal power and force of character with himself, and was glad to get rid of him.

"But I have not gi'n up smuggling," added the man, with a smile. "It do pay pretty well, and is more heartylike than this sort o' thing."

"I'd advise you to fall back on mining," said Oliver. "It is hard work, I know, but it is honest labour, and as far as I have seen, there does not appear to be a more free, hearty, and independent race under the sun than Cornish miners."

Joe Tonkin shook his head and smiled dubiously.

"You do think so, sur, but you haven't tried it. I don't like it. It don't suit me, it don't. No, no; there's nothin' like a good boat and the open sea."

"Things are looking a little better at Botallack just now, Joe," said Oliver, after a pause. "I'd strongly advise you to try it again."

The man remained silent for a few minutes, then he said — "Well, Mr. Trembath, I don't mind if I do. I'm tired o' this work, and as my time is up this very day, I'll go over tomorrow and see 'bout it. There's a man at Newlyn as I've got somethin' to say to; I'll go see him tonight, and then —"

"Come along, Oliver," shouted Tregarthen at that moment; "it's time to go."

Oliver bade Tonkin good-afternoon, and, turning hastily away, followed his friend.

The two proceeded arm in arm up Market-Jew Street, and turning down towards the shore, walked briskly along in the direction of the picturesque fishing village of Newlyn, which lies little more than a mile to the westward of Penzance.

CHAPTER XXII.

*Shows how Oliver and his Friend went to Newlyn and saw
the Mackerel Market, and found some Difficulties and
Mysteries Awaiting them there.*

The beach opposite Newlyn presented a busy scene when Oliver Trembath
and his friend Charlie Tregarthen reached it.

Although the zenith of the season was over, mackerel fishing was still going
on there in full vigour, and immense crowds of men, women, and children covered the sands. The village lies on the heights above, and crowds of people were
leaning over the iron rails which guard the unwary or unsteady passenger from
falling into the sea below. A steep causeway connects the main street above with
the shore beneath; and up and down it horses, carts, and people were hurrying
continuously.

True, there was not at that time quite as much bustle as may be witnessed
there at the present day. The railway has penetrated these remote regions of the
west, and now men work with a degree of feverish haste that was unknown then.
While hundreds of little boats (tenders to the large ones) crowd in on the beach,
auctioneers with long heavy boots wade knee-deep into the water, followed and
surrounded by purchasers, and, ringing a bell as each boat comes in, shout —
"Now, then, five hundred, more or less, in this boat; who bids? Twenty shillings
a hundred for five hundred — twenty shillings — say nineteen — I'm bid nineteen — nineteen-and-six — say nineteen-an — twenty — twenty shillings I'm bid —
say twenty-one — shall I make it twenty-one shillings for any person?" etc.

The bells and voices of these auctioneers, loud though they be, are mild
compared with the shouts of men, women, and children, as the fish are packed
in baskets, with hot haste, to be in time for the train; and horses with laden carts
gallop away over the sands at furious speed, while others come dashing back for
more fish. And there is need for all this furious haste, for trains, like time and
tide, wait for no man, and prices vary according to trains. Just before the starting
of one, you will hear the auctioneers put the fish up at 20s., 25s., and even 30s. a
hundred, and in the next half-hour, after the train is gone, and no chance
remains of any more of the fish being got into the London market by the following morning, the price suddenly falls to 8s. a hundred, sometimes even less.
There is need for haste, too, because the quantity of fish is very great, for there
are sometimes two hundred boats at anchor in the bay, each with four thousand
fish on the average, which must all be washed and packed in four or five hours.
Yes, the old days cannot be compared with the present times, when, between the
months of April and June, the three hundred boats of Mounts Bay will land
little short of three thousand tons of mackerel, and the railway, for the mere carriage of these to London, Manchester, Birmingham, etc., will clear above
£20,000!

Nevertheless, the busy, bustling, hearty nature of the scene on Newlyn beach in days of yore was not so very different as one might suppose from that of the present time. The men were not less energetic then than now; the women were not less eager; the children were quite as wild and mischievous, and the bustle and noise apparently, if not really, as great.

"What interests you?" asked Charlie Tregarthen, observing that his companion gazed pointedly at some object in the midst of the crowd.

"That old woman," said Oliver; "see how demurely she sits on yonder upturned basket, knitting with all her might."

"In the midst of chaos," observed Tregarthen, laughing; "and she looks as placidly indifferent to the noise around her as if it were only the murmuring of a summer breeze, although there are two boys yelling at her very ear at this moment."

"Perhaps she's deaf," suggested Oliver.

Tregarthen said he thought this highly probable, and the two remained silent for some time, watching, from an elevated position on the road leading down to the sands, the ever-changing and amusing scene below. Talk of a pantomime, indeed! No Christmas pantomime ever got up in the great metropolis was half so amusing or so grand as that summer pantomime that was performed daily on Newlyn sands, with admission to all parts of the house – the stage included – for nothing! The scenery was painted with gorgeous splendour by nature, and embraced the picturesque village of Newlyn, with its irregular gables, variously tinted roofs, and whitewashed fronts; the little pier with its modest harbour, perfectly dry because of the tide being out, but which, even if the tide had been in, and itself full to overflowing, could not apparently have held more than a dozen of the larger fishing-boats; the calm bay crowded with boats of all sizes, their brown and yellow sails reflected in the clear water, and each boat resting on its own image. On the far-off horizon might be seen the Lizard Point and the open sea, over which hung red and lurid clouds, which betokened the approach of a storm, although, at the time, all nature was quiet and peaceful. Yes, the scenery was admirably painted, and nothing could exceed the perfection of the acting. It was so *very* true to nature!

Right in front of the spot where the two friends stood, a fisherman sat astride of an upturned basket, enjoying a cup of tea which had been brought to him by a little girl who sat on another upturned basket at his side, gazing with a pleased expression into his rugged countenance, one cheek of which was distended with a preposterously large bite of bread and butter. The great Mathews himself never acted his part so well. What admirable devotion to the one engrossing object in hand! What a perfect and convincing display of a hearty appetite! What obvious unconsciousness of being looked at, and what a genuine and sudden burst of indignation when, owing to a touch of carelessness, he capsized the cup, and poured the precious tea upon the thirsty sand. At the distance from which Oliver and his friend observed him, no words were audible, but none were necessary. The man's acting was so perfect that they knew he was scolding the little girl for the deed which he himself had perpetrated. Then there was something peculiarly touching in the way in which he suddenly broke into a short laugh, and patted the child's head while she wiped out the cup, and refilled it from the little brown broken-nosed teapot hitherto concealed under her ragged shawl to keep it warm. No wizard was needed to tell, however, that this was quite an unnecessary piece of carefulness on the little girl's part, for any brown teapot in the world, possessing the smallest amount of feeling, would have instantly made hot and strong tea out of cold water on being pressed against the bosom of that sunny child!

Just beyond this couple, three tired men, in blue flannel shirts, long boots, and sou'-westers, grouped themselves round a bundle of straw to enjoy a pipe: one stretched himself almost at full length on it, in lazy nonchalance; another sat down on it, and, resting his elbows on his knees, gazed pensively at his pipe as he filled it; while the third thrust his hands into his pockets, and stood for a few seconds with a grand bend at the small of his back (as if he felt that his muscles worked easily), and gazed out to sea. The greatest of the old masters could have painted nothing finer.

Away to the right, an old man might be seen tying up the lid of a basket full of fish beside his cart, and dividing his attention between the basket and the horse, which latter, much to his surprise, was unwontedly restive that evening, and required an unusual number of cautions to remain still, and of threats as to the punishment that would follow continued disobedience, all of which afforded the most intense and unutterable delight to a very small precocious boy, who, standing concealed on the off side of the animal, tickled its ear with a straw every time it bent its head towards the bundle of hay which lay at its feet. No clown or pantaloon was there to inflict condign punishment, because none was needed. A brother carter standing by performed the part, extempore. His eye suddenly lit on the culprit; his whip sprang into the air and descended on the urchin's breech. Horror-struck, his mouth opened responsive to the crack, and a yell came forth that rose high above the surrounding din, while his little legs carried him away over the sands like a ragged leaf driven before the wind.

To the left of this scene (and ignorant of it, for the stage was so large, the actors were so numerous, and the play so grand, that few could do more than attend to their own part) a cripple might be seen with a crutch hopping actively about. He was a young man; had lost his leg, by an accident probably, and was looking about for a cast-away fish for his own supper. He soon found one. Whether it was that one had been dropped accidentally, or that some generous-hearted fish-dealer had dropped one on purpose, we cannot tell, but he did get one — a large fat one, too — and hobbled away as quickly as he could, evidently rejoicing.

The cripple was not the only one who crossed the stage thus lightly burdened. There were several halt and maimed, and some blind and aged ones there, whose desires in regard to piscatorial wealth extended only to one, or perhaps two, and they all got what they wanted. That was sufficient for the evening's supper — for the morrow there was no need to care; they could return to get a fresh supply evening after evening for many a day to come, for it was a splendid mackerel season — such as had not been for many years — so said the sages of the village.

There were other groups, and other incidents that would have drawn laughter as well as tears from sympathetic hearts, but we must forbear. The play was long of being acted out – it was no common play; besides, it is time for *our* actors to come upon the stage themselves.

"I see old Hitchin," exclaimed Oliver Trembath, starting suddenly out of a reverie, and pointing into the thickest of the crowd.

"How can you tell? you don't know him," said his companion.

"Know him! Of course I do; who could fail to know him after the graphic description the lawyer gave of him? See – look yonder, beside the cart with the big man in it arranging baskets. D'you see?"

"Which? the one painted green, and a scraggy horse with a bag hanging to its nose?"

"No, no; a little further to the left, man – the one with the broken rail and the high-spirited horse. There, there he is! a thin, dried-up, wrinkled, old shabby –"

"Ah! that's the man," exclaimed Tregarthen, laughing. "Come along, and let's try to keep our eyes on him, for there is nothing so difficult as finding any one in a crowd."

The difficulty referred to was speedily illustrated by the fact that the two friends threaded their way to the spot where the cart had stood, and found not only that it was gone, but that Hitchin had also moved away, and although they pushed through the crowd for more than a quarter of an hour they failed to find him.

As they were wandering about thus, they observed a very tall broad-shouldered man talking earnestly in undertones to a sailorlike fellow who was still broader across the shoulders, but not quite so tall. It is probable that Oliver would have paid no attention to them, had not the name of Hitchin struck his ear. Glancing round at the men he observed that the taller of the two was Joe Tonkin, and the other his friend of the Land's End, the famous Jim Cuttance.

Oliver plucked his companion by the sleeve, and whispered him to stand still. Only a few words and phrases reached them, but these were sufficient to create surprise and arouse suspicion. Once, in particular, Tonkin, who appeared to be losing his temper, raised his voice a little, exclaiming – "I tell 'ee what it is, Cuttance, I do knaw what you're up to, an' I'll hinder 'ee ef I can."

The man confirmed this statement with a savage oath, to which Cuttance replied in kind; nevertheless he was evidently anxious to conciliate his companion, and spoke so low as to be nearly inaudible.

Only the words, "Not tonight; I won't do it tonight," reached the ears of the listeners.

At this point Tonkin turned from the smuggler with a fling, muttering in an undertone as he went, "I don't b'lieve 'ee, Cuttance, for thee'rt a liard, so I'll watch 'ee, booy."

Oliver was about to follow Tonkin, when he observed Hitchin himself slowly wending his way through the crowd. He had evidently heard nothing of the conversation that appeared to have reference to himself, for he sauntered along with a careless air, and his hands in his pockets, as though he were an uninterested spectator of the busy scene.

Oliver at once accosted him, "Pray, sir, is your name Hitchin?"

"It is," replied the old man, eyeing his interrogator suspiciously.

"Allow me to introduce myself, sir — Oliver Trembath, nephew to Mr. Thomas Donnithorne of St. Just."

Mr. Hitchin held out his hand, and said that he was happy to meet with a nephew of his old friend, in the tone of a man who would much rather not meet either nephew or uncle.

Oliver felt this, so he put on his most insinuating air, and requested Mr. Hitchin to walk with him a little aside from the crowd, as he had something of a private nature to say to him. The old man agreed, and the two walked slowly along the sands to the outskirts of the crowd, where young Tregarthen discreetly left them.

The moment Oliver broached the subject of the advance of money, Hitchin frowned, and the colour in his face betrayed suppressed anger.

"Sir," said he, "I know all that you would say to me. It has already been said oftener than there is any occasion for. No one appears to believe me when I assert that I have met with heavy losses of late, and have no cash to spare — not even enough to pay my debts."

"Indeed, sir," replied Oliver, "I regret to hear you say so, and I can only apologise for having troubled you on the subject. I assure you nothing would have induced me to do so but regard for my uncle, to whom the continuance of this mine for some time would appear to be a matter of considerable importance; but since you will not —"

"*Wilt* not!" interrupted Hitchin angrily, "have I not said *can not*? I tell you, young man, that there is a scoundrel to whom I owe a large sum for — for — well, no matter what it's for, but the blackguard threatens that if I don't — pshaw! —"

The old man seemed unable to contain himself at this point, for he turned angrily away from Oliver, and, hastening back towards the town, was soon lost again in the crowd.

Oliver was so taken by surprise, that he stood still gazing dreamily at the point where Hitchin had disappeared, until he was roused by a touch on the shoulder from Charlie Tregarthen.

"Well," said he, smiling, "how fares your suit?"

Oliver replied by a burst of laughter.

"How fares my suit?" he repeated; "badly, very badly indeed; why, the old fellow's monkey got up the moment I broached the subject, and I was just in the middle of what I meant to be a most conciliating speech, when he flung off as you have seen."

"Odd, very odd," said Tregarthen, "to see how some men cling to their money, as if it were their life. After all, it *is* life to some — at least all the life they have got."

"Come now, don't moralise, Charlie, for we must act just now."

"I'm ready to act in any way you propose, Oliver; what do you intend to do? Issue your commands, and I'll obey. Shall we attack the village of Newlyn single-handed, and set fire to it, as did the Spaniards of old, or shall we swim off to the fleet of boats, cut the cables, bind the men in charge, and set sail for the mackerel fishing?"

"Neither, my chum, and especially not the latter, seeing that a thunder-cloud is about to break over the sea ere long, if I do not greatly misjudge appearances in the sky; but, man, we must see this testy old fellow again, and warn him of the danger which threatens him. I feel assured that that rascal Cuttance means him harm, for he let something fall in his anger, which, coupled with what we have already heard from the smuggler himself, and from Tonkin, convinces me that evil is in the wind. Now the question is, how are we to find him, for searching in that crowd is almost useless?"

"Let us go to his house," suggested Tregarthen, "and if he is not at home, wait for him."

"Do you know where his house is?"

"No, not I."

"Then we must inquire, so come along."

Pushing once more through the throng of busy men and women, the friends ascended the sloping causeway that led to the village, and here asked the first man they met where Mr. Hitchin lived.

"Right over top o' hill," replied the man.

"Thank you. That'll do, Charlie, come along," said Oliver, turning into one of the narrow passages that diverged from the main street of Newlyn, and ascending the hill with giant strides; "one should never be particular in their inquiries after a place. When I'm told to turn to the right after the second turning to the left, and that if I go right on till I come to some other turning, that will conduct me point blank to the street that enters the square near to which lies the spot I wish to reach, I'm apt to get confused. Get a general direction if possible, the position indicated by compass is almost enough, and *ask again*. That's my plan, and I never found it fail."

CHAPTER XXIII.

In which is Recorded a Visit to an Infant-School; a Warning to a Thankless Old Gentleman; also a Storm, and a Sudden as well as Surprising End of a Mine, besides Dark Designs.

Oliver Trembath's plan of "asking again" had to be put in practice sooner than had been anticipated, for the back alleys and lanes of Newlyn were a little perplexing to a stranger.

"Let us inquire here," said Tregarthen, seeing the half-open door of a very small cottage, with part of a woman's back visible in the interior.

"By all means," said Oliver, pushing open the door and stooping low as he entered.

The visitors were instantly transfixed by thirty pair of eyes — all of them bright blue, or bright black — few of them elevated much more than two feet from the ground, and not one of them dimmed by the smallest approach to a wink. Nay, on the contrary, they all opened so wide when the strangers entered that it seemed as if either winking or shutting were in future out of the question, and that to sleep with eyes wide open was the sad prospect of the owners thereof in all time coming.

"An infant-school," murmured Tregarthen.

The very smallest boy in the school — an infant with legs about five inches long, who sat on a stool not more than three inches high — appeared to understand what he said, and to regard it as a personal insult, for he at once began to cry. A little girl with bright red hair, a lovely complexion, and a body so small as to be scarce worth mentioning, immediately embraced the small boy, whereupon he dried his eyes without delay.

"You have a nice little school here," said Oliver.

"Iss, sur; we do feel proud of it," said the good-looking motherly dame in charge, with a little twitch of her shoulders, which revealed the horrible fact that both her arms had been taken off above the elbows, "the child'n are very good, and they do sing bootiful. Now then, let the gentlemen hear you — 'O that'll be' — come."

Instantly, and in every possible pitch, the thirty mouths belonging to the thirty pair of eyes opened, and "O that will be joyful," etc., burst forth with thrilling power. A few leading voices gradually turned the torrent into a united channel, and before the second verse was reached the hymn was tunefully sung, the sweet voice of the little girl with the bright hair being particularly distinguishable, and the shrill pipe of the smallest boy sounding high above the rest as he sang, "O that will be doyful, doyful, doyful, doyful," with all his might and main.

When this was finished Tregarthen asked the schoolmistress what misfortune had caused the loss of her arms, to which she replied that she had lost them in a coach accident. As she was beginning to relate the history of this sad affair,

Oliver broke in with a question as to where old Mr. Hitchin's house was. Being directed to it they took leave of the infant-school, and soon found themselves before the door of a small cottage. They were at once admitted to the presence of the testy old Hitchin, who chanced to be smoking a pipe at the time. He did not by any means bestow a welcome look on his visitors, but Oliver, nevertheless, advanced and sat down in a chair before him.

"I have called, Mr. Hitchin," he began, "not to trouble you about the matter which displeased you when we conversed together on the beach, but to warn you of a danger which I fear threatens yourself."

"What danger may that be?" inquired Hitchin, in the tone of a man who held all danger in contempt.

"What it is I cannot tell, but —"

"Cannot tell!" interrupted the old man; "then what's the use of troubling me about it?"

"Neither can I tell of what use my troubling you may be," retorted Oliver with provoking coolness, "but I heard the man speak of you on the beach less than an hour ago, and as you referred to him yourself I thought it right to call —"

At this point Hitchin again broke in — "Heard a man speak of me — what man? Really, Mr. Trembath, your conduct appears strange to me. Will you explain yourself?"

"Certainly. I was going to have added, if your irascible temper would have allowed me, that the notorious smuggler, Jim Cuttance —"

Oliver stopped, for at the mention of the smuggler's name the pipe dropped from the old man's mouth, and his face grew pale.

"Jim Cuttance!" he exclaimed after a moment's pause; "the villain, the scoundrel — what of him? what of him? No good, I warrant. There is not a rogue unhanged who deserves more richly to swing at the yard-arm than Jim Cuttance. What said he about me?"

When he finished this sentence the old man's composure was somewhat restored. He took a new pipe from the chimney-piece and began to fill it, while Oliver related all that he knew of the conversation between the two smugglers.

When he had finished Hitchin smoked for some minutes in silence.

"Do you really think," he said at length, "that the man means to do me bodily harm?"

"I cannot tell," replied Oliver; "you can form your own judgment of the matter more correctly than I can, but I would advise you to be on your guard."

"What says your friend?" asked Hitchin, turning towards Tregarthen, of whom, up to that point, he had taken no notice.

Thus appealed to, the youth echoed Oliver's opinion, and added that the remark of Cuttance about his intention not to do something unknown *that* night, and Joe Tonkin's muttered expressions of disbelief and an intention to watch, seemed to him sufficient to warrant unusual caution in the matter of locks, bolts, and bars.

As he spoke there came a blinding flash of lightning, followed by a loud and prolonged peal of thunder.

Oliver sprang up.

"We must bid you good-night," he said, "for we have to walk to St. Just, and don't wish to get more of the storm than we can avoid."

"But you cannot escape it," said Hitchin.

"Nevertheless we can go as far as possible before it begins, and then take shelter under a bush or hedge, or in a house if we chance to be near one. I would rather talk in rain any day than drive in a kittereen!"

"Pray be persuaded to stop where you are, gentlemen," said the old man in a tone of voice that was marvellously altered for the better. "I can offer you comfortable quarters for the night, and good, though plain fare, with smuggled brandy of the best, and tobacco to match."

Still Oliver and Tregarthen persisted in their resolution to leave, until Hitchin began to plead in a tone that showed he was anxious to have their presence in the house as protectors. Then their resolution began to waver, and when the old man hinted that they might thus find time to reconsider the matter of the Wherry Mine, they finally gave in, and made up their minds to stay all night.

According to the opinion of a celebrated poet, the best-laid plans of men as well as mice are apt to miscarry. That night the elements contrived to throw men's calculations out of joint, and to render their cupidity, villainy, and wisdom alike ineffectual.

A storm, the fiercest that had visited them for many years, burst that night on the southern shores of England, and strewed her rocks and sands with wrecks and dead bodies. Nothing new in this, alas! as all know who dwell upon our shores, or who take an interest in, and read the records of, our royal and noble Lifeboat Institution. But with this great subject we have not to do just now, further than to observe, as we have said before, that in those days there were no lifeboats on the coast.

Under the shelter of an old house on the shore at Penzance were gathered together a huge concourse of townspeople and seafaring men watching the storm. It was a grand and awful sight — one fitted to irresistibly solemnise the mind, and incline it, unless the heart be utterly hardened, to think of the great Creator and of the unseen world, which seems at such a season to be brought impressively near.

The night was extremely dark, and the lightning, by contrast, peculiarly vivid. Each flash appeared to fill the world for a moment with lambent fire, leaving the painful impression on observers of having been struck with total blindness for a few seconds after, and each thunderclap came like the bursting of artillery, with scarcely an interval between the flash and crash, while the wind blew with almost tropical fury.

The terrible turmoil and noise were enhanced tenfold by the raging surf, which flew up over the roadway, and sent the spray high above and beyond the tops of the houses nearest to the shore.

The old house creaked and groaned in the blast as if it would come down, and the men taking shelter there looked out to sea in silence. The bronzed veterans there knew full well that at that hour many a despairing cry was being uttered, many a hand was stretched wildly, helplessly, and hopelessly from the midst of the boiling surf, and many a soul was passing into eternity. They would have been ready then, as well as now, to have risked life and limb to save fellow-creatures from the sea, but ordinary boats they knew could not live in such a storm.

Among the watchers there stood Jim Cuttance. He had been drinking at a public-house in Penzance, and was at the time, to use his own expression, "three sheets in the wind" — that is, about half-drunk. What his business was nobody knew, and we shall not inquire, but he was the first to express his belief that the turret and bridge of the Wherry Mine would give way. As he spoke a vivid flash of lightning revealed the stout timbers of the mine standing bravely in the storm, each beam and chain painted black and sharp against the illumined sky and the foaming sea.

"She have stud out many a gale," observed a weather-beaten old seaman; "p'raps she won't go down yet."

"I do hope she won't," observed another.

"She haven't got a chance," said Cuttance.

Just then another flash came, and there arose a sharp cry of alarm from the crowd, for a ship was seen driving before the gale close in upon the land, so close that she seemed to have risen there by magic, and appeared to tower almost over the heads of the people. The moments of darkness that succeeded were spent in breathless, intense anxiety. The flashes, which had been fast enough before, seemed to have ceased altogether now; but again the lightning gleamed — bright as full moonlight, and again the ship was seen, nearer than before — close on the bridge of the mine.

"'Tis the Yankee ship broken from her anchors in Gwavus Lake," exclaimed a voice.

The thunder-peal that followed was succeeded by a crash of rending timber and flying bolts that almost emulated the thunder. Certainly it told with greater power on the nerves of those who heard it.

Once again the lightning flashed, and for a moment the American vessel was seen driving away before the wind, but no vestige of Wherry Mine remained. The bridge and all connected with it had been completely carried away, and its shattered remnants were engulfed in the foaming sea.

It deserved a better fate; but its course was run, and its hour had come. It passed away that stormy night, and now nothing remains but a few indications of its shaft-mouth, visible at low water, to tell of one of the boldest and most singular of mining enterprises ever undertaken and carried out by man.

There was one spectator of this imposing scene who was not very deeply impressed by it. Jim Cuttance cared not a straw for storms or wrecks, so long as he himself was safe from their influence. Besides, he had other work in hand that night, so he left the watchers on the beach soon after the destruction of the bridge. Buttoning his coat up to the neck, and pulling his sou'-wester tight over his brows, he walked smartly along the road to Newlyn, while many of the fishermen ran down to the beach to render help to the vessel.

Between the town of Penzance and the village of Newlyn several old boats lay on the grass above high-water mark. Here the smuggler stopped and gave a loud whistle. He listened a moment and than repeated it still louder. He was answered by a similar signal, and four men in sailor's garb, issuing from behind one of the boats, advanced to meet him.

"All right, Bill?" inquired Cuttance.

"All right, sur," was the reply.

"Didn't I tell 'ee to leave them things behind?" said Cuttance sternly, as he pointed to the butt of a pistol which protruded from the breast-pocket of one of the men; "sure we don't require powder and lead to overcome an old man!"

"No more do we need a party o' five to do it," replied the man doggedly.

To this Cuttance vouchsafed no reply, but, plucking the weapon from the man, he tossed it far into the sea, and, without further remark, walked towards the fishing village, followed by his men.

By this time the thunder and rain had abated considerably, but the gale blew with increased violence, and, as there were neither moon nor stars, the darkness was so intense that men less acquainted with the locality would have been obliged to proceed with caution. But the smugglers knew every foot of the ground between the Lizard and the Land's End, and they advanced with rapid strides until they reached the low wall that encompassed, but could not be said to guard, old Mr. Hitchin's garden-plot.

The hour was suited for deeds of darkness, being a little after midnight, and the noise of the gale favoured the burglars, who leaped the wall with ease and approached the back of the cottage.

In ordinary circumstances Hitchin would have been in bed, and Cuttance knew his habits sufficiently to be aware of this; his surprise, therefore, was great when he found lights burning, and greater still when, peeping through a chink of the window-shutter, he observed two stout fellows seated at the old man's table. Charles Tregarthen he had never seen before, and, as Oliver Trembath sat with his back to the window, he could not recognise him.

"There's company wi' the owld man," said Cuttance, returning to his comrades; "two men, young and stout, but we do knaw how to manage they!"

This was said by way of an appeal, and was received with a grin by the others, and a brief recommendation to go to work without delay.

For a few minutes they whispered together as to the plan of attack, and then, having agreed on that point, they separated. Cuttance and the man whom he had called Bill, went to the window of the room in which Hitchin and his guests were seated, and stationed themselves on either side of it. The sill was not more than breast high. The other three men quickly returned, bearing a heavy boat's-mast, which they meant to use as a battering-ram. It had been arranged that Cuttance should throw up the window, and, at the same moment, his comrades should rush at the shutter with the mast. The leader could not see their faces, but there was light sufficient to enable him to distinguish their dark forms standing in the attitude of readiness. He therefore stepped forward and made a powerful effort to force up the window, but it resisted him, although it shook violently.

Those inside sprang up at the sound, and the smugglers sank down, as if by mutual consent, among the bushes which grew thickly near the window.

"I told you it was only the wind," said Oliver Trembath, who had opened the shutter and gazed through the window for some time into the darkness, where, of course, he saw nothing.

Well was it for him that Cuttance refused to follow Bill's advice, which was to charge him through the window with the mast. The former knew that, with the window fastened, it would be impossible to force an entrance in the face of such a youth as Tregarthen, even although they succeeded in rendering the other *hors de combat*, so he restrained Bill, and awaited his opportunity.

Oliver's remark appeared to be corroborated by a gust of wind which came while he was speaking, and shook the window-frame violently.

"There it is again," he said, turning to his host with a smile. "Depend upon it, they won't trouble you on such a night as this."

He closed and refastened the shutter as he spoke, and they all returned to their places at the table.

Unfortunately Oliver had not thought of examining the fastening of the window itself. Had he done so, he would have seen that it was almost wrenched away. Cuttance saw this, however, and resolved to make sure work of it next time.

When the men with the battering-ram were again in position, he and Bill applied their united strength to the window, and it instantly flew up to the top. At same moment, bolts and bars gave way, and the shutter went in with a crash. Making use of the mast as a rest, Cuttance sprang on the window-sill and leaped into the room.

The whole thing was done with such speed, and, if we may so express it, with such simultaneity of action, that the bold smuggler stood before the astonished inmates almost as soon as they could leap from their chairs. Cuttance ducked to evade a terrific blow which Oliver aimed at him with his fist, and in another instant grappled with him. Tregarthen rushed to the window in time to meet Bill, on whose forehead he planted a blow so effectual that that worthy fell back into the arms of his friends, who considerately let him drop to the ground, and made a united assault on Charlie.

Had Oliver Trembath possessed his wonted vigour, he would speedily have overcome his adversary despite his great strength, but his recent illness had weakened him a little, so that the two were pretty equally matched. The consequence was that, neither daring to loosen his hold in order to strike an effective blow, each had to devote all his energies to throw the other, in which effort they wrenched, thrust, and swung each other so violently round the room that chairs and tables were overturned and smashed, and poor old Hitchin had enough to do to avoid being floored in the *mêlée*, and to preserve from destruction the candle which lighted the scene of the combat.

At first Oliver had tried to free his right hand in order to strike, but, finding this impossible, he attempted to throw the smuggler, and, with this end in view, lifted him bodily in the air and dashed him down, but Cuttance managed to throw out a leg and meet the ground with his foot, which saved him. He was a noted wrestler. He could give the famous Cornish hug with the fervour of a black bear, and knew all the mysteries of the science. Often had he displayed his great muscular power and skill in the ring, where "wrestlers" were wont to engage in those combats of which the poet writes:

> *"They rush, impetuous, with a shock*
> *Their arms implicit, rigid, lock;*
> *They twist; they trip; their limbs are mixed;*
> *As one they move, as one stand fixed.*
> *Now plant their feet in wider space,*
> *And stand like statues on their base."*

But never before had Jim Cuttance had to deal with such a man as Oliver Trembath, who swung him about among the chairs, and crashed him through the tables, until, seizing a sudden opportunity, he succeeded in flinging him flat on the floor, where he held him down, and planted his knee on his chest with such force that he nearly squeezed all the breath out of him.

No word did Jim Cuttance utter, for he was incapable of speech, but the colour of his face and his protruding tongue induced Oliver to remove his knee.

Meanwhile Charlie Tregarthen had enough to do at the window. After he had tumbled Bill out, as we have described, two of the other men sprang at him, and, seizing him by the collar of his coat, attempted to drag him out. One of these he succeeded in overthrowing by a kick on the chest, but his place was instantly taken by the third of the bearers of the battering-ram, and for a few minutes the struggle was fierce but undecided. Suddenly there arose a great shout, and all three tumbled head over heels into the shrubbery.

It was at this moment that Oliver rose from his prostrate foe. He at once sprang to the rescue; leaped out of the window, and was in the act of launching a blow at the head of the first man he encountered, when a voice shouted — "Hold on, sur."

It is certain that Oliver would have declined to hold on, had not the voice sounded familiar. He held his hand, and next moment Charlie appeared in the light of the window dragging a struggling man after him by the nape of the neck. At the same time Joe Tonkin came forward trailing another man by the hair of the head.

"Has Cuttance got off?" inquired Tonkin.

"No," replied Oliver, leaping back into the room, just in time to prevent Jim, who had recovered, from making his escape.

"Now, my man, keep quiet," said Oliver, thrusting him down into a chair. "You and I have met before, and you know that it is useless to attempt resistance."

Cuttance vouchsafed no reply, but sat still with a dogged expression on his weather-beaten visage.

Hitchin, whose nerves were much shaken by the scene of which he had been a trembling spectator, soon produced ropes, with which the prisoners were bound, and then they were conducted to a place of safe keeping — each of the victors leading the man he had secured, and old Hitchin going before — an excited advance-guard. The two men whom Tregarthen knocked down had recovered, and made their escape just before the fight closed.

Oliver Trembath walked first in the procession, leading Jim Cuttance.

"I gave you credit for a more manly spirit than this," said Oliver, as he walked along. "How could you make so cowardly an attack on an old man?"

Cuttance made no reply, and Oliver felt sorry that he had spoken, for the remembrance of the incident at the Land's End was strong upon him, and he would have given all he possessed to have had no hand in delivering the smuggler up to justice. At the same time he felt that the attempt of Cuttance was a dastardly one, and that duty required him to act as he did.

It seemed to Oliver as if Joe Tonkin had divined his thoughts, for at that moment he pushed close to him and whispered in his ear, "Jim Cuttance didn't mean to rob th' owld man, sur. He only wanted to give he a fright, an' make un pay what he did owe un."

This was a new light on the subject to Oliver, who at once formed his resolution and acted on it.

"Cuttance," he said, "it is not unlikely that, if brought to justice, you will swing for this night's adventure."

He paused and glanced at the face of his prisoner, who still maintained rigid silence.

"Well," continued our hero, "I believe that your intentions against Mr. Hitchin were not so bad as they would appear to be —"

"Who told 'ee that?" asked the smuggler sternly.

"No matter," replied Oliver, drawing a knife from his pocket, with which he deliberately cut the cords that bound his prisoner. "There — you are free. I hope that you will make better use of your freedom in time to come than you have in time past, although I doubt it much; but remember that I have repaid the debt I owe you."

"Nay," replied Cuttance, still continuing to walk close to his companion's side. "I did give you life. You have but given me liberty."

"I'd advise you to take advantage of that liberty without delay," said Oliver, somewhat nettled by the man's remark, as well as by his cool composure, "else your liberty may be again taken from you, in which case I would not give much for your life."

"If you do not assist, there is no one here who can take me *now*," replied Cuttance, with a smile. "However, I'm not ungrateful — good-night."

As he said this, the smuggler turned sharp to the right into one of the numerous narrow passages which divide the dwellings of Newlyn, and disappeared.

Charles Tregarthen, who was as sharp as a needle, observed this, and, leaving his man in charge of Tonkin, darted after the fugitive. He soon returned, however, wiping the perspiration from his brow, and declaring that he had well-nigh lost himself in his vain endeavours to find the smuggler.

"How in all the world did you manage to let him go?" he demanded somewhat sharply of Oliver.

"Why, Charlie," replied his friend, with a laugh, "you know I have not been trained to the duties of a policeman, and it has always been said that Jim Cuttance was a slippery eel. However, he's gone now, so we had better have the others placed in safe custody as soon as possible."

Saying this he passed his arm through that of old Mr. Hitchin, and soon after the smugglers were duly incarcerated in the lock-up of Penzance.

CHAPTER XXIV.

Exhibits the Managing Director and the Secretary of Wheal Dooem in Confidential Circumstances, and Introduces the Subject of "Locals".

About this time that energetic promoter of mining operations, Mr. George Augustus Clearemout, found it necessary to revisit Cornwall.

He was seated in an easy-chair in a snug little back-office, or board-room, in one of the airiest little streets of the City of London, when this necessity became apparent to him. Mr. Clearemout did not appear to have much to do at that particular time, for he contented himself with tapping the arm of his easy-chair with the knuckles of his right hand, while he twirled his gold watch-key with his left, and smiled occasionally.

To judge from appearances it seemed that things in general were prospering with George Augustus. Everything about him was new, and, we might almost say, gorgeous. His coat and vest and pantaloons had a look and a cut about them that told of an extremely fashionable tailor, and a correspondingly fashionable price. His rings, of which he wore several, were massive, one of them being a diamond ring of considerable value. His boots were faultlessly made, quite new, and polished so highly that it dazzled one to look at them, while his linen, of which he displayed a large quantity on the breast, was as white as snow – not London snow, of course! Altogether Mr. G.A. Clearemout was a most imposing personage.

"Come in," he said, in a voice that sounded like the deep soft whisper of a trombone.

The individual who had occasioned the command by tapping at the door, opened it just enough to admit his head, which he thrust into the room. It was a shaggy red head belonging to a lad of apparently eighteen; its chief characteristics being a prolonged nose and a retracted chin, with a gash for a mouth, and two blue holes for eyes.

"Please, sir, Mr. Muddle," said the youth.

"Admit Mr. Muddle."

The head disappeared, and immediately after a gentleman sauntered into the room, and flung himself lazily into the empty armchair which stood at the fireplace *vis-à-vis* to the one in which Mr. Clearemout sat, explaining that he would not have been so ceremonious had he not fancied that his friend was engaged with some one on business.

"How are you, Jack?" said George Augustus.

"Pretty bobbish," replied Jack. (He was the same Jack whom we have already introduced as being Mr. Clearemout's friend and kindred spirit.)

"Any news?" inquired Mr. Clearemout.

"No, nothing moving," said Jack languidly.

"H'm, I see it is time to stir now, Jack, for the wheel of fortune is apt to get stiff and creaky if we don't grease her now and then and give her a jog. Here is a little pot of grease which I have been concocting and intend to lay on immediately."

He took a slip of paper from a large pocket-book which lay at his elbow on the new green cloth-covered table, and handed it to his friend, who slowly opened and read it in a slovenly way, mumbling the most of it as he went on:

"**Wheal Dooem,**

"'In St. Just, Cornwall — mumble — *m-m* — in 10,000 shares. An old mine, *m-m* — every reason to believe — m-m — splendid lodes visible from — *m-m*. Depth of Adit fifty fathoms — *m-m* — depth below Adit ninety fathoms. Pumps, whims, engines, etc., in good working order — *m-m* — little expense — Landowners, Messrs. — *m* — Manager at the Mine, Captain Trembleforem — *m-m* — thirteen men, four females, and two boys — *m-m* — water — wheels — stamps — *m-m* — Managing Director, George Augustus Clearemout, Esq., 99 New Gull Street, London — *m-m* — Secretary, John Muddle, Esq. — *ahem* — '"

"But, I say, it won't do to publish anything of this sort just yet, you know," said Secretary Jack in a remonstrative tone, "for there's nothing doing at all, I believe."

"I beg your pardon," replied the managing director, "there is a good deal doing. I have written to St. Just appointing the local manager, and it is probable that things are really under way by this time; besides, I shall set out for Cornwall tomorrow to superintend matters, leaving my able secretary in charge here in the meantime, and when he hears from me this paper may be completed and advertised."

"I say, it looks awful real-like, don't it?" said Jack, with a grin. "Only fancy if it should turn out to be a good mine after all — what a lark *that* would be! and it might, you know, for it *was* a real one once, wasn't it? And if you set a few fellows to sink the what-d'ye-call-'ems and drive the thingumbobs, it is possible they may come upon tin and copper, or something of that sort — wouldn't it be jolly?"

"Of course it would, and that is the very thing that gives zest to it. It's a speculation, not a swindle by any means, and admirably suits our easy consciences. But, I say, Jack, you *must* break yourself off talking slang. It will never do to have the secretary of the Great Wheal Dooem Mining Company talk like a street boy. Besides, I hate slang even in a blackguard — not to mention a blackleg — so you must give it up, Jack, you really must, else you'll ruin the concern at the very beginning."

Secretary Jack started into animation at this.

"Why, George," he said, drawing himself up, "I can throw it off when I please. Look here — suppose yourself an inquiring speculator — ahem! I assure you, sir, that the prospects of this mine are most brilliant, and the discoveries that have been made in it since we commenced operations are incredible — absolutely incredible, sir. Some of the lodes (that's the word, isn't it?) are immensely rich, and upwards of a hundred feet thick, while the part that runs under the sea, or *is* to run under the sea, at a depth of three thousand fathoms, is probably as rich in copper ore as the celebrated Botallack, whose majestic headland, bristling with machinery, overhangs the raging billows of the wide Atlantic, etc., etc. O George, it's a great lark entirely!"

"You'll have to learn your lesson a little better, else you'll make a great mess of it," said Clearemout.

"A muddle of it — according to my name and destiny, George," said the secretary; "a muddle of it, and a fortune *by* it."

Here the secretary threw himself back in the easy-chair, and grinned at the opposite wall, where his eye fell on a large picture, which changed the grin into a stare of surprise.

"What have we here, George," he said, rising, and fitting a gold glass in his eye — "not a portrait of Wheal Dooem, is it?"

"You have guessed right," replied the other. "I made a few sketches on the spot, and got a celebrated artist to put them together, which he has done, you see, with considerable effect. Here, in the foreground, you observe," continued the managing director, taking up a new white pointer, "stands Wheal Dooem, on a prominent crag overlooking the Atlantic, with Gurnard's Head just beyond. Farther over, we have the celebrated Levant Mine, and the famous Botallack, and the great Wheal Owles, and a crowd of other more or less noted mines, with Cape Cornwall, and the Land's End, and Tolpedenpenwith in the middle-distance, and the celebrated Logan Rock behind them, while we have Mounts Bay, with the beautiful town of Penzance, and St. Michael's Mount, and the Lizard in the background, with France in the remote distance."

"Dear, *dear* me! quite a geographical study, I declare," exclaimed Secretary Jack, examining the painting with some care. "Can you really see all these places at once from Wheal Dooem?"

"Not exactly from Wheal Dooem, Jack, but if you were to go up in a balloon a few hundred yards above the spot where it stands, you might see 'em all on a very clear day, if your eyes were good. The fact is, that I regard this picture as a triumph of art, exhibiting powerfully what is by artists termed 'bringing together' and great 'breadth,' united with exceedingly minute detail. The colouring too, is high — very high indeed, and the *chiaroscuro* is perfect —"

"Ha!" interposed Jack, "all the *chiar* being on the surface, and the *oscuro* down in the mine, eh?"

"Exactly so," replied Clearemout. "It is a splendid picture. The artist regards it as his *chef d'oeuvre*, and you must explain it to all who come to the office, as well as those magnificent geological sections rolled-up in the corner, which it would be well, by the way, to have hung up without delay. They arrived only this morning. And now, Jack, having explained these matters, I will leave you, to study them at your leisure, while I prepare for my journey to Cornwall, where, by the way, I have my eye upon a sweet little girl, whose uncle, I believe, has lots of tin, both in the real and figurative sense of the word. Something may come of it — who knows?"

Next morning saw the managing director on the road, and in due time he found his way by coach, kittereen, and gig to St. Just, where, as before, he was hospitably received by old Mr. Donnithorne.

That gentleman's buoyancy of spirit, however, was not quite so great as it had been a few months before, but that did not much affect the, spirits of Clearemout, who found good Mrs. Donnithorne as motherly, and Rose Ellis as sweet, as ever.

It happened at this time that Oliver Trembath had occasion to go to London about some matter relating to his deceased mother's affairs, so the managing director had the field all to himself. He therefore spent his time agreeably in looking after the affairs of Wheal Dooem during the day, and making love to Rose Ellis in the evening.

Poor Rose was by no means a flirt, but she was an innocent, straightforward girl, ignorant of many of the world's ways, and of a trusting disposition. She found the conversation of Mr. Clearemout agreeable, and did not attempt to conceal the fact. Mr. Clearemout's vanity induced him to set this down to a tender feeling, although Rose never consciously gave him, by word or look, the slightest reason to come to such a conclusion.

One forenoon Mr. Clearemout was sitting in Mr. Donnithorne's dining-room conversing with Rose and Mrs. Donnithorne, when the old gentleman entered and sat down beside them.

"I had almost forgotten the original object of my visit this morning," said the managing director, with a smile, and a glance at Rose; "the fact is that I am in want of a man to work at Wheal Dooem, a steady, trustworthy man, who would be fit to take charge — become a sort of overseer; can you recommend one?"

Mr. Donnithorne paused for a moment to reflect, but Mrs. Donnithorne deeming reflection quite unnecessary, at once replied — "Why, there are many such men in St. Just. There's John Cock, as good a man as you could find in all the parish, and David Trevarrow, and James Penrose — he's a first-rate man; You remember him, my dear?" (turning to her worse half) — "one of our locals, you know."

"Yes, my dear, I remember him perfectly. — You could not, Mr. Clearemout, get a better man, I should say."

"I think you observed, madam," said Mr. Clearemout, "that this man is a 'local.' Pray, what is a local?"

Rose gave one of her little laughs at this point, and her worthy aunt exclaimed — "La! Mr. Clearemout, don't you know what a local preacher is?"

"Oh! a *preacher*? Connected with the Methodist body, I presume?"

"Yes, and a first-rate man, I assure you."

"But," said Mr. Clearemout, with a smile, "I want a miner, not a preacher."

"Well, he is a miner, and a good one too —"

"Allow *me* to explain, my dear," said Mr. Donnithorne, interrupting his spouse. "You may not be aware, sir, that many of our miners are men of considerable mental ability, and some of them possess such power of speech, and so earnest a spirit, that the Wesleyan body have appointed them to the office of local preaching. They do not become ministers, however, nor are they liable to be sent out of the district like them. They don't give up their ordinary calling, but are appointed to preach in the various chapels of the district in which they reside, and thus we accomplish an amount of work which could not possibly be overtaken by the ordinary ministry."

"Indeed! but are they not untrained men, liable to teach erroneous doctrine?" asked Mr. Clearemout.

"They are not altogether untrained men," replied Mr. Donnithorne. "They are subjected to a searching examination, and must give full proof of their Christianity, knowledge, and ability before being appointed."

"And good, excellent Christian men many of them are," observed Mrs. Donnithorne, with much fervour.

"Quite true," said her husband. "This James Penrose is one of our best local preachers, and sometimes officiates in our principal chapel. I confess, however, that those who have the management of this matter are not always very judicious in their appointments. Some of our young men are sorely tempted to show off their acquirements, and preach *themselves* instead of the gospel, and there are one or two whom I could mention whose hearts are all right, but whose brains are so muddled and empty that they are utterly unfit to teach their fellows. We must not, however, look for perfection in this world, Mr. Clearemout. A little chaff will always remain among the wheat. There is no system without some imperfection, and I am convinced that upon the whole our system of appointing local preachers is a first-rate one. At all events it works well, which is one of the best proofs of its excellence."

"Perhaps so," said Mr. Clearemout, with the air of a man who did not choose to express an opinion on the subject; "nevertheless I had rather have a man who was *not* a local preacher."

"You can see and hear him, and judge for yourself," said Mr. Donnithorne; "for he is, I believe, to preach in our chapel tomorrow, and if you will accept of a seat in our pew it will afford my wife and myself much —"

"Thank you," interrupted Mr. Clearemout; "I shall be very glad to take advantage of your kind offer. Service, you say, begins at —"

"Ten precisely," said Mr. Donnithorne.

CHAPTER XXV.

*Shows the Miner in his Sunday Garb, and Astonishes
Clearemout, besides Relating some Incidents of an Accident.*

The sun rose bright and hot on Sunday morning, but the little birds were up before the great luminary, singing their morning hymn with noisy delight. It was a peaceful day. The wind was at rest and the sea was calm. In the ancient town of St. Just it was peculiarly peaceful, for the numerous and untiring "stamps" — which all the week had continued their clang and clatter, morning, noon, and night, without intermission — found rest on that hallowed day, and the great engines ceased to bow their massive heads, with the exception of those that worked the pumps. Even these, however, were required to do as little work as was compatible with the due drainage of the mines, and as their huge pulsations were intermittent — few and far between — they did not succeed in disturbing the universal serenity of the morning.

If there are in this country men who, more than any other, need repose, we should say they are the miners of Cornwall, for their week's work is exhausting far beyond that of most other labourers in the kingdom. Perhaps the herculean men employed in malleable-iron works toil as severely, but, besides the cheering consciousness of being well paid for their labour, these men exert their powers in the midst of sunlight and fresh air, while the miners toil in bad air, and get little pay in hard times. Sunday is indeed to them the Sabbath-day — it is literally what that word signifies, a day of much-required rest for body, soul, and spirit.

Pity that the good old word which God gave us is not more universally used among Christians! Would it not have been better that the translation Rest-day had been adopted, so that even ignorant men might have understood its true signification, than that we should have saddled it with a heathen name, to be an apple of discord in all generations? However, Sunday it is, so Sunday it will stand, we suppose, as long as the world lasts. After all, despite its faulty origin, that word is invested with old and hallowed associations in the minds of many, so we enter our protest against the folly of our forefathers very humbly, beseeching those who are prone to become nettled on this subject to excuse our audacity!

Well, as we have said, the Sunday morning to which we refer was peaceful; so would have been Maggot's household had Maggot's youngest baby never been born; but, having been born, that robust cherub asserted his right to freedom of action more violently than ever did the most rabid Radical or tyrannical Tory. He "swarmed" about the house, and kicked and yelled his uttermost, to the great distress of poor little Grace, whose anxiety to get him ready for chapel was gradually becoming feverish. But baby Maggot had as much objection to go to chapel as his wicked father, who was at that time enjoying a pipe on the cliffs, and intended to leave his family to the escort of David Trevarrow. Fortunately, baby gave in about half-past nine, so that little Grace had him washed and dressed, and on his way to chapel in pretty good time, all things considered.

No one who entered the Wesleyan Chapel of St. Just that morning for the first time could have imagined that a large proportion of the well-dressed people who filled the pews were miners and balmaidens. Some of the latter were elegantly, we might almost say gorgeously, attired, insomuch that, but for their hands and speech, they might almost have passed for ladies of fashion. The very latest thing in bonnets, and the newest mantles, were to be seen on their pretty heads and shapely shoulders.

As we have said before, and now repeat, this circumstance arose from the frequency of the visits of the individual styled "Johnny Fortnight," whose great aim and end in life is to supply miners, chiefly the females among them, with the necessaries, and unnecessaries, of wearing apparel.

When the managing director entered Mr. Donnithorne's pew and sat down beside his buxom hostess, he felt, but of course was much too well bred to express astonishment; for his host had told him that a large number of the people who attended the chapel were miners, and for a time he failed to see any of the class whom he had hitherto been accustomed to associate with rusty-red and torn garbs, and dirty hands and faces. But he soon observed that many of the stalwart, serious-looking men with black coats and white linen, had strong, muscular hands, with hard-looking knuckles, which, in some instances, exhibited old or recent cuts and bruises.

It was a new sight for the managing director to behold the large and apparently well-off families filing into the pews, for, to say truth, Mr. Clearemout was not much in the habit of attending church, and he had never before entered a Methodist chapel. He watched with much curiosity the gradual filling of the seats, and the grave, quiet demeanour of the people. Especially interesting was it when Maggot's family came in and sat down, with the baby Maggot in charge of little Grace. Mr. Clearemout had met Maggot, and had seen his family; but interest gave place to astonishment when Mrs. Penrose walked into the church, backed by her sixteen children, the eldest males among whom were miners, and the eldest females tin-dressers, while the little males and females aspired to be miners and tin-dressers in the course of time.

"That's Penrose's family," whispered Mr. Donnithorne to his guest.

"What! the local's family?"

Mr. Donnithorne nodded.

Soon after, a tall, gentlemanly man ascended the pulpit.

The managing director was disappointed. He had come there to hear a miner preach, and behold, a clergyman!

"Who is he?" inquired Clearemout.

But Mr. Donnithorne did not answer. He was looking up the hymn for Mrs. D., who, being short-sighted, claimed exemption from the duty of "looking up" anything. Besides, he was a kind, good man at heart — though rather fond of smuggling and given to the bottle, according to Oliver Trembath's account of him — and liked to pay his wife little attentions.

But there were still greater novelties in store for the London man that morning. It was new to him to hear John Wesley's beautiful hymns sung to equally beautiful tunes, which were not, however, unfamiliar to his ear, and sung with a degree of fervour that quite drowned his own voice, powerful and deep though it was. It was a new and impressive thing to hear the thrilling, earnest tones of the preacher as he offered up an eloquent extempore prayer — to the petitions in which many of the people in the congregation gave utterance at times to startlingly fervent and loud responses — not in set phraseology, but in words that were called forth by the nature of each petition, such as "Glory to God," "Amen," "Thanks be to Him" — showing that the worshippers followed and sympathised with their spokesman, thus making his prayer their own. But the newest thing of all was to hear the preacher deliver an eloquent, earnest, able, and well-digested sermon, without book or note, in the same natural tone of voice with which a man might address his fellow in the street — a style of address which riveted the attention of the hearers, induced them to expect that he had really something important to say to them, and that he thoroughly believed in the truth of what he said.

"A powerful man," observed the managing director as they went out; "your clergyman, I suppose?"

"No, sir," replied Mr. Donnithorne with a chuckle, "our minister is preaching elsewhere today. That was James Penrose."

"What! the miner?" exclaimed Clearemout in astonishment.

"Ay, the local preacher too."

"Why, the man spoke like Demosthenes, and quoted Bacon, Locke, Milton, and I know not whom all — you amaze me," said Mr. Clearemout. "Surely all your local preachers are not equal to this one."

"Alas, no! some of the young ones are indeed able enough to spout poetry and quote old authors, and too fond they are of doing so; nevertheless, as I have said to you before, most of the local preachers are sober-minded, sterling Christian men, and a few of them have eminent capabilities. Had Penrose been a younger man, he would probably have entered the ministry, but being above forty, with an uncommonly large family, he thinks it his duty to remain as he is, and do as much good as he can."

"But surely he might find employment better suited to his talents?" said Clearemout.

"There is not much scope in St. Just," replied Mr. Donnithorne, with a smile, "and it is a serious thing for a man in his circumstances to change his abode and vocation. No, no, I think he is right to remain a miner."

"Well, I confess that I admire his talents," returned Clearemout, "but I still think that an ordinary miner would suit me better."

"Well, I know of one who will suit you admirably. He is common enough to look at, and if you will accompany me into the mine tomorrow I'll introduce you to him. I'm not fond of descending the ladders nowadays, though I could do it very well when a youth, but as the man I speak of works in one of the levels near the surface, I'll be glad to go down with you, and Captain Dan shall lead us."

True to his word, the old gentleman met Mr. Clearemout the following morning at nine o'clock, and accompanied him down into the mine.

Their descent was unmarked by anything particular at first. They wore the usual suit of underground clothing, and each carried a lighted candle attached to his hat. After descending about thirty fathoms they left the main shaft and traversed the windings of a level until they came to a place where the sound of voices and hammers indicated that the miners were working. In a few seconds they reached the end of the level.

Here two men were "driving" the level, and another — a very tall, powerful man — was standing in a hole driven up slanting-ways into the roof, and cutting the rock above his head. His attitude and aspect were extremely picturesque, standing as he did on a raised platform with his legs firmly planted, his muscular arms raised above him to cut the rock overhead, and the candle so placed as to cause his figure to appear almost black and unnaturally gigantic.

"Stay a minute, Captain Dan," said Mr. Donnithorne. "That, Mr. Clearemout, is the man I spoke of — what think you of his personal appearance?"

Clearemout did not reply for a few minutes, but stood silently watching the man as he continued to wield his heavy hammer with powerful strokes — delivering each with a species of gasp which indicated not exhaustion, but the stern vigour with which it was given.

"He'll do," said Clearemout in a decided tone.

"Hallo! James," shouted Mr. Donnithorne.

"Hallo! sir," answered the man looking back over his shoulder.

"There's a gentleman here who wants to speak to you."

The miner flung down his tools, which clattered loudly on the hard rock, as he leaped from his perch with the agility of one whose muscles are all in full and constant exercise.

"What! not the local —"

Before the managing director could finish his sentence Mr. Donnithorne introduced him to James Penrose, and left the two for a time to talk together.

It need scarcely be added that Clearemout was quite willing to avail himself of the services of the "local," but the local did not meet his proposals so readily as he would have wished. Penrose was a cautious man, and said he would call on Mr. Clearemout in the evening after he had had time to consider the matter.

With this reply the other was fain to rest satisfied, and shortly after he returned to the bottom of the shaft with his friends, leaving the hardy miner to pursue his work.

At the bottom of the shaft they were accosted by a, sturdy little man, who told them that a large piece of timber was being sent down the shaft, and it would be advisable to wait until it reached the bottom.

"Is it on the way, Spankey?" asked Captain Dan.

"Iss, sur, if it haven't walked into the thirty-fathom level in passin'."

Spankey was a humorous individual addicted to joking.

"Are you married, Spankey?" asked Clearemout, looking down with a grin at the dirty little fellow beside him.

"Iss, sur. Had, two wives, an' the third wan is waitin' for me, 'spose."

"Any children, Spankey?"

"Iss, six, countin' the wan that died before it could spaik."

At this point the beam was heard coming down. In a few seconds it made its appearance, and was hauled a little to one side by Spankey, who proceeded to unwind the chain that had supported it.

"I'll give 'em the signal, Captain Dan, to haul up the chain before thee do go on the ladders."

The signal was given accordingly, and the engine immediately began to draw up the chain by which the beam had been lowered.

This chain had a hook at one end of it, and, as ill-luck would have it, the hook caught Spankey by the right leg of his trousers, and whisked him off his feet. Almost before those beside him could conceive what had happened, the unfortunate man went up the shaft feet foremost, with a succession of dreadful yells, in the midst of which could be heard a fearful rending of strong linen.

Fortunately for Spankey, his nether garments were not only strong, but new, so that when the rend came to the seam at the foot, it held on, else had that facetious miner come down the shaft much faster than he went up, and left his brains at the bottom as a memorial of the shocking event!

With palpitating hearts, Captain Dan, Clearemout, and old Donnithorne ran up the ladders as fast as they could. In a few minutes they reached the thirty-fathom level, and here, to their great relief, they found Spankey supported in the arms of stout Joe Tonkin.

That worthy, true to his promise to Oliver Trembath, had gone to work in Botallack Mine, and had that very day commenced operations in the thirty-fathom level referred to. Hearing the terrible screams of Spankey, he rushed to the end of the level just as the unfortunate man was passing it. The risk was great, but Tonkin was accustomed to risks, and prompt to act. He flung his arms round Spankey, drew him forcibly into the level, and held on for life. There was a terrible rend; the leg of the trousers gave way at the hip, and went flapping up to grass, leaving the horrified miner behind.

"Not gone dead yet, sur, but goin' fast," was Spankey's pathetic reply to Captain Dan's anxious inquiries.

It was found, however, that, beyond the fright, the man had received no damage whatever.

The only other noteworthy fact in reference to this incident is, that when Captain Dan and his companions reached the surface, they were met by the lander, who, with a face as pale as a ghost, held up the torn garment. Great was this man's relief, and loud the fit of laughter with which he expressed it, when Spankey, issuing from the mouth of the shaft, presented his naked limb, and claimed the leg of his trousers!

CHAPTER XXVI.

Tells of a Discovery and a Disaster.

That afternoon another accident occurred in the mine, which was of a much more serious nature than the one just recorded, and which interfered somewhat with the plans of the managing director of the Great Wheal Dooem Mining Company.

Not long after his interview with Clearemout, James Penrose finished a blast-hole, and called to Zackey Maggot to fetch the fuse.

Zackey had been working for a week past in connection with Penrose, and, at the time he was called, was engaged in his wonted occupation of pounding "tamping" wherewith to fill the hole.

Wherever Zackey chanced to be at work, he always made himself as comfortable as circumstances would admit of. At the present time he had discovered a little hollow or recess in the wall of the level, which he had converted into a private chamber for the nonce.

There was a piece of flat rock on the floor of this recess, which Zackey used as his anvil, and in front of which he kneeled. At his side was a candle, stuck against the wall, where it poured a flood of light on objects in its immediate neighbourhood, and threw the boy's magnified shadow over the floor and against the opposite wall of the level. Above his head was a small shelf, which he had ingeniously fixed in a narrow part of the cell, and on this lay a few candles, a stone bottle of water, a blasting fuse, and part of his lunch, which he had been unable to consume, wrapped in a piece of paper. A small wooden box on the floor, and a couple of pick-hilts, leaning against the wall, completed the furniture of this subterranean grotto.

Zackey, besides being a searcher after metals, possessed an unusual amount of metal in himself. He was one of those earnest, hard working, strong hearted boys who pass into a state of full manhood, do the work of men, and are looked upon as being men, before they have passed out of their "teens." The boy's manhood, which was even at that early period of his life beginning to show itself, consisted not in his looks or his gait, although both were creditable, but in his firmness of purpose and force of character. What Zackey undertook to do he always did. He never left any work in a half-finished state, and he always employed time diligently.

In the mine he commenced to labour the moment he entered, and he never ceased, except during a short period for "kroust," until it was time to shoulder his tools, and mount to the regions of light. Above ground, he was as ready to skylark as the most volatile of his companions, but underground he was a pattern of perseverance — a true Cornish miner in miniature. His energy of character was doubtless due to his reckless father, but his steadiness was the result of "Uncle Davy's" counsel and example.

"Are you coming, Zackey?" shouted Penrose, from the end of the level.

"Iss, I'm comin'," replied the boy, taking the fuse from the shelf, and hastening towards his companion.

Penrose had a peculiar and pleased expression on his countenance, which Zackey observed at once.

"What do 'ee grizzle like that for?" inquired the boy.

"I've come on a splendid bunch of copper, Zackey," replied the man; "you and I shall make money soon. Run away to your work, lad, and come back when you hear the shot go off."

Zackey expressed a hope that the prophecy might come true, and returned to his cell, where he continued pounding diligently — thinking the while of rich ore and a rapid fortune.

There was more reason in these thoughts than one might suppose, for Cornish miners experience variety of fortune. Sometimes a man will labour for weeks and months in unproductive ground, following up a small vein in the hope of its leading into a good lode, and making so little by his hard toil that on pay day of each month he is compelled to ask his employer for "subsist" — or a small advance of money — to enable him to live and go on with his work. Often he is obliged to give up in despair, and change to a more promising part of the mine, or to go to another mine altogether; but, not unfrequently, he is rewarded for his perseverance by coming at last to a rich "lode," or mass, or "bunch" of copper or tin ore, out of which he will rend, in a single month, as much as will entitle him to thirty or forty, or even a hundred pounds, next pay day.

Such pieces of good fortune are not of rare occurrence. Many of the substantial new cottages to be seen in St. Just at the present day have been built by miners who became suddenly fortunate in this way, so that, although the miner of Cornwall always works hard, and often suffers severe privation, he works on with a well-grounded expectation of a sudden burst of temporal sunshine in his otherwise hard lot.

Zackey Maggot was dreaming of some such gleam of good fortune, and patiently pounding away at the tamping, when he heard the explosion of the blast. At the same moment a loud cry rang through the underground caverns. It was one of those terrible, unmistakable cries which chill the blood and thrill the hearts of those who hear them, telling of some awful catastrophe.

The boy leaped up and ran swiftly towards the end of the level, where he called to his companion, but received no answer. The smoke which filled the place was so dense that he could not see, and could scarcely breathe. He ran forward, however, and stumbled over the prostrate form of Penrose. Zackey guessed correctly what had occurred, for the accident was, and alas! still is, too common in the mines. The shot had apparently missed fire. Penrose had gone forward to examine it, and it exploded in his face.

To lift his companion was beyond Zackey's power, to leave him lying in such dense smoke for any length of time would, he knew, ensure his suffocation, so he attempted to drag him away, but the man was too heavy for him. In his extremity the poor boy uttered a wild cry for help, but he shouted in vain, for there was no one else at work in the level. But Zackey was not the boy to give way to despair, or to act thoughtlessly, or in wild haste in this emergency. He suddenly recollected that there was a rope somewhere about the level. He sought for and found it. Fastening an end of it round the body of the man, under the armpits, he so arranged that the knot of the loop should reach a few inches beyond his head, and on this part of the loop he spread a coat, which thus formed a support to the head, and prevented it being dragged along the ground. While engaged in this operation the poor boy was well-nigh suffocated with smoke, and had to run back once to where the air was purer in order to catch a breath or two. Then, returning, he seized the rope, passed it over his shoulder, and bending forward with all his might and main dragged the man slowly but steadily along the floor of the level to a place where the air was comparatively pure.

Leaving him there he quickly fixed a candle in his hat, and carrying another in his hand, to avoid the risk of being left in darkness by an accidental stumble or gust of air, Zackey darted swiftly along the level and ran up the ladders at his utmost speed. Panting for breath, and with eyes almost starting from their sockets, he rushed into the engine-house, and told the man in charge what had occurred; then he dashed away to the counting-house and gave the alarm there, so that, in a very few minutes, a number of men descended the shaft and gathered round the prostrate miner. The doctor who had taken Oliver Trembath's place during his absence was soon in attendance, and found that although no bones had been broken, Penrose's face was badly injured, how deep the injury extended could not at that time be ascertained, but he feared that his eyes had been altogether destroyed.

After the application of some cordial the unfortunate man began to revive, and the first words he uttered were, "Praise the Lord" — evidently in reference to his life having been spared.

"Is that you, Zackey?" he inquired after a few moments.

"No, it is the doctor, my man. Do you feel much pain in your head?" he asked as he knelt beside him.

"Not much; there is a stunned feeling about it, but little pain. You'd better light a candle."

"There are candles burning round you," said the doctor. "Do you not see them? There is one close to your face at this moment."

Penrose made no answer on hearing this, but an expression of deep gravity seemed to settle on the blackened features.

"We must get him up as soon as possible," said the doctor, turning to Captain Dan, who stood at his elbow.

"We're all ready, sir," replied the captain, who had quietly procured ropes and a blanket, while the doctor was examining the wounds.

With great labour and difficulty the injured man was half hauled, half carried, and pushed up the shaft, and laid on the grass.

"Is the sun shining?" he asked in a low voice.

"Iss, it do shine right in thee face, Jim," said one of the miners, brushing away a tear with the back of his hand.

Again the gravity of Penrose's countenance appeared to deepen, but he uttered no other word; so they brought an old door and laid him on it. Six strong men raised it gently on their shoulders, and, with slow steps and downcast faces, they carried the wounded miner home.

CHAPTER XXVII.

Indicates that "We little know what Great Things
from Little Things may rise."

Soon after this accident to James Penrose, the current of events at the mines was diverted from its course by several incidents, which, like the obstructing rocks in a rapid, created some eddies and whirlpools in the lives of those personages with whom this chronicle has to do.

As the beginning of a mighty inundation is oft-times an insignificant-looking leak, and as the cause of a series of great events is not unfrequently a trifling incident, so the noteworthy circumstances which we have still to lay before our readers were brought about by a very small matter – by a baby – *the* baby Maggot!

One morning that cherubical creature opened its eyes at a much earlier hour than usual, and stared at the ceiling of its father's cottage. The sun was rising, and sent its unobstructed rays through the window of Maggot's cottage, where it danced on the ceiling as if its sole purpose in rising had been to amuse the Maggot baby. If so, it was pre-eminently successful in its attempts, for the baby lay and smiled for a long time in silent ecstasy.

Of course, we do not mean to say that the sun itself, or its direct rays, actually danced. No, it was too dignified a luminary for that, but its rays went straight at a small looking-glass which was suspended on the wall opposite to the window, and this being hung so as to slope forward, projected the rays obliquely into a tub of water which was destined for family washing purposes; and from its gently moving surface they were transmitted to the ceiling, where, as aforesaid, they danced, to the immense delight of Maggot junior.

The door of the cottage had been carelessly closed the previous night when the family retired to rest, and a chink of it was open, through which a light draught of summer air came in. This will account for the ripple on the water, which (as every observant reader will note) ought, according to the laws of gravitation, to have lain perfectly still.

The inconstancy of baby Maggot's nature was presently exhibited in his becoming tired of the sun, and the restlessness of his disposition displayed itself in his frantic efforts to get out of bed. Being boxed in with a board, this was not an easy matter, but the urchin's limbs were powerful, and he finally got over the obstruction, sufficiently far to lose his balance, and fall with a sounding flop on the floor.

It is interesting to notice how soon deceit creeps into the hearts of some children! Of course the urchin fell sitting-wise – babies always do so, as surely as cats fall on their feet. In ordinary circumstances he would have intimated the painful mishap with a dreadful yell; but on this particular occasion young Maggot was bent on mischief. Of what sort, he probably had no idea, but there must have been a latent feeling of an intention to be "bad" in some way or other, because, on reaching the ground, he pursed his mouth, opened his eyes very wide, and looked cautiously round to make sure that the noise had awakened no one.

His father, he observed, with a feeling of relief, was absent from home — not a matter of uncommon occurrence, for that worthy man's avocations often called him out at untimeous hours. Mrs. Maggot was in bed snoring, and wrinkling up her nose in consequence of a fly having perched itself obstinately on the point thereof. Zackey, with the red earth of the mine still streaking his manly countenance, was rolled-up like a ball in his own bed in a dark recess of the room, and little Grace Maggot could be seen in the dim perspective of a closet, also sound asleep, in her own neat little bed, with her hair streaming over the pillow, and the "chet" reposing happily on her neck.

But that easily satisfied chet had long ago had more than enough of rest. Its repose was light, and the sound of baby Maggot falling out of bed caused it to rise, yawn, arch its back and tail, and prepare itself for the mingled joys and torments of the opening day. Observing that the urchin rose and staggered with a gleeful expression towards the door, the volatile chet made a dash at him sidewise, and gave him such a fright that he fell over the door step into the road.

Again was that tender babe's deceitfulness of character displayed, for, instead of howling, as he would have done on other occasions, he exercised severe self-restraint, made light of a bruised shin, and, gathering himself up, made off as fast as his fat legs could carry him.

There was something deeply interesting — worthy of the study of a philosopher — in the subsequent actions of that precocious urchin. His powers in the way of walking were not much greater than those of a very tipsy man, and he swayed his arms about a good deal to maintain his balance, especially at the outset of the journey, when he imagined that he heard the maternal voice in anger and the maternal footsteps in pursuit in every puff of wind, grunt of pig, or bark of early-rising cur. His entire soul was engrossed in the one grand, vital, absorbing idea of escape! By degrees, as distance from the paternal roof increased, his fluttering spirit grew calmer and his gait more steady, and the flush of victory gathered on his brow and sparkled in his eye, as the conviction was pressed home upon him that, for the first time in his life, he was *free*! free as the wind of heaven to go where he pleased — to do what he liked — to be *as bad as possible*, without let or hindrance!

Not that baby Maggot had any stronger desire to be absolutely wicked than most other children of his years; but, having learnt from experience that the attempt to gratify any of his desires was usually checked and termed "bad," he naturally felt that a state of delight so intense as that to which he had at last attained, must necessarily be the very quintessence of iniquity. Being resolved to go through with it at all hazards, he felt proportionately wild and reckless. Such a state of commotion was there in his heaving bosom, owing to contradictory and conflicting elements, that he felt at one moment inclined to lie down and shout for joy, and the next, to sink into the earth with terror.

Time, which proverbially works wonderful changes, at length subdued the urchin to a condition of calm goodness and felicity, that would have rejoiced his mother's heart, had it only been brought on in ordinary circumstances at home.

There is a piece of waste ground lying between St. Just and the sea — a sort of common, covered with heath and furze — on which the ancient Britons have left their indelible mark, in the shape of pits and hollows and trenches, with their relative mounds and hillocks. Here, in the days of old, our worthy but illiterate forefathers had grubbed and dug and turned up every square foot of the soil, like a colony of gigantic rabbits, in order to supply the precious metal of the country to the Phoenicians, Jews, and Greeks.

The ground on this common is so riddled with holes of all sizes and shapes, utterly unguarded by any kind of fence, that it requires care on the part of the pedestrian who traverses the place even in daylight. Hence the mothers of St. Just are naturally anxious that the younger members of their families should not go near the common, and the younger members are as naturally anxious that they should visit it.

Thither, in the course of time — for it was not far distant — the baby Maggot naturally trended; proceeding on the principle of "short stages and long rests." Never in his life — so he thought — had he seen such bright and beautiful flowers, such green grass, and such lovely yellow sand, as that which appeared here and there at the mouths of the holes and old shafts, or such a delicious balmy and sweet-scented breeze as that which came off the Atlantic and swept across the common. No wonder that his eyes drank in the beautiful sights, for they had seen little of earth hitherto, save the four walls of his father's cottage and the dead garden wall in front of it; no wonder that his nostrils dilated to receive the sweet odours, for they had up to that date lived upon air which had to cross a noisome and stagnant pool of filth before it entered his father's dwelling; and no wonder that his ears thrilled to hear the carol of the birds, for they had previously been accustomed chiefly to the voices of poultry and pigs, and to the caterwauling of the "chet."

But as every joy has its alloy, so our youthful traveller's feelings began to be modified by a gnawing sensation of hunger, as his usual hour for breakfast approached. Still he wandered on manfully, looking into various dark and deep holes with much interest and a good deal of awe. Some of the old shafts were so deep that no bottom could be seen; others were partially filled up, and varied from five to twenty feet in depth. Some were nearly perpendicular, others were sloped and irregular in form; but all were more or less fringed with gorse bushes in full bloom. In a few cases the old pits were concealed by these bushes.

It is almost unnecessary to say that baby Maggot's progress, on that eventful morn, was — unknown to himself — a series of narrow escapes from beginning to end — no not exactly to the end, for his last adventure could scarcely be deemed an escape. He was standing on the edge of a hole, which was partially concealed by bushes. Endeavouring to peer into it he lost his balance and fell forward. His ready hands grasped the gorse and received innumerable punctures, which drew forth a loud cry. Head foremost he went in, and head foremost he went down full ten feet, when a small bush caught him, and lowered him gently to the ground, but the spot on which he was landed was steep; it sloped towards the bottom of the hole, which turned inwards and became a sort of cavern. Struggling to regain his footing, he slipped and rolled violently to the bottom, where he lay for a few minutes either stunned or too much astonished to move. Then he recovered a little and began to whimper. After which he felt so much better that he arose and attempted to get out of the hole, but slipped and fell back again, whereupon he set up a hideous roar which continued without intermission for a quarter of an hour, when he fell sound asleep, and remained in happy unconsciousness for several hours.

Meanwhile the Maggot family was, as may well be believed, thrown into a state of tremendous agitation. Mrs. Maggot, on making the discovery that baby had succeeded in scaling the barricade, huddled on her garments and roused her progeny to assist in the search. At first she was not alarmed, believing that she should certainly find the self-willed urchin near the house, perhaps in the cottage of the Penroses. But when the cottages in the immediate neighbourhood had been called at, and all the known places of danger round the house examined, without success, the poor woman became frantic with terror, and roused the whole neighbourhood. Every place of possible and impossible concealment was searched, and at last the unhappy mother allowed the terrible thought to enter her mind that baby had actually accomplished the unheard-of feat of reaching the dreaded common, and was perhaps at that moment lying maimed or dead at the bottom of an ancient British shaft!

Immediately a body of volunteers, consisting of men, women, and children, and headed by Mrs. Maggot, hastened to the common to institute a thorough search; but they searched in vain, for the holes were innumerable, and the one in which the baby lay was well concealed by bushes. Besides, the search was somewhat wildly and hastily made, so that some spots were over-searched, while others were almost overlooked.

All that day did Mrs. Maggot and her friends wander to and fro over the common, and never, since the days when Phoenician galleys were moored by St. Michael's Mount, did the eyes of human beings pry so earnestly into these pits and holes. Had tin been their object, they could not have been more eager. Evening came, night drew on apace, and at last the forlorn mother sat down in the centre of a furze bush, and began to weep. But her friends comforted her. They urged her to go home and "'ave a dish o' tay" to strengthen her for the renewal of the search by torch-light. They assured her that the child could easily exist longer than a day without food, and they reminded her that her baby was an exceptional baby, a peculiar baby — like its father, uncommonly strong, and, like its mother, unusually obstinate. The latter sentiment, however, was *thought*, not expressed.

Under the influence of these assurances and persuasions, Mrs. Maggot went home, and, for a short time, the common was deserted.

Now it chanced, curiously enough, that at this identical point of time, Maggot senior was enjoying a pipe and a glass of grog in a celebrated kiddle-e-wink, with his friend Joe Tonkin. This kiddle-e-wink, or low public-house, was known as Un (or Aunt) Jilly's brandy-shop at Bosarne. It was a favourite resort of smugglers, and many a gallon of spirit, free of duty, had been consumed on the premises.

Maggot and his friend were alone in the house at the time, and their conversation had taken a dolorous turn, for many things had occurred of late to disturb the equanimity of the friends. Several ventures in the smuggling way had proved unsuccessful, and the mines did not offer a tempting prospect just then. There had, no doubt, been one or two hopeful veins opened up, and some good "pitches" had been wrought, but these were only small successes, and the luck had not fallen to either of themselves. The recent discovery of a good bunch by poor Penrose had not been fully appreciated, for the wounded man had as yet said nothing about it, and little Zackey had either forgotten all about it in the excitement of the accident, or was keeping his own counsel.

Maggot talked gloomily about the advisability of emigration to America, as he sent clouds of tobacco smoke up Un Jilly's chimney, and Tonkin said he would try the mines for a short time, and if things didn't improve he would go to sea. He did not, however, look at things in quite the same light with his friend. Perhaps he was of a more hopeful disposition, perhaps had met with fewer disappointments. At all events, he so wrought on Maggot's mind that he half induced him to deny his smuggling propensities for a time, and try legitimate work in the mines. Not that Joe Tonkin wanted to reform him by any means, but he was himself a little out of humour with his old profession, and sought to set his friend against it also.

"Try your luck in Botallack," said Joe Tonkin, knocking the ashes out of his pipe, preparatory to quitting the place, "that's my advice to 'ee, booy."

"I've half a mind to," replied Maggot, rising; "if that theere cargo I run on Saturday do go the way the last did, I'll ha' done with it, so I will. Good-hevenin', Un Jilly."

"Good-hevenin', an' don't 'ee go tumblin' down the owld shafts," said the worthy hostess, observing that her potent brandy had rendered the gait of the men unsteady.

They laughed as they received the caution, and walked together towards St. Just.

"Lev us go see if the toobs are all safe," said Maggot, on reaching the common.

Tonkin agreed, and they turned aside into a narrow track, which led across the waste land, where the search for the baby had been so diligently carried on all that day.

Night had set in, as we have said, and the searchers had gone up to the town to partake of much-needed refreshment, and obtain torches, so that the place was bleak and silent, as well as dark, when the friends crossed it, but they knew every foot of the ground so thoroughly, that there was no fear of their stumbling into old holes. Maggot led the way, and he walked straight to the old shaft where his hopeful son lay.

There were three noteworthy points of coincidence here to which we would draw attention. It was just because this old shaft was so well concealed that Maggot had chosen it as a place in which to hide his tubs of smuggled brandy; it was owing to the same reason that the town's-people had failed to discover it while searching for the baby; and it was — at least we think it must have been — just because of the same reason that baby Maggot had found it, for that amiable child had a peculiar talent, a sort of vocation, for ferreting out things and places hidden and secret, especially if forbidden.

Having succeeded in falling into the hole, the urchin naturally discovered his father's tubs. After crying himself to sleep as before mentioned, and again awakening, his curiosity in respect to these tubs afforded him amusement, and kept him quiet for a time; perhaps the fact that one of the tubs had leaked and filled the lower part of the old shaft with spirituous fumes, may account for the baby continuing to keep quiet, and falling into a sleep which lasted the greater part of the day; at all events, it is certain that he did not howl, as might have been expected of him in the circumstances. Towards evening, however, he began to move about among the tubs, and to sigh and whimper in a subdued way, for his stomach, unused to such prolonged fasting, felt very uncomfortable. When darkness came on baby Maggot became alarmed, but, just about the time of his father's approach, the moon shone out and cast a cheering ray down the shaft, which relieved his mind a little.

"Joe," said Maggot in a whisper, and with a serious look, "some one have bin here."

"D'ee think so?" said Tonkin.

"Iss I do; the bushes are broken a bit. Hush! what's that?"

The two men paused and looked at each other with awe depicted on their faces, while they listened intently, but, in the words of the touching old song, "the beating of their own hearts was all the sound they heard."

"It wor the wind," said Maggot.

"Iss, that's what it wor," replied Tonkin; "come, lev us go down. The wind can't do no harm to we."

But although he proposed to advance he did not move, and Maggot did not seem inclined to lead the way, for just then something like a sigh came from below, and a dark cloud passed over the moon.

It is no uncommon thing to find that men who are physically brave as lions become nervous as children when anything bordering on what they deem supernatural meets them. Maggot was about the most reckless man in the parish of St. Just, and Tonkin was not far behind him in the quality of courage, yet these two stood there with palpitating hearts undecided what to do.

Ashamed of being thought afraid of anything, Maggot at last cleared his throat, and, in a husky voice, said — "Come, then, lev us go down."

So saying he slid down the shaft, closely followed by Tonkin, who was nearly as much afraid to be left alone on the bleak moor as he was to enter the old mine.

Now, while the friends were consulting with palpitating hearts above, baby Maggot, wide-awake and trembling with terror, listened with bated breath below, and when the two men came scrambling down the sides of the shaft his heart seemed to fill up his breast and throat, and his blood began to creep in his veins. Maggot could see nothing in the gloomy interior as he advanced, but baby could see his father's dark form clearly. Still, no sound escaped from him, for horror had bereft him of power. Just then the dark cloud passed off the moon, and a bright beam shone full on the upper half of the baby's face as he peeped over the edge of one of the tubs. Maggot saw two glaring eyeballs, and felt frozen alive instantly. Tonkin, looking over his comrade's shoulder, also saw the eyes, and was petrified on the spot. Suddenly baby Maggot found his voice and uttered a most awful yell. Maggot senior found his limbs, and turned to fly. So did Tonkin, but he slipped and fell at the first step. Maggot fell over him. Both rose and dashed up the shaft, scraping elbows, shins, and knuckles as they went, and, followed by a torrent of hideous cries, that sounded in their ears like the screaming of fiends, they gained the surface, and, without exchanging a word, fled in different directions on the wings of terror!

Maggot did not halt until he burst into his house, and flung himself into his own chair by the chimney corner, whence he gazed on what was calculated to alarm as well as to perplex him. This was the spectacle of his own wife taking tea in floods of tears, and being encouraged in her difficult task by Mrs. Penrose and a few sympathising friends.

With some difficulty he got them to explain this mystery.

"What! baby gone lost?" he exclaimed; "where away?"

When it was told him what had occurred, Maggot's eyes gradually opened, and his lips gradually closed, until the latter produced a low whistle.

"I think that I do knaw where the cheeld is," he said; "come along, an' I'll show un to 'ee."

So saying, the wily smith, assuming an air of importance and profound wisdom, arose and led his wife and her friends, with a large band of men who had prepared torches, straight to the old shaft. Going down, but sternly forbidding any one to follow he speedily returned with the baby in his arms, to the surprise of all, and to the unutterable joy of the child's mother.

In one sense, however, the result was disastrous. Curious persons were there who could not rest until they had investigated the matter further, and the tubs were not only discovered, but carried off by those who had no title to them whatever! The misfortune created such a tumult of indignation in the breast of Maggot, that he was heard in his wrath to declare he "would have nothin' more to do with un, but would go into the bal the next settin' day."

This was the commencement of that series of events which, as we have stated at the beginning of this chapter, were brought about by that wonderful baby — the baby Maggot.

CHAPTER XXVIII.

Describes Setting-Day at the Mine, etc.

That very evening, while Maggot was smoking his pipe by the fireside, his son Zackey referred to the bunch of copper which Penrose had discovered in the mine. After a short conversation, Maggot senior went to the wounded man to talk about it.

"'Twas a keenly lode, did 'ee say?" asked Maggot, after he had inquired as to the health of his friend.

"Yes, and as I shall not be able to work there again," said Penrose sadly, "I would advise you to try it. Zackey is entitled to get the benefit of the discovery, for he was with me at the time, and, but for his aid, dear boy, I should have been suffocated."

Maggot said no more on that occasion about the mine, being a man of few words, but, after conversing a short time with the wounded man, and ascertaining that no hope was held out to him of the recovery of his sight, he went his way to the forge to work and meditate.

Setting-day came — being the first Saturday in the month, and no work was done on that day in Botallack, for the men were all above ground to have their "pitches" for the next month fixed, and to receive their wages — setting-day being also pay day.

Some time before the business of the day commenced, the miners began to assemble in considerable numbers in the neighbourhood of the account-house. Very different was their appearance on that occasion from the rusty-red fellows who were wont to toil in the dark chambers far down in the depths below the spot where they stood. Their underground dresses were laid aside, and they now appeared in the costume of well-off tradesmen. There was a free-and-easy swing about the movements of most of these men that must have been the result of their occupation, which brings every muscle of the body into play, and does not — as is too much the case in some trades — over-tax the powers of a certain set of muscles to the detriment of others.

Some there were, however, even among the young men, whose hollow cheeks and bloodless lips, accompanied with a short cough, told of evil resulting from bad air and frequent chills; while, on the other hand, a few old men were to be seen with bright eyes and ruddy cheeks which indicated constitutions of iron. Not a few were mere lads, whose broad shoulders and deep chests and resolute wills enabled them to claim the title, and do the work, of men.

There were some among them, both young and old, who showed traces of having suffered in their dangerous employment. Several were minus an eye, and one or two were nearly blind, owing to blast-holes exploding in their faces. One man in particular, a tall and very powerful fellow, had a visage which was quite blue, and one of his eyes was closed — the blue colour resulting from unburnt grains of powder having been blown into his flesh. He had been tattooed, in fact, by a summary and effective process. This man's family history was peculiar. His father, also a miner, had lived in a lonely cottage on a moor near St. Just, and worked in Balaswidden Mine. One night he was carried home and laid at his wife's feet, dead – almost dashed to pieces by a fall. Not long afterwards the son was carried to the same cottage with his right eye destroyed. Some time later a brother dislocated his foot twice within the year in the mine; and a few months after that another brother fell from a beam, descended about twenty-four feet perpendicularly, where he struck the side of the mine with his head, and had six or seven of his teeth knocked out; glancing off to one side, he fell twenty feet more on the hard rock, where he was picked up insensible. This man recovered, however, under the careful nursing of his oft and sorely tried mother.

Maggot was present on this setting-day, with a new cap and a new blue cloth coat, looking altogether a surprisingly respectable character. A good deal of undertoned chaffing commenced when he appeared.

"Hallo!" exclaimed one, "goin' to become an honest man, Maggot?"

"Thinkin' 'bout it," replied the smith, with a good-humoured smile.

"Why, if I didn't knaw that the old wuman's alive," said another, "I'd say he was agoin' to get married again!"

"Never fear," exclaimed a third, "Maggot's far too 'cute a cunger to be caught twice."

"I say, my dear man," asked another, "have 'ee bin takin' a waalk 'pon the clifts lately?"

"Iss, aw iss," replied the smith with much gravity.

"Did 'ee find any more daws 'pon clift?" asked the other, with a leer.

There was a general laugh at this, but Maggot replied with good-humour – "No, Billy, no – took 'em all away last time. But I'm towld there's some more eggs in the nest, so thee'll have a chance some day, booy."

"I hope the daws ain't the worse of their ducking?" asked Billy, with an expression of anxious interest.

"Aw, my dear," said Maggot, looking very sad, and shaking his head slowly, "didn't 'ee hear the noos?"

"No, not I."

"They did catch the noo complaint the doctor do spaik of – bronkeetis I think it is – and although I did tie 'em up wi' flannel round their necks, an' water-gruel, besides 'ot bottles to their feet, they're all gone dead. I mean to have 'em buried on Monday. Will 'ee come to the berryin, Billy?"

"P'raps I will," replied Billy, "but see that the gravedigger do berry 'em deep, else he'll catch a blowin' up like the gravedigger did in Cambourne last week."

"What was that, booy? Let us hear about it, Billy," exclaimed several voices.

"Well, this is the way of it," said Billy: "the owld gravedigger in Cambourne was standin' about, after mittin' was over, a-readin' of the tombstones, for he'd got a good edjication, had owld Tom. His name was Tom – the same man as put a straw rope to the bell which the cows did eat away, so that he cudn't ring the people to mittin'. Well, when he was studdyin' the morials on the stones out comes Captain Rowe. He was wan o' the churchwardens, or somethin' o' that sort, but I don't knaw nothin' 'bout the church, so I ain't sure – an' he calls owld Tom into the vestry.

"'Now look here, Tom,' says the captain, very stern, 'they tell me thee 'rt gettin' lazy, Tom, an' that thee do dig the graves only four fut deep. Now, Tom, I was over to St. Just t'other day to a berryin', and I see that they do dig their graves six fut or more deeper than you do. That won't do, Tom, I tell 'ee. What's the meanin' of it?'

"This came somewhat suddent on owld Tom, but he wor noways put out.

"'Well, you do see, Cap'n Rowe,' says he, 'I do it apurpose, for I do look at the thing in two lights.'"

"'How so?' asked the captain.

"'Why, the people of St. Just only think of the berryin', but *I* do think of the resurrection; the consekince is that they do dig too deep, an' afore the St. Just folk are well out of their graves, *ours* will be a braave way up to heaven!'"

The laugh with which this anecdote was received had scarcely subsided when the upper half of one of the account-house windows opened, and the fine-looking head and shoulders of old Mr. Cornish appeared.

The manager laid an open book on the window-sill, and from this elevated position, as from a pulpit, he read out the names, positions, etc., of the various "pitches" that were to be "sett" for the following month. One of the mine captains stood at his elbow to give any required information – he and his three brother captains being the men who had gone all over the mine during the previous month, examined the work, measured what had been done by each man or "pare" of men, knew the capabilities of all the miners, and fixed the portion that ought to be offered to each for acceptance or refusal.

The men assembled in a cluster round the window, and looked up while Mr. Cornish read off as follows:

"John Thomas's pitch at back of the hundred and five. By two men. To extend from the end of tram-hole, four fathom west, and from back of level, five fathom above."

For the enlightenment of the reader, we may paraphrase the above sentence thus:

"The pitch or portion of rock wrought last month by John Thomas is now offered anew – in the first place, to John Thomas himself if he chooses to continue working it at our rate of pay, or, if he declines, to any other man who pleases to offer for it. The pitch is in the back (or roof) of the level, which lies one hundred and five fathoms deep. It must be wrought by two men, and must be excavated lengthwise to an extent of four fathoms in a westerly direction from a spot called the tram-hole. In an upward direction, it may be excavated from the roof of the level to an extent of five fathoms."

John Thomas, being present, at once offered "ten shillings," by which he meant that, knowing the labour to be undergone, and the probable value of the ore that would have to be excavated, he thought it worth while to continue at that piece of work, or that "pitch," if the manager would give him ten shillings for every twenty shillings' worth of mineral sent to the surface by him; but the captain also knew the ground and the labour that would be required, and his estimate was that eight shillings would be quite sufficient remuneration, a fact which was announced by Mr. Cornish simply uttering the words, "At eight shillings."

"Put her down, s'pose," said John Thomas after a moment's consideration.

Perhaps John knew that eight shillings was really sufficient, although he wanted ten. At all events he knew that it was against the rules to dispute the point at that time, as it delayed business; that if he did not accept the offer, another man might do so; and that he might not get so good a pitch if he were to change.

The pitch was therefore sett to John Thomas, and another read off: — "Jim Hocking's pitch at back of the hundred and ten. By one man. To extend," etc.

"Won't have nothin' to do with her," said Jim Hocking.

Jim had evidently found the work too hard, and was dissatisfied with the remuneration, so he declined, resolving to try his chance in a more promising part of the mine.

"Will any one offer for this pitch?" inquired Mr. Cornish.

Eight and six shillings were sums immediately named by men who thought the pitch looked more promising than Jim did.

"Any one offer more for this pitch?" asked the manager, taking up a pebble from a little pile that lay at his elbow, and casting it into the air.

While that pebble was in its flight, any one might offer for the pitch, but the instant it touched the ground, the bargain was held to be concluded with the last bidder.

A man named Oats, who had been in a hesitating state of mind, here exclaimed "Five shillings" (that is, offered to work the pitch for five shillings on every twenty shillings' worth sent to grass); next instant the stone fell, and the pitch was sett to Oats.

Poor James Penrose's pitch was the next sett.

"James Penrose's *late* pitch," read the manager, giving the details of it in terms somewhat similar to those already sett, and stating that the required "pare," or force to be put on it, was two men and a boy.

"Put me down for it," said Maggot.

"Have you got your pare?" asked Mr. Cornish.

"Iss, sur."

"Their names?"

"David Trevarrow and my son Zackey."

The pitch was allocated in due form at the rate of fifteen shillings per twenty shillings' worth of mineral sent up — this large sum being given because it was not known to be an unusually good pitch — Penrose having been too ill to speak of his discovery since his accident, and the captain having failed to notice it. When a place is poor looking, a higher sum is given to the miner to induce him to work it. When it is rich, a lower sum is given, because he can make more out of it.

Thus the work went on, the sums named varying according to the nature of the ground, and each man saying "Naw," or "Put me down," or "That won't do," or "I won't have her," according to circumstances.

While this was going on at the window, another and perhaps more interesting scene was taking place in the office. This apartment presented a singular appearances. There was a large table in the centre of it, which, with every available inch of surface on a side-table, and on a board at the window, was completely covered with banknotes and piles of gold, silver, and copper. Each pile was placed on a little square piece of paper containing the account-current for the month of the man or men to whom it belonged. Very few men laboured singly. Many worked in couples, and some in bands of three, five, or more. So much hard cash gave the place a wealthy appearance, and in truth there was a goodly sum spread out, amounting to several hundreds of pounds.

The piles varied very much in size, and conveyed a rough outline of the financial history of the men they belonged to. Some large heaps of silver, with a few coppers and a pile of sovereigns more than an inch high, lying on two or more five-pound notes indicated successful labour. Nevertheless, the evidence was not absolutely conclusive, because the large piles had in most cases to be divided between several men who had banded together; but the little square account-papers, with a couple of crowns on them, told of hard work and little pay, while yonder square with two shillings in the centre of it betokened utter failure, only to be excelled by another square, on which lay *nothing*.

You will probably exclaim in your heart, reader, "What! do miners sometimes work for a month, and receive only two shillings, or *nothing* as wages?"

Ay, sometimes; but it is their own seeking if they do; it is not forced upon them.

There are three classes of miners — those who work on the surface, dressing ore, etc., who are paid a weekly wage; those who work on "tribute," and those who work at "tut-work." Of the first we say nothing, except that they consist chiefly of balmaidens and children — the former receiving about 18s. a month, and the latter from 8s. to 20s., according to age and capacity.

In regard to "tributers" and "tut-workers," we may remark that the work of both is identical in one respect — namely, that of hewing, picking, boring, and blasting the hard rock. In this matter they share equal toils and dangers, but they are not subjected to the same remunerative vicissitudes.

When a man works on "tribute" he receives so many shillings for every twenty shillings' worth of ore that he raises during the month, as already explained. If his "pitch" turns out to be rich in ore, his earnings are proportionably high; if it be poor, he remains poor also. Sometimes a part of the mineral lode becomes so poor that it will not pay for working, and has to be abandoned. So little as a shilling may be the result of a "tributer's" work for a month at one time, while at another time he may get a good pitch, and make £100 or £200 in the same period.

The "tutman" (or piecework man), on the other hand, cuts out the rock at so much per fathom, and obtains wages at the rate of from £2, 10s. to £3 a month. He can never hope to make a fortune, but so long as health and strength last, he may count on steady work and wages. Of course there is a great deal of the work in a mine which is not directly remunerative, such as "sinking" shafts, opening up and "driving" (or lengthening) levels, and sinking "winzes." On such work tutmen are employed.

The man who works on "tribute" is a speculator; he who chooses "tut-work" is a steady labourer. The tributer experiences all the excitement of uncertainty, and enjoys the pleasures of hope. He knows something, too, about "hope deferred;" also can tell of hope disappointed; has his wits sharpened, and, generally, is a smart fellow. The tut-worker knows nothing of this, his pay being safe and regular, though small. Many quiet-going, plodding men prefer and stick to tut-work.

In and about the counting-room the men who had settled the matter of their next month's work were assembled. These – the cashier having previously made all ready – were paid in a prompt and businesslike manner.

First, there came forward a middle-aged man. It was scarcely necessary for him to speak, for the cashier knew every man on the mine by name, and also how much was due to him, and the hundreds of little square accounts-current were so arranged that he could lay his hands on any one in an instant. Nevertheless, being a hearty and amiable man, he generally had a word to say to every one.

"How's your son, Matthew?" he inquired of the middle-aged man, putting the square paper with its contents into his hand.

"He's braave, sir. The doctor do say he'll be about again in a week."

Matthew crumpled up his account-current – notes, gold, silver, copper and all – in his huge brown hand, and, thrusting the whole into his breeches pocket, said "Thank 'ee," and walked away.

Next, there came forward a young man with one eye, an explosion having shut up the other one for ever. He received his money along with that of the three men who worked in the same "pare" with him. He crumpled it up in the same reckless way as Matthew had done, also thrust it into his pocket, and walked off with an independent swagger. Truly, in the sweat, not only of his brow, but, of every pore in his body, had he earned it, and he was entitled to swagger a little just then. There was little enough room or inducement to do so down in the mine! After this young man a little boy came forward saying that his "faither" had sent him for his money.

It was observable that the boys and lads among those who presented themselves in the counting-room, were, as a rule, hearty and hopeful. With them it was as with the young in all walks of life. Everything looked bright and promising. The young men were stern, yet free-and-easy – as though they had already found life a pretty tough battle, but felt quite equal to it. And so they were, every one of them! With tough sinews, hard muscles, and indomitable energy, they were assuredly equal to any work that man could undertake; and many of them, having the fear of God in their hearts, were fitted to endure manfully the trials of life as well. The elderly men were sedate, and had careworn faces; they knew what it was to suffer. Many of them had carried little ones to the grave; they had often seen strong men like themselves go forth in the morning hale and hearty, and be carried to their homes at evening with blinded eyes or shattered limbs. Life had lost its gloss to them, but it had not lost its charms. There were loving hearts to work for, and a glorious end for which to live, or, if need be, to die — so, although their countenances were sedate they were not sad. The old men — of whom there were but two or three — were jolly old souls. They seemed to have successfully defied the tear and wear of life, to have outlived its sorrows, and renewed their youth. Certainly they had not reached their second childhood, for they stepped forth and held out their hands for their pay as steadily as the best of the young ones.

When about one-half of the number had been paid, a woman in widow's weeds came forward to take up the pay due to her son — her "wretched Harry," as she styled him. All that was due was seven-and-sixpence. It was inexpressibly sad to see her retire with this small sum — the last that her unsettled boy was entitled to draw from the mines. He had worked previously in the neighbouring mine, Wheal Owles, and had gone to Botallack the month before. He was now off to sea, leaving his mother, who to some extent depended on him, to look out for herself.

The next who came forward was a blind man. He had worked long in the mine — so long that he could find his way through the labyrinth of levels as easily in his blind state as he did formerly with his eyesight. When his eyes were destroyed (in the usual way, by the explosion of a hole), he was only off work during the period of convalescence. Afterwards he returned to his familiar haunts underground; and although he could no longer labour in the old way, he was quite able to work a windlass, and draw up the bucket at a winze. For this he now pocketed two pounds sterling, and walked off as vigorously as if he had possessed both his eyes!

Among others, a wife appeared to claim her husband's pay, and she was followed by Zackey Maggot, who came to receive his own and Penrose's money.

"How does Penrose get on?" inquired the cashier, as he handed over the sum due.

"Slowly, sur," said Zackey.

"It is a bad case," said one of the captains, who sat close by; "the doctor thinks there is little or no chance for his eyesight."

Poor Zackey received his pay and retired without any demonstration of his wonted buoyancy of spirit, for he was fond of Penrose, almost as much so as he was of uncle David Trevarrow.

The varied fortune experienced in the mine was exhibited in one or two instances on this occasion. One man and a boy, working together, had, in their own phraseology, "got a sturt" — they had come unexpectedly on a piece of rich ground, which yielded so much tin that at the end of the month they received £25 between them. The man had been receiving "subsist," that is, drawing advances monthly for nearly a year, and, having a wife and children to support, had almost lost heart. It was said that he had even contemplated suicide, but this little piece of good fortune enabled him to pay off his debt and left something over. Another man and boy had £20 to receive. On the other hand, one man had only 2s. due to him, while a couple of men who had worked in poor ground found themselves 2s. in debt, and had to ask for "subsist."

Some time previous to this, two men had discovered a "bunch of copper," and in the course of two months they cleared £260. At a later period a man in Levant Mine, who was one of the Wesleyan local preachers, cleared £200 within a year. He gave a hundred pounds to his mother, and with the other hundred went off to seek his fortune in Australia!

After all the men had been paid, those who wished for "subsist," or advances, were desired to come forward. About a dozen of them did so, and among these were representatives of all classes – the diligent and strong, the old and feeble, and the young. Of course, in mining operations as in other work, the weak, lazy, and idle will ever be up to the lips in trouble, and in need of help. But in mining the best of men may be obliged to demand assistance, because, when tributers work on hopefully day after day and week after week on bad ground, they must have advances to enable them to persevere – not being able to subsist on air! This is no hardship, the mine being at all times open to their inspection, and they are allowed to select their own ground. Hence the demand for "subsist" is not necessarily a sign of absolute but only of temporary poverty. The managers make large or small advances according to their knowledge of the men.

There was a good deal of chaffing at this point in the proceedings – the lazy men giving occasion for a slight administration of rebuke, and the able men affording scope for good-humoured pleasantry and badinage.

In Botallack, at the present time, about forty or fifty men per month find it necessary to ask for "subsist."

Before the wages were paid, several small deductions had to be made. First, there was sixpence to be deducted from each man for "the club." This club consisted of those who chose to pay sixpence a month to a fund for the temporary support of those who were damaged by accidents in the mine. A similar sum per month was deducted from each man for "the doctor," who was bound, in consideration of this, to attend the miners free of charge. In addition to this a shilling was deducted from each man, to be given to the widow and family of a comrade who had died that month. At the present time from £18 to £20 are raised in this way when a death occurs, to be given to the friends of the deceased. It should be remarked that these deductions are made with the consent of the men. Any one may refuse to give to those objects, but, if he do so, he or his will lose the benefit in the event of his disablement or death.

Men who are totally disabled receive a pension from the club fund. Not long ago a miner, blind of one eye, left another mine and engaged in Botallack. Before his first month was out he exploded a blast-hole in his face, which destroyed the other eye. From that day he received a pension of £1 a month, which will continue till his death – or, at least as long as Botallack shall flourish – and that miner may be seen daily going through the streets of St. Just with his little daughter, in a cart, shouting "Pilchards, fresh pilcha-a-rds, breem, pullock, fresh pullock, *pil-cha-a-rds*" — at the top of his stentorian voice — a living example of the value of "the club," and of the principle of insurance!

At length the business of the day came to a close. The wages were paid, the men's work for another month was fixed, the cases of difficulty and distress were heard and alleviated, and then the managers and agents wound up the day by dining together in the account-house, the most noteworthy point in the event being the fact that the dinner was eaten off plates made of pure Botallack tin.

Once a quarter this dinner, styled the "account-dinner," is partaken of by any of the shareholders who may wish to be present, on which occasion the manager and agents lay before the company the condition and prospects of the mine, and a quarterly dividend (if any) is paid. There is a matter-of-fact and Spartanlike air about this feast which commands respect. The room in which it is held is uncarpeted, and its walls are graced by no higher works of art than the plans and sections of the mine. The food is excellent and substantial, but simple. There is abundance of it, but there are no courses — either preliminary or successive — no soup or fish to annoy one who wants meat; no ridiculous *entremêts* to tantalise one who wants something solid; no puddings, pies, or tarts to tempt men to gluttony. All set to work at the same time, and enjoy their meal *together*, which is more than can be said of most dinners. All is grandly simple, like the celebrated mine on which the whole is founded.

But there is one luxury at this feast which it would be unpardonable not to mention — namely the punch. Whoever tastes this beverage can never forget it! Description were useless to convey an idea of it. Imagination were impotent to form a conception of it. Taste alone will avail, so that our readers must either go to Cornwall to drink it, or for ever remain unsatisfied. We can only remark, in reference to it, that it is potent as well as pleasant, and that it is also dangerous, being of an insinuating nature, so that those who partake freely have a tendency to wish for more, and are apt to dream (not unreasonably, but too wildly) of Botallack tin being transformed into silver and gold.

CHAPTER XXIX.

Details, among other Things, a Deed of Heroism.

To work went Maggot and Trevarrow and Zackey on their new pitch next day like true Britons. Indeed, we question whether true Britons of the ancient time ever did go to work with half the energy or perseverance of the men of the present day. Those men of old were mere grubbers on the surface. They knew nothing of deep levels under the ocean. However, to do them justice, they made wonderfully extensive tunnels in mother earth, with implements much inferior to those now in use.

But, be that as it may, our trio went to work "with a will." Maggot was keen to get up as much of the rich mineral as possible during the month – knowing that he would not get the place next month on such good terms. Trevarrow, besides having no objections to make money when he could for its own sake, was anxious to have a little to spare to James Penrose, whose large family found it pinching work to subsist on the poor fellow's allowance from the club. As to Zackey, he was ready for anything where Uncle Davy was leader. So these three resolved to work night and day. Maggot took his turn in the daytime and slept at night; Trevarrow slept in the daytime and worked at night; while the boy worked as long as he could at whatever time suited him best.

As they advanced on the lode it became larger and richer, and in a day or two it assumed such proportions as to throw the fortunate workers into a state of great excitement, and they tore out and blasted away the precious mineral like Titans.

One day, about kroust-time, having fired two holes, they came out of the "end" in which they wrought and sat down to lunch while the smoke was clearing away.

"'Tes a brave lode," said Maggot.

"It is," responded Trevarrow, taking a long draught of water from the canteen.

"What shall us do?" said Maggot; "go to grass to slaip, or slaip in the bal?"

"In the bal, if you do like it," said Trevarrow.

So it was agreed that the men should sleep in the mine on boards, or on any dry part of the level, in order to save the time and energy lost in ascending and descending the long ladders, and thus make the most of their opportunity. It was further resolved that Zackey should be sent up for dry clothes, and bring them their meals regularly. Trevarrow did not forget to have his Bible brought to him, for he was too serious a man to shut his eyes to the danger of a sudden run of good fortune, and thought that the best way to guard against evil would be to devote nearly all his short periods of leisure time to the reading of "the Word."

You may be sure that Maggot afterwards laughed at him for this, but he did not concern himself much about it at the time, because he was usually too hungry to talk at meal-times, and too sleepy to do so after work was over.

They were still busily discussing the matter of remaining in the mine all night, when they heard the kibble descending the shaft, near the bottom of which they sat, and next moment a man came to the ground with considerable violence.

"Why, Frankey, is that thee, booy?" said Maggot, starting up to assist him.

"Aw dear, iss; I'm gone dead a'most! aw dear! aw dear!"

"Why, whatever brought 'ee here?" said Trevarrow.

"The kibble, sure," replied the man, exhibiting his knuckles, which were cut and bleeding a good deal. "I did come by the chain, anyhow."

This was indeed true. Frankey, as his mates called him, was at that time the "lander" in charge of the kibbles at the surface. It was his duty to receive each kibble as it was drawn up to the mouth of the shaft full of ore, empty it, and send it down again. Several coils of chain passing round the large drum of a great horse-windlass, called by the miners a "whim," was the means by which the kibbles were hoisted and lowered. The chain was so arranged that one kibble was lowered by it while the other was being drawn up. Frankey had emptied one of the kibbles, and had given the signal to the boy attending the horse to "lower away," when he inadvertently stepped into the shaft. With ready presence of mind the man caught the chain and clung to it, but the boy, being prevented by a pile of rubbish from seeing what had occurred, eased him down, supposing him to be the kibble!

This "easing down" a great number of fathoms was by no means an easy process, as those know well who have seen a pair of kibbles go banging up and down a shaft. It was all that poor Frankey could do to keep his head from being smashed against rocks and beams; but, by energetic use of arms and legs, he did so, and reached the bottom of the shaft without further damage than a little skin rubbed off his knees and elbows, and a few cuts on his hands. The man thought so little of it, indeed, that he at once returned to grass by the ladder-way, to the unutterable surprise and no little consternation of the boy who had "eased him down."

The air at the "end" of the level in which Maggot and Trevarrow worked was very bad, and, for some time past, men had been engaged in sinking a winze from the level above to connect the two, and send in a supply of fresh air by creating a new channel of circulation. This winze was almost completed, but one of the men employed at it had suddenly become unwell that day, and no other had been appointed to the work. As it was a matter of great importance to have fresh air, now that they had resolved to remain day and night in the mine for some time, Maggot and Trevarrow determined to complete the work, believing that one or two shots would do it. Accordingly, they mounted to the level above, and were lowered one at a time to the bottom of the unfinished winze by a windlass, which was turned by the man whose comrade had become unwell.

For nearly two hours they laboured diligently, scarce taking time to wipe the perspiration from their heated brows. At the end of that time the hole was sufficiently deep to blast, so Maggot called out — "Zackey, my son, fetch the fuse and powder." The boy was quickly lowered with these materials, and then drawn up.

Meanwhile Maggot proceeded to charge the hole, and his comrade sat down to rest. He put in the powder and tamping, and asked the other to hand him the tamping-bar.

"Zackey has forgot it," said Trevarrow, looking round.

"It don't matter; hand me the borer."

"No, I won't," said Trevarrow decidedly, as he grasped the iron tool in question. "Ho! Zackey booy, throw down the tampin'-bar."

This was done, and the operation of filling the hole continued, while Trevarrow commented somewhat severely on his companion's recklessness.

"That's just how the most o' the reckless men in the bal do get blaw'd up," he said; "they're always picking away at the holes, and tamping with iron tools; why, thee might as well put a lighted match down the muzzle of a loaded gun as tamp with an iron borer."

"Come, now," said Maggot, looking up from his work with a leer, "it warn't that as made old Kimber nearly blow hisself up last week."

"No, but it was carelessness, anyhow," retorted Trevarrow; "and lucky for him that he was a smart man, else he'd bin gone dead by this time."

Maggot soon completed the filling of the hole, and then perpetrated as reckless a deed as any of his mining comrades had ever been guilty of. Trevarrow was preparing to ascend by the windlass, intending to leave his comrade to light the fuse and come up after him. Meanwhile Maggot found that the fuse was too long. He discovered this after it was fixed in the hole, and, unobserved by his companion, proceeded to cut it by means of an iron tool and a flat stone. Fire was struck at the last blow by the meeting of the iron and the stone, and the fuse ignited. To extinguish it was impossible; to cut it in the same way, without striking fire, was equally so. Of course there was plenty of time to ascend by the windlass, but *only one* at a time could do so. The men knew this, and looked at each other with terrible meaning in their eyes as they rushed at the bucket, and shouted to the man above to haul them up. He attempted to do so, but in vain. He had not strength to haul up two at once. One could escape, both could not, and to delay would be death to both. In this extremity David Trevarrow looked at his comrade, and said calmly — "Escape, my brother; a minute more and I shall be in heaven."

He stepped back while he spoke — the bucket went rapidly upwards, and Trevarrow, sitting down in the bottom of the shaft, covered his eyes with a piece of rock and awaited the issue.

The rumbling explosion immediately followed, and the shaft was filled with smoke and flame and hurling stones. One of these latter, shooting upwards, struck and cut the ascending miner on his forehead as he looked down to observe the fate of his self-sacrificing comrade!

Maggot was saved, but he was of too bold and kindly a nature to remain for a moment inactive after the explosion was over. At once he descended, and, groping about among the débris, soon found his friend — alive, and almost unhurt! A mass of rock had arched him over — or, rather, the hand of God, as if by miracle, had delivered the Christian miner.

After he was got up in safety to the level above they asked him why he had been so ready to give up his life to save his friend.

"Why," said David quietly, "I did think upon his wife and the child'n, and little Grace seemed to say to me, 'Take care o' faither' — besides, there are none to weep if I was taken away, so the Lord gave me grace to do it."

That night there were glad and grateful hearts in Maggot's cottage — and never in this world was a more flat and emphatic contradiction given to any statement, than that which was given to David Trevarrow's assertion — "There are noneto weep if I was taken away."[8]

8 A short but beautiful account of the above incident will be found in a little volume of poems, entitled *Lays from the Mine, the Moor, and the Mountain*, written by John Harris, a Cornish miner.

CHAPTER XXX.

Reveals some Astonishing Facts and their Consequences.

Sorrow and trouble now began to descend upon Mr. Thomas Donnithorne like a thick cloud.

Reduced from a state of affluence to one bordering on absolute poverty, the old man's naturally buoyant spirit almost gave way, and it needed all the attentions and the cheering influence of his good wife and sweet Rose Ellis to keep him from going (as he often half-jestingly threatened) to the end of Cape Cornwall and jumping into the sea.

"It's all over with me, Oliver," said he one morning, after the return of his nephew from London. "A young fellow like you may face up against such difficulties, but what is an old man to do? I can't begin the world over again; and as for the shares I have in the various mines, they're not worth the paper they're writ upon."

"But things may take a turn," suggested Oliver; "this is not the first time the mines have been in a poor condition, and the price of tin low. When things get very bad they are likely to get better, you know. Even now there seems to be some talk among the miners of an improved state of things. I met Maggot yesterday, and he was boasting of having found a monstrous bunch, which, according to him, is to be the making of all our fortunes."

Mr. Donnithorne shook his head.

"Maggot's geese are always swans," he said; "no, no, Oliver, I have lost all hope of improvement. There are so many of these deceptive mines around us just now — some already gone down, and some going — that the public are losing confidence in us, and, somewhat unfairly, judging that, because a few among us are scoundrels, we are altogether a bad lot."

"What do you think of Mr. Clearcmout's new mine?" asked Oliver.

"I believe it to be a genuine one," said the old gentleman, turning a somewhat sharp glance on his nephew. "Why do you ask?"

"Because I doubt it," replied Oliver.

"You are too sceptical," said Mr. Donnithorne almost testily; "too much given to judging things at first sight."

"Nay, uncle; you are unfair. Had I judged of you at first sight, I should have thought you a —"

"Well, what? a smuggling old brandy-loving rascal — eh? and not far wrong after all."

"At all events," said Oliver, laughing, "I have lived to form a better opinion of you than that. But, in reference to Clearemout, I cannot shut my eyes to the fact that the work doing at the new mine is very like a sham, for they have only two men and a boy working her, with a captain to superintend; and it is said, for I made inquiries while in London, that thirty thousand pounds have been called up from the shareholders, and there are several highly paid directors, with an office-staff in the City drawing large salaries."

"Nonsense, Oliver," said Mr. Donnithorne more testily than before; "you know very well that things must have a beginning, and that caution is necessary at first in all speculations. Besides, I feel convinced that Mr. Clearemout is a most respectable man, and an uncommonly clever fellow to boot. It is quite plain that you don't like him — that's what prejudices you, Oliver. You're jealous of the impression he has made on the people here."

This last remark was made jestingly, but it caused the young doctor to wince, having hit nearer the truth than the old gentleman had any idea of, for although Oliver envied not the handsome stranger's popularity, he was, almost unknown to himself, very jealous of the impression he seemed to have made on Rose Ellis.

A feeling of shame induced him to change the subject of conversation, with a laughing observation that he hoped such an unworthy motive did not influence him.

Now, while this conversation was going on in the parlour of Mr. Donnithorne's cottage, another dialogue was taking place in a small wooden erection at the end of the garden, which bore the dignified name of "Rose's Bower." The parties concerned in it were George Augustus Clearemout and Rose Ellis.

A day or two previous to the conversation to which we are about to draw attention, the managing director had undergone a change in his sentiments and intentions. When he first saw Rose he thought her an uncommonly sweet and pretty girl. A short acquaintance with her convinced him that she was even sweeter and prettier than at first he had thought her. This, coupled with the discovery that her uncle was very rich, and that he meant to leave a large portion of his wealth, if not all of it, to Rose, decided Clearemout, and he resolved to marry her. Afterwards he became aware of the fact that old Mr. Donnithorne had met with losses, but he was ignorant of their extent, and still deemed it worth while to carry out his intentions.

George Augustus had been a "managing director" in various ways from his earliest infancy, and had never experienced much opposition to his will, so that he had acquired a habit of settling in his own mind whatever he meant to do, and forthwith doing it. On this occasion he resolved to sacrifice himself to Rose, in consideration of her prospective fortune — cash being, of course, Mr. Clearemout's god.

Great, then, was the managing director's surprise, and astonishing the condition of his feelings, when, on venturing to express his wishes to Rose, he was kindly, but firmly, rejected! Mr. Clearemout was so thunderstruck — having construed the unsophisticated girl's candour and simplicity of manner into direct encouragement — that he could make no reply, but, with a profound bow, retired hastily from her presence, went to his lodgings, and sat down with his elbows on the table, and his face buried in his large hands, the fingers of which appeared to be crushing in his forehead, as if to stifle the thoughts that burned there. After sitting thus for half an hour he suddenly rose, with his face somewhat paler, and his lips a little more firmly compressed than usual.

It was an epoch in his existence. The man who had so often and so successfully deceived others had made the wonderful discovery that he had deceived himself. He had imagined that money was his sole object in wishing to marry Rose. He now discovered that love, or something like it, had so much to do with his wishes that he resolved to have her without money, and also without her consent.

Something within the man told him that Rose's refusal was an unalterable one. He did not think it worth while to waste time in a second attempt. His plans, though hastily formed, required a good deal of preliminary arrangement, so he commenced to carry them out with the single exclamation, "I'll do it!" accompanied with a blow from his heavy fist on the table, which, being a weak lodging-house one, was split from end to end. But the managing director had a soul above furniture at that moment. He hastily put on his hat and strode out of the house.

Making good use of a good horse, he paid sundry mysterious visits to various smuggling characters, to all of whom he was particularly agreeable and liberal in the bestowal of portions of the thirty thousand pounds with which a too confiding public had intrusted him. Among other places, he went to a cottage on a moor between St. Just and Penzance, and had a confidential interview with a man named Hicks, who was noted for his capacity to adapt himself to circumstances (when well paid) without being troubled by conscientious scruples. This man had a son who had once suffered from a broken collarbone, and whose ears were particularly sharp. He chanced to overhear the conversation at the interview referred to, and dutifully reported the same to his mother, who happened to be a great gossip, and knew much about the private affairs of nearly everybody living within six miles of her. The good woman resolved to make some use of her information, but Mr. Clearemout left the cottage in ignorance, of course, of her resolution.

Having transacted these little pieces of business, the managing director returned home, and, on the day following, sought and obtained an interview with Rose Ellis in her bower.

Recollecting the subject of their last conversation, Rose blushed, as much with indignation as confusion, at being intruded upon, but Mr. Clearemout at once dispersed her angry feelings by assuring her in tones of deferential urbanity that he would not have presumed to intrude upon her but for the fact that he was about to quit Cornwall without delay, and he wished to talk with her for only a few minutes on business connected with Mr. Donnithorne.

There was something so manly and straightforward in his tone and manner that she could not choose but allow him to sit down beside her, although she did falter out something about the propriety of talking on her uncle's business affairs with Mr. Donnithorne himself.

"Your observation is most just," said Mr. Clearemout earnestly; "but you are aware that your uncle's nature is a delicate, sensitive one, and I feel that he would shrink from proposals coming from me, that he might listen to if made to him through you. I need not conceal from you, Miss Ellis, that I am acquainted with the losses which your uncle has recently sustained, and no one can appreciate more keenly than I do the harshness with which the world, in its ignorance of details, is apt to judge of the circumstances which brought about this sad state of things. I cannot help feeling deeply the kindness which has been shown me by Mr. Donnithorne during my residence here, and I would, if I could, show him some kindness in return."

Mr. Clearemout paused here a few moments as if to reflect. He resolved to assume that Mr. Donnithorne's losses were ruinous, little imagining that in this assumption he was so very near the truth! Rose felt grateful to him for the kind and delicate way in which he referred to her uncle's altered circumstances.

"Of course," continued the managing director, "I need not say to *you*, that his independent spirit would never permit him to accept of assistance in the form which would be most immediately beneficial to him. Indeed, I could not bring myself to offer money even as a loan. But it happens that I have the power, just now, of disposing of the shares which he has taken in Wheal Dooem Mine at a very large profit; and as my hope of the success of that enterprise is very small, I —"

"Very small!" echoed Rose in surprise. "You astonish me, Mr. Clearemout. Did I not hear you, only a few nights ago, say that you had the utmost confidence in the success of your undertaking?"

"Most true," replied the managing director with a smile; "but in the world of business a few hours work wonderful changes, sometimes, in one's opinion of things — witness the vacillations and variations 'on 'Change' — if I may venture to allude before a lady to such an incomprehensible subject."

Rose felt her vigorous little spirit rise, and she was about to return a smart reply in defence of woman's intelligence even in business matters, but the recollection of the altered relative position in which they now stood restrained her.

"Yes," continued Mr. Clearemout, with a sigh, "the confidence which I felt in Wheal Dooem has been much shaken of late, and the sooner your uncle sells out the better."

"But would it be right," said Rose earnestly, "to sell our shares at a high profit if things be as you say?"

"Quite right," replied Clearemout, with a bland smile of honesty; "*I* believe the mine to be a bad speculation; my friend, we shall suppose, believes it to be a good one. Believing as I do, I choose to sell out; believing as he does, he chooses to buy in. The simplest thing in the world, Miss Ellis. Done every day with eyes open, I assure you; but it is not every day that a chance occurs so opportunely as the present, and I felt it to be a duty to give my friend the benefit of my knowledge before quitting this place — for ever!"

There was something so kind and touching in the tone of the managing director that Rose was quite drawn towards him, and felt as if she had actually done him an unkindness in refusing him.

"But," continued her companion, "I can do nothing, Miss Ellis, without your assistance."

"You shall have it," said Rose earnestly; "for I would do anything that a woman might venture, to benefit my dear, dear uncle, and I feel assured that you would not ask me to do anything wrong or unwomanly."

"I would not indeed," answered Clearemout with emotion; "but the world is apt to misjudge in matters of delicacy. To ask you to meet me on the cliffs near Priest's Cove, close to Cape Cornwall, tonight, would appear wrong in the eyes of the world."

"And with justice," said Rose quickly, with a look of mingled dignity and surprise.

"Nevertheless, this is absolutely needful, if we would accomplish the object in view. A friend, whom I know to be desirous of purchasing shares in the mine is to pass round the cape in his yacht this evening. The idea of offering these shares to him had not occurred to me when I wrote to say that I would meet him there. He cannot come up here, I know, but the stroke of a pen, with one of the family to witness it, will be sufficient."

It was a bold stroke of fancy in the managing director to put the matter in such a ridiculously unbusinesslike light, but he counted much on Rose's ignorance. As for poor Rose herself, she knew not what to say or do at first, but when Clearemout heaved a sigh, and, with an expression of deep sadness on his countenance, rose to take leave, she allowed a generous impulse to sway her.

"Your answer, then, is — No," said Clearemout, with deep pathos in his tone.

Now, it chanced that at this critical point in the conversation, Oliver Trembath, having left the cottage, walked over the grass towards a small gate, near which the bower stood. He unavoidably heard the question, and also the quick, earnest reply — "My answer, Mr. Clearemout, is — Yes. I will meet you this evening on the cliff."

She frankly gave him her hand as she spoke, and he gallantly pressed it to his lips, an act which took Rose by surprise, and caused her to pull it away suddenly. She then turned and ran out at the side of the bower to seek the solitude of her own apartment, while Clearemout left it by the other side, and stood face to face with the spellbound Oliver.

To say that both gentlemen turned pale as their eyes met would not give an adequate idea of their appearance. Oliver's heart, as well as his body, when he heard the question and reply, stood still as if he had been paralysed. This, then, he thought, was the end of all his hopes — hopes hardly admitted to himself, and never revealed to Rose, except in unstudied looks and tones. For a few moments his face grew absolutely livid, while he glared at his rival.

On the other hand, Mr. Clearemout, believing that the whole of his conversation had been overheard, supposed that he had discovered all his villainy to one who was thoroughly able, as well as willing, to thwart him. For a moment he felt an almost irresistible impulse to spring on and slay his enemy; his face became dark with suppressed emotion; and it is quite possible that in the fury of his disappointed malice he might have attempted violence — had not Oliver spoken. His voice was husky as he said — "Chance, sir — unfortunate, miserable chance – led me to overhear the last few words that passed between you and –"

He paused, unable to say more. Instantly the truth flashed across Cleare-mout's quick mind. He drew himself up boldly, and the blood returned to his face as he replied – "If so, sir, you cannot but be aware that the lady's choice is free, and that your aspect and attitude towards me are unworthy of a gen-tleman."

A wonderful influence for weal or woe oft-times results from the selection of a phrase or a word. Had Clearemout charged Oliver with insolence or pre-sumption, he would certainly have struck him to the ground; but the words "unworthy of a gentleman" created a revulsion in his feelings. Thought is swifter than light. He saw himself in the position of a disappointed man scowling on a successful rival who had done him no injury.

"Thank you, Clearemout. Your rebuke is merited," he said bitterly; and, turning on his heel, he bounded over the low stone wall of the garden, and has-tened away.

Whither he went he knew not. A fierce fire seemed to rage in his breast and burn in his brain. At first he walked at full speed, but as he cleared the town he ran – ran as he had never run before. For the time being he was absolutely mad. Over marsh and moor he sped, clearing all obstacles with a bound, and making straight for the Land's End, with no definite purpose in view, for, after a time, he appeared to change his intention, if he had any. He turned sharp to the left, and ran straight to Penzance, never pausing in his mad career until he neared the town. The few labourers he chanced to pass on the way gazed after him in sur-prise, but he heeded not. At the cottage on the moor where he had bandaged the shoulder of the little boy a woman's voice called loudly, anxiously after him, but he paid no attention. At last he came to a full stop, and, pressing both hands tightly over his forehead, made a terrible effort to collect his thoughts. He was partially successful, and, with somewhat of his wonted composure, walked rap-idly into the town.

CHAPTER XXXI.

Describes a Marred Plot, and tells of Retributive Justice.

Meanwhile the gossiping woman of the cottage on the moor, whose grateful heart had never forgotten the little kindness done to her boy by the young doctor, and who knew that the doctor loved Rose Ellis, more surely, perhaps, than Rose did herself, went off in a state of deep anxiety to St. Just, and, by dint of diligent inquiries and piecing of things together, coupled with her knowledge of Clearemout's intentions, came to a pretty correct conclusion as to the state of affairs.

She then went to the abode of young Charles Tregarthen, whom she knew to be Oliver's friend, and unbosomed herself. Charlie repaid her with more than thanks, and almost hugged her in his gratitude for her prompt activity.

"And now, Mrs. Hicks," said he, "you shall see how we will thwart this scoundrel. As for Oliver Trembath, I cannot imagine what could take him into Penzance in the wild state that you describe. Of course this affair has to do with it, and he evidently has learned something of this, and must have misunderstood the matter, else assuredly he had not been absent at such a time. But why go to Penzance? However, he will clear up the mystery ere long, no doubt. Meanwhile we shall proceed to thwart your schemes, good Mr. Clearemout!"

So saying, Charlie Tregarthen set about laying his counter-plans. He also, as the managing director had done, visited several men, some of whom were miners and some smugglers, and arranged a meeting that evening near Cape Cornwall.

When evening drew on apace, four separate parties converged towards Priest's Cove. First, a boat crept along shore propelled by four men and steered by Jim Cuttance. Secondly, six stout men crept stealthily down to the cove, led by Charlie Tregarthen, with Maggot as his second in command. Thirdly, Rose Ellis wended her way to the rendezvous with trembling step and beating heart; and, fourthly, George Augustus Clearemout moved in the same direction.

But the managing director moved faster than the others, having a longer way to travel, for, having had to pay a last visit to Wheal Dooem, he rode thence to St. Just. On the way he was particularly interested in a water-wheel which worked a pump, beside which a man in mining costume was seated smoking his pipe.

"Good-evening," said Clearemout, reining up.

"Good-hevenin', sur."

"What does that pump?" asked the managing director, pointing to the wheel.

"That, sur?" said the miner, drawing a few whiffs from his pipe; "why, that do pump gold out o' the Londoners, that do."

The managing director chuckled very much, and said, "Indeed!"

"Iss, sur," continued the miner, pointing to Wheal Dooem, "an' that wan theere, up over hill, do the same thing."

The managing director chuckled much more at this, and displayed his teeth largely as he nodded to the man and rode on.

Before his arrival at the rendezvous, the boat was run ashore not far from the spot where Tregarthen and his men were concealed. As soon as the men had landed, Charlie walked down to them alone and accosted their leader.

"Well, Cuttance, you're a pretty fellow to put your finger in such a dirty pie as this."

Cuttance had seen the approach of Tregarthen with surprise and some alarm.

"Well, sur," said he, without any of the bold expression that usually characterised him, "what can a man do when he's to be well paid for the job? I do confess that I don't half like it, but, after all, what have we got to do weth the opinions of owld aunts or uncles? If a gurl do choose to go off wi' the man she likes, that's no matter to we, an' if I be well paid for lendin' a hand, why shouldn't I? But it do puzzle me, Mr. Tregarthen, to guess how yow did come to knaw of it."

"That don't signify," said Tregarthen sternly. "Do you know who the girl is?"

"I don't knaw, an' I don't care," said Jim doggedly.

"What would you say if I told you it was Miss Rose Ellis?" said Charlie.

"I'd say thee was a liard," replied Cuttance.

"Then I do tell you so."

"Thee don't mean that!" exclaimed the smuggler, with a blaze of amazement and wrath in his face.

"Indeed I do."

"Whew!" whistled Jim, "then that do explain the reason why that smooth-tongued feller said he would car' her to the boat close veiled up for fear the men should see her."

A rapid consultation was now held by the two as to the proper mode of proceeding. Cuttance counselled an immediate capture of the culprit, and pitching him off the end of Cape Cornwall; but Tregarthen advised that they should wait until Clearemout seized his victim, otherwise they could not convict him, because he would deny any intention of evil against Rose, and pretend that some other girl, who had been scared away by their impetuosity, was concerned, for they might depend on it he'd get up a plausible story and defeat them.

Tregarthen's plan was finally agreed to, and he returned to his men and explained matters.

Soon afterwards the managing director appeared coming down the road.

"Is all right?" he inquired of Cuttance, who went forward to meet him.

"All right, sur."

"Go down to the boat then and wait," he said, turning away.

Ere long he was joined by Rose, with whom he entered into conversation, leading her over the cape so as to get out of sight of the men, but young

Tregarthen crept among the rocks and never for a moment lost sight of them. He saw Clearemout suddenly place a kerchief on Rose's mouth, and, despite the poor girl's struggles, tie it firmly so as to prevent her screaming, then he threw a large shawl over her, and catching her in his arms bore her swiftly towards the boat.

Tregarthen sprang up and confronted him.

Clearemout, astonished and maddened by this unexpected interference, shouted — "Stand aside, sir! *You* have no interest in this matter, or right to interfere."

Charlie made no reply, but sprang on him like a tiger. Clearemout dropped his burden and grappled with the youth, who threw him in an instant, big though he was, for Tregarthen was a practised wrestler, and the managing director was not. His great strength, however, enabled him to get on his knees, and there is no saying how the struggle might have terminated had not Cuttance come forward, and, putting his hard hands round Clearemout's throat, caused that gentleman's face to grow black, and his tongue and eyes to protrude. Having thus induced him to submit, he eased off the necklace, and assisted him to rise, while the men of both parties crowded round.

"Now, then, boys," cried Jim Cuttance, "bear a hand, one and all, and into the say with him."

The managing director was at once knocked off his legs, and borne shoulder-high down to the beach by as many hands as could lay hold of him. Here they paused:

"All together, boys — one — two — ho!"

At the word the unfortunate man was shot, by strong and willing arms, into the air like a bombshell, and fell into the water with a splash that was not unlike an explosion.

Clearemout was a good swimmer. When he came to the surface he raised himself, and, clearing the water from his eyes, glanced round. Even in that extremity the quickness and self-possession of the man did not forsake him. He perceived, at a glance, that the boat which, in the excitement of the capture, had been left by all the men, had floated off with the receding tide, and now lay a short distance from the shore.

At once he struck out for it. There was a shout of consternation and a rush to the water's edge. Maggot shot far ahead of the others, plunged into the sea, and swam off. Observing this, and knowing well the courage and daring of the man, the rest stopped on the shore to witness the result.

Clearemout reached the boat first, but, owing to exhaustion, was unable to raise himself into it. Maggot soon came up and grasped him by the throat, both men managed to get their arms over the gunwale, but in their struggle upset the boat and were separated. Clearemout then made for the shore with the intention of giving himself up, and Maggot followed, but he was not equal in swimming to the managing director, whose long steady strokes easily took him beyond the reach of his pursuer. He reached the shore, and stalked slowly out of the water. At the same moment Maggot sank and disappeared.

The consternation of his comrades was so great that in the confusion their prisoner was unheeded. Some sprang into the sea and dived after Maggot; others swam to the boat, intending to right it and get the boat-hooks.

Suddenly those who had remained on the beach observed something creep out of the sea near to some rocks a little to the right of the place where they stood. They ran towards it.

"Hallo! is that you, old Maggot?" they cried.

It was indeed the valiant smith himself! How he got there no one ever knew, nor could himself tell. It was conjectured that he must have become partially exhausted, and, after sinking, had crept along the bottom to the shore! However, be that as it may, there he was, lying with his arm lovingly round a rock, and the first thing he said on looking up was – "Aw! my dear men, has any of 'ee got a chaw of baccy about 'ee?"

This was of course received with a shout of laughter, and unlimited offers of quids while they assisted him to rise.

Meanwhile Tregarthen was attending to Rose, who had swooned when Clearemout dropped her. He also kept a watch over the prisoner, who, however, showed no intention of attempting to escape, but sat on a stone with his face buried in his hands.

The men soon turned their attention to him again, and some of the more violent were advancing to seize him, with many terrible threats of further vengeance, when Rose ran between them, and entreated them to spare him.

Tregarthen seconded the proposal, and urged that as he had got pretty severe punishment already, they should set him free. This being agreed to, Charlie turned to the managing director, and said, with a look of pity, "You may go, sir, but, be assured, it is not for your own sake that we let you off. You know pretty well what the result would be if we chose to deliver you up to justice; we care more, however, for the feelings of this lady – whose name would be unavoidably and disagreeably brought before the public at the trial – than we care for your getting your merited reward. But, mark me, if you ever open your lips on the subject, you shall not escape us."

"Iss," added Jim Cuttance, "ann remember, you chucklehead, that if you do write or utter wan word 'bout it, after gettin' back to London, there are here twelve Cornish men who will never rest till they have flayed thee alive!"

"You need have no fear," said Clearemout with a bitter smile, as he turned and walked away, followed by a groan from the whole party.

"Now, lads," said Cuttance after he was gone, "not wan word of this must ever be breathed, and we'll howld 'ee responsible, David Hicks, for t' wife's tongue; dost a hear?"

This was agreed to by all, and, to the credit of these honest smugglers, and of Mrs. Hicks, be it said, that not a syllable about the incident was ever heard of in the parish of St. Just from that day to this!

CHAPTER XXXII.

Touches on Love and on Pilchard Fishing.

There can be no doubt that "Fortune favours the brave," and Maggot was one of those braves whom, about this time, she took special delight in favouring.

Wild and apparently reckless though he was, Maggot had long cherished an ambitious hope, and had for some time past been laying by money for the purpose of accomplishing his object, which was the procuring of a seine-net and boats for the pilchard fishery. The recent successes he had met with in Botallack enabled him to achieve his aim more rapidly than he had anticipated, and on the day following that in which Clearemout received his deserts, he went to Penberth Cove to see that all was in readiness, for pilchards had recently appeared off the coast in small shoals.

That same day Oliver Trembath, having spent a night of misery in Penzance, made up his mind to return to St. Just and face his fate like a man; but he found it so difficult to carry this resolve into effect that he diverged from the highroad — as he had done on his first memorable visit to that region — and, without knowing very well why, sauntered in a very unenviable frame of mind towards Penberth Cove.

Old Mr. Donnithorne possessed a pretty villa near the cove, to which he was wont to migrate when Mrs. D. felt a desire for change of air, and in which he frequently entertained large parties of friends in the summer season. In his heart poor Mr. Donnithorne had condemned this villa "to the hammer," but the improved appearance of things in the mines had induced him to suspend the execution of the sentence. News of the appearance of pilchards, and a desire to give Rose a change after her late adventure, induced Mr. Donnithorne to hire a phaeton (he had recently parted with his own) and drive over to Penberth.

Arrived there, he sauntered down to the cove to look after his nets — for he dabbled in pilchard fishing as well as in other matters — and Rose went off to have a quiet, solitary walk.

Thus it came to pass that she and Oliver Trembath suddenly met in a lonely part of the road between Penberth and Penzance. Ah, those sudden and unexpected meetings! How pleasant they are, and how well every one who has had them remembers them!

"Miss Ellis!" exclaimed Oliver in surprise.

"Mr. Trembath!" exclaimed Rose in amazement.

You see, reader, how polite they were, but you can neither see nor conceive how great was the effort made by each to conceal the tumult that agitated the breast and flushed the countenance, while the tongue was thus ably controlled. It did not last long, however. Oliver, being thrown off his guard, asked a number of confused questions, and Rose, in her somewhat irrelevant replies, happened to make some reference to "that villain Clearemout."

"Villain?" echoed Oliver in undisguised amazement.

"The villain," repeated Rose, with a flushed face and flashing eye.

"What? why? how? — really, excuse me, Miss Ellis — I — I — the villain — Clearemout — you don't —"

There is no saying how many more ridiculous exclamations Oliver might have made had not Rose suddenly said — "Surely, Mr. Trembath, you have heard of his villainy?"

"No, never; not a word. Pray do tell me, Miss Ellis."

Rose at once related the circumstances of her late adventure, with much indignation in her tone and many a blush on her brow.

Before she had half done, Oliver's powers of restraint gave way.

"Then you never loved him?" he exclaimed.

"Loved him, sir! I do not understand —"

"Forgive me, Rose; I mean — I didn't imagine — that is to say — oh! Rose, can it be — is it possible — my *dear* girl!"

He seized her hand at this point, and — but really, reader, why should we go on? Is it not something like a violation of good taste to be too particular here? Is it not sufficient to say that old Mr. Donnithorne came suddenly, and of course unexpectedly, on them at that critical juncture, rendering it necessary for Rose to burst away and hide her blushing face on her uncle's shoulder, while Oliver, utterly overwhelmed, turned and walked (we won't say fled) at full speed in the direction of the cove.

Here he found things in a condition that was admirably suited to the state of his feelings. The fishermen of the cove were in a state of wild excitement, for an enormous shoal of pilchards had been enclosed in the seine-nets, and Maggot with his men, as well as the people employed by Mr. Donnithorne, were as much over head and ears in fishing as Oliver was in love. Do you ask, "Why all this excitement?" We will tell you.

The pilchard fishing is to the Cornish fisherman what the harvest is to the husbandman, but this harvest of the sea is not the result of prolonged labour, care, and wisdom. It comes to him in a night. It may last only a few days, or weeks. Sometimes it fails altogether. During these days of sunshine he must toil with unwonted energy. There is no rest for him while the season lasts if he would not miss his opportunity. The pilchard is a little fish resembling a small herring. It visits the southern coasts of England in autumn and winter, and the shoals are so enormous as to defy calculation or description. When they arrive on the coast, "huers" — sharp-sighted men — are stationed on the cliffs to direct the boatmen when to go out and where to shoot their seine-nets. When these are shot, millions of pilchards are often enclosed in a single net.

To give an idea of the numbers of fish and the extent of the fishing, in a few words, we may state the fact that, in 1834, one shoal of great depth, and nearly a mile broad, extended from Hayle River to St. Ives, a distance of two and a half miles. A seine was shot into this mass, and 3,600 hogsheads were carried to the curing cellars. As there are 3,000 pilchards in each hogshead, the catch amounted to nearly eleven million fish! The value of these might be £3 a hogshead, and the clear profit about £1 a hogshead, so that it is no wonder we hear of fortunes having been made in a few hauls of the pilchard seines. At the same time, losses are sometimes very heavy, owing to gales arising and breaking or carrying away the nets. Such facts, combined with the uncertainty of the arrival or continuance of the fish on any particular part of the coast, tend to induce that spirit of eager, anxious excitement to which we have referred as being so congenial to Oliver Trembath's state of mind at the time of which we write.

On the beach the young doctor found Maggot and his men launching their boats, and of course he lent them a hand.

"Pilchards been seen?" he inquired.

"Iss, iss, doctor," was the smith's curt reply; "jump in, an' go 'long with us."

Oliver accepted the invitation, and was rowed towards a part of the bay where the sea appeared to be boiling. The boat was a large one, attended by several others of smaller dimensions. The boiling spot being reached, Maggot, whose whole being was in a blaze of enthusiasm, leaped up and seized the end of a seine-net — three hundred fathoms long by fourteen deep — which he began to throw overboard with the utmost energy, while the boat was rowed swiftly round the mass of fish. David Trevarrow assisted him, and in less than four minutes the whole net was in the sea. One of the other boats, meanwhile, had fastened another net to the first, and, rowing in an opposite direction from it, progressed in a circular course, dropping its net as it went, until the two met — and thus an immense shoal of pilchards were enclosed.

The nets being floated on the surface with corks, and their lower ends sunk to the bottom with leads, the fish were thus securely imprisoned. But the security was not great; a gale might arise which would sweep away the whole concern, or the pilchards might take a fancy to make a dash in one particular direction, in the event of which they would certainly burst the net, and no human power could save a single fin. In order to prevent this, the men in the smaller boats rowed round the seine, beat the sea with their oars, hallooed, and otherwise exerted themselves to keep the fish in the centre of the enclosure. Meanwhile a little boat entered within the circle, having a small net, named a "tuck-net," which was spread round the seine, inside, and gradually drawn together, until the fish were raised towards the surface in a solid, sweltering mass. The excitement at this point became tremendous. Thousands of silvery fish leaped, vaulted, and fluttered in a seething mass on the sea. Maggot roared and yelled his orders like a Stentor. Even mild David Trevarrow lost self-command, and shouted vociferously.

"Hand the basket!" cried Maggot.

A large basket, with a rope attached to one handle, was produced. Maggot seized the other handle, and thrust it down among the wriggling pilchards. Trevarrow hauled on the rope, lifted the basket out of the sea, and a cataract of living silver was shot into the boat, accompanied by a mighty cheer. Basketful after basketful followed, until the men stood leg-deep in fish.

"Hold on a bit!" cried Maggot, as, with rolled-up sleeves, dishevelled hair, and glaring eyes, he threw one leg over the side of the boat, the more easily to continue his work.

"Have a care," cried Oliver at that moment, stretching out his hand; but he was too late. The excitable smith had overbalanced himself, and was already head and shoulders deep down among the pilchards, which sprang high over him, as if in triumph!

To catch him by the legs, and pull him back into the boat, was the work of a moment, but the proceedings were not interrupted by the mishap. A laugh greeted the smith as he was turned head up, and immediately he braced himself to his arduous labour with renewed energy.

The boat filled, it was rowed to the shore, and here was received by eager and noisy men, women, and children, by whom the precious contents were carried to the "cellars," or salting-houses, where they were packed in the neatest possible piles, layer on layer, heads and tails, with a sprinkling of salt between.

Maggot's family had followed him to Penberth. Mrs. M. was there, busy as a bee — so was Zackey, so was little Grace, and so was the baby. They all worked like Trojans, the only difference between baby Maggot and the others being, that, while they did as much work as in them lay, he undid as much as possible; was in every one's way; fell over and into everything, including the sea, and, generally, fulfilled his mission of mischief-maker with credit. The chet was there too! Baby Maggot had decreed that it should accompany him, so there it was, living on pilchards, and dragging out its harassed existence in the usual way. What between salt food, and play, kicks, cuffs, capers, and gluttony, its aspect at that time was more demoniacal, perhaps, than that of any other chet between John o' Groat's and the Land's End.

Volumes would scarcely contain all that might be written about this wonderful scene, but enough has been said to indicate the process whereby Maggot secured and salted some hundreds of thousands of pilchards. The enclosing of the fish was the result of a few minutes' work, but the salting and packing were not ended for many days. The result, however, was that the lucky smith sent many hogsheads of pilchards the way of most Cornish fish — namely, to the Mediterranean, for consumption by Roman Catholics, and in due course he received the proceeds, to the extent of three thousand pounds.

Thus did Maggot auspiciously begin the making of his fortune — which was originated and finally completed by his successful mining operations at Botallack.

And let it be observed here, that he was neither the first nor the last poor man who became prosperous and wealthy by similar means. There are men, not a few, now alive in Cornwall, who began with hammer and pick, and who now can afford to drink in champagne, out of a golden flagon, the good old Cornish toast — "Fish, tin, and copper."

THE END